THE CRY OF THE JETS

John Du Cane was educated at Eton, Cranwell and Cambridge.

A former pilot in the Royal Air Force, he spent many years in Aviation and almost thirty as a Member of Parliament.

He divides his time between Chile and the Isle of Man.

THE CRY OF THE JETS

John Du Cane

THE CRY OF THE JETS

Olympia Publishers
London

www.olympiapublishers.com
OLYMPIA PAPERBACK EDITION

Copyright © John Du Cane 2012

The right of John Du Cane to be identified as author of
this work has been asserted in accordance with sections 77 and 78 of
the Copyright, Designs and Patents Act 1988.

All Rights Reserved

No reproduction, copy or transmission of this publication
may be made without written permission.
No paragraph of this publication may be reproduced,
copied or transmitted save with the written permission of the
publisher, or in accordance with the provisions
of the Copyright Act 1956 (as amended).

Any person who commits any unauthorised act in relation to
this publication may be liable to criminal
prosecution and civil claims for damage.

A CIP catalogue record for this title is
available from the British Library.

ISBN: 978-1-84897-226-1

This is a work of fiction.
Names, characters, places and incidents originate from the writer's
imagination. Any resemblance to actual persons, living or dead, is
purely coincidental.

First Published in 2012

Olympia Publishers
60 Cannon Street
London
EC4N 6NP

Printed in Great Britain

Dedication

This book is dedicated to those who gave their lives for liberty during the Cold War.

Acknowledgments

The author expresses his heartfelt thanks to Tracey Maloney for her patient and meticulous typing of the manuscript.

CHAPTER 1

It was snowing when the 12.25 diesel electric train from King's Cross drew into Grantham Station. The platforms were grey. The sky was grey, and a darkish blue anonymous bus stained with grey slush, awaited to take the carefully selected flight cadets to the most formative institution of their lives.

The driver in rough serge battledress vouchsafed only two comments; that this bus was indeed going to the Royal Air Force College and that the College Warrant Officer would meet the passengers on arrival. The countryside was featureless. A raw wind had exposed the red soil of the Kesteven heathland. The snow, which had built up at the edges of the fields, accentuated the rectangular pattern of the limestone walls.

Once on the straight Roman road from Ancaster, the imposing tower of Cranwell soon loomed above the windswept landscape with its terrestrial lighthouse occulting clearly through the lowering murk. For William Jamieson, at just eighteen and fresh from Stowe, such a sombre edifice reminded him reassuringly of school. He recalled the comment he had overheard at the Aircrew Selection Centre the year before that Cranwell is like a public school for those who have never been to one.

Such thoughts seemed academic now as the bus swept past the College. It turned abruptly right alongside what had to be the Station Headquarters, judging from the Royal Air Force ensign fluttering on a lofty pole in front. The bus halted at a line of low brick built huts at the edge of the airfield, whose orange windsock was extended stiffly against the snowy wastes behind.

The driver was right. At the foot of the bus steps stood a rigid towering figure. His moustache bristled. His toecaps gleamed seemingly impervious to slush. A brass tipped pace stick was tucked into his armpit at right angles to the ground. His neck was subsumed into a fearsome rectilinear geometry from peaked cap to shoulder blade to pace stick, and then via knife edge trouser creases to big black boots and snow.

"Out of the vehicle, gentlemen," he thundered. "At the double. Into the briefing room. Bring your kit." He extended his arm imperiously and pointed with his pace stick towards a squat neo Georgian building, slightly apart from the huts abutting a square expanse of snow delineated at each corner with triangular light blue marker flags.

The cadets, some fifty in number, installed themselves hesitantly on metal hard backed chairs in front of a stage with a solitary lectern. Four sergeants stood beside the wall and alternately barked: "Hurry up; put your kit under your chair; sit up; stop nattering; look bright," and finally, "stand for the College Warrant Officer."

The Warrant Officer strode in from the snow and instantly took charge. "Sit down, gentlemen. Today you are joining the Royal Air Force" he began. "You are starting a new life. Your old life is over and of no interest to me. Now you look horrible but with time and effort I will make you into gentlemen and a credit to the Service. My name is Mr Izzard and I am lucky in having four distinguished non-commissioned officers to assist me in my thankless task. Please identify yourselves."

"Sergeant Langholm, sir."
"Sergeant Price, sir."
"Sergeant McCabe, sir."
"Sergeant Plumtree, sir."

"I will now divide you young gentlemen into squadrons, he continued. "Bring me the nominal roll, Sergeant Langholm. Everyone present?"

"The bus driver reported a full complement, sir, " replied the sergeant. "I don't care. Some flight cadets may have got cold feet and have slipped away already. When I call your name just say, sir." The cadets did so. "Entry present and correct. A good start gentlemen." Then a random process of selection assigned each cadet to a squadron and more importantly to each of the four squadrons its own drill sergeant.

Will Jamieson, Jamie to his friends, found himself in C squadron and the squadron's drill sergeant was Sergeant McCabe. To all of his dozen charges the sergeant addressed personal words of welcome: "Mr Jamieson, your name may be Scottish but you sound very lah-di-dah to me. Mr Carrick, so you're from Pudsey are you? There's no muck here only plenty of brass to polish. Mr Lascelles, a scholarship boy from Winchester College. Well at Cranwell we do everything by the book so you should be very happy. Mr Jones, you're our man from Glamorgan – a rugby star I see. The only kicking around here will be done by me, Taffy boy. I'll kick your backside mercilessly from now on for every misdemeanour.

"You lucky gentlemen are going to be in hut 150 at the end of the lines behind the gap in the hangars, so you'll get the full benefit of the eine kleine nachtmusik – the roar of the jets as they run up for night flying. There'll be no point in cosy talk, of chatting late into the night because no one will hear a word you say. Anyway the nights are for bull – bootshine and blancoeing, floor polishing and the ironing of your uniforms, not converzationes.

"And another thing. I have assigned to you four a special mentor, a Kiwi, a navigator, Mr McGilligan. He's already been here for a term and so knows his way round. He should do. Before long he'll be a one winged wonder so there's no excuse for you lot getting lost on camp or being late. I expect split second timing. And to give you a foretaste of formation flying you will march everywhere in squads, not just when you're in uniform, but in plain clothes as well. Finally remember that gentlemen wear hats at all times so I expect not just the normal courtesies to officers of a salute in uniform but in plain clothes, too. In this case a respectful removal of headdress and in sports clothing a smart eyes right or left. Is that clear? Back to you, Mr Izzard, sir."

The Warrant Officer strode to the front and gave further precise instructions, "You know your places now, gentlemen," he resumed. "You have your squadrons, your huts and your mentors. Soon you will fulfil your first and most important duty to get your shaggy heads shorn. With a decent haircut you might just be presentable enough to march this evening by squadrons to the College Hall where you will be attested in the rank of Aircraftsman Second Class by the Assistant Commandant Group Captain Vigors. Your drill sergeant will ensure that you do it correctly but now the Officer Commanding Cadet Wing, Wing Commander Tophill, will welcome you and introduce you to your Flight Commanders. Attention!"

Out of a side door at the back of the stage emerged a Wing Commander of medium build, verging on middle age with a sallow complexion, smooth shiny black hair, in Number One uniform with a gleaming waist buckle restricting an incipient paunch. His Cadet Wing ground tour had clearly already taken a toll on his physique, although the mauve and white diagonally striped ribbon of the Distinguished Flying Cross, the green and purple vertically striped ribbon of the General Service Medal and the all grey ribbon of the Queen's Commendation for Valuable Service in the air gave evidence of an active earlier career – Korea and the Malayan Emergency probably and some outstanding flying exploit, which did not quite merit an Air Force Cross.

Behind him at a respectful distance followed four slimmer looking Flight Lieutenants in well-tailored officers' battle dress with black buttons. Three were pilots and one somewhat red faced and fuller figured than the others a navigator. The Wing Commander advanced to the lectern on the front of which hung the Royal Air Force College shield with its three white droop winged cranes above a brief Latin motto. The Flight Lieutenants positioned themselves in line abreast to the back of the stage and looked attentively serious. The Wing Commander cast a wearied eye on the cadets below, "Be seated, gentlemen," he began in a technocratic classless monotone. "Welcome to the Royal Air Force College. You have looked forward to this moment for a long time. I assure you that Cranwell will exceed all your expectations. My job is to ensure that in three strenuous years you are worthy to pass out with the Queen's Commission. You will then be no ordinary officers. You will be the repository of the highest standards and traditions of the Royal Air Force, the favoured few to whom a Permanent Commission is awarded; the backbone of the Service.

"In return we expect nothing but the best. What does it say below the College coat of arms? Superna Petimus – we seek the higher things. I and my officers and non commissioned officers, indeed all members of the College staff whether of the Cadet, Flying or Academic Wings will do our utmost to make sure that you live up to the expectations of those who selected you. You probably feel well satisfied to have shown at the Aircrew Selection Centre, Biggin Hill, the aptitude necessary to fly and to have convinced the Selection Board here at Cranwell that you have officer potential. However, I can assure you that getting into Cranwell is the easy part. Passing out is much more difficult and on average only half of every entry graduate.

"You will be assessed at every stage of your training and your aptitude will be judged critically. Cranwell style leadership is special. Your life here will be so challenging that nothing in your subsequent Service career will daunt you. We require you to lead by example and expect that a Cranwell graduate will be able to outperform his fellow officers in all his duties. You can always recognise an Old Cranwellian because he does things properly.

"Many of you will have joined the Royal Air Force above all in order to fly and indeed airpower is our business. However, most essentially it is leadership and officer qualities which we seek from you. The majority of you are destined for the General Duties that is the flying branch of the Service, but we have Equipment and Secretarial branch cadets among you also. Everybody has a vital role to play. You will be trained to the same high level and, although you probably cannot wait to join your first flying squadron, ground tours are just as important as flying. The more senior you become the more of them you will do. I'm sure your Flight Commanders would agree, wouldn't you gentlemen?" The four Flight Lieutenants nodded in unison, each doubtless privately longing to be back on a squadron.

"Your Flight Commanders are responsible for every aspect of your progress. They will see you through the Junior Entries until you transfer to the main College in your final year to fly Vampire advanced jet trainers or Meteors whereupon their Senior Entries counterparts will take over. Your Squadron Commanders whom you will meet at attestation this evening will provide continuity of oversight and will monitor you all the way to graduation. Normally you will not see much more of me unless serious concerns arise about you, in which case your senior officers may ask you to report to me for interview. Your Flight Commanders will assure your normal welfare and the drill sergeants will instil in you the self-respect, which comes from the maintenance of proper pride and personal bearing and the careful attention to detail at all times. Any questions?"

A lanky somewhat spotty cadet in the middle row leant back in his chair and languorously raised a hand. Before the cadet could utter a word the Warrant Officer pre-empted him sharply, "Flight Cadet stand up when you address an officer. Name and squadron please!"

"Garrity, sir, B squadron."

"Go ahead," instructed the Wing Commander.

"Could you tell us, sir," continued the cadet hesitantly, "when we will be allowed off the station?"

"Good question, Garrity," the Wing Commander replied. "The mid-term break will take place in just over eight weeks time, from 1300 hours on Saturday 27 February until 2359 hours on Sunday 28 February." The cadets looked serious.

"Of course Wednesdays and Saturdays are sports afternoons," Wing Commander Tophill went on. "Here at Cranwell, team sports are a duty. When they are over you may leave the station. Remember you must be back by 2159 hours on Wednesdays and Sundays and 2359 hours on Saturdays. However, I think you'll be too tired for the first few weeks. You'll have your kit to prepare for inspections and the hut to clean out, not to mention academic studies to attend to and perhaps extra parades to fill your spare time."

A fresh faced confident looking cadet in the front row rose eagerly to his feet. "Who told you to stand?" snapped Warrant Officer Izzard. The cadet blushed and sat down hurriedly. "Well I suppose I just have time for one more question," said the Wing Commander. "Now stand to attention to address Wing Commander Tophill. Make it brief."

"Blackham, A Squadron, sir. When do we start flying?"

"After mid-term break you will fly once a month till the end of the year as trainee navigators in Valetta aircraft, flying classrooms, to see how you perform in the air under pressure. We want student pilots who understand the principles of air navigation and who will fit more easily into a crew. If all goes well your last few sorties of the year will be in Varsity aircraft, which you will find a little faster, better equipped, quieter and more comfortable."

"From Pig to Superpig, how lucky we will be," whispered Blackham's neighbour audibly.

"Listen to the Wing Commander and you might learn something," snapped the Warrant Officer.

"Those who do not make the grade we could consider for one of the ground branches. If you subsequently cannot cope with your pilot training you might just be recoursed as a navigator if you've impressed your navigation instructors with your ability during the first year. That way everyone benefits. Flying Wing gets the best out of you. If you have officer qualities they will not be wasted and the Treasury has to fund fewer washouts. Your training is expensive. It is my task to see that the country gets good value for money. My Flight Commanders will constantly monitor the taxpayer's investment in you. I hand you over to them now. Carry on, Mr Izzard."

The College Warrant Officer stamped to attention and repositioned his pace stick in the erect position clutched in his armpit. "Flight Cadets will move to Flight Commanders' briefings by squadrons," he barked. With his spare left arm he indicated the rooms, which abutted the central hall.

"A squadron to Portal room. B squadron to Tedder room. C squadron to Slessor room. D squadron to Harris room. Look sharp! Move."

Once installed in their briefing room Jamieson had a moment to look at his surroundings and to assess his C squadron colleagues. In addition to Peter Carrick, Peter Lascelles and David Jones his future hut mates, there were three faces he recognised – Ian McIntyre the tall dour Scotsman he had met at summer camp with the Air Cadets down at Thorney Island. There was also James Kelly the Cockney from Dagenham who, he was amazed to see had somehow passed the Cranwell Selection Board at Daedalus House. He had been the humorist of his syndicate always laughing at other people's misfortunes when they came to grief on the obstacle course. Then there was Carl Higgins the Middlesex man from Pinner near Harrow on the Hill, with whom he had slipped away from the Aircrew Selection Centre at Biggin Hill to do some under age drinking down the road.

There was not long to reflect on his future before in swept Sergeant McCabe. "Attention, gentlemen. You will listen to the Flight Commander. He will advise you of your duties for the next action packed forty-eight hours. Flight Lieutenant Bracewell will put all your anxieties to rest and inform you of just what is expected from you on C squadron. Sit down! Attention!"

In came a small red faced Flight Lieutenant from behind the cadets. Jamieson could just discern a first sign of wear on the elbows and seat of Bracewell's battledress. Instead of standing at the end of the room he seated himself at a small trestle table with a white Perspex chinagraph board behind him. From the left top pocket of his battledress blouse above his single Navigator's Wing he withdrew a packet of Camel cigarettes and immediately lit up.

Bracewell's reputation had preceded him. James Kelly who had an elder brother in the Senior Entry, the winner of a prize cadetship from the RAF Apprentice School at Halton had tipped Jamie off about the Flight Commanders. There was Bill Brennan of A squadron, the tall red haired old Cranwellian from Northern Ireland, a Canberra pilot, punctilious and proper, ultra correct at all times but a fearsome martinet. B squadron's Flight Commander was the legendary Bill Barton, very charming and laid back – "gash" – in Air Force parlance. After a tour on Treble One squadron flying Hunters and in their aerobatic team he had gone to the Central Flying School and won the aerobatic trophy, been rewarded with an instructional tour at Cranwell on Vampires from which he had been talent spotted for three more years at Cranwell, this time on a ground tour.

Henry Hargreaves of D Squadron was the intellectual of the Flight Commanders, a graduate of Cambridge University, a maths scholar. He had spent two tours on Shackletons in Coastal Command first at Ballykelly, then Kinloss. The arcane world of oceanic navigation, sonar and anti-submarine warfare suited him. Thin and pipe smoking, at Cranwell he seemed almost a recluse and very remote from his cadets who liked him nonetheless because he caused them no trouble. Jack Bracewell of C squadron was the joker in the pack. He had joined the Air Force straight from school on a short service commission but had already made a name for himself.

First he had survived baling out at night from a Meteor NF12 of 25 squadron at Waterbeach. The compressor of the aircraft's starboard Derwent engine had exploded setting fire to the wing. He had climbed out, missed the tail and pulled his parachute ripcord very early. A strong north-easterly wind had miraculously carried him to the beach at Cromer. His pilot who abandoned the aircraft later was never seen again.

Then followed a tour on Javelins up at Leeming where his exceptional facility as an operator of airborne interception radar and good fortune to crew with the Squadron Commander led to his being granted a permanent commission notwithstanding his rough diamond reputation and notorious binges in the Mess bar. His rages at Flight Cadets were legendary. His wife Pam who had not taken happily to their move from a rented house in idyllic Cambridge with its attendant social life to a married quarter on base in the North Riding of Yorkshire had left him.

Mosquito Close at Leeming had been bad enough for her but Hampden Avenue at Cranwell was even worse. "At least there was some life on the squadron," she moaned, "here in beastly Lincolnshire there is none. Your bloody Air Force treats us wives like cattle to be moved from one field to the next," she had complained over breakfast before the last Passing Out parade. "Now you expect me after being ignored for the last three and a half months of this dreary term to dress up in my best ladylike outfit to join the Commandant, his shrew of a wife and all the other bitchy Godforsaken officers' wives to have sherry with a bunch of callow Pilot Officers and their ghastly doting parents."

Her reserved seat in the second row facing the parade remained empty nor did she appear at the subsequent cocktail party, but on his return to their quarter Bracewell saw that a note was stuck to the door of the sitting room. It simply read: GONE TO LONDON. I DO NOT EXPECT YOU TO FOLLOW. PAM. No wonder he seemed bitter and twisted to cadets but at least his address was brief, delivered in a sedentary position through a cloud of cigarette smoke.

"Gentlemen, first the good news. You have been assigned to C squadron. It is the best. Keep it that way. Now the bad news. I will be your Flight Commander until that far off day when the lucky few who are still left go up to the Senior Entries to fly Vampires. After two years I shall also lose the brainy ones – that is the Navigators of course plus the Equippers and Secretarials, too, who keep the show on the road.

"However, that is for the future. My job is to see that you learn to be commanded, a task I have largely delegated to the exemplary Sergeant McCabe here and to your squadron Under Officers and Senior Flight Cadets to whom the College in its wisdom entrusts much authority in matters of discipline. I am sure that the Senior Entries will make themselves known to you very shortly.

"Sergeant McCabe will soon knock you into shape, a process which will begin this very afternoon with the march up to the College for attestation. Drills and the parade ground will become a familiar part of your life. You will begin the course with a parade outside right now and you will finish it with a parade on graduation day. There'll be plenty of drill in the three years in between because we believe that before you give orders you have to learn to take orders and that discipline on the ground translates into discipline in the air. In flying strict discipline is the best way to stay alive.

"Remember that the College staff are watching you all the time and so am I. I will see your progress reports and if they are outstandingly good or bad so will your Squadron Commander, Squadron Leader Chivvers. You will meet him at attestation. When I have finished you will assemble outside for haircut parade. Then you will reclaim your luggage and take it to your hut. You will immediately reform outside to be marched up to the College and down again. On return you are to report to the Junior Mess for supper before being marched to your huts to meet your mentors who have had the privilege of coming back to the College a few hours early after their leave to greet you.

"Tomorrow reveille is at 0600 hours sharp and after breakfast you will parade on the drill square at 0630 to march to the clothing store for kitting out. As soon as you have got your new uniforms on you will parade again to learn the first rudiments of drill. Then you will be presentable enough for Sergeant McCabe to march you to the Education Site to be briefed by the Wing Commander Commanding, Education Wing and his senior instructors. When you get back you will parade again after lunch for more drill before being marched first to the Ground Defence Section and then to the Chief Physical Training Instructor.

"In the evening you will work on the marking and adjustment of your newly issued clothing and on the preparation of your hut under the supervision of your mentor for the first visits from the senior entries. The day after tomorrow will be a normal working day that is reveille at 0630, drill parade at 0730, then academics from 0900. After lunch you will do more academics followed by Ground Defence and finally Physical Training in the gymnasium. The evening will be spent preparing your drill kit for inspection. Any questions?" An apprehensive silence ensued. "Take them away, Sergeant McCabe," growled the chain smoking Flight Lieutenant Bracewell.

CHAPTER 2

Round the back of the Junior Headquarters was a low wooden hut. At one end bicycles were stored. At the other were piled flagpoles, coils of white rope, a dais, a folded awning and a wheeled machine for drawing lines with lime. In between the two were four haircutting booths manned by young aircraftsmen probably on National Service. Sergeant McCabe marched his charges in single file from the briefing hall to the hairdressing section where they were halted, turned into line and finally stood easy. They then went in one at a time to have their heads shorn with electric clippers; a process, which took at most three minutes per Flight Cadet. Even so the last few cadets were already frozen to the marrow before receiving attention. The gnawing east wind which picked up humidity and low cloud in the North Sea en route from Russia became familiar to all at Cranwell. As Pam Bracewell used repetitively to observe: "There is nothing to block the wind between Siberia and Cranwell and I'm sure life in a Siberian Gulag is just as fun."

The march up to the main College by squadrons was easy enough. Most of the cadets had been in the Air Training Corps or Cadet Force at school. On arrival at College Hall Warrant Officer Izzard was on the steps to greet them, pace stick at the ready. "Thank you, Sergeant McCabe," he began. "You gentlemen look almost presentable after your haircuts. From today you will march everywhere – by squadrons, by Entry, by Flight, by squad even in twos or threes. The gentleman at the back right of the squad will be in charge. Of course if you are in plain clothes you will wear hats at all times so if you do not have a smart one in your luggage you must go to Gieves the tailor's shop near the station post office over lunch tomorrow and buy one."

When instructed the cadets followed Sergeant McCabe in single file up the main steps of the College, a route they would never again be allowed to take until they slow marched off their passing out parade to the strains of Auld Lang Syne. They then skirted the edge of the rotunda in the middle of which was a table with a Bible and a copy of the Queen's regulations of the Royal Air Force together with a pile of forms, an office stamp, ink blotter and fountain pen.

Above hung standards of the Royal Air Force College and Flying Training Command. On the walls were full length portraits of Her Majesty Queen Elizabeth II and of Marshal of the Royal Air Force His Royal Highness Prince Philip in full dress uniform, the Royal Air Force College's founder Marshal of the Royal Air Force Lord Trenchard, General Jan Smuts and of Air Commodore Longmore the first Commandant.

Sergeant McCabe ushered the cadets into an anteroom. Magazines lay on the table – Country Life, Punch, Horse and Hound, RAF Quarterly, The Field, Spectator, Economist, Flight and Lincolnshire Life. On the walls were pictures of aerial combats some signed by the participants and some with small etched or photographic portraits of the distinguished old Cranwellians involved. Few were still serving or alive.

"Sit down, gentlemen," ordered Sergeant McCabe. "The Squadron Commander will soon make himself known to you." Shortly afterwards in walked a tall Squadron

Leader with crinkly brown hair, probably a little over thirty years of age with the single red and white diagonally stripped medal ribbon of the Air Force Cross below his pilot's wings.

"Please be seated, gentlemen," he began calmly. "My name is Squadron Leader,Chivvers and I command C squadron. After attestation I will welcome you individually, but thereafter you will normally see very little of me although I shall be following your progress with intense interest. Carry on, Sergeant McCabe."

The Sergeant took charge. "I shall call you out by name, gentlemen, in alphabetical order. You will then walk smartly out through this door halting in front of the Assistant Commandant at the small table. The Squadron Commander will introduce you by name to Group Captain Vigors. He will ask you to swear the oath of allegiance to Her Majesty the Queen, her heirs and successors and to sign on in the Service in the rank of Aircraftsman second class.

"To yourselves, myself, your Flight and Squadron Commanders and all the College staff you are Flight Cadets, gentlemen and prospective officers but to Whitehall and the Ministry of Defence unless and until you receive the Queen's Commission you will have assumed the lowest rank in the Service. You will have taken the Queen's shilling with all the responsibilities and obligations that entails. Your life will no longer be your own. I will be constantly on hand to see you never get bored."

Sergeant McCabe called out the cadets in alphabetical order. First was the Pakistani: "Mr Ahmed. Sergeant." One of the two Commonwealth cadets in the C Squadron Entry he leapt instantly to attention at the drill sergeant's summons and strutted rather than marched exaggeratedly out. When called, Mr Allen, Mr Carrick, Mr Chu, Mr Ellington, Mr Farquharson and Mr Jamieson followed.

Once out of the anteroom door Jamie discerned a small mahogany table behind which stood the Assistant Commandant with his gold braided cap beside him on a chair. His chest looked heavy with medals. His Royal Air Force wings were complemented below by a smaller winged badge of the elite wartime Pathfinder Force. Jamie spotted the magenta of the DSO, the DFC, the Aircrew Northern Europe and World War Two stars, Defence medal and some other ribbons, which he could not recognise in the split second before Mr Izzard took vociferous charge.

"Attention. Flight Cadet Jamieson you will take the oath of allegiance in your left hand and the Bible in your right. Now repeat clearly the text of the oath to the Group Captain." This done, his barking of orders resumed: "Sign the proforma, Mr Jamieson," the College Warrant Officer resumed. "Blot it properly. It is an official document. No smudges." Whereupon Squadron Leader Chivvers did the introduction: "Assistant Commandant, Sir, Flight Cadet Jamieson."

Jamie manoeuvred round the other side of the table, halted and grasped the extended hand of the Assistant Commandant. "You wouldn't be related to Jock Jamieson would you by any chance?" he began. "We were briefly at Ludford Magna together in '43 on Lancasters. Hardly knew him, I'm afraid. His outfit was on the other side of the airfield and I went off very soon down to Warboys to join Don Bennett's Pathfinder lot. I wonder what became of Jock. I know he had done a great many missions. He must have had a guardian angel because I was told his aircraft at Ludford never suffered any serious damage. He was very pious by reputation and they said he used to say his prayers kneeling beside the bed in the Nissen hut."

"He's my father, sir. He did another tour afterwards in Mosquitoes at Upwood. He loved that aeroplane. He went all the way through without a scratch," replied

Jamieson. "I think it affected him so much that he went into the church when it was all over. He's Vicar of Bideford now."

"Move on, Mr Jamieson," snapped Mr Izzard precluding any further reminiscences and keeping the proceedings expeditious and businesslike. "Report now to the Squadron Commander." Squadron Leader Chivvers was standing at ease behind the Assistant Commandant, his tall lean figure dwarfing the thick set Group Captain. "Flight Cadet Jamieson, welcome to C Squadron," he declared. "I see you've had a Flying Scholarship. That should help with your flying next year, but till then it's attention to detail we're looking for and the right attitude in everything you do. Carry on."

The others followed quickly: David (Taff) Jones, Peter Lascelles, Ian McIntyre, Freddie Parker and Paul Whiteman. Once attested Sergeant McCabe briskly formed the cadets into a squad and soon they were marching off to the South Brick Lines and to their three huts, which for the next seven months would have to count as home.

Flight Cadet Eamonn (Kiwi) McGilligan was awaiting his charges at the door of Hut 150. "You have half an hour till supper and if you're not in the Mess on time the meal will be off," he warned them. "You have a lot to do." The outside door entered onto a tiled washroom area with five hand basins with a shower and wc to one side.

Through another door lay the main body of the hut with five metal beds around a central black coke stove and the mentor's bed first on the left. A small shoe box with drawers lay to one side of each bed, a wooden wardrobe on the other. The floor was shiny pale brown linoleum. The walls were without decoration and simple green curtains covered single glazed metal framed windows.

"You will place your bags on top of your wardrobe. The wardrobe shelves are for your uniforms and issue clothing. Your civilian clothes can go in the shoe box drawers or stay in your bag. The wire hangers are for your uniforms and great coat. You will remove your shoes on entering the hut and use the felt footpads at all times for moving around. You will have to polish the lino so this rule will soon make sense.

"You may have noticed that on each bed there are two sheets, two woollen blankets, plus a pillow and pillow case. You will fold the bedclothes in the regulation manner like mine, ready at all times for inspection. The Flight Commander will inspect the hut every Friday; Sergeant McCabe will inspect it every Tuesday; the Squadron Commander every month and the Assistant Commandant every term. The Under Officer or Senior Flight Cadet on duty can come in and inspect it at any time so make sure that the hut is always immaculate likewise your kit because if they are not you will be on a charge and then restrictions.

"There are four restrictions parades a day at 0630 hours, 1830, 2120 and 2200 so you will have plenty of opportunities on restrictions for extra drill. This and the additional inspections involved will I fear bring still more restrictions if your kit is not absolutely perfect. That is why I keep a spare set of as many items as possible IPO, which means for inspection purposes only. Once something is used it only has to be cleaned, polished or refolded, which takes time and gets tedious. So keep one set of everything for use, if you can; another solely for inspection.

"A final word for health and happiness. We receive two scuttles of coke every week and no kindling, so fire control and stove management are key Cranwell skills, which you will soon learn. After having a fire you will remove all cinders and ashes and keep both the stove and chimney blacked right up to the roof, ready for inspection at all times.

"From tomorrow you crows can expect the senior entries to come and visit you. I am afraid they won't be quiet social visits. Crowing gives senior cadets a chance to see what you're made of. Remember to call Senior Flight Cadets and Under Officers, sir. Some can give you an even harder time than Sergeant McCabe and Mr Izzard, but they're not all like that and some are even human. Anyway don't worry about that now. The Flying Fornicator, the 7.29 express from King's Cross gets in to Grantham too late for them to trouble you tonight! I suggest you form up outside and march quickly to the mess before it closes. I'll be here to answer any further questions you may have on return."

Supper in the Junior Mess was the standard Air Force meal Jamie had already received at Biggin Hill and Daedalus House, the traditional fry up of baked beans, chips, bacon, sausages, greasy eggs and tinned tomatoes plus white bread and margarine and a mug of tea – identical in fact to the legendary night flying suppers which had sustained Bomber Command aircrews in World War II and which still followed night flying at the College.

Jamie and the rest at last had a brief moment to think. He wondered how the Chinese cadet from Singapore Sam Chu would cope with the cold. Maybe the Pakistani Yousuf Ahmed was suffering, too, but probably less so. Much of Pakistan is very cold in winter. What were the officers really like? He heard more over supper about Squadron Leader Chivvers the Squadron Commander. He had been in 56 Squadron at Waterbeach, the first to get the Swift when it came into service.

There were several casualties in the squadron, mostly from the aircraft's tendency to pitch up viciously in tight manoeuvres. Chivvers had gone on to the Central Fighter Establishment to develop combat tactics on the aircraft for which he had been awarded the much coveted Air Force Cross before the Service gave up on the Swift as an interceptor in favour of the more docile Hunter. He was then posted to Geilenkirchen on Swift FR5s in the low level fighter reconnaissance role as a Flight Commander.

Now Chivvers was back at Cranwell on promotion twelve years after winning the Sword of Honour and taking the passing out parade. If he did not put up a black he should be a Wing Commander on his next tour commanding his own squadron. Jamie thought Chivvers' name was familiar, then he recalled the memorable afternoon at Geilenkirchen, which he had visited on a navigational exercise by Varsity during Combined Cadet Force summer camp at Thorney Island.

What a trip it had been staying in the mess like an officer, being brought tea in bed first thing by the batman, the exciting pre-flight briefing for a triangular cross country exercise to Le Touquet airfield nestling beside the wooded villa filled dunes of Paris plage to the French fighter base at St Dizier followed by a descent into a low level sector over the pine clad hills of the Eifel. For most of the flight Jamie had been prone in a replica of the bomb aimer's station in the Varsity's nose with the fields and farmsteads of north-west Europe passing beneath.

On arrival at Geilenkirchen they were taken straight to the balcony of the station's control tower, "You will now witness a demonstration of RAF Geilenkirchen's role in the Second Allied Tactical Air Force," proclaimed their host the Wing Commander, Flying. Before the schoolboys could even wonder what it was an explosion of sound struck them. Two Swifts well spaced in battle formation passed below the balcony, parallel to the runway and then broke in opposite directions. When the roar of the jets subsided the Wing Commander explained. "You see we have to go in low and very fast. That way our aircraft could be past the objective with their target pictures taken before the Warsaw Pact defences even knew they were coming. See if you can spot them in advance next time round."

Jamie and his friends scoured the skyline. Nothing to be seen. Then he saw it – the arrowhead planform of a Swift banking vertically with grey vortices swirling from its swept wings silhouetted briefly between a pine copse and a large hangar. "There it is!" he exclaimed, but the sentence was drowned by the other aircraft tearing past over the signals square below in the opposite direction. The two Swifts crossed over the centre of the airfield before pulling up into three vertical rolls in full reheat disappearing into the summertime clouds of puffy white cumulus.

"That's it, boys," said the Wing Commander. "We'll just watch them rejoin the circuit and land, then you can talk to the pilots in the crew room." Five minutes later the pair of Swifts reappeared in close formation higher than before and not so fast. First the leader broke left halfway down the runway onto the downwind leg followed three seconds later by the number two. Both aeroplanes lowered their wheels and began a tightly curved approach straightening out just as they passed the white stripes at the threshold of the runway. Their tyres audibly kissed the runway with a puff of blue smoke and they taxied in with their canopies back to the dispersal where the ground crew marshalled them expeditiously to their shutdown position.

To talk to the pilots Flight Lieutenant Chivvers and Flying Officer 'Manx' Quine felt a privilege indeed. Even to enter the Two squadron crew room was like trespassing a sanctuary. The coffee bar was cluttered with mugs, some with crests and emblems, some with jokey inscriptions. Magazines like Air Clues, Flight and Aviation Week littered the tables together with Accident Reports and Flight Safety bulletins.

The walls were decorated with a collage of busty pinups interspersed with silhouettes of Warsaw Pact aircraft with their NATO codenames. Photographs were hanging of squadron groups at Weapon Camp at Sylt, at Twenthe on exchange, at Ramstein for the Tactical Air Forces photo reconnaissance competition, and older pictures from World War II with dogs and pipe smoking pilots at dispersal or swinging themselves in or out of aircraft cockpits. Pride of place on the back of the door was the slogan in dark red capitals "It takes two to tango" and a black and white cut out of a Two Squadron pilot in bow tie and mess kit with a Hispanic diva in dancing pose with an outsize black numeral 2 between them. Such exotic memories for Jamie seemed far removed from the realities of Flight Cadet life at Cranwell.

Amazingly when he returned to their hut he found that Kiwi McGilligan had already lit the fire. Around the stove it was hot. Beside the walls and windows it was glacially cold but with socks and sweater on the cold in bed was tolerable. Although their fatigue was profound the experience of arrival at the College was too intense to pass unremarked.

"I quite liked, Sergeant McCabe," observed Carrick. "The other sergeants' language was far worse."

"Give him time to reveal his true nature," replied Lascelles pessimistically. "What do we do, Kiwi, if there's just more and more snow? How will we drill? Will we ever be able to fly? I heard that one year Cranwell was snowbound almost till Easter."

"Well I assure you that you will not miss out on the drill," replied McGilligan, "they use the hangars for drill in extremely bad weather and as for flying you're programmed to do hardly any this term anyway."

"Let's just see what delights tomorrow brings," observed Jamie. "It's time to sleep."

CHAPTER 3

It was black outside with an icy east wind howling around the huts when McGilligan's alarm clock went off at 0545 hours. He did not linger in bed. "Wake up all of you," he cried, "you'll need to be shaved, showered and out by 0605 with your bedclothes folded correctly if you're to have any chance of getting to breakfast and of being on parade on time. If you're late for parade you'll begin your first full day with a charge, which I do not recommend."

In the event there was time for a hurried shower and bed making or for a proper breakfast, but not for both. Lascelles who was deliberate and slow in all he did, opted out of breakfast. The others bolted some cereal but the tea was too hot to drink in the two minutes available and the service of the regulation fry up impossibly slow.

Out on the parade square by 0628 hours for kit issue those with caps or hats were glad of them. Those with gloves were particularly happy. Further overnight snowfall muffled their drill movements as Sergeant McCabe brought the squadron to attention. The piercing wind accentuated Lascelles' hunger pangs and China Chu's light footwear, ideal for the sweaty heat of Singapore made his snowy trudge to East Camp even more miserable. The dark morning and relentless cold were completely alien to him.

The Clothing Store was a classic 1920s red brick slate roofed structure beside yet another snow covered parade ground with which doubtless Aircraftsman Ross was all too familiar during his escape to Cranwell from the Lawrence of Arabia Legend thirty years before. Around the other sides of the square, airmen were emerging into the bitter gloom mess tin and enamel mug in hand to proceed hunched like Lowry's mill town matchstick men towards the Airmen's Mess.

Inside the Clothing Store each cadet received a blue holdall into which he stuffed a coarse blue battledress; black shoes without toecaps; black drill boots with toecaps; standard issue shirts with detached starchable collars and softer aircrew shirts with integral collars; two blue pullovers, one lightweight and v necked, the other heavy duty with patched shoulders and elbows; black socks for daily use and white socks for flying and PT; several pairs of the notorious and baggy drawers cotton cellular; a housewife or needle pouch containing a thimble, needle and thread; a black tie; a thick greatcoat with brass buttons; blue blancoable anklets and a blue blancoable belt both with brass buckles for drill; a white blancoable belt also with brass buckles for ceremonial parades; a beret with RAF cap badge set in a white disc; a pair of flying overalls plus dinghy knife, which had to be separately signed for; a pair of exquisitely soft kid leather flying gloves; a pair of black flying boots; a pair of black woollen gloves and a pair of smooth buttonable brown leather gloves for ceremonial parades; two white shirts with detached starchable winged collars and a black bow tie for Mess Guest Nights.

"Check all items against the issue list, gentlemen," insisted Sergeant McCabe. "If they don't fit you can change them later," he claimed optimistically. "Your Number One dress hat will be issued after fitting by Bates the hatters and your Number One uniform also after fitting, by Gieves the tailors. You will receive a protective flying helmet or 'bone dome' next year if you are lucky enough to proceed to pilot training. Now you will march back to your huts as a squad to pack your kit away. Tonight you will mark it, iron your uniforms, adjust them if necessary and polish and blanco your drill items. Tomorrow you will be inspected with all your equipment."

The lightening sky revealed the unredeemed blackness of East Camp dominated by three storied barrack blocks named in honour of five Royal Air Force winners of the Victoria Cross – Cheshire, Learoyd, Gibson, Edwards and Nicholson. There was a Sergeants' Mess, an Airmen's Mess, the Motor Transport section, NAAFI, and of especial interest to the Flight Cadets who otherwise never ventured into East Camp, a gymnasium and an indoor swimming pool for physical training, parachute and dinghy drills.

South brick lines were positively homely compared to East Camp. The huts snuggled up against the back of the hangars, which doubtless would come to noisy life when improved weather permitted flying to begin. In the other direction they looked towards the College, a symbol of power and purpose to whose lofty corridors all were drawn by expectant aspiration and from which on graduation over thirty years of respect and responsibility as permanent commissioned officers beckoned.

For the inmates of East Camp twenty-two years of largely unrecognised service was the most that the airmen could hope for unless they earned a long service and good conduct medal or could slip the confined horizons of their enlisted caste on commission from the ranks.

After a group photograph in front of the Junior Mess the cadets assembled on the parade ground by squadrons in their new uniforms, greatcoats and boots. Then came an inspection, which revealed a multitude of dress defects. Some battledresses were too big, some too small or tight, likewise boots, shirts, greatcoats and berets. "Swap them among yourselves or change them," was the sergeant's injunction.

No concession was made to wind or snow or cold. "You will parade out here at all times, unless I declare the weather so severe as to warrant a hangar parade," declared Sergeant McCabe. "After half term you will be issued with rifles for arms drill. They will be kept permanently padlocked to your beds when not in use. Until then I want you to get the basis of foot drill right and I will go on at you until you do. You will now march smartly as a squad to your academic instructors in West Camp."

The tramp to a cluster of huts known as West Site was a welcome respite. The home of the academic Wing was the antithesis of the dreamy towers and spires of Oxford and Cambridge. The squat wooden huts were the most basic imaginable but possessed of central heating and as far as could be discerned weatherproof. Two academic hierarchies would control the Flight Cadets' destiny. First came the crucial technical and scientific training team run by the kindly lugubrious Wing Commander Blackett known affectionately by the cadets as Dr Volta. Under his benign tutelage came the more practical aeronautical subjects – mathematics, physics, meteorology, aerodynamics, navigation, instruments, thermodynamics, powerplants, radio, structures and weapons.

Second were the so-called humanities run by Wing Commander (Worldly) Wise – the history and customs of the Royal Air Force, service writing, which subsumed English and war studies with lecturers drawn from each of the three armed services plus one from the United States Air Force. The overall Head of Academics was a civilian who only seemed to appear for prize givings, Mess Guest Nights, Passing Out Parades and Graduation Balls.

The message of both Chief Instructors was the same. "There are exams," they explained at the end of each term. "You are required to reach a minimum standard in all subjects. If you do not you will be suspended or recoursed. In addition you will have two free periods a week in which you can take an optional subject like military history or a foreign language. In your final term you will do a thesis on a subject of your choice upon which you will be marked."

The cadets knew that few of them would excel equally at the sciences and humanities although one or two notorious brainboxes like Kiwi McGilligan managed to do so. Most had come in via the College's competitive entry examination with its bias towards science and mathematics. Some more literary types like Lascelles, fearful of maths and the sciences, managed to slip in without an entrance exam by passing A Levels. However, they paid for their special dispensation later since all the aerodynamics, radio, thermodynamics, structures, and meteorology they were taught seemed to come down to arcane formulae and abstruse mathematical calculations, sources of much toil and travail for the arts men.

That evening the Senior Entries were to call on the crows. The door of hut 150 burst open and in swept what Jamie instantly recognised as an Under Officer with a thin v shaped stripe on his sleeve, and two Senior Flight Cadets with gold buttons on their white shoulder flashes. Their timing was shrewd. Supper was over and the cadets of hut 150 were working furiously to get their kit up to scratch for the next day's inspection by Sergeant McCabe.

The Under Officer first addressed Kiwi McGilligan. "How are the new boys doing, mentor?"

"A steady progress so far Under Officer Peterson," replied Kiwi. "I think their kit will be up to scratch by morning, sir."

"Well I do not share your confidence," he answered. He turned to Lascelles who had leapt to attention with the rest. "Give me your belt. Look at the rear of the belt buckles, Flight Cadet, and tell me what you see."

"Ordinary buckle brass, sir."

"No it is not. It is extraordinarily dirty brass. In future you will polish the back of each buckle to shine as brightly as the front. To remember my comments you'd better start the whole thing again. I want to see you put the belt under the tap. Then when I've gone reblanco it and last but not least address yourself to both sides of each buckle without allowing any spot of brasso to spoil the webbing. If you cannot do it now you will soon learn to do so for restrictions parades."

One of the Senior Flight Cadets had homed in on Jones. "Why are you looking pleased with yourself Taffy boy?" he taunted.

"I don't think I am," replied Jones.

"Well, pick up a drill boot and look at your face in the toecap and tell me what you see."

"Nothing sir."

"Of course not. It's shitty with no real shine at all. So you've got nothing to be pleased about. You'll need to polish both boots including the soles all night to get them up to standard. When you can see your reflection in the toecaps then you can stop."

"Sir," acknowledged Jones crestfallen. If he was going to shine boots all night how was he going to mark his clothes, press his battledress, iron his shirt and collar, blanco his webbing and polish the buckles? These were the daily quandaries which faced the new entry all along the South Brick Lines as crowing persisted throughout the first fortnight and beyond.

Drill Sergeants, Flight and Squadron Commanders soon found several scores of faults to which were added the Senior Entries' ample tally. Charges built up for most of the crows although some marked men suffered much worse than others. Lascelles was a particular target. He seemed almost provocatively laid back. He exuded a cultivated insouciance, which brought upon him many accusations of dumb insolence. Parker just did not seem to be able to do anything right and Carrick was always behind the clock, congenitally incapable of arriving punctually for parade or accomplishing any task on time.

In the last week of January wind, gloom, grey skies and blizzards gave way to bright sunshine and severe frosts. The cadets were detailed to clear the parade grounds with salty sand and shovels. On the south airfield the fuel bowsers sported snowploughs from their front bumpers and at last the College's true purpose was revealed. From eight in the morning until dark the whining wail of the Vampires' Goblin engines almost drowned out the lustily bellowed orders of the drill sergeants.

After three and a half weeks of snowbound inactivity Flying Wing had much catching up to do. Graduation day was an immovable date at the end of July. All two hundred and seventy flight hours of pilot training and each and every exercise – the formation flying, tail chasing, high level aerobatics, high and low level navigation, night and instrument flying plus much else besides had to be satisfactorily accomplished for a cadet to pass out and to earn a pilot's coveted flying badge.

This exciting flying activity brought a sense of purpose and real interest to even the lowliest new cadet's routine. Senior Flight Cadets and Under Officers in unstarched aircrew shirts, flying boots and pilot's parkas bicycled past the marching and drilling crows on their way to Met. briefing and the Flight Line. Early morning drill often coincided with a weather check, which would allow a star Vampire instructor to impress the Junior Entries on the parade ground with loops and rolls, Cuban and vertical eights, Derry and Immelmann turns and the whole repertoire of aerobatic artistry to which drill sergeants remained obstinately impervious.

A furtive skyward glimpse to count the points of a hesitation roll or to judge the symmetry of a vertical eight would bring an instant charge upon a Flight Cadet. Doubtless this misanthropic tradition of the NCOs even applied in the immediate post war years when early morning Met reconnaissance beat ups and impromptu aerobatic displays were often the prerogative of the Commandant himself, Air Commodore Batchy Atcherley.

Such was the urgency of the catch up programme that when the weekend came and the Senior Entries had to continue flying on Saturday to complete the syllabus, Sergeant McCabe made a special announcement at the end of morning drill: "The Officer Commanding Cadet Wing has expressed his concern that the recent inclement weather could have led Flight Cadets to lose physical fitness. As you know all football is still off due to ice and thick snow on the pitches. He has therefore organised a cross-country run for all Flight Cadets of the Middle and Junior Entries. Cheer up Lascelles, don't look so sad," he continued. "The course will extend right round the north airfield through the wood at the western end and out onto the High Dyke, the old Roman road to Lincoln and back.

"You will all take part except for the two cadets from each Junior Entry squadron who will act as markers. I, gentlemen, am going to show you how reasonable I can be. I know it will be so cold that the markers would rather be running but being on restrictions would be even worse. So the privileged pair will be those I previously charged for letting their eyes wander on parade towards aircraft overhead. Out on the north airfield and the High Dyke you will ensure that the runners do not take short cuts but complete the full circuit. You will also be able to watch all the air activity you could only glimpse during drill. I nominate the two aforementioned peeping toms for this purpose – Mr Jamieson and Mr Lascelles. Get warmly kitted out gentlemen and be in position by 1400 hours."

It would have been fanciful to imagine that Junior Entry Cadets could have actually prevented the Middle Entries from skiving had they wished to. Cadet Wing Officers in aircrew parkas and great coats were huddled at the start post behind the College where the run also finished, but none of them ventured onto the distant wastes of the north airfield let alone beyond the woods to the High Dyke. As every cadet's performance had to be monitored and each individual time recorded Wing Commander Tophill commanding the Cadet Wing had thoughtfully laid on NCO physical training instructors as pacemakers to accompany the runners and ensure that they neither wandered from the course nor lagged nor faked injury, but strode out purposefully past the markers culminating in a sprint finish in front of their squadron officers.

When the runners had gone past him out and back Lascelles trudged over to Jamieson and admitted: "Would you believe it, Jamie, I almost enjoyed standing out here in the cold. Quite incredibly I even saw a bird cross this windswept arctic tundra. Any female creature is such a rare appearance that I actually felt my pulse rise. She was walking her dog back to the officers' married quarters."

"I had no luck behind the wood, Peter, but I did have a good view of the aeroplanes. There were stream take offs, formation landings and wonderful breaks into the circuit. Do you know that one Vampire broke level with the controller's caravan and touched down in forty-four seconds. Look they're still at it," he replied.

Dusk was gathering over the Kesteven heathland and although it was not yet dark the aircraft had their navigation lights on and the circuit was humming with Vampires hurrying home. First a four ship formation broke left onto the downwind leg at five second intervals, level and in leisurely style unlike the previous forty-four second singleton.

"Look, Peter," he exclaimed, "that's just how you should not rejoin, I bet he can't see a thing below him…" The sentence was not finished before the impact. The single-seater pitched instantaneously vertically downwards and exploded loudly in a mushroom of fire. The two-seater staggered on briefly like a wounded butterfly and fluttered into a copse beyond the runway. Within a minute a red glow was discernible and dense black smoke billowed from the woodland. The crash alarm hooted and fire engines and an ambulance could be seen struggling over the rough ground through bramble bushes and saplings towards the crash sites.

For a couple of minutes Jamie and Peter did not speak, then Peter observed "You were right to be worried, Jamie. I wonder how many more of such horrors we can expect before we pass out."

"I don't know Peter," Jamie replied, "but Taffy Jones took the bus to Lincoln last Saturday afternoon and in the twilight he reckons he saw a couple of hundred new white headstones in the Cranwell village churchyard. Some of those will be wartime of course and not all Flight Cadets by any means, but hardly any entry escapes the grim reaper entirely in its three years."

When they got back to the hut Kiwi McGilligan was emerging from the shower after his run. "What was all that about?" he asked. "I heard a double bang and the crash alarm. So often they're spurious these alarms – undercarriage light failures, very low fuel states, false fire warnings, that kind of thing but this one sounded different to me. I could hear what seemed like the bell of an ambulance in the distance, too."

"I'm afraid it was, Kiwi," Jamie answered. "Two Vampires collided just beyond the end of the runway. The single-seater stood no chance. They don't have bang seats anyway. He just went straight in. He hit a T11 climbing out. It staggered on for a bit and wobbled into the woods. It must have caught fire because there was a pall of thick black smoke beyond the trees. I only hope they could get out because the emergency vehicles did not seem to have been able to get through the bushes and scrub."

High Tea in the Junior Mess was alive with rumours. "Did anyone else see it happen?" asked Jamieson.

"Well we all heard the bangs and the crash alarm. Some of us dashed out of our huts and saw the smoke. It must have been quite close," said Higgins.

"I'm on restrictions at 9.20 and 10.00 pm and my mentor has told me that Under Officer Groves will not be taking it so I fear the worst. He was so officious at the 0630 parade asking why my tie had only a half and not a whole Windsor knot. I've never heard of Duty Under Officers or Senior Flight Cadets being excused restrictions."

"They would not want to be," observed Farquharson, "putting crows like us on charges is their chief pleasure in life."

"I reckon the roll call of Cadet Wing has been reduced by at least one this afternoon," said Lascelles. "No qualified flying instructor would rejoin the circuit straight ahead in a dive like that. As for the T11 it might have been an instructor with a pupil who were hit, but whoever was on board the fuselage is made of plywood and you are more or less sitting on top of a centrifugal turbojet surrounded by fuel so I don't think that's the kind of structure in which to land in the woods. Anyway they were too low when they collided for them to eject even if the pilot ever knew what happened."

The conversation was interrupted by a breathless Flight Cadet Ellington. "Bad news from south airfield this afternoon, I'm afraid. Three dead – one Senior Flight Cadet, one Under Officer and a QFI. I was rehydrating myself in the pub in Leasingham after the run when a farmer came in who had tried to help with his tractor when the aircraft came down. The crash crew told him it was Under Officer Groves who was hit in the T11. It was not even an instructional trip. He had volunteered for the ride to keep a QFI company on an air test at the end of the day so the aeroplane could be serviceable first thing on Monday and, as for Senior Flight Cadet Thomas, it was his first solo flight in an FB9."

CHAPTER 4

The next day dawned grey and cold with light snow flurries sweeping across the north airfield on the edge of which stood the College chapel, a black all iron World War One hangar whose outer structure had remained unaltered since Cranwell's days as HMS Daedalus, a Royal Naval Air Station during the Great War. Breakfast was leisurely from 0830 hours but inevitably the Sabbath Day at the College was celebrated with parades – first the Church Parade proper consisting of an inspection on the drill square and march as a squad to the sanctified hangar and then after the service the Cadet Wing march past the Commandant and Assistant Commandant by squadrons with each squadron commander leading, the only occasion when Cadet Wing executives actually marched with their flight cadets.

By 0930 hours the junior entries were duly out on the square in front of their Mess. Although Cadet Wing officers regarded impeccable turnout as akin to Godliness a Cranwell Sunday afforded some concessions. Best blue uniforms were the order instead of rough serge battledress with brown leather not black woollen gloves. Shoes were worn not drill boots. No anklets were required and peaked caps were donned not berets. Each cadet wore a great coat with well buffed brass buttons plus a perfectly blancoed blue belt on top with gleaming buckles.

Carl Higgins had taken the bus from East Camp to the Green Man in Lincoln the night before, his first sortie away from the station. The Saturday night Cinderella deadline of 2359 hours for cadets to return to the College plus the early departure time of the last bus to Cranwell village had been pacemakers for his drinking. His face was ashen and each drill movement even without studded boots jarred his aching head. Sergeant McCabe was onto him at once spotting traces of brasso within the interstices of the crosses in the crowns of his great coat buttons.

"If you had spent as much time on your buttons as you did on your beer last night, Mr Higgins, you would be marching off more worthily to worship this morning. I shall see to it that you get more time these coming evenings for polishing brass than for swilling beer. Then by next Church Parade you'll have discovered that piety here is no substitute for attention to detail and impeccable kit. So, Mr Higgins, I am charging you for filthy buttons on Church Parade."

After his brief homily to Higgins and the squad Sergeant McCabe seemed satisfied. "Roman Catholics and Jews may now fall out," he bellowed. No one could remember a Jew at Cranwell, but one Roman Catholic James Kelly came to attention, turned to his right and moved off. "And where do you think you're going, Mr Kelly?" snapped Sergeant McCabe. "Just because you're a Papist doesn't mean you can skive off. Report to Flight Lieutenant Brennan in his office at once and he will ensure that you attend RC Mass. As soon as it is over report outside the College chapel for the march past at 1130 hours sharp."

Up they marched to the chapel skirting the College, the squad swinging along the old interwar flight lines where Douglas Bader and Peter Townsend had trained, with Sergeant McCabe striding stiffly alongside his pace stick at times folded under his arm, at other times extended and tapping out the pace like a metronomic geometrical compass.

On arrival a quarter of an hour early for the service Jamieson had tried to look around. The hangar was cavernous and dusty somewhat moth eaten standards hung from its corrugated iron roof. At the far end on the platform in front of the altar sat the College band and the cadet choir. "Can you sing, Jamie?" asked Ellington.

"If you can it's worth it. In the choir you're excused Church Parade to attend choir practice." In the front rows sat the officers and their behatted overdressed wives and cowed looking children. Lascelles felt a stirring of excitement. Would the girl he had spotted on the north airfield with her dog the day before put in an appearance?

In came the Cadet Wing executives in reverse order of seniority – first the Flight Lieutenants, then the Squadron Leaders with Messrs Bates' No 1 dress caps under their arms and brown leather gloves studiously in hand. "There she is!" exclaimed Peter Lascelles to Jamie. "I'd recognise that walk anywhere." Her parents were a wingless rather grey faced Squadron Leader, her mother somewhat brassy with exceptionally high heels and a very flowery blouse beneath an open fur collared coat.

Peter's bird had long legs, which swung easily at the hips as she progressed self-consciously under the critical eyes of many flight cadets towards the officers' pews up front. Soon came the Wing Commanders followed by a clanking of medals, which heralded the Station Commander, Assistant Commandant and the notoriously gruff voiced, laconic and moustachioed Commandant himself. The College chaplain followed shortly behind at a respectful distance as the band struck up the Trumpet Voluntary.

The service was muscular but not devoid of religious feeling. The crash of the day before lent it greater intensity. Traditional hymns, a psalm, and an anthem from the choir plus two Biblical lessons one read by an officer, one by a cadet were as on all previous Sundays. There was no special address by the Commandant, no tribute from any Cadet Wing officer or cadet to his fellows who had so recently been killed. However, the chaplain who had experienced all too many such events at the various stations on which he served chose his text from St John's Gospel well: "Greater love hath no man than this that a man lay down his life for his friends.

"You may not realise it ladies and gentlemen," he began, "but in the church's year we are still commemorating the feast of the Epiphany in which the infant Jesus is revealed to the world through the persons of the three wise men who came from the east to worship him and to pay him tribute. We are here this morning as on every Sunday morning to pay our tribute to Christ who gave his life for our salvation. Unlike the Magi we have no gifts to offer him but only as the Holy Communion service states 'ourselves, our souls and bodies to be a full, lively and sufficient sacrifice'.

"Service of all kinds demands sacrifice and in serving our neighbour we are also serving our Lord. As military men and women our service is special because it can entail the total sacrifice of our lives. That's what Under Officer Groves, Senior Flight Cadet Thomas and Flight Lieutenant Ackroyd made yesterday. We all know that it is a sacrifice which any of us may be called upon to make in the Royal Air Force. No one of us likes it. It causes grief to families and friends and we all share a terrible sense of loss, but it is necessary to keep us and our country free; a price worth paying.

"The Royal Air Force and most certainly the Royal Air Force College, Cranwell, are like an extended family. You may not realise it but each of you is valued. You are carefully selected and monitored. You will bear special responsibilities for which very few are worthy. Your qualities are on trial all the time to see if they match those required by the Service. On Remembrance Sundays in commemoration of the fallen we proclaim 'they shall not grow old as we that are left grow old. Age shall not weary them nor the years condemn.' It is often said that the best die young. The three who died yesterday left many treasured memories and a strong sense of unfulfilled promise but they died before the disappointments and failures of later life could tarnish their memory. Let us take their examples to heart fortified in the knowledge that Christ sacrificed himself for us and that our three brothers died doing what they loved best for the freedom of their families and friends and the continued liberty of our nation and the Commonwealth."

Padre Cinderton was not the kind of chaplain who normally aroused emotions but he was well regarded. It was said that his wife baked good cakes for those who attended his evening confirmation classes and that the cadets who volunteered for his Moral Leadership courses, the spiritual retreats at the Royal Air Force Chaplains' school on the edge of the Cotswolds experienced the next best thing to paradise for a cadet. They constituted the perfect antidote to College life – a lazy weekend in the Gloucestershire countryside with Mess Stewards to serve the meals at polished mahogany tables, chintz sofas on which to laze, extensive gardens and a total absence of kit inspections and drill sergeants.

Christian faith was innate at the College but unstated. A gem of a chapel in the main building converted from the crash site of an aircraft in World War II and a consecrated hut on the way to Station Headquarters held Holy Communion services on Sunday mornings, which were not unattended. However, few would speak mystically about flying like the pilot poet John Magee in High Flight who 'reached out and touched the hand of God'. Yet at this moment of common bereavement Padre Cinderton had got the commemoration of the fallen flight cadets just right.

The service ended as ever with the Walford Davies anthem sung by the choir, which Peter Lascelles very much still the Wykehamist scholar epigramatically called 'sit deus in capite' – 'God be in my head… and at my departing.' Did this include sudden death Jamie mused and rationalised that it meant always being spiritually prepared, living this day as if one's last and entrusting one's soul to God in advance ready for any eventuality.

Once the anthem died away the band struck up the stirring tune for the hymn St Patrick's Breastplate – "I bind unto myself today, the strong name of the Trinity" as the flight cadets filed out first precluding any ogling of the officers' daughters. Perhaps the band master had concluded that the whole congregation needed a spiritual uplift. The College band's brassy exit blast was confident and bold.

Outside, Mr Izzard the Station Warrant Officer had his weekly opportunity to impress the Commandant by exerting his formidable authority even over the nominal Parade Commander, Wing Commander Greg Tophill. His bellowing began, "Form up, form up, gentlemen: by squadrons of course, facing the west door." Soon by dint of much courteous shuffling around by squadron drill sergeants of the Cadet Wing officers who seemed exceptionally unfamiliar with drill and looked ungainly with their full dress belts and swords, the parade had been turned into line by Mr Izzard.

The band whose members were notably of all shapes and sizes and capped with Ruritanian blue plumed headgear took up the familiar chords of the Lincolnshire Poacher. At the head of C squadron padded Squadron Leader Chivvers. His ungainly gait had earned him the cadets' sobriquet of Snowshoes. Even when approaching the saluting base he walked his inimitable walk whilst the band reverted to Walford Davies' Royal Air Force March, so eminently suitable for striding out.

"C Squadron, eyes right!" cried Snowshoes bringing his sword down to a forty-five degree angle. Just as Peter had hoped she was perfectly placed behind the Commandant's dais. The minute that the squadron took to march past gave him time not just to catch the Air Commodore's eye but to gaze over his shoulder to the small family group behind. The blousy mother was easily recognisable. The Squadron Leader was probably Education or Secretarial branch thought Peter. He seemed to have anonymity written all over him. Their daughter wore no hat, had auburn hair and a clearly curvaceous figure, which her unbuttoned coat happily revealed.

"Eyes front!" commanded Snowshoes and he brought his sword up to the carry whilst the cadets marched purposefully on to the dismissal point of the East Wing of the College.

Peter's life had gained a new purpose in just a few minutes. How could he actually meet the girl? He never saw her father during the day. Perhaps he had some tedious administrative job in Station Headquarters or endured the living death of teaching enlisted personnel in East Camp.

What on earth did the girl do? Most young girls of her age were away at University or sharing a flat in London with other secretaries. Living at home on the married patch of Cranwell north airfield might have its compensations but Peter could hardly imagine what they were. It must be almost as frustrating as being a Flight Cadet, so at least they should have something in common if only they could meet. Longing looks at Church Parade were not going to get him very far. He would have to discuss the problem with Jamie Jamieson who had at least seen her but experienced no interest. He probably still harboured the delusion that he could find his intellectual soul mate in Lincolnshire. Lascelles who was genuinely intellectual had given up on this idea after the first snowbound week.

CHAPTER 5

February was no warmer than January. The 0630 hours restrictions parades were especially unpleasant with numb unfeeling fingers resting on rifles and frozen ears protruding beneath tight berets, which always seemed to sear painfully into the forehead. However, after the first month came the news that all the junior entry except the handful of Equipment and Secretarial cadets had been waiting for. "Tomorrow you fly, gentlemen," announced Sergeant McCabe at the morning drill parade. "You will have a very early lunch in the Mess and report outside at 1230 hours bringing your navigation bag plus the issue holdall with your flying gear in. I will inspect you and your kit before you embark for Barkston Heath."

"What can we expect, Kiwi?" Jamie asked Kiwi McGilligan the hut 150 mentor as he blancoed his belt and anklets for next morning's parade.

"Oh, the usual milk run up North," Kiwi replied. "It will be just dead simple map reading, straightforward visual navigation plus a little time and distance work. The subsequent few flights will be similar, but you'll be using the pinpoints you've identified to plot your track on a chart whilst keeping a navigation log of your progress. On further trips it will build up to dead reckoning, air plots, radio bearings and establishing your position electronically with Gee culminating eventually in some blind and night navexes. As you are all pilots you won't be let loose on the astronavigation, with sextants, star shots, etc., which separates the GD/N men like me from the General Duties/Pilot boys like you."

Next morning they marched off to the East Camp swimming pool for dinghy drill. The chlorine laden water steamed and stank. The cadets learned how difficult it is to inflate a rubber dinghy, to set it the right way up and to board it even in a calm heated pool in daylight. As they would later discover to repeat the operation in the open sea in winter especially at night or in bad weather is infinitely more challenging.

After lunch the now familiar anonymous blue bus took them along the High Dyke to Barkston Heath, a journey they would repeat many scores of times in the months ahead till each stone wall, bush and tree became familiar. How the Roman legionaries must have hated the Lincolnshire winters. Perhaps Ancaster was their last staging and bathing post on the long tramp to Lincoln. For the cadets Ancaster, with its mellow limestone houses, high spired church and a gem of a bow windowed red brick miniature country house represented an oasis of calm rural village life between Mr Izzard's fearsome domain at Cranwell and the Nissen hutted, black hangared wilderness of Barkston Heath.

At least the cadets could with confidence expect to return for supper not so the airborne forces who had left Barkston Heath's asphalt runways a decade and a half before to drop on Arnhem. Now Barkston had been stripped of everything irrelevant to its role as a relief landing ground for Cranwell. On arrival the cadets trooped into a wooden hut where they were met by a Flight Sergeant in flying overalls.

"This way," he indicated, "for Met briefing, gentlemen and afterwards you will go across the corridor for your parachutes and for the issue of flying rations." The Met briefing room was sparse with a few posters on the wall of cloud formations –

cumulus, stratus, cirrus and their particular forms – nimbus, lenticular, mammatus and so on.

Behind the platform at the end was a large topographical chart of the United Kingdom and Ireland with airways and danger areas clearly marked and an assortment of coloured pins superimposed upon particular airfields. In one corner was a green radio facilities chart and in another a white board for chinagraph inscriptions with a few key titles – Airfield Status, Diversions, Altimeter pressure settings of the airfield elevation QNH and sea level QFE, Royal Flights and special warnings.

"Take a seat, gentlemen," instructed the grizzled Flight Sergeant. "You will first receive a navigation briefing from your Chief Navigation Instructor, then a flight briefing from the officer commanding Varsity and Valetta flight and finally a meteorological briefing. You must listen and if necessary take notes because the briefings will not be repeated."

In strode Squadron Leader Ashley, a tall, benign, spectacled, slightly stooped figure whose unusual patience and tolerance in the classroom the cadets had come to admire. Then followed Flight Lieutenant Zopoloski, DFC, DFM, VM, one of a handful of brave Poles who had stayed on in the Royal Air Force rather than face retribution from the communist authorities in Poland. "Better to finish my career as a Pig pilot at Barkston Heath than clean pigsties in my ruined truncated country," had been his explanation. The other three pilots were all NCOs – a couple of Warrant Officers, one with an Air Force Medal, the other with a long service and distinguished conduct ribbon and finally a tiny rotund bald-headed Flight Sergeant whose short legs must have only just reached the rudder pedals of a Valetta. Following them was "Cunimb Jim" the College meteorologist dressed as ever in tweed jacket and corduroys, a figure the cadets would get to know well and on whose judgement lives could depend.

"This afternoon, gentlemen," began Squadron Leader Ashley, "you start your flying training. We shall be operating four Valettas on a triangular cross country navex from Barkston Heath to St Abb's Head then across to Crosby in Eden and back to base. You will use your 1:500,000 topographical charts to mark the track and time points and you'll log your progress noting on a sheet of paper the prominent pinpoints you obtain and precisely when you identified them.

"During the sortie one of my instructing team" – and he pointed to three colleagues who had slipped in at the back – "may ask you questions and of course if you need assistance or advice of any kind when airborne speak to them. They are there to help.

"This time you're excused the flight planning and you'll simply need to concentrate on the track which will take you initially over the easily recognisable landmarks of Lincolnshire's bomber country – past Cranwell, RAF Swinderby, RAF Waddington, the city of Lincoln and RAF Scampton northwards more or less following the old Roman road past the disused bomber base at Hemswell, across the Humber skirting the Vale of York with its many airfields, RAF Church Fenton and so on, over the Tees Valley with RAF Middleton St George to one side and RAF Thornaby to the other.

"Then we cross the Tyne – Newcastle and Gateshead stand out well on their respective sides of the river and Woolsington, Newcastle Airport, soon after. Then you will see RAF Acklington and the Farne Islands and before you know it we will be turning over St Abb's Head on a south westerly heading for Crosby in Eden just north of Carlisle. It's a pretty featureless stretch of Cheviot Hills and Northumberland moors but your navigation instructor will give you the actual wind vector so you can work out our groundspeed and using the Dalton computer estimate the timings to Crosby and to potential diversions like RAF Ouston, RAF Leeming and so on.

"From Crosby we will descend as soon as we are past Carlisle to fly a low level sector before resuming our cruising altitude. By then the haze over the industrial areas and thickening evening mist will make pinpointing difficult especially up sun. We hope to touch down at base at five-minute intervals from 1700 hours. If that is all clear to you I now invite Flight Lieutenant Zopoloski to read the aircraft detail for this afternoon and to give the flight safety briefing."

Flight Lieutenant Zopoloski looking incongruous in best blue and decidedly left wing low from the mass of medal ribbons on his chest stood up and from the front gave his brief heavily accented instructions.

"Flight Cadets," he began, "my three colleagues and I will command the four Valetta navigation training aircraft in which you are to fly this afternoon. The details of today's exercise are on the blackboard at the door with the full routeing giving captain's name, registration markings and radio call signs for each aeroplane, embarkation times and the names of the navigation trainees; that is you.

"On board the captain's orders will be obeyed at once without question. You will wear your parachute harness and life jackets at all times, only clipping on the parachute if you are required to abandon the aircraft in flight. You have been instructed on the use of your safety equipment during dinghy drill so remember that at this time of year it is imperative if you end up in the sea, to board the life raft very quickly. Otherwise you will not survive. Enjoy the flight. If any of you are unwell eat your aircrew rations. They will raise your blood sugar level and make you feel better."

Finally Cunimb Jim gave his weather briefing in a doleful voice. "An anticyclone covers the British Isles," he intoned, "with a westerly drift around the north of the UK so the visibility should improve the further north you fly. By evening I anticipate thickening smoke haze over the conurbations of industrial Lancashire and the West Midlands. Radiation fog can be expected early in the night especially in the Vale of York and over the Fens. However, you should be safely down well before it develops. Your Master Diversion airfields will be Leuchars in Fife and Waddington near Lincoln. If Barkston Heath is closed for any reason your local diversions are Cranwell and Waddington. I don't expect any mist at Cranwell till 1900 hours and at Waddington till an hour or so later. Any questions?"

"Why do we trainees need to know the Master Diversion airfields? Surely that's a matter for the aircraft's captain," suggested Parker.

"The safety of the aeroplane, Flight Cadet, is a matter for the whole crew," replied Zopoloski. "If we need to divert you may be called on as navigators to give the captain a heading, time and distance to the nearest appropriate airfield. A Master Diversion airfield has all the facilities to handle any type of aircraft day or night. Binbrook would be fine for Canberras during operating hours or Leeming for a Javelin but the faithful piston engined Valetta uses a different fuel – avgas not avtur – for a start."

Jamie was impressed that an officer like Polzol as he was always affectionately known to the cadets could still take such an evident interest in his job at Barkston which contrasted so dramatically with his early life. When the Germans invaded his country in 1939 he had escaped by biplane from Poland to Romania and then by sea to England where after a quick conversion course he had been posted as an NCO pilot straight to 303 (Polish) Squadron at Northolt, the highest scoring squadron of Fighter Command in the Battle of Britain. For many years he remained a fighter pilot first on Spitfires in England, North Africa and Italy and then after the war on Meteors and Vampires at Wunstorf and Celle.

Now as specialist aircrew he could expect to fly navigation trainers, target tugs and communications aircraft into late middle-age with no chance of promotion. Before the war as a cadet and latterly a flying instructor at the Polish Air Force Academy he had aspired to be a General in the Polish Air Force. His wartime record was exemplary. Hardly any other Polish officer had won both the British Distinguished Flying Medal and Distinguished Flying Cross as well as Poland's highest award for gallantry, the Virtutis Militari – in his case for landing a blazing Spitfire back at Northolt in October 1940. He still bore the scar tissue of his burns upon his face below where his goggles had been.

In the bar over a beer he would have argued that he had simply fought for Poland to be free. He and his Polish friends had certainly helped to win the Battle of Britain. Poland had indeed been freed from Nazi tyranny but then lost its liberty and half its territory to the equivalent evil of communism. He would never return to a Soviet satrapy. Furthermore his brothers who had fought as soldiers under General Anders and survived the assault on Monte Cassino were also both in Britain, one in Bradford the other in Ealing. Like him they had married English girls. The Polish Parish and ex-Combatants' clubs were like a second home to them and Polzol had always felt so thoroughly welcome in the Royal Air Force that it was part of an extended family to him now.

Kitting out with parachutes and Mae Wests as aircrew life jackets were still affectionately known did not take long – a glance to ensure the seal on the jacket's CO_2 bottle was intact, the garment's rubberised fabric undamaged, a check inside the top of the packed parachute to confirm that the safety thread on top of the rip cord connection was in place and an adjustment of the parachute harness to a tightness which permitted walking but which made it difficult to stand erect.

The aircrew rations would soon become familiar and ever welcome – a Mars bar, Kit Kat and Blue Riband bar. They proved over the months ahead a good antidote, as Polzol had recommended, to the all too frequent nausea as the Pigs and Superpigs pitched, rolled and performed their characteristically unaerodynamic wallowings in the turbulent lower layers.

Jamie found himself in the squat little Flight Sergeant's aircraft with Higgins, Farquharson, Whiteman and Jones. Perhaps because they had the most junior captain the crew was assigned the most senior navigation instructor – Squadron Leader Ashley. The cadets installed themselves expectantly in their rear facing seats with an array of knobs and dials in front of them.

Flying classroom was no misnomer for the interior of a Valetta. There was a radio, airspeed indicator, altimeter, gee set, remote sensing magnetic compass and a plotting table plus lamp for every student. There was a good view out for those not above the wings and an array of glass bubbles or astrodomes along the top of the fuselage for those taking sun or star shots.

It felt positively homely as the two big Hercules radial engines coughed and spluttered into life, belching blue smoke. The captain called up each cadet by name over the intercom, confirmed with the navigation instructor that all was well and taxied out to the holding point where the engines were run up for pitch control, magneto, oil pressure and slow running checks.

Then following a green light from the black and white control caravan at the end of the runway the Valetta lumbered into the air to a clattering roar from its straining engines. Jamie had a sense of deep fulfilment, of an intense ambition accomplished and looking at his friends they clearly shared his satisfaction. The aircraft swung gently northwards over Grantham and he glimpsed the baroque splendour of Belton House as they turned. In a few minutes they were through the patchy, tufted cumulus leaving the gloomy haze behind and entering a realm of clarity and light.

Only a green faced Higgins looked less than happy. "I ate all my chocolate taxiing out," he confided to Jamie as he leant queasily across. By the time the 'Pig' was in the cruise 'Honkers' Higgins had filled his first sick bag. For some learning to fly would never be fun but a constant exercise in willpower and determination. By the time they were in the descent towards base Honkers had filled two more.

The navigation on this first trip was not really challenging. Lincoln dominated the initial part of the route as they droned across Lincolnshire's bomber country slipping between Swinderby with its taxiway through the woods alongside the Fosse Way and the nuclear bomber base of Waddington, past Scampton of Dambusters' fame leaving Hemswell's massive hangars to starboard. Once across the Humber the Vale of York was no more difficult to mapread. It was, however, misty over Teesside with a thick industrial haze and RAF Thornaby could only just be made out among the smoke stacks.

As the weather cleared towards the Tyne, Monkwearmouth then Jarrow and the land of St Cuthbert and the Venerable Bede appeared. Then came RAF Acklington. The cadets who had spent much of the time between pinpoints grimacing at each other from the astrodomes could easily make out the spume specked shores of the Farne Islands and beyond them further north the outline of Lindisfarne cut off now by high tide as they soon set course south westward from St Abb's Head towards the descending wintry sun.

Rural Northumberland looked undulating, unspoilt, featureless and short of pinpoints to log. Just discernible down-sun were the far distant outline of Hadrian's Wall, the river Tyne beyond and Hexham Abbey. Crosby in Eden airfield seemed moribund and deserted given over entirely to sheep as they descended to low level.

Low flying was a new and exhilarating experience and even at a leisurely three nautical miles a minute the Pig appeared to cover the route much faster than before. Five hundred feet above ground is not very low but the peaks and dales of the North Pennines were scenically glorious albeit navigationally mysterious as they flashed past too fast for most cadets to pinpoint. Only the snow capped crest of Cross Fell towering above Alston in its little hollow was unambiguously clear to identify.

Jamie's aircraft was the first home to Barkston Heath. The cadets were exuberant as they climbed down onto the tarmac. No banter came from Higgins as he gingerly made his way to earth with three sick bags and a parachute pack in one hand, his inner flying helmet or 'electric hat' and navbag in the other. Parachutes and Mae Wests were handed in and signed off at the Safety Equipment section. Squadron Leader Ashley collected the cadets' navigation logs and his eager pupils embussed excitedly still comparing how many towns, rivers and airfields they had identified on route. Only Flight Lieutenant Zopoloski's aircraft remained airborne.

Then a green Verey light shot skyward from the runway controller's caravan arching towards Grantham through the misty dusk. On the distant ear there came the roar of two powerful engines at full throttle and soon the red and green navigation lights of a steeply descending Valetta could be discerned. Abreast of the caravan it pivoted on its wingtip into a sharp climbing turn to port. Downwind the engines' note changed as the propellers were put into fine pitch. Down came the undercarriage at the apogee of Zopoloski's upward arc, which maintained itself symmetrically downward culminating in a three pointed arrival beside the caravan.

"Even Pigs in the right hands can cut a dash, Jamie," observed Lascelles, "but still a posting to Transports or Shackletons would be the kiss of death to me."

"Your future depends entirely on what vacancies there are when you pass out," replied Jamie, "but at least we train on pensioned off fighters because that's what Vampires and Meteors are. So if you get your wings you'll be able to boast justifiably that you could have flown fighters but you ended up on something bigger and better because you are sociable, can manage a crew and are not cut out to be a split arse loner into early middle age."

CHAPTER 6

By early March Jamie had learned that the Per Ardua beagles kennelled beyond East Camp towards Cranwell village offered a reliable means of escape from the College on both Wednesday and Saturday sports afternoons. Whether it was chasing elusive hares over the clinging clays of the Trent Valley or puffing up and down the Lincoln Edge the exertions were well worthwhile – at least as strenuous as official sports but infinitely more fun. Sherry at the meet was always welcome but better by far was the host farmer's tea at the end of the day.

It was at Caythorpe whose spire lay just off the western end of Cranwell's main runway that Jamie met Jane Hetherington who seemed to come home to Lincolnshire from her secretarial course in London most weekends. Her parents' farm was close by at Fulbeck within the circuit pattern of the College Vampires, which practised circuits and landings on the nearby satellite airfield.

Jamie had noticed a green gumbooted blonde in tweed hacking jacket and designer headscarf at two previous meets and over tea had been unable to prize her away from the local young farmers. However, at Caythorpe a tactical opportunity presented itself. She snagged her sleeve on barbed wire crossing a fence and Jamie had been on hand to free her.

Her smile and thanks warmed Jamie's heart as no experience at Cranwell had ever done so far. He readily abandoned his efforts to head off the hare and keep up with the hounds in favour of a leisurely stroll with Janey as she preferred to be called, back to the farmhouse for tea. She was reassured that he was no ordinary grammar school boy as she had heard so many flight cadets were and he was excited that her conversation abounded with the superlatives of the London social circuit and lacked the flat intonation of Lincolnshire altogether. She promised to try to come to next Saturday's meet.

Luckily for Jamie one of the more elderly whips had just yielded to stiff joints and lack of breath and he was designated by Air Commodore Chris Hawkins in charge of the College Beagles, as replacement. Jamie took himself at the next opportunity to Gieves the tailors and duly kitted himself out with a black riding cap and black hunting jacket with pale blue lapels, a crisp white stock and large gold fastening pin, white breeches, pale blue stockings and black hockey boots. He felt well able to satisfy Air Commodore Hawkins with his physical stamina and practical competence with the hounds yet confident that he could impress Janey, too, if she put in an appearance.

He was lucky. The following Saturday dawned clear but not frosty. There would be a good scent. Two days without rain meant that the going was reasonable. You could see right across the Vale of Trent in the early spring sunshine and the stone walls and orange tiled roofs of Navenby stood out well atop the cliff or Lincoln Edge. At the meet itself there was no sign of Jane. She had probably stayed in London for a party, Jamie thought to himself as the beagles trotted off down the lane with the Air Commodore behind them. Jamie was positioned to one side occasionally flicking his whip to keep the hounds from dashing into the wrong field and another whip Fred Holmes a local solicitor was deployed similarly on the pack's further flank.

Soon they were into a big field near the top of the Edge drawing it wide for a hare. Almost immediately Fred Holmes was calling view halloo and pointed to the crest line where a hare jinked over the top of the hill. Air Commodore Hawkins root tooted his horn. The pack gave vociferous tongue their cries echoing excitedly across the countryside as the hunt followers raced after them.

For a change the hunt went well with the hounds streaming along the skyline. The soil of the plough up on the heath was not heavy and on the grassland and stubble Jamie's new hockey boots positively flew. The Air Commodore was as usual well up with the chase and sweating hard called through foam flecked lips – "Look to it! Tally ho! Go, go, go!" whilst still hooting away on his horn.

Suddenly the hare dashed into a small covert with the hounds in hot pursuit. "Go round the side, Fred," called Air Commodore Hawkins. "Don't lose her."

"There she is, sir!" shouted Jamie as the hare shot out towards the main Grantham – Lincoln road with about half a dozen hounds right on its tail. He hardly saw what happened next. The hare was bowled over by the leading hound.

"Tear him and eat him," exclaimed the Air Commodore. Jamie looked to where now a full dozen hounds were milling around. There was no vestige of the hare left to be seen and he glanced beyond the hounds to the village where a green Land Rover had parked beside the gate giving to the killing field.

Out stepped Janey in tight fawn jodhpurs, which accentuated the curve of her inner thighs and an exceedingly short hacking jacket, which revealed rather than covered her trim behind. "Perfect timing, Jane," said Jamie sensing the stirrings of desire. "Did you follow us in the vehicle? What a chase!"

"No, Jamie," she replied, "my mother had taken it to go shopping in Lincoln and as usual returned late. You'd better get back to the hounds or the Master will be calling you names. See you at tea."

Evening haze was thickening down the valley bottom and wisps of wood smoke from a score of cottage fires lent an aroma of family hearthside comfort to the gathering dusk. No more hares had appeared and the Master called for home. Jamie, Fred and Air Commodore Hawkins corralled the hounds whilst the Per Ardua huntsmen chivvied them up the ramp into their box for the trip back to their East Camp kennels.

Tea was very welcome. A huge kettle had been heated on the Aga and the meet hostess had prepared a tempting spread of scones and cakes to regale the hunt followers. "Didn't young Jamie do well on his first sortie as whip?" proclaimed the Air Commodore loud and clear.

"Thank you, Master," Jamie replied modestly.

"Don't you remember the interview at my Selection Board when you asked me if I liked country sports?" Jamie continued. "I said I loved them and was very keen to pursue them at the College. So my honour was at stake today. I'm glad you felt it was satisfied, sir."

The courtesies complete, Jane was in conversation with the host. "I'm definitely not going to miss the Game Fair this year, Jane," Jamie overheard.

"Tell your father to come, too. He might pick up some tips to get a better return from all those pheasant chicks he rears."

"I could not fail to hear that, Jane," interjected Jamie. "I've only had one day's shooting since I came to the College. Bill Prentice of the Senior Entry who was at

Stowe with me took pity on me. We walked up Barkston Heath one Saturday afternoon and actually came back with a rabbit, a wood pigeon and a hare."

"If you're really good, Jamie," said Jane intriguingly, "I might even introduce you to my father who is always complaining about the rabbits and pigeons on our land, and who knows what could happen. However, you've got to prove yourself first."

"Well, let me start at once," replied Jamie. "See you at the Black Bull at Leadenhan at 8.00 pm tonight. Can you make it Jane?"

Jamie glanced at her shiny blonde hair, downey pink cheeks flushed from the hunt and cold breeze and close fitting v-necked cashmere pullover topped by a silk foulard for the few tantalising seconds she took to reply: "That would be nice. See you then."

Jamie was too excited to continue the conversation. How would he get there? He had no car. The huntsman's van had already departed for the kennels. He rushed up to his fellow whip and exclaimed, "Fred, could you possibly drop me off at the College gates on your way back to Sleaford?"

"Delighted old boy. I'm going right away. Follow me."

Back at hut 150 Jamie remembered that he had solved only half the problem. How would he get to Leadenham? Of course the bus to Newark must stop there. Quick shower. On with the aftershave. Don shooting cap instead of church parade trilby. Put on polished brown shoes, well tailored cavalry twill trousers and checked Van Heusen shirt. He had surely to be the country gentleman to please a country girl like Jane.

To the station Post Office. Hurry! The bus to Newark he knew went only three times on Saturdays. Dammit the last had left half an hour ago. Just have to leg it. He set off at a jog past the garage at Byard's Leap. Surely some cadet passing en route to an evening out in Nottingham would take pity on him and stop. No luck. It was dark but by dint of steady jogging he made it sweatily to the pub with a minute to spare.

How would he get back? There would certainly be no buses. What if Jane took against him? No chance of a lift then. Too bad if he was late back. It did not matter. One look at her and he knew she was worth a charge and at least a fortnight's restrictions.

That evening she was hardly the simple country girl he had imagined at the meet. Smooth brown close cut leather skirt, silk blouse, Ferragamo shoes and a mysterious scent were the hallmarks of a girl well used to party time in London. Perhaps she had been a debutante, thought Jamie. Maybe she went to country house parties, charity balls, nightclubs in Mayfair and all the traditional English summer season's events which Jamie missed but which his Stowe friends now enjoyed. Bannish self pity! They would never fly.

Night times of chicken in the basket washed down with beer at the fireside of the pub with Jane and flying by day, this must be the sum of all happiness, thought Jamie. Her unquestioning acceptance of his life amazed him. Without asking he had the lift back he needed – but the long way round with a lingering stop on the High Dyke. This was a bonus beyond all his youthful expectations.

By the time the short Easter break came, Cranwell life was stepping into a familiar routine. Restrictions parades both early and late were less grim since the incipient spring brought lighter mornings and evenings. The Valetta sorties became more challenging as the cadets plotted their way around the country on navigation charts calculating wind vectors and estimated times of arrival and taking radio bearings from the various stations along their route.

The new entry had already lost three of its number before the first leave. Flight Cadet Inman was perpetually late, untidy and disorganised. On a charge hearing he confessed to his Flight Commander that he had only joined the Royal Air Force to please his bullying martinet of a father who had served as a Regular in the ranks and knew no other life. He was given a rail warrant and took the next train home. Flight Cadet Gregory hated the wallowing Valetta flights so much that he was mercifully chopped at the recommendation of Squadron Leader Ashley as unfit for flying duties pending possible remustering in a ground branch. Flight Cadet Winters blew his top at the Duty Under Officer for failing his belt three times the same day on restrictions parade and was also judged to be unacceptably insolent before both the Flight and Squadron Commanders. He was immediately sent packing for lack of officer qualities.

Easter leave at home was an unreal experience. It seemed that parents, family and friends just could not comprehend the reality of life at Cranwell. There was no point in explaining what it felt to be up at 0530 hours to prepare for a ceremonial parade in wintertime; the numbness of fingers on rifles in the Siberian cold; the nights spent blancoeing webbing beneath the table by torchlight; the hopes of an evening off base constantly dashed by restrictions parades; and the navigation plots torn up before the eyes for slips in symbology or infinitesimal errors of ground speed, heading, track or timing. Reality was no longer the haven of home but bellowing drill sergeants, fastidious Under Officers and perpetual fatigue.

At leave's end Flight Cadets stood out at King's Cross beside the Flying Fornicator 1929 hours express train to Grantham in their tweed jackets and hats, some leaning out of windows, some on the platform in intense embrace with girlfriends and fiancées. Arrival at Grantham brought reunion with the uncompromising Kesteven landscape, without the psychosomatic shock of early January. No NCO awaited them at the station only a duty bus driver and soon they were bowling along the High Dyke towards Winkling Willie, Cranwell's familiar occulting light atop the College tower.

Spring had its compensations. North Airfield boasted it show of cowslips, the neighbouring covert was deep in bluebells. Skylarks soared skyward from the Roman road and in mid-May the nightingales arrived. Peter Lascelles who was an expert ornithologist reckoned they were the Northernmost in the country. Lascelles spent much time on North Airfield in search of his personal vision – the girl from the married quarters.

Marching around was almost pleasant as spring yielded to summer and battledress tops were shed in favour of shirt sleave order. The two senior entries seemed to spend all their time flying. The middle year were often away at Barkston Heath mastering the long legged dumpy radial engined Piston Provost. The junior entries were either on drill or at their academic studies. In the classroom nothing exciting ever happened, but when they heard the crash alarm go off the cadets knew it often meant high drama.

One Senior Flight Cadet had an explosive engine failure on take off and his Vampire careered across fields and through stone walls almost to the High Dyke. Another lost his engine above cloud, glided through it in hopes of reaching Waddington for a flame out landing only to find when he emerged into the clear at four hundred feet that the airfield was too distant to reach. He and his instructor ejected, his parachute tangling in telephone wires on the descent. He only needed to twist and press his quick release box to step down the one inch to the ground.

Another instructor using some spare time on an air test to demonstrate ground attack techniques to his eager pupil managed to fly his Vampire through the upper branches of a tree returning to base like a witch's broomstick. All these excitements of the South Airfield flightline were relayed swiftly on the grapevine to the Junior Mess.

Even the lower orders had their memorable moments. Flight Lieutenant Zopoloski's Pig sprang an oil leak over the Bristol Channel and diverted to St Mawgan on one engine to the delight of its complement of cadets who missed a ceremonial parade next morning. Taffy Jones claimed their booze-up in Newquay was his happiest experience since he arrived at Cranwell.

Another Pig had an undercarriage collapse at Barkston Heath. It was said that the NCO pilot had expensively underestimated the crosswind and that the aircraft after a spectacular ground loop ended up blocking the runway in a pool of the crash crew's foam with Barkston Heath's resident Piston Provosts diverted to the grass runwayed satellite of Spitalgate.

Carrick who had done a flying scholarship at Yeadon as an Air Training Corps cadet and still rated his flying skill highly declared when they got back to the crew room: "It was an accident just waiting to happen. I saw on the approach the windsock sticking way out to port but the clown of a Flight Sergeant didn't kick off the drift at all. I'll be able to impress my many Yorkshire girlfriends of my heroic emergence from the foam soaked fuselage of a crashed Valetta." The Board of Inquiry's verdict was more prosaic. The venerable Valetta's port oleo leg had suffered a fatigue fracture and the maligned captain of the aircraft had done well to keep the aircraft on the runway and almost undamaged.

CHAPTER 7

The summer term saw the cadets develop an affection for their adopted county. Spring had arrived cold and late. The daffodils did not disappear until the end of May and the hawthorn, lilac and laburnum blossom lingered till the middle of June. Peter Lascelles had discovered that the College third cricket eleven played matches all around Cranwell.

Up to the last days of May this meant long vigils in the field with many sweaters under a leaden sky as the unceasing north-east wind swept in from the North Sea, but thereafter sunlit afternoons at Heckington and Leasingham, Carlton Scroop and Beckingham were a rustic antidote to the inexorable routine of College life. Team membership even exempted players from the early evening restrictions parade, which was an added bonus.

The cricket season had started well for Peter. The side's first match was at home against Burton Coggles on a mown strip of the North Airfield with immense boundaries. He himself had hardly scored. Chasing a total of 97 he came in first wicket down to confront a rotund, red necked ruddy faced purveyor of distinctly military medium paced bowling much of it directed from a short length against the head and shoulders of the batsmen.

The first ball was a long hop and wide of the off stump. He slashed it past cover for four, the second was a yorker, which he grubbed out from the base of his middle stump. The third delivery was short and reared up towards his face. Peter squared up to it and pulled it off the end of his nose imperiously but loftily towards square leg.

On most village grounds the ball would have flown over the pub and into the orchard beyond, but at Cranwell North the legside boundary was almost infinitely far away. Peter holed out to a distant fielder cunningly placed on the extreme boundary halfway towards the old tin hangars and the College chapel.

His early dismissal had an unexpected compensation. First the anonymous wingless Squadron Leader and father of the married patch mystery girl, came up to him and commiserated: "Bad luck, Lascelles. The timing was perfect but the placing of your stroke abysmal. I expect the boundaries were shorter at Winchester."

"How do you know who I am?" replied Lascelles.

"It's my job to. I am on the staff of the Wing Commander, Cadet Wing. You do not see me much because I operate behind the scenes keeping the paperwork under control at College Headquarters. But there's not much that I don't know about you and your fellow Flight Cadets.

"I am also OC Cricket and find myself on duty here this afternoon as the College First and Second Elevens are playing away and my deputies have gone with them. I expect you'll be staying to watch till the end of the innings so don't disappear. I'll introduce you to my wife and daughter who should be here shortly to help prepare tea for the players."

Sure enough the girl and her mother duly arrived about half an hour before the tea interval and unloaded a couple of capacious wicker hampers and some large thermos flasks from the boot of their car.

"Can I give you a hand?" suggested Peter optimistically, relieving the mother of the bigger hamper and a thermos flask and depositing them on a trestle table inside the small marquee.

"Oh you are kind," she replied. "Do I know you?"

"I doubt it," answered Peter. "This is only my second term and my first cricket match."

"How is it going?" she inquired.

"For our side quite well. We got them all out for under a hundred in less than two hours and we were catching their total fast until an opening batsman and then myself gave our wickets away. By the way I am Peter Lascelles, C Squadron."

"I am Mrs Harrison and this is my daughter Lizzie."

The Squadron Leader's wife beckoned to the girl to come over. She was tall, slim and looked athletic with tight blue jeans, knee length brown leather boots, polo necked sweater under an open suede jacket topped off by sunglasses at the ready above her forehead in spite of the sullen grey sky.

"Hello, I'm Elizabeth. I see you've met my mother," said Lizzie.

"Yes indeed and your father, too," Peter replied. "He knew rather a lot about me. I'll have to watch my behaviour in future. I'm Peter Lascelles from the Junior Entry."

"Pleased to meet you," Lizzie answered. "I don't often come to the North Airfield like this because we normally watch the First Eleven on the Orange in front of the College. Forgive me. I must set out the tea. The players will be in here in two minutes."

By four thirty when they all tramped in for tea more of the College Third Eleven had given their wickets away mostly to the bucolic and rubicund dispenser of military medium bowling but others to a guileful leg spinner whose floating deliveries were just asking to be despatched. Some victims were stumped, others holed out going for a big hit over the College chapel.

"I see your lot, Under Officer Tomlinson, need much more net practice. I can't imagine anyone being promoted to the Second Eleven on today's showing," observed Squadron Leader Harrison. "I expect you to organise a training session in batting technique on Monday evening. The nets are just by the Married Quarters so I shall be able to observe the attendance and commitment of the players from my back garden."

Peter almost dropped his doughnut when he overhead Harrison's conversation with Under Officer Tomlinson.

"Did you hear that, Elizabeth?" he asked as she offered him some fruit cake. "We've got net practice Monday night right beside your garden. You'd better close your window shutters before I come in to bat. I say again on reflection don't do that. I might miss a tantalising glimpse of you. You're already a marked lady. Do you remember that afternoon in January – the day of the cross country run when the Vampires crashed?"

"How could I forget it?" she answered.

"How could I also," he replied. "But for a very different reason; that's you. I was a marker for the cross country run out on North Airfield. Seeing you and your dog was the highlight of what had been a cold and dreary afternoon until the terrible collision, of course. What's your dog's name by the way – the cocker spaniel?" he continued eagerly to maintain the flow of conversation.

"Jamie."

"Just like my best friend at the College, Jamie Jamieson. I bet your Jamie is the more intelligent," he went on. "Mine is often hopelessly impractical. I sometimes wonder if he'll get through. However, none of us really know whether we'll make it. I just live for today, but this time I'll make an exception, I'll live for Monday, that is if you'll let me take you and Jamie for a walk once the nets are over?"

"Indeed I will Peter," she replied, "so long as the nets don't go on too late."

Monday evening's net practice was well attended apart from one unfortunate team member who was on restrictions parade. The weather had been glorious – the first day of Lincolnshire summer, ideal for flying and perfect for dreaming of flying in claustrophobic classrooms. The whine of Goblin engines was incessant from the Vampires overhead and at least the Junior Entry had been outside a second time after early morning drill to position radioactive sources on the grass beside the Ground Defence section and to plot the intensity of their emissions.

"Don't imagine, gentlemen that you'll just be dropping atomic bombs on the Ruskies. You'll be on the receiving end of them as well and I'm going to teach you PROTECSHUN," bellowed the wrinkly rock ape of a sergeant of the RAF Regiment before issuing Geiger counters and chart paper for the plotting of radioactive contour maps. Ground Defence Training numbed the brain and dulled the spirit of aspiring aviators so it was an especial relief for Peter to throw away anklets, beret and boots to don white flannels and sweater and to dash off to the North Airfield.

Under Officer Tomlinson had already taken charge and Peter was detailed to put in a lengthy spell of bowling. This was good as the batsmen had their backs to the officers' Married Quarters but the bowler looked straight at them and as luck would have it the modest sized Squadron Leader's quarter of the OC Cricket was the closest of them all. There was the man himself dutifully mowing the lawn doubtless at the behest of his blousy wife, pipe in mouth and serious of purpose. He stopped to empty the first collection of grass cuttings, advanced to the fence and shouted encouragement.

"Keep them at it, Tomlinson."

The evening was cool with a clear view to the edge of the Fens and a light north-easterly breeze from the sea. The heady smell of cut grass was exhilarating. Peter looked beyond the mauve lilac – it bloomed late in Lincolnshire – and a blaze of gold from a small laburnum tree to an open window. No Lizzie there leaning provocatively out to draw attention to herself with a brief word to her father. No glimpse of her inside either, but an open bedroom window offered hope and to Peter's vivid imagination the promise of better things to come.

By half past eight it was getting too dark to bat and most of the cadets had drifted off except Under Officer Tomlinson who stayed to the last to set a good example. Peter bowled away at him loyally to get in his good books for future restrictions parades and in the expectation of seeing Lizzie later. They had just drawn stumps when Jamie shot out down the track from the married patch towards East Camp and the Motor Transport section. Where Jamie the cocker went Liz was sure to follow.

Indeed she did. Loose limbed and long legged she looked rather too elegant for a country walk. She again wore her smooth suede jacket half open, this time over a clinging pink silk blouse and pleated magenta skirt. Her delicate light brown shoes with a simulated buckle on top looked better suited for a walk in Hyde Park or the Tuilleries gardens than for striding along the rough and puddled surface of the High Dyke.

"Oh, there you are," she exclaimed catching sight of Peter in his blue sports jacket and traditional cricket whites.

"Hello Elizabeth," he replied. "Your dog seems to be looking forward to his walk as much as I have. He's raced away almost to East Camp already."

"Jamie is a character; a softy at home, but an inveterate sheep chaser who's never happier than when he's picking a fight with another dog. Don't try to stroke him. He nips ferociously. He's good at ridding me of unwelcome attentions. Not that you're in that category, Peter."

The evening breeze from the Fens was a delight. It soothed the cheeks and gently rustled Lizzie's auburn hair. They skirted the Northern fringe of the airfield till they reached the covert at its Western end.

"Climb over, follow me, Lizzie," suggested Peter. "I often come here in the evening with Taffy Jones, one of my hutmates. He's a great naturalist and like me he loves the wood anemonies, the wild garlic, the celendines, bluebells and dog violets and it's great for warblers, too – chiff chaff, whitethroat, blackcap and willow wrens. He can recognise them all by their song. Now that the nightingales have come it's a special joy. You hear them all the more clearly once the cry of the jets has ended."

"You know, Peter. I have passed this place many times on my daily dog walks but I've never before crossed the fence. Could you help me?" She extended a warm soft hand while he trod down the lower strand of barbed wire for her to slip through.

"I'll lead the way. Let's go out onto the High Dyke," he urged. "We'll take the path of the Roman legions, Lizzie. Lindum Hill would have been almost in sight from here. We're about halfway from Ancaster to Lincoln and I expect the legionaries' sandals were sturdier than your dainty shoes. Where did you get them?"

"In Düsseldorf in the Königsallee actually," she replied. "It's a stylish place for clothes shopping and Düsseldorf was the nearest big city to our last home at Wildenrath."

"Did you like Germany, Lizzie?" asked Peter. "I've never been there although I'm looking forward to our entry's visit to the Sauerland for survival camp this summer. We're due to fly out the day after the passing out parade."

"It's wonderful, Peter. Everything is clean, affordable and well organised. With his local allowances and cheap fuel tokens Dad could take us from Wildenrath all over the country and into Holland and Belgium, too."

"Jamie's been," replied Peter, "and he also loved it. He went to Geilenkirchen with the Air Cadets and they took him to Monschau in the Eifel Hills. He tells of black and white timbered houses, scented pineclad slopes, of pretty terraced restaurants with fabulous beer and trout streams running by.

"Were you working there, Lizzie?" asked Peter.

"Yes I was indeed," she answered. "Because I'm tall and lanky and they seemed to like the English look – whatever that is – after a short course I got jobs modelling for fashion houses in Düsseldorf. It was great. Dad used to let me borrow the car. He didn't need it during the week. He could walk to his work on the station in the accounts section. Mum put me up to it. She had modelled herself in her younger days and said that it was better than being stuck behind a typewriter."

Once out on the High Dyke they strode out purposefully towards Lincoln. Jamie the cocker shot off after a hare.

"He ought to go out with his namesake. Jamie's a great supporter of the beagles." Peter stopped. "Aren't they wonderful – the yellow hammers. Taffy taught me their song: 'A little bit of bread and no cheese'. It's a rather incongruous phrase on the heathland, but quite unmistakeable. Out here there are lapwing, meadow pipits, stonechats, wheatears and above all the skylarks. Look up, Lizzie! Higher and higher soar the tittering skylarks. I'm not sure Vaughan Williams would have approved such a frivolous description of their musical ascent, but do you know a better?"

"I agree, Peter." Lizzie answered. "You can be quite poetic."

"This is the life, Lizzie," Peter replied. "I really love it – thanks to your company of course. Usually I'm preparing my kit for the evening restrictions parades about this time."

"Are you often in trouble, Peter?" Lizzie inquired.

"No more than the rest of us, but the officiousness of some of the Senior Entry really upsets me. Given a little power it goes to their heads and they become little Hitlers."

Lincolnshire is a land of big skies and wide horizons. The sun was setting in the fiery West. Lizzie broke the spell.

"Time to go home. Mum and Dad will be getting anxious."

"Why do you still stay with them, Lizzie?" asked Peter.

"Well there's not much opportunity in Lincoln, Grantham, Newark or Sleaford for a girl like me, is there?" she replied. "Anyway I'm an only child and I like my parents' company and they appreciate me. I don't know what Mum would do on the married patch without me, the other wives are so bitchy."

"And what about your father?" Peter inquired.

"It's a lovely life for him," Lizzie admitted. "His contemporaries are mostly Wing Commanders or Group Captains now but he loves the Air Force. He wanted to fly but he couldn't. He's colour blind and all the top jobs always go to the fliers. I know Mum and Dad always wanted to have a home of their own and to put down roots, but we have to move every two or three years. I was born in Singapore and since then we've lived in Germany of course and Leuchars, St Athan, Uxbridge, Middleton St George, Coltishall and Abingdon."

"How lucky I am," said Peter, "that you're here with me and not strutting the catwalks in London. Let's just sit down on this tree trunk a minute or two, listen to the nightingales and watch the sun go down."

"I can't imagine anything lovelier," said Lizzie. "Sit, Jamie, sit!" Very soon the sun had set, but even a mere couple of silent minutes seemed to bring a closer bond between them.

"Let me help you through the fence, Lizzie," Peter suggested, "and you'll soon be back home for a late but welcome dinner."

As she prepared to negotiate the snagging strands of wire Peter leant forward and kissed her full and slightly parted lips.

"That was nice, Peter," she breathed. "As they say in Germany Luft und Liebe – open air and love – go well together. Don't you agree?"

"Mostly certainly I do, Lizzie. I'll walk you back to the married patch and if I hurry I should be in the hut by the witching hour of 2159 hours."

The cricket season progressed. The pitches became browner and harder. Wild roses and honeysuckle filled the hedgerows on the road to Oasby where Lizzie and Peter passed many happy evening hours in the pub. Taffy Jones spent most of the half term weekend on the beach at Oxwich with his girlfriend Myfanwy from Swansea and Carrick disappeared to his native Yorkshire with Sylvia the trainee teacher he had met at a Saturday night social at Retford College of Education.

Jamie's half term was idyllic. Jane had wangled him an invitation to join the long weekend house party, which Colonel and Mrs Carlton were hosting at their big house below Wellingore village.

Jane was in her element. She knew everybody. Gregarious and funny, nobody could quite understand why she had attached herself to Jamie even if he was a Stoic.

"Is it true that your father is a parson?" the fellow guests from London kept inquiring. "What's it like in the Air Force? Do they pay you properly? What do you do in Lincolnshire without a car?"

"Well actually Jane drives me in the Land Rover which seems ideal to me," Jamie answered. "A cadet in the entry above me drove himself into a Fenland dyke after a session in the pub and was drowned. With Janey as my glamorous chauffeuse life is much safer and less inhibiting."

"What do you do during the week without her?"

"Well I'm only allowed off the base on Wednesday nights after games and on Sundays after church and then only till 10.00 pm so it is scarcely a hardship. Anyway I'm often on restrictions parades and cannot get out at all so the lack of a car is no sacrifice. What's more I'm fully occupied whilst Janey's away during the week," Jamie replied.

The Carltons whose last posting before his retirement had been to Rome where the Colonel was Military Attaché were kindness and generosity personified. Their own children, one a Merchant Banker in London, the other still at Cambridge were not spoilt with possessions. They were privileged rather by the warmth and hospitality of their parents whose wholehearted welcome to the young made the household a focus of fun and entertainment from all over Lincolnshire. It was a source of reciprocation throughout the county from which by association Janey and Jamie benefited effortlessly.

Tea on arrival at Wellingore on Friday afternoon was followed by drinks and then dinner. A late breakfast of kidneys and scrambled eggs preceded tennis before a salad lunch accompanied by Chablis. In the heat of the afternoon there was croquet till a strawberry teatime spent under the trees. Then came more tennis till Pimms was brought to the courtside. Finally all dashed off to change for the black-tie dinner dance to which even more young people were invited from further afield.

Jane was such a joy to be with. She danced electrifyingly thigh against thigh and the more frenzied sequences were followed by languorous sittings out in the heavily scented gardens. When at last the music and dancing stopped the floorboards of the big house creaked upstairs to the comings and goings of the guests whose indiscretions could be absolved in the General Confession at Matins next morning in the parish church. Soon came Sunday lunch with minted roast lamb washed down with claret followed by summer pudding and raspberries and cream. All too soon Jamie's heady half term was over. House guests departed for London and Jane dropped Jamie off at the iron gates in front of the College.

The second part of the summer term before the graduation of the Senior Entry passed in a blur of hyperactivity. Two more of the Junior Entry were chopped. The last navigational flight of the term was by Varsity, a luxurious experience after the heaving clattering of Valettas. The sky over South Airfield was crowded with numerous formations of Vampires – senior cadets completing the final qualifying exercises before winning their wings and their instructors preparing for the big Fly Past over the Passing out Parade.

There were mercifully no more major dramas since the terrible collision back in January. One cadet on a solo cross-country by Vampire supposedly to Linton on Ouse in Yorkshire set his gyro 180° wrong and landed at Oakington in Cambridgeshire. His arrival was hardly the discreet affair to be expected after such a basic and shameful error. He came in too high and too fast topping the crest on the main runway at a good 70 knots. He descended the hill with smoke pouring from his brakes before coming to rest with his nose poking through the perimeter fence just short of the Huntingdon to Cambridge Road. He was chopped and left the College next day.

Usually it was the Senior Entries on Vampires who set off the crash alarm but Kiwi McGilligan the mentor of hut 150 achieved it in a glider. His father was a gliding instructor at a club on the edge of the Southern Alps and Kiwi had gained much gliding experience at an early age. He was now working up assiduously for the silver C qualification. Kiwi persuaded the pilot of the College Tiger Moth Tug to tow him towards the base of a huge cumulonimbus, which towered imperiously over Lincoln. Once in the column of shuddering, thumping, thundering and hailing unstable air Kiwi soon became totally disorientated and parachuted out, landing on the disused airfield of Coleby Grange. The crash ambulance brought him back to the Junior Mess in time for tea where the universal advice was for Kiwi to stick to navigation and to leave piloting to the more capable cadets trained to do it.

In the height of the summer heat the tempo of drill increased. The Sergeants were even less forgiving than before. First the Junior Entries joined the Seniors for Squadron Parades and then for the final week the whole Cadet Wing was rehearsing early each morning on the main parade ground in front of the College and in one of the South Airfield hangars, which had been emptied of aircraft for a wet weather ceremony if required.

The last two dress rehearsals were with full bands and taken solely by the Senior Under Officer winner of the Sword of Honour. His was the big responsibility to give commands in time to keep the marching squadrons within the confines of the parade square. Mr Izzard was quick to charge any cadet he deemed to be accelerating towards the marker ropes. For cadets to do this to an unpopular Under Officer on a routine parade was for them fair game but the Passing out Parade and its rehearsals were serious business, not to be sabotaged, with a standard which Mr Izzard insisted must be better than that of the Brigade of Guards because "those pansy pongoes have no brains and do less drill than you".

The Reviewing Officer was to be Air Chief Marshal Sir Thomas Swallowfield the much decorated and highly extrovert Air Officer Commanding, Royal Air Force Germany. He was due to arrive the evening beforehand to stay at the Lodge with the Commandant. There are aviator's Air Marshals and political Air Marshals. The ebulient Sir Thomas was very much in the first category.

The cadets were in their huts with the doors and windows open, polishing and ironing and blancoeing their ceremonial kit. The banter was suddenly disturbed by a loud tearing sound as of ripping calico. "I'd recognize that noise anywhere," exclaimed Jamie. "It's a Hunter. I was brought up in Bideford with 229 OCU across the water at Chivenor. They have Hunters."

"So did 233 OCU at Pembrey. The Gower sky was full of them when I was a boy. Ymlaen – forward, was their motto," remarked Taffy. They both ran out to see a two seat T7 Hunter with barndoor air brake extended curving onto the downward leg "That's the AOC arriving," said Taffy. "I'm glad he's left the Pembroke and

Devon behind at the Communications Squadron in favour of a real gentleman's carriage. They say that he insists that his ADCs be Hunter qualified. Now I understand why."

The morning of the parade dawned sunny and hot. Chairs were arranged in lines in front of the square. The rose beds around the orange had been manicured; the roses all dead headed. A narrow red well-dusted carpet extended from the saluting base to the main gates. Guests and officers unhurriedly assumed their allotted seats filling up from the back in order of seniority. Soon came the traditional march on from the wings of the College and then standing easy the long wait for the Reviewing Officer. Emotion was high on this perfect English summer morning as Vaughan Williams' Greensleeves wafted across the gravelled parade ground from the College steps where stood the band to the spectators and the welcoming party beyond.

Peter could see Lizzie three rows from the back. There was her mother in some fancy feathered headgear and there was her gauntly grey faced father in best blue uniform wholly devoid of any flying badge or medal. He must feel seriously underdressed for such an occasion, thought Peter. By contrast the Assistant Commandant's left shoulder almost sagged under the weight of his decorations whilst the magenta ribbon round his neck and starlike order it suspended hanging low above his spreading waistline added to an appearance too Ruritanian for such a gallant combat aviator. Lizzie wore no hat but she had clearly chosen her summery outfit well. Her pale blue suit seemed even at the distance of the cadets' ranks tasteful and appropriate, elegantly simple compared to the elaborate creations of so many officers' wives and Flight Cadets' mothers.

The Air Marshal's limousine arrived soundlessly at the College gates where he was greeted by the Commandant. The Senior Under Officer called the parade to attention and the select group of Air Chief Marshal Swallowfield, the Commandant and their respective Aide de Camp and Personal Staff Officer proceeded to the saluting base for the general salute. The parade went ahead. The band beat out the Lincolnshire Poacher, Scipio, Slow March from Saul and Imperial Echoes – all the old and stirring favourites never for a lifetime to be forgotten.

Sir Thomas stopped at Jamie on his inspection down the ranks, "How is it going, Flight Cadet?" he asked him.

"Well, so far, sir."

"Of course, of course – your training young man, not the parade."

"Well, sir. I'd like to get on fighters in Germany, Hunters if possible."

"Quite right, too, Flight Cadet. Good choice."

"Next time, Mr Jamieson," hissed Sergeant McCabe when the Reviewing Officer had passed, "just answer the Air Marshal's question. Don't give the C in C a personal wish list. Your passing out is a VERY long way away."

The marches past the saluting base in slow and quick time were impressive. The dressing of the squadrons was good and the cadets maintained impeccable line abreast without any whiplash effect whatever. Peter was able to see Lizzie clearly during the eyes right and left. How exciting it would be to hold her tight that night at the Graduation Ball. However, he also could not escape the vision of her mother who was displaying a mutton dressed up as lamb appearance in a décoleté dress, which even from the parade square could be seen to reveal more flesh than was called for on such a proud and formal occasion.

Thirty-two Vampires had thundered past to the second in immaculate formation and no cadet had committed the chargeable offence of fainting on parade. The proceedings were moving smoothly to their culmination. Mr Izzard and his four drill sergeants must be well satisfied.

The Air Marshal's address was short and memorable. "Your performance on parade was outstanding today, gentlemen. Your parents can rightly be proud of you. That's as it should be at Cranwell, but it also shows not only that you can maintain its high traditions, but that you've already acquired what I hope will prove its lasting legacy – discipline. Discipline is essential to all accomplishments. Discipline will keep you safe in the air. Discipline wins battles, but in the Royal Air Force we need discipline tempered by initiative. When I was your age and very junior in the Service I learned a good lesson. Never ask permission, it can only be refused. Justify your action afterwards preferably with success. Probably you've learned that, too. God speed!"

Soon the band struck up Auld Lang Syne and the Senior Entry turned inwards and slow marched off parade up the College steps to sherry under the rotunda and the parents' lunch in College Hall. It was a profoundly moving moment. Narrow Pilot Officer's braid looked very fresh upon their sleeves. The wings the Commandant had pinned on them the evening before were resplendent in the summer sun. The brass buckles and buttons of their Number One uniforms gleamed. The toe caps of their new Northampton shoes shone. Their leather gloves were pristine and buttoned up and their black banded officers' caps were clearly straight from Messrs Bates the hatters and had not yet been rendered conformal with operational contours in a flying boot.

The cadet squadrons still on the square felt bereft without their Senior Entries and front ranks. How many of the new Pilot Officers would be left a year or two from this glad glorious morning? Collisions, high ground, bad weather, engine, structural and system failures as well as inevitable aerial misjudgements – the pilot error of the accident reports, or even enemy action would all take their inexorable toll. Banish such baleful melancholy thought Jamie. The band were playing in quick time again. The squadrons turned outward and marched off to Walford Davies' Royal Air Force march.

Before squadron dismissal at their respective wings of the College the drill sergeants were united in their message, "Remember that the Graduation Ball tonight is a parade, gentlemen. You will be properly dressed at all times and above all no PDAs, no public displays of affection. Have a good leave."

Hut 150 had a table of its own at the Ball. Kiwi McGilligan was with his Entry elsewhere but Janey, Elizabeth, Peter Lascelle's girlfriend, Sylvia from the Teacher Training College at Retford who seemed somewhat loosely attached to Peter Carrick and the exotic Natasha daughter of Flight Lieutenant Zopoloski the celebrated Polzol of Barkston Heath the surprise guest of Taffy Jones made up the party.

"How did you keep such a super secret, Taffy?" asked Carrick. "How on earth did you meet?"

"You cynical lot will never believe it," Taffy replied, "but it was divine destiny. You know my parents have a guest house at Oxwich near Swansea. Well Natasha came down to Gower last summer to surf at Rhosilli Bay with a group of friends from Nottingham University but it was far too hot and calm for waves at Rhosilli so she and her best friend came over to Oxwich for a bit of a sunbathing and sophistication and that's where I came in."

"But what does such a cracker from Krakow see in a ginger headed freckle faced rugby fanatic like you – product of the celebrated sheep shaggers' Academy of Gowerton Grammar?" joked Jamie.

"First of all she's not from Krakow, Poland but Barkston, Lincolnshire as you know and as for Gowerton Grammar it is not just the finishing school for half the Welsh Rugby XV but actually produces intellectuals for university. I was offered a place at Bristol University myself but against my better judgement I opted for the benighted Cranwell Towers."

The Junior Entry in best blue with white shirt, winged collar and black bow tie could not match the style of the Senior Entries and instructors in their loin hugging grey blue Mess kit but the drink flowed so freely and the light entertainment section of the college band was such a compelling dance orchestra that distinctions rapidly disappeared, as did Sylvia with a graduating member of the Senior Entry, Hank Peterson, who had been a regular at Retford Teacher Training College for the past three years not only of herself but of many of her fellow students, too. Peter Carrick who was dour at the best of times, morosely took to the bar and the beer.

Lizzie who had come the short distance from the married quarters to the College Hall in her mother's Morris Minor offered it as transport for an early breakfast at Barkston which Natasha invitingly made available as her parents were away in the Cotswolds for her father's yearly standards check with the Central Flying School at Little Rissington. Before they left the Ball at four in the morning Natasha in swirling skirt demonstrated with Taffy how the waltz should be danced in Central European style whilst Janey and Liz smooched out the last dance with their heavy footed public school partners Jamie and Peter.

"Chez Natasha is a lot better than Harry Ramsden's Fish and Chips on the A1. Let's move!" said Peter and they followed Lizzie out to her little car parked under the pine trees at the back of the College kitchens. Six was not an undue load. Taffy Jones said he had returned once from the pub in an Under Officer's Morris 1000 with seven on board. This time Lizzie and Peter Lascelles had their own seats in front whilst Janey and Natasha sat on Jamie's and Taffy's legs at the back.

By the time that they were out on the High Dyke the Eastern horizon was greying. On arrival at Barkston the outline of the village was clearly visible and the stone silhouette of Natasha's Virginia creeper covered home stood out against the lightening sky.

A rosary decked alabaster figure of the Blessed Virgin Mary and larger picture in the hall of Krakow Cathedral and a signed photograph in the kitchen of a Squadron group around a Spitfire with the white and red checked square of Poland on its nose were the sole indications of a Polish heritage, apart from the large vodkas, which Natasha dispensed all round.

On came the records, the dancing resumed and the guests soon repaired to her bedroom, her sister's and the sofa downstairs. The Air Force is indeed a life of contrasts mused Peter as quiveringly eager he snuggled up to Lizzie in a Polish stranger's bed whilst Jane and Jamie continued where they had left off at Colonel Carlton's house party four weekends before.

At eight thirty Natasha's alarm clock sounded, "How do you do it, Natasha?" exclaimed Taffy.

"Well, I'm usually out of here by 0700 to catch the bus to Lincoln for my vacation job in the cathedral bookshop. This is leisure. I've got the day off – I'm allowed one a month till my term resumes. And you, David, have to be back at the

College to prepare your kit ready to take off to Gütersloh at midday so you and your friends had better move fast. Enjoy the breakfast I promised and get on your way quickly to the College. Anyway my parents are due back later today so I must clear up all traces of the disreputable company I keep."

Cornflakes together with a hard-boiled egg, brown bread, salami and gherkins were rapidly consumed. "Thanks a million Natasha," said Lizzie.

"Do come across and call on me soon, Liz," Natasha replied. "The place will seem very quiet without this lot." Soon the group were heading back along the cornflower and poppy lined High Dyke to Cranwell where Lizzie dropped off the cadets at the gates. Janey's Land Rover was still hidden under the pine trees at the back of the College.

"Why don't you come and visit me in London, Lizzie?" suggested Jane. "I expect you could do with a change of scene. Come and see how the London look compares with Düsseldorf. I'm sure we could have a lot of fun together."

Lizzie's mother was bustling around the diminutive kitchen of their modest Married Quarter when she returned. "Did you enjoy yourself, dear? I hope you didn't drink too much. I still remember the first RAF Guest Night your father took me to. I had a terrible hangover next day. It lasted until teatime. I expect a Graduation Ball is worse or is it better with all that dancing and exercise?"

"I'm fine mother. Natasha Zopoloski insisted we stick to vodka all evening and after the Ball she gave us a good breakfast at her home. Vodka is very pure and healthy. My head is as clear as a bell."

Back on the South Brick lines the cadets hurriedly transferred all their kit from the five-man huts at the back of the Flight line to their new individual rooms in the Barrack Blocks beside the drill square ready for next term. Kiwi McGilligan had already gone and the sullen Carrick was staying on as mentor of Hut 150 in his place to look after the new entry. Blue holdalls were quickly filled with the essentials of a life in the field for survival camp and the cadets duly paraded on the square at 1130 ready for departure by Valetta to Germany.

Sgt McCabe was almost affable: "What shall I do without you these five long weeks, gentlemen? I received no criticisms from the Reviewing Officer yesterday and no Flight Commander has charged anyone for an excess of alcohol or for PDAs at the Ball last night. Congratulations! I want you to maintain these standards of discipline on survival camp. Reluctantly I hand you over to the tender loving care of the NCOs of the Royal Air Force Regiment for the duration, but I assure you that any reports of bad behaviour or poor turnout will come back to me and will not be overlooked. Beware of the Fräuleins by the way. They are very seductive and very possessive. I should know, I've been married to one these last seven years."

CHAPTER 8

Briefing at Barkston Heath for the flight to Germany was at noon with take off scheduled for an hour later. All the familiar NCO aircrew were there plus Polzol looking uncharacteristically informal in shirtsleeve order. The air was stuffy and the briefing room was unusually full with all the Equipment and Secretarial cadets present as well as the normal complement of their aircrew counterparts.

Polzol opened the proceedings with a billiard cue pointer in hand. "I hope the Graduation Ball was a success and that you feel up to a long flight to the heart of West Germany." I bet he doesn't know what success I had with the warm lovely welcoming Natasha last night thought Taffy Jones. "We head off south-east at five minute intervals in four Valettas skirting Cottesmore and then Wittering watching out for any bomber traffic en route as we do so, towards Marham then avoiding the Thetford Danger Area, overflying Honington and coasting out over Clacton. Our diversions in Belgium will be Ostend and Beauvechain and in Germany we've got the clutch of RAF bases – Laarbruch, Brüggen and Wildenrath and of the three Wildenrath's the best equipped to accept uninvited visitors.

"I hope we shall arrive at Gütersloh in time for the opening of the Mess bar. I'm looking forward to my return. Last time I was in an intruder Mosquito and my surprise night-time appearance in the circuit was far from welcome.

"Just one last thing, gentlemen. It will be a much more turbulent sortie than any you've experienced so far but we have to be punctual for you to get to the bivouac site in the Sauerland before dark so we can't postpone departure. Anyway it is no bad thing for our Flight Cadet fellow passengers from the Ground Branches to learn how their General Duties counterparts actually earn their flying pay. I invite the Duty Meteorological Officer to tell you more."

As ever in his wonted tweed jacket and cavalry twill trousers in spite of the heat and humidity the College Metman strode to the dais in front of the assembled cadets and Navigation Flight personnel. Polzol handed him the billiard cue and Cunimb Jim addressed himself to the synoptic chart on the wall with its spider's web of isobars, wind arrows and sharply delineated frontal systems. "I may be misquoting him but I think it was King Charles II who said that an English summer consisted of three fine days and then a thunderstorm," he began. "Well we've just had a whole week of unusually hot weather. Yesterday afternoon Benson and Abingdon recorded 90°, Northolt 89°, Odiham 88° and Farnborough 87°. We were lucky here at Cranwell. A sea breeze from the cool North Sea kept the temperature down to a maximum of 79° but pressure has been falling fast. The warm front from an intense depression over the Hebrides went through last night although you probably did not notice it at the Ball. Later this afternoon the cold front is due to follow.

"You can see a black wall of cloud out West over Grantham. The tops of the embedded cumulonimbus are reaching just short of 40,000 feet and you can expect very bad weather on the first part of your route – intense rain, frequent hail, lightning, extreme turbulence and moderate to severe icing. In the worst affected areas there will be extensive nimbostratus down to ground level, which will make any diversions marginal at best – unless you go well behind or ahead of the front. As your training schedule does not permit a later departure I suggest you strap in tightly and press on to Germany where the conditions should be very considerably better."

The Equipment and Secretarial cadets did not know what to expect as their General Duties friends helped them on with parachute harnesses and showed them how to snap on and unbuckle the chest parachutes. Carl (Honkers) Higgins knew all too well what was coming. The flight to the long awaited outdoor adventure for the entry of survival camp in Germany meant nauseous en route purgatory for him. His friends would no doubt be praying for deliverance intact from the gut wrenching bone jarring turbulence. His prayer would be for the immediate deliverance of sudden death.

Constrained by their parachute webbing the cadets waddled out to the aircraft navigation bags and parachute in hand. Once on board Jamie lent across to Peter Carrick and observed: "Isn't it nice not to have to do any work on this trip – just like a holiday flight."

"I'd prefer to be calculating our position and plotting the track to Germany," replied Carrick. "Then at least we'd have something to think about other than our stomachs. I'll settle mine by eating all the aircrew rations before we even start up." Almost immediately the big Hercules radial engines spluttered into life spewing black smoke onto the tarmac and the four squat aircraft fishtailed out of dispersal moving off like a gaggle of geese down the taxitrack to the holding point at the end of the runway. There they ran up the engines, set flaps, tested the controls and waited for a green Aldis light from the control caravan to depart Westward through the rain into an ominously threatening sky.

Almost as soon as the wheels were up the turbulence struck lifting them one moment to the heavens and dropping them the next juddering instant towards earth. The cadets endured a medley of sensations all unpleasant as the Pigs thumped and banged and creaked and groaned and wallowed and heaved and fell and twisted and hammered on their way. There was no possibility of happy face pulling out of the astrodromes, little alleviation to be found in scoffing Mars bars, Blue Ribands or Kit Kat chocolate. All the cadets felt clammy with sweat and prepared a ready sickbag.

How could a metal structure built by human hands endure such torture? Surely the rivets must be popping. Imaginations went into overdrive. Would not the wing spars be fatigued after so many years of service? Do tailplanes easily snap off, rudders bend or ailerons and elevators come unhinged? Prayerfulness was a solace but God does not strike bargains thought Peter Lascelles as ice chunks detached by the Denver boots of inflatable rubber on the front of the wing clattered down the fuselage but at least faith could instil an acceptance of His will. Peter, like the others, soon found he could not fight the turbulence only let himself go as relaxedly as possible with the flow. Another Cranwell lesson had been learned that in the air as well as on the ground even the most dire experiences are finite as they eventually eluded the grip of the Cold Front and sailed on into the stiller air over East Anglia.

The southern North Sea and Belgium slipped serenely by and as they passed just north of the Ruhr a long gentle descent towards Gütersloh began. Time had been lost to the turbulence but a straight in approach saved five minutes and Polzol reckoned that with luck he should just be in time for the first round at the bar in one of Hermann Goering's favourite Officers' Messes.

From the portholes of the Pigs the view looked excitingly operational. Net covered blast pens were distributed around the perimeter. Camouflaged buildings surrounded the dark green control tower and the Battle Flight pair of Hunters were at readiness on the Operational Readiness platform at the end of the runway with their pilots strapped in ready to scramble at any incursion into the Air Defence Interception Zone along the inner German border. The Valettas taxied to station Flight at the furthest extremity of the flight line where four three ton trucks were standing by to take the Flight Cadets into the hills.

The Warrant Officer from the Ground Defence section of the College awaited them with a Corporal of the RAF Regiment. His shirt was starched, his toecaps gleamed and a stable belt in Royal Air Force stripes contained his ample stomach whilst suspending his well-pressed trousers. The only concession to the field conditions from which he had come was a beret in place of the regulation peaked cap, which had been left at Cranwell with his pace stick.

"All aboard the vehicles, gentlemen, by squadrons," rasped the Warrant Officer. "Leave your bags in the last lorry. Instruct the drivers to move off, corporal." After two hours driving they reached the campsite at dusk. It lay among rolling dark pine clad hills between Marsberg and Brilon. Large communal tents had already been pitched around a white flag pole. Notices on boards outside denoted the purpose of each tent – Officers' Mess, Flight Cadets' Mess, Sergeants' Mess, Officer Commanding's Quarters, Stores, Kitchen, Exercise Planning Section, Survival Camp HQ and of course the Cadets', Officers', Sergeants' and other ranks accommodation.

On arrival the Camp Warrant Officer, Mr Gidley, immediately took charge. "Form up by Squadrons in front your tents facing the flagpole," he ordered. "Three instructors from Flying Wing have volunteered to be your Squadron Officers for the duration. They will report on your performance to Cadet Wing at the conclusion of this camp. They will be assisted by three NCOs of the Ground Defence Section and by one other NCO from RAF Germany's Alpine Survival School at Bad Kohlgrub in Bavaria who will lend his specialist expertise.

"Before I hand you over to the Officer Commanding, Wing Commander Jolly, we need a fluent German speaker who can assist us in procuring fresh supplies from Brilon market and in liaising with the local community as required. Anyone interested?"

"I could do it, sir," said Carl Higgins coming swiftly to attention. "I lived in Germany for three years as a boy. My father was in the Embassy in Bonn and I made a lot of German friends. I got German 'A' level at school."

"Just the man we're looking for, Mr Higgins," replied the warrant officer. "Report to the Junior Ground Defence Officer Flight Lieutenant Perkins after this parade. He is acting as Camp Adjutant and will give you your instructions. A final point, gentlemen, before I present you to Wing Commander Jolly. This will be the last occasion on which you will wear battledress until the return flight. From now on the rig is camouflage fatigues with wet weather boots. You will wear your berets and field green belt at all times. Here comes the camp commander! Attention!"

The rotund, greying and somewhat purple nosed figure of Wing Commander Jolly emerged from the headquarters tent followed by the immaculate tall and slender figure of his Sandhurst trained Adjutant. Jamie wondered to himself why someone would spend two years at Sandhurst and not opt for a good Army regiment. Perhaps Perkins came from an Air Force family and got chopped from flying training or had failed the aircrew selection tests but still wanted to reach Air Marshal in a combat branch.

"At ease, gentlemen," ordered the Wing Commander. "Welcome to Survival Camp. This is one of the most important parts of your Cranwell course and it will give the directing staff ample opportunities to judge your attitude under pressure and officer qualities. You will have plenty of time to demonstrate your endurance, initiative and self-discipline. We are here to test you not to break you and to impart the skills, which should enable you to survive on land in Northern Europe, extract yourself safely from enemy territory, rejoin your unit and resume flying operations.

"The first week will build up your stamina. You will do route marches initially by squadrons, then in crews of four and finally in pairs. You will be responsible for your own navigation and you will sustain yourselves by day with aircrew survival rations, returning to the camp each night for a debrief and cooked meal.

"The second week will begin with three days of survival technique training. You will learn first aid, to make parachute shelters – A-frames and teepees as well as bashas of branches and foliage. You will be taught to trap, snare, fish and live off the land; how to lie up during the day and to move tactically at night to evade capture. The third night you'll do a navigational exercise in crews of four finding your own way to the designated bivouac location where you will erect a parachute shelter in which to spend the night, returning by a different route next day. The final forty-eight hours will be spent in escape and evasion. We are lucky to have the participation of the Army Air Corps who are assigning Auster aircraft and Skeeter helicopters from Detmold to the search as well as of the second battalion of the Irish Guards who are coming down from Minden to join in as well. These will constitute the enemy and will do everything in their power to catch and interrogate you.

"You will be dropped off in pairs by lorry the first night with instructions to reach a primary or secondary rendezvous by the same time the following night. There your contact, one of the course staff, will question you for useful intelligence on the route you have taken and for the dispositions of the enemy and then give you a further rendezvous – your point of egress from the exercise area. If you fail to reach it on time you will lose marks and be required to wait an extra 24 hours to be picked up.

"If captured you will be interrogated. Remember to give only your service number, rank and name. You may be put through some pretty prolonged discomfort and intimidation and deprived of rest by your captors so it is best not to be caught. If you are captured on a road, railway line or in a built-up area an adverse report will be submitted to your Cadet Wing Squadron Commander. We expect cadet pairs to stay together and only to split in the most exceptional circumstances, which will have to be justified to the directing staff afterwards. Any questions?" There were none.

A strong smell of curry wafted from the camp kitchen and the Warrant Officer was asked to dismiss the parade. The cadets reckoned that survival camp curry and rice washed down with tea and followed by apple pie and custard excelled by far what the Junior Mess at Cranwell had to offer.

Afterwards Carl Higgins strolled over to the Camp Headquarters where Perkins the Adjutant was drafting the operation order for the next day's march under a hurricane lamp. "What is it, Higgins?" he asked looking up and over his reading glasses.

"I'm your German speaker, sir. Will you need me tomorrow?"

"Most certainly," the adjutant replied. "Meet me here after the Squadron route march and we will go into Brilon together in the Land Rover. The market doesn't close till late. I'll have a beer while you're buying the list of fresh food I give you to supplement and vary the interminable curries. Thereafter you'll be able to go on your own with the Duty Corporal which will be much easier. Goodnight, Higgins."

For cadets brought up in the country a strenuous fortnight under parachute canopy or canvas in the Sauerland was an energetic delight. For the town dwellers among them and for those unused to much walking and the outdoor life it was more of a challenge. After over six active months at the College physical fitness was not the problem so much as psychological unpreparedness and insufficient willpower on the part of an unhappy minority.

None were actually sent home but trailing on route marches, untidiness in camp or dress, inability to reach rendezvous on time, to map read accurately across country in all weathers or build a sturdy parachute shelter at the end of a long day betrayed a fatal lack of motivation soon spotted by the directing staff and usually confirmed by suspension from training in subsequent terms.

Jamie Jamieson was in his element. He had spent much time trekking on Exmoor as a boy so that he hardly ever got tired. The scent of the pines was exhilarating, the wild raspberries and blueberries succulent and the constant roar of criss-crossing contour hugging low flying Starfighters, Sabres, Hunters, Swifts and Canberras overhead leant a sense of present purpose to the mental inspiration derived from books he had read about famous wartime escapers like Airey Neave and Basil Embry and the legendary heroes of the Wooden Horse, the Great Escape and Colditz Castle.

His friends from Hut 150 were also impressively positive though of them the more introverted Peter Carrick less enthusiastically so in spite of many youthful expeditions with family and friends to the Pennine Moors and Yorkshire Dales. These had, however, given him an enviable tolerance of midges which for the less bitter blooded made lying up on escape and evasion a Chinese torture of the first magnitude.

Jamie was lucky to crew with Carl Higgins for escape and evasion. He had been putting his daily victualing missions to Brilon with the duty Corporal to good use. They would return with the Land Rover full of plums, apples, pears, raspberries, fresh milk and cream, many bars of chocolate, dark wholemeal bread, sticky cakes, crate upon crate of beer and several bottles of Schnapps – all the provisions in short of which downed airmen on the run could only dream. The Wing Commander and his directing staff were clearly determined to lead by exhortation not example although to his credit Nigel Perkins the Adjutant did come on the route marches and teamed up with a flying instructor on Meteors to complete a successful escape and evasion exercise with the cadets.

Carl Higgins and Jamie had always got on well. Perhaps their family backgrounds of service were intrinsically similar. Both were sociable people. Higgins' bonhomie and readiness to chat with the locals were invaluable. His first sortie to Brilon with Flight Lieutenant Perkins satisfactorily reassured the Adjutant that Higgins could evidently converse fluently in German and that by bargaining he seemed to be able to obtain good deals from the market stallholders. However, Perkins was unwilling to linger for a beer on the way back. He insisted that he had to write up the camp's daily diary but said that in future he had no objection to Higgins' doing so, provided that he returned to camp on time, did not boast about it to his friends and made sure that the driver kept off the alcohol.

This was enough to provide a life changing opportunity for Higgins. Next day he and the Corporal driver were back in Brilon by late afternoon. The necessary purchases were swiftly made and Corporal Davies was happy to look after the Land Rover in the town square in return for a packet of cigarettes, plastic cup of coffee and a Frankfurter hot dog. Higgins meanwhile bought himself a copy of Die Welt and installed himself at a boulevard café table with a Sachetorte und ein helles Bier – a creamcake and a lager beer.

His concentration was broken by penetrating feminine laughter and he had not yet finished the first page of his newspaper before a girl at a neighbouring table, probably he guessed a secretary on her way home was asking him for a light. "Ich rauche nicht," he replied, and indicated towards Corporal Davies smoking visibly in the Land Rover reading a book who he felt sure would be happy to oblige.

When she moved off her dark haired friend turned to Carl and asked, "Are you English? In the Army I presume."

"Royal Air Force actually. I'm Flight Cadet Higgins," Carl replied.

"We get a lot of English soldiers here and you're the first I've seen reading a German newspaper," she observed.

"Well you're the first German I've heard speaking English at this café – with an impeccable accent, too."

"I was in Oxford all last year working as an au pair. It was wonderful. The father was a philosophy lecturer, a Fellow of Christ Church. I was like one of the family."

"That's funny. It was my father's old college. He read philosophy, politics and economics – PPE they call it – before becoming a diplomat. I spent three years as a boy in the Rhineland in your Hauptdorf, Bonn. It's supposed to be so boring but I was very happy there. I love Germany."

"I lost my father when I was very young. I hardly knew him. He disappeared on the Eastern Front. He was near Kursk the last time that Mutti heard from him. We lost our home as well. It was in Schlesien near Breslau. I remember leaving it as a girl with Mutti and my sister Dörthe with all our belongings in a horse and cart. It was so cold until we got to Dresden. We took a train, almost the last out of the Hauptbahnhof on the morning of the terrible destruction of 13 February because Mutti could not face celebrating Karneval without Papi, to stay with my aunt in Westfalen near Lippstadt. We settled here in Brilon after the war. My mother was a teacher and brought us up on her own."

Carl who had been totally absorbed noticed that the light seeking friend was back, smoking cigarette in hand. He looked at his watch. "Mein Gott! Sechs Uhr ja! I must be back at camp by 1830 hours. Auf wiedersehn."

"Good bye. I often drop in here to relax after work. I'm called Angela, Angela Lammersdorf – von Lammersdorf in fact but we're a little bit reticent about the von these days. I'll explain later if I see you again, Mr Higgins."

"I'm so happy we met. My name is Carl by the way. Only the Sergeants call me Mr Higgins. I must rush. Cheers!"

The following day Carl had hoped for another sortie to Brilon with the NCO duty driver. He was eager to resume his tantalisingly unfinished conversation with Angela but the course got back late from demonstrations of parashelter building and living off the land because two cadets had failed to repack their parachutes properly and had been disciplined with a half-hour run in the forest with full Bergen rucksack, webbing pouches and water bottle. Nigel Perkins declared on return that the staff had enough fresh food for messing and that anyway there was to be an unscheduled night march by compass bearing to the distant ski lift building and back.

Luckily next day everything was back on timetable at camp and Corporal Davies was on driving duty once more. The Camp Commander had taken the Land Rover so they set off in the three ton truck instead. This was lucky. It could not be overlooked so easily in town and Angela was disappointingly not to be seen at the café of two day before.

After the routine food purchases were done Corporal Davies was happily installed in the cab of the lorry with his hot dog, coffee and paperback and Carl settled down to read another serious newspaper the Frankfurter Allgemeine Zeitung whilst still nurturing the hope that Angela would turn up. She did. "Lucky you came by truck, Carl. My other colleague Bärbel insisted we go to a different café but as soon as I saw what I hoped was your lorry I managed to slip away and here I am. Let's have a Dortmunder each. It's my favourite beer and since you didn't come yesterday we need to celebrate your reappearance today."

"It's great to be back in your delightful company, Fräulein von Lammersdorf. I think your name sounds so elegant and distinguished. Why are you shy about the 'von'?" asked Higgins.

"I promised to explain," replied Angela. "After the war families like ours were unwilling to give any reminder of what we called the good old says especially in the East where my uncle Wolfgang now lives. Everyone imagines that if you're 'von' anything you're very – how do you put it – posh; if not an aristocrat at least landed gentry.

"There's been quite a social revolution even in the Bundesrepublik after the two world wars. In the first Mutti lost two of her brothers, one in the Uhlans at Tannenberg in 1914 and one in the Air Service in 1916. He was in Oswald Boelcke's squadron on the Western Front. The Nazis were always suspicious of people like us. Then came the Red Army's invasion in 1945.

"The Western Allies let the Soviet Russian invaders hand over my Silesian homeland to the communist Poles. Our estate has been broken up long ago and Onkel Wolfgang tells us that the family home has been turned into a training school for the managers of workers' co-operatives.

"We were never Nazis but poor Herr Doktor Wolfgang my uncle is treated with great suspicion by his medical colleagues. He only stays in the Russian sector of Berlin out of loyalty to his patients. As for us we prefer to live quietly. We do not even go to meetings of Silesian exiles."

"That's what amazes me about your country, Angela. In just over fifty years you've all gone through such heart rending drama and yet chatting to you in the warm evening sunshine at this delightful café everything seems so normal. Yet I cannot get it out of my mind that young men of my age in the same blue uniform as I wear were bombing your cities flat less than fifteen years ago," Higgins observed.

"That's true, Carl," Angela replied, "but many of Mutti's generation brought such shame upon Germany and appearances are deceptive. Our behaviour in those years was not normal and we are paying the price. We can never now go home to where I was born and Uncle Wolfgang tells us that people in what I call Mitteldeutschland, East Germany to you, are very poor and have as little freedom as in Nazi times. We just have to keep faith that 'es gibt nur eines Deutschland, unteilbares' that there's only one Germany, indivisible. I hope the slogan comes true before too long. We're all quite prosperous here in the Bundesrepublik but I doubt if the Poles will ever give up my family's Silesian homeland."

"Do you realise, Angela, what a joy these moments snatched with you on my way back to survival camp are for me? It is amazing that I met you and do you know how privileged I am? I am the only cadet allowed out of the camp. Normally the officers and sergeants watch us every minute but there's no one else they can trust with the shopping and the officers can't do without their special food and beer. Also none of my fellow cadets could express such appreciation of you as I do, meine Schatzi Angela – Angela my little treasure."

"I would have slipped off home long ago, Carl, if I were not happy, too," Angela answered directly. "I hope you'll be able to come on a shopping expedition here tomorrow as well, but these visits are such a rush. I've got an idea. I know a woodland Schwimmbad which is just off the road to your camp. If you would allow me to hide in the back of your lorry I'll bang on the cab when we reach the track through the forest which leads there. I'll show it to you right away and if you like it just come to the pool tomorrow evening and I'll be waiting for you there. Don't worry about me tonight. I can catch the bus back to Brilon."

"All right, Schatzi, but you realise that if we're found out I'll be sent straight home to England and chopped," Carl warned.

Corporal Davies the driver was a willing accomplice. German propensity for sun worship was legendary and he was hopeful that there would be no shortage of pretty girls sunbathing at the poolside. His optimism was fully justified. To Carl the limpid green waters of the pine forest lagoon were enchanting. The surrounding tree line was masked by a purple fringe of foxgloves and willowherb and a grassy sward dotted with sunbathers led down to the water's edge. There was a little jetty on one side from which a rowing boat lay moored and on the other was a diving platform a good five metres high from which little boys were jumping excitedly into the water.

Next day dawned hot – ideal for the twenty twenty route march in Wing Commander Jolly's view – twenty kilometres of quick time speed marching by squadrons with Bergen rucksacks each weighing over twenty kilograms plus a 303 Lee Enfield rifle for each man. The RAF Regiment NCOs were in their element. They had the merit of keeping the pace up with a ceaseless stream of invective so that Higgins got back in plenty of time for his late afternoon sortie to Brilon with Corporal Davies. It had unusually fervent support from Flight Lieutenant Perkins, the Adjutant. "After today's march, Higgins," he instructed, "I want you to double the beer purchase tonight. Now get moving!"

CHAPTER 9

Carl Higgins and Corporal Davies fairly rattled into Brilon in the Land Rover and equally rapidly out again after their shopping to the schwimmbad in the woods. Davies was happy enough to wait with his paperback and a can of beer while Carl went off to the jetty at the end of which he had promised to meet Angela. He soon spotted her in a royal blue lycra one piece swimming costume stretched out on a pale blue towel big enough for two. At her feet were a small wicker hamper and a thermos flask.

"Welcome, Carl. Relax. Lie down and enjoy the sunshine. You've done well to get here so punctually. I wasn't expecting you till 6.00 pm so we have an extra half-hour to enjoy together. I know you English like a cup of tea about this time so I've brought the thermos and made gurken sandwiches. I learned how to prepare delicate cucumber sandwiches when I was at Oxford but German bread is browner with a stronger flavour which makes them even better."

"I can't wait to find out," Carl replied.

"After tea we can have a swim and then if you've got time – wir können im Wald spazieren gehen – we can go for a walk in the woods. You know how we Germans love to go a wandering, hiking with funny hats and mountain boots an Alpenstock in hand," Angela jokingly proposed.

"I'm all for it but I can't linger too long. The Camp Commander has a meeting with his directing staff at 8.00 pm and dinner at 8.30 pm. I can't imagine them sitting down happily for a meal unless they have their beer and schnapps available," Carl explained.

Angela's tea was even more delicious than Carl expected and culminated in an exotic looking chocolate cake of her own confection amply crowned with a generous topping of Schlag – Westphalian whipped cream at its richest. Before Carl could have any ideas of sleeping off such an unwarranted treat, Angela was urging him on: "Time to swim. It's warm in there."

Off they trotted across the close cropped grass. Spring had long since gone and it was high summer in its prime but still the lines of Rupert Brooke came unseasonably back to Carl: "And when the day is young and sweet gild gloriously the bare feet that run to bathe. Du lieber Gott!" Indeed they had God's blessing now. Du liebste Angela… Dearest Angela.

Her olive skinned limbs seemed at one with the olive waters of the forest pool. Carl had a vision of brown eyes, brown hair and gently swirling eddies as she swam the easy strokes of one for whom to swim was as natural as for a water nymph. The experience was short but intense. Angela was calling to Carl, "Let's get dry quickly!" as she made strongly for the grassy bank. "I want to show you my little secret in the wood," she suggested with an inviting smile. She deftly dabbed down her silky hair and towelled dry her skin hugging lycra swimsuit seemingly personally designed for just such a divine embodiment of the female form. "Now follow me."

A little path led from the back of the boathouse, invisible to the sunbathers on the shore. Angela trod it surefootedly between bramble bushes and raspberry canes until a bed of soft brown pine needles was reached beneath a canopy of pine trees. About five minutes further in lay a tiny pine girt pool of crystal clear water. "Try this, Carl," said Angela and she dived straight in from a tree stump. The Schwimmbad beyond the trees was temperate from the summer sun but this pure water of the inner forest was glacial and tingled the skin excitingly. The thermal shock was better than a sauna. Shafts of sunlight through loftily imperious pines trees illuminated for Carl a cameo of timeless Teutonic bliss.

"Did this surprise you, Carl?" asked Angela breathlessly. "It's icy in here but I can soon warm you up. I can see you're freezing. Give me your towel. Let me dry you, please." She stood tiptoe barefooted on his feet looking straight into his eyes and tenderly rubbed him down and planting what she called a Küßchen on his mouth and others followed. "Look your lips are blue," she observed. "You need bigger kisses to warm you up and we can use the towel better like this," she suggested, extending it over a mattress of ferns and woodland grasses. "Let me give you a hug. We Silesians never feel the cold. Don't be shy. No one ever comes here," she reassured him as she slipped the lycra swimsuit down and off her legs.

Once in her arms Carl's circulation was stirringly restored. The pupils of Angela's eyes seemed as wide and bottomless as the lagoon itself; her kisses, too, were infinitely deep. "I feel as if I've been waiting for you all my life, my bold English pilot but you've only been here a week," she sighed. "And you my well named Angela have ushered me into paradise. I never knew such joy and fulfilment could be shared so naturally. 'Blessed Communion, fellowship divine' is a phrase from a hymn sung on All Saints Day in England. It describes us doesn't it? Your loving takes me to another plane. We are one flesh. How will I ever be able to return to Cranwell knowing that I leave behind a vision of perfect womanhood beyond most men's imagining?"

"A bold pilot like you must be strong, Carl," Angela replied with steady self-assurance. "We shall enjoy every moment together while you're here and then we must have faith. There is nothing more important as Martin Luther has reminded us. By faith we are saved. Our future is in God's hands. That's one lesson I learned from the war."

"Look the shadows are getting longer, Angela. I must go quickly and return to the camp by dinner time or the officers will be suspicious and never let me come again."

"That would be too bad, Carl," Angela answered firmly, "I said we must enjoy every moment together and I meant it. We never know what tomorrow brings. I hope to see you then."

"You shall if my duties permit it," Carl answered optimistically.

Carl ran off towards the waiting Land Rover and cast a long look backwards as he ran. There she was still sitting in the warming rays of the evening sun and waving to him. He waved back somewhat weakly as he ran. Fears of a cross examination on return and confinement to camp made him sprint to Corporal Davies.

"Drive fast this time Corporal. If the Wing Commander's debrief finishes early I'm done for."

Luckily for Carl the Camp Commander had been at his most long-winded. Although he arrived at the Headquarters tent a full ten minutes late Higgins could distinctly hear Wing Commander Jolly's pompous intonation: "Even some of you, gentlemen, are not setting the standards we require for Flight Cadets. I know that officers from Flying Wing may be unaccustomed to such matters and that things may be more relaxed down on the Flight Line but I do expect you to maintain a good example at all times – that means you wear your berets and belts however hot it is and however strenuous the activity.

"What's more," he droned on, "I shall not need to remind you gentlemen, that although your duties may take you into sand and mud you should at least start the day with polished boots for which as directing staff you are responsible because in a survival camp everyone has to look after himself without the luxury of batmen." The Wing Commander is clearly enjoying the sound of his own voice thought Higgins as he slipped round to the back of the Officers' Mess Tent and discreetly left the crates of beer and Schnapps and box of special foods in the usual place beneath the dining table.

The following day passed quickly enough with First Aid instruction and a briefing on the medical aspects of survival. The Chief Ground Defence NCO returned to his favourite theme: "PROTECSHUN – get out of the wind, make a weatherproof shelter, get and keep dry and although Napoleon's Army may have marched on its stomach as downed aircrew you must look after your feet. They're the only means of locomotion you possess. You can go for days without food so there's no need for you to eat any of your survival rations the first day – if at all if you live intelligently off the land. Drinking sufficient water, however, is essential. Manage its consumption responsibly and ensure that it is pure, preferably boiled or if that would be too dangerous do not forget to use your purification tablets."

Carl Higgins began to get anxious. The instruction was degenerating into a question and answer session and the First Aid element had not even begun. Finally they broke for gobbled haversack rations before being called to attention by the Warrant Officer. "You will now march as an Entry at the double," he resumed, "to Willi Gross' saw mill where Corporal Davies will instruct you in the principles of First Aid." Off they trotted in metronomic step with Corporal Davies in the lead until they reached a clearing littered with tree trunks, stacks of logs and piles of pinewood planks beside an empty corrugated iron workshop. "Sit down, gentlemen. Make yourselves comfortable," began the RAF Regiment Corporal whose speciality apart from driving was First Aid.

Notwithstanding his soft lilting Welsh voice Corporal Davies began firmly with a familiar theme, "Remember gentlemen baling out, forced landing or a crash are going to be traumatic experiences and you are likely to end up in harsh terrain in extremes of heat, cold or precipitation," he began. "So what the casualty will need first of all to minimise the shock is PROTECSHUN. Don't move him unless you absolutely have to but keep him warm or cool according to the weather and shielded from wind, snow, rain or sun." The Corporal was thorough but repeated much that Carl had learnt at school from the St John's Ambulance man's visit.

Higgins' thoughts were elsewhere, with Angela who he felt sure would be at the Schwimmbad as early as possible today. Like so many Germans she said she was punctually at her desk in the insurance office by eight in the morning and always left correspondingly early at 5.00 o'clock sharp. For her not just work but leisure were a serious business. Carl felt that Corporal Davies would not wish his First Aid instruction to overrun. He, too, enjoyed his early evening trips to Brilon although for him the incentive was not as heart-poundingly attractive as for Carl.

As Carl had expected Corporal Davies kept strictly to time and insisted that the cadets return to camp at the double. On arrival once they were halted, turned into line and dismissed he came up to Higgins and inquired smilingly, "The usual this evening, Mr Higgins?" Carl did not even bother to shower – a dip in the Schwimmbad with Angela was infinitely preferable. He piled straight into the lorry bumping off down the track to Brilon to fulfil what Nigel Perkins the Adjutant had shouted at them on departure, "The standard requirements gentlemen please."

Never had Carl rushed round the market stalls so expeditiously. He knew where everything was to be found. The stallholders greeted him familiarly, "Dieselbe Einkäufe wie gewöhnlich?", "The same purchases as usual?" Carl did not even bother to haggle with them but he did manage to negotiate from one, "ein kleines Geschenck für meinen Kamerad", "a small present for my comrade" of a basket of strawberries for free, "und einen Blumenstrauß für meine Freundin," "and a bunch of flowers for my girlfriend."

The strawberries ought to keep Corporal Davies sweet thought Carl and perhaps enhance his chances of a good mark for First Aid in the final assessment at the end of survival camp. Aching heart and soul together with the irresistible impulsion of desire propelled him urgently back to the cab of the lorry. "Off we go, Corporal Davies, to the swimming pool post haste," Carl instructed.

"I see we are in a hurry now, Mr Higgins," replied Corporal Davies sardonically. "Aren't you tired after those two long marches in double time?"

"They were nothing, Corporal," Carl insisted cheerfully, "that a dip in the pool can't put right."

"I prefer to rest it off in the cab under the trees," answered Corporal Davies. "I've brought my portable radio and I'll eat your strawberries at leisure."

The scene was unusual when Carl arrived. Angela's pale blue towel lay in the same place as before. She had brought the picnic hamper and thermos again. Wonderful girl thought Carl. A book, her clothes, shoes and sunglasses were grouped together beside the towel but where was Angela? She surely would not have gone off to what he regarded as their own magic lagoon in the forest without him. She was not that kind of girl. Something was strange. There were no sunbathers stretched out on the grass. Everyone seemed to be gathered at the water's edge.

Carl approached an onlooker, "Was ist los?", "What's happening?", he asked. "Es gab einen Unfall", "there's been an accident" was the laconic reply. A large group of people were on the jetty peering down into the olive green waters below. The little rowing boat had been loosed from its moorings. One man was at the oars, the other leaning over the stern and prodding away below him with a boathook. "Mach schnell!", "Hurry up!" someone shouted down to the boatmen.

Where was Angela wondered Carl apprehensively. If a swimmer had got into trouble Carl felt sure that she would with strong and stylish strokes have been the first on the scene to buoy him up. Another snatch of German reached him, "Es ist ein Mädchen", "It's a girl" and made his apprehension turn to agony. Could it be Angela herself who had suffered the accident? His stomach felt as if it had been smitten by a hard kicked football. There was no royal blue swimsuit to be seen. If she was not at the pool she would be looking for him.

His anguished thoughts were interrupted by a cry from a bystander, "Schauen Sie mal", "Look!" The man with the boathook was clearly struggling. "Hilfe! Schnell!!", "Help! Quickly!" he exclaimed. Two able bodied men, one fully clothed leapt straight down into the water and swam vigorously to the boat which was down by the stern about a yard off the end of the jetty. They dived under water and then after much struggling Carl saw that the barb of the boathook was snagged on a royal blue shoulder strap. All the demons of hell could not inflict more torture upon him.

Two more young men jumped into the pool and helped push the rowing boat to shore with its inert human catch towed behind.

Angela was pulled through a muddy reed bed and onto the grass. Her face was pallid. Her eyes were largely white with pupils directed upward towards heaven and a pale frothy stream of liquid was exuding from the corner of her mouth. Her breasts seemed flaccid. Her mound once tumescent now was flat. Her curves, her silken hair and well shaped legs were a sensual irrelevance almost too painful to behold.

Carl watched her being turned over to the resuscitation position and a burly German apply measured pressure to her lungs. She exhaled a pinkish blend of blood and bubbly foam. He could stand no more. He raced to the lorry. Corporal Davies was slumbering in the cab. How could anyone sleep at a time like this. "Wake up Corporal! You're the First Aider. We need you now. A girl is unconscious. She may have drowned."

Corporal Davies was at her side in no more than a few seconds. People deferred to his uniform and evident authority and made way for him. He turned Angela over and tried to revive her mouth to mouth. Then he was massaging her heart. So it went on it seemed for ever. Carl wished that he could have wept. He wanted to do so but this was tragedy beyond tears. A green and yellow ambulance with two police motorcycle outriders arrived in a cloud of dust. A professional crewman applied a stethoscope to Angela's heart and tried her pulse. "Es ist unnützlich. Sie ist tot", "It's useless. She is dead," the senior one pronounced. Angela was put on a stretcher, wrapped in a blue plastic sheet matching her half lowered swimsuit and raised into the ambulance.

Carl ran and picked up her things from the grass and handed them to the driver. "Ich mag lhr ein kleines küßchen geben", "I would like to give her a little kiss." He went in at the back of the ambulance, put a hand on Angela's bare shoulder, stooped down and touched her already cooling forehead with his lips. "Farewell meine liebste Angela. I loved you dearly but I never had the time to tell you."

"You knew her then?" the crewman inquired.

"Sie war meine Freundin", "She was my girlfriend," Carl replied, "but I didn't even know where she lived."

The rear doors were shut and Carl watched the ambulance pull away down the track towards Brilon. People drifted back from the water's edge to their towels and clothes but Carl just stood there until he felt a heavy hand upon his shoulder, "Shouldn't we be going Mr Higgins?" How terribly sad, sir. It's only the second drowning I've been involved with. The other was at White Sands Bay near St David's when a holidaymaker got pulled under by the undertow when trying to belly board in big waves. Even a First Aider can't always help but at least he can try. It is even worse just to look on. We must go now, sir."

Twice Corporal Davies had called him "sir". His respect was comforting because Carl felt total desolation. "You knew her didn't you, Mr Higgins?"

"Indeed I did but not for long. She was more important to me than anyone I've ever known. I've never experienced such complete happiness in anyone else's company. It was as if she was the mirror image of my soul."

"What do you think happened, Mr Higgins?" Corporal Davis enquired.

"When I kissed her my final farewell I saw she had a big bruise by her left temple. I imagine that instead of using the diving board she dived off the jetty and too steeply bashing her head on the rocks which you can just see below water at the far end. Everyone was probably so preoccupied with tanning themselves in the sunshine that they never noticed what had happened until it was too late," Carl replied.

"Let's hurry on back, sir," Corporal Davis proposed. "Remember dinner is later than normal tonight, Mr Higgins, as the Wing Commander is to brief everyone for the Grand Finale, the Escape and Evasion, which begins tomorrow."

Wing Commander Jolly in verbose and sonorous style outlined his plans for the next two days' exercise to the assembled cadets sitting on folding camp chairs around the flagpole. Carl was so utterly drained and shocked by the afternoon's tragedy at the Schwimmbad that he hardly remembered a word that the Camp Commander said. Only two instructions stuck in his mind: "Don't mark the map," Wing Commander Jolly insisted. "You can't afford to compromise the rendezvous or your escape route to the enemy. If you do you will be putting friendly personnel and fellow crews in grave jeopardy. Remember, gentlemen, this exercise is serious. The next time you perform escape and evasion may be for real so now as on an operational squadron we allow you to pick your fellow crewmen. This should ensure good cooperation between you, mutual support and maximise effectiveness."

Taffy Jones teamed up with Peter Carrick and Lascelles with Blackham. Somewhat incongruously the two Commonwealth cadets paired, the lanky Flight Cadet Ahmed with the tubby little 'China' Chu and less surprisingly Carl Higgins with Jamie Jamieson. All the cadets were pleased to see Nigel Perkins the Camp Adjutant crew with Flying Officer Matthews, a tall athletic flying instructor on Meteors. "I'm really looking forward to this, Higgins," observed the Adjutant who had become quite familiar with Carl from his foraging expeditions to Brilon. "Bob Matthews should be in his element. He's in the Royal Air Force ski team for both downhill and cross country. The only thing we'll really miss are your provisions from the market. Blueberries, standard issue dry compo biscuits and stream water will hardly make up for the calories foregone from your excellent pork chops, sausages, Tilsitter cheese and beer."

"Don't worry, sir," Carl replied. "My friends feel that you're really one of us although I'm sure that there were many more of this type of exercise in your two years at Sandhurst. Here we have to endure the rigours of Survival Camp for only seventeen days in the whole of our three years at the College. Listen, sir, Wing Commander Jolly is giving us our final timings."

The Wing Commander went wordily on, "Please set your watches, gentlemen. It is now exactly 21.30 hours Central European Time. Get it right. Remember that rendezvous will only be manned from one minute before to one minute after the stipulated time. I suggest you collect your parachute packs and aircrew survival rations from the Quartermaster's tent forthwith and get your heads down at once for a few hours' rest. Reveille will be at 02.00 hours and the lorries will depart for the DZs, the dropping zones, at 02.30. By 03.00 at the latest you should be moving off from where your lorry left you giving you at least five miles to cover in the darkness before you can lie up at dawn for which you must choose your spot carefully, secure from ground and aerial searches because the Irish Guards will be lying in wait for you and the Army Air Corps will complement their searches for you at first light."

Getting out of their sleeping bags was an effort of will and after a snatched breakfast of bread and jam and tea the cadets were on their way with an officer in the cab to direct the driver to the correct dropping off point and an NCO in the back of the lorry to ensure that the cadets did not peep through the tarpaulin cover to identify their position.

All Carl and Jamie were given was the timing and description of the rendezvous – a wood cutter's shelter beside a woodland stream running North to South through a clearing in the forest; its bearing of 105° magnetic and distance of fifteen nautical miles from drop off, which they had to cover in exactly twenty-four hours.

Higgins held the compass and Jamie followed him some five yards behind keeping Carl's ill defined silhouette in sight but sufficiently distant to escape separately if ambushed. Every five minutes they would stop and listen as the night-time silence betrayed the tiniest movement. Luckily a half moon through a hazy layer of cirrus made it easier to avoid obstacles, tree trunks and bushes along the way.

As they proceeded Carl counted their strides halting at exactly the five mile point. A Homerian rosy fingered dawn revealed an undulating landscape of seemingly endless pine forests. Luckily some hundred yards further on was a clearing with bramble bushes into which Carl and Jamie painfully inserted themselves. The leaves lent invisibility from air and ground whilst the thorns would put off most searchers who would imagine that cadets on the run would take shelter in barns, bothies and logger's huts.

Fortuitously Jamieson and Higgins had manoeuvred themselves into the ideal observation post. They felt confident about their security though apprehensive lest the searching infantry be accompanied by tracker dogs. Blackberry pickers had left swathes of flattened grass so the evaders' footsteps could in no way be distinguished. The extent of the clearing and its location on a pronounced knoll gave Carl and Jamie a clear view in all directions above all down into the valley below along which ran a metalled road and a line of high tension cables suspended from ugly steel pylons.

"Let's take turns to kip and to keep watch. One hour on, one hour off," suggested Carl.

"I agree," replied Jamie, "provided you allow me to crash out first" curling himself up in a foetus position with his head on his as yet unopened parachute pack. "You've had all those relaxing hours in Brilon, Carl, sipping coffee with the local beauties no doubt whilst we untutored barbarians who speak no language but our own have endured the evening chores, extra duties and endless nagging of the Rock Ape Warrant Officer. You maintain the look out. I'm knackered. Good night or rather good morning."

All too quickly Jamieson had dozed off leaving Carl feeling strangely lonely and vulnerable. He envied Jamie his easy public school confidence; his seemingly steady County girlfriend and unspoken self-assurance that he would replicate his father's charmed flying career unscathed by the vagaries and tragedies of Royal Air force service.

Carl had not confided to anyone yet about dear Angela's terrible death. No other cadet knew she had even existed. Only Corporal Davies shared his secret sorrow. Angela had been looking forward so much to one more meeting after the escape and evasion exercise was over before he flew back to Cranwell.

He was going to suggest to her that they spend a week of his summer leave camping in the Harz mountains and if that went well he had been hoping to persuade her to come across to the Graduation Ball at Christmas. She would take the ferry from the Hook of Holland and he remembered that a train went straight from Harwich to Lincoln via Sleaford. Friends had taken it in reverse on a posting to RAF Germany. She would have stayed at the White Hart in Lincoln right beside the

Cathedral Close, which he had already earmarked for his parents for his own Passing Out Parade two and a half years hence. He had worked it all out but why had he mentally made so many plans when a cadet's life is so uncertain? He forced himself back from such cruelly poignant daydreams to the current task of vigilance.

Down the valley a small column of three ton trucks preceded by a Land Rover flying a blue pennant and followed by another bristling with radio aerials was moving steadily down the road. About halfway along the procession stopped. Carl could clearly make out what looked like four sections of infantry disembark and fan out to each side of the road and then proceed in line abreast towards the first copse of pine trees.

Soon his watch was interrupted by the unmistakable sound of a light aircraft so different from the howl of the more frequent "widowmaker" Starfighters of the Luftwaffe. He looked up to see the ungainly shape of an Army Spotter aircraft in military camouflage – undoubtedly an Auster, probably an AOP9 he thought to himself.

Although its high wing gave the crew a good downward view he felt perfectly secure.

Taffy Jones had flown the civil version the Autocrat at Fairwood Common. He related how the flaps are on the cabin roof and how you have to operate the throttle, flaps and control column like a cross armed dingbat. The aeroplane was well named. It certainly had a will of its own. He had only managed to land it on the fifth attempt after many ignominious kangaroo hops down the runway. He did not envy the poor observers. The pongo pilots probably flew in hobnailed boots and operated the ultra sensitive controls through muscle bound and brawny tattooed arms.

As the day progressed Army activity in the valley intensified. Another column of trucks proceeded further along the road disgorging rather more troops this time. A second Auster passed right overhead but did not return. The soldiers moved steadily forward so the cadets had not been spotted.

Then came a more worrying development. A pair of Skeeters appeared over the hill behind them, one flying each side of the road. Both hovered up to the first copse and landed at its edge. The crewman got out and walked through the wood presumably to look for cadets on the run by which time his helicopter had flown round to the other side to pick him up again. They did this once more then the third time Carl witnessed a chilling sight.

The day was hot and the Skeeter's lack of power was notorious. The nearer helicopter got airborne once the observer was back on board and rose a few feet into the air beginning to turn into wind to climb away but in doing so the tail rotor struck a high tension cable. The pylons were out of view beyond the clumps of pine trees leaving the cables very hard to see. There was a brilliant blue flash. The tail rotor detached itself from the fuselage cascading down into the wheat field below and the helicopter began to gyrate crazily smashing into tall pines at the edge of the copse before bursting into flames, which quickly spread to the wood itself.

This all happened so fast that by the time Carl could wake Jamie the blaze had become an inferno with a pall of black smoke billowing upward. The other Skeeter was circling above doubtless radioing for assistance and to direct the emergency vehicles to the scene of the crash. The cadets could see the soldiers abandon their line search and race towards the flames. Once there they could only be macabre spectators and two peeled off running down the field to open the gate onto the field and act as guides to the crash crews. A distant wailing of sirens soon presaged a speeding convoy of two German ambulances, a massive six-wheeled fire tender with a foam cannon on top and huge cross country tyres, and two Army style Volkswagen police vehicles.

"This is just too bad, Carl," said Jamie. "Our time as Junior Entry began with the two Vampires crashing off the end of Cranwell South's main runway and ends with another fatal air accident during our escape and evasion exercise. Our training seems to be a cruel business costly in blood and treasure to get us up to the standard the Service requires. What stupid unnecessary deaths!"

Before long the smoke had cleared and only four soldiers remained at the site no doubt to guard the wreckage from ghoulish souvenir hunters and protect evidence for the inquiry. Now there was no longer danger of a forest fire the German vehicles had been replaced by crash vehicles from Güttersloh with red, white and blue roundels and a Royal Air Force Wessex helicopter had landed nearby. The sun was getting low and the midges were beginning to bite.

Carl and Jamie huddled together with aircrew parkas over their heads to deter the insects whilst Carl smoked furiously to keep the midges out. Jamie continued his whispered monologue. "Now I understand why they have those slogans all over the crewroom walls – 'Never assume: check'. If the guy rejoining at Cranwell had looked beneath him before rejoining the circuit there would have been no collision. If the poor old pongo helicopter pilot had looked carefully behind him before lifting off he would have kept his tail rotor on and saved his life."

"It's certainly gruesome for us," Carl replied between smoke puffs. "I just hope we learn by what we have seen. It's been a more effective lesson than a hundred flight safety posters on the wall."

Carl and Jamie studied the map and confirmed the bearing and distance to the rendezvous, nine and a half nautical miles mostly forest trek on a bearing of 115° magnetic. Their route to the rendezvous did not look too difficult – almost solidly pinewoods with a large clearing at the six mile point in the middle of which was a forest pool surrounded by what was indicated on the map as boggy ground. They would have to be careful there and execute a precisely measured dog leg. As for the logger's shelter it seemed well isolated and could be approached downhill from the edge of the forest so the cadets could observe it carefully for potential ambushes before making expeditious contact with the friendly personnel waiting for them there.

Carl and Jamie chumped some survival biscuits washed down with a few mouthfuls of water before extricating themselves from the bramble bush. It was half an hour after sunset the time when officially night flying began and certainly dark enough to get moving with confidence. This they did crossing the cornfield boldly to the woodlands beyond. Once beneath the pines it became truly dark. As during the previous night they took turns to lead on the compass bearing stopping every five minutes to listen intently for enemy movement. Their only surprise was at a loud succession of guttural grunts followed by the sound of hasty scampering. They assumed they had disturbed a wild boar but the soldiers were nowhere in evidence, at least not in Carl and Jamie's part of the forest – probably comfortably consuming a well cooked evening meal they guessed.

The sole minor drama arose when they emerged from the pinewoods at what was evidently their pre-identified clearing. The watery half moon reflected weakly on a different woodland pool and they were hardly out of the pines before they were sinking into a deep peat bog. They extricated themselves as quickly as they could and felt sure the whole British Army could hear the suction as they carefully withdrew their boots, which they were eager not to leave behind.

Off they went on a dog leg round the obstacle maintaining forty-five degrees to the right for five minutes, then turning ninety degrees left and proceeding for a further five minutes before going forty-five degrees right again on their original bearing. They continued on for two more hours until the wood began to thin and eventually they emerged into an open field. It sloped down towards a stream which they could hear clearly probably some thousand yards away.

They were half an hour early so there was still plenty of time to locate the rendezvous hut. "There it is, Carl," whispered Jamie, "at two o'clock to us probably eight hundred yards away." Indeed there lay a low one storey building emitting no light nor sound of movement. Perhaps the two directing staff had already been caught and the Army would now be lying in wait there for them as well.

On reflection Jamie dismissed the idea. He could see no vehicle beside the hut. Their briefing had explained there was no other hut anywhere near and the stream was in the right position relative to it and ran on the correct bearing. Anyway the pongos would doubtless have much better things to do than charge through the forest all night. Carl felt sure that they had long since taken to their sleeping bags.

Then he saw it – a tiny red glow at the further end of the black silhouette of a building. It could only be a lighted cigarette. Soldiers would certainly not smoke in an ambush position. When it came to discipline the directing staff were long on the preaching of it much shorter on its personal practice. "Let's move Carl," suggested Jamie. "It's 0245 hours by my infallible aircrew Rolex. The cigarette will be a perfect homing beacon. The ground looks downhill and we should get to the rendezvous at the appointed time."

They made good speed down the gentle slope towards the point of red light which as they arrived they could just see emanated from the end of a white ebony cigarette holder, which the weak moonlight revealed to be clasped in the jaw of an officer more elegantly dressed than members of the directing staff in flying boots, into which were tucked his trousers, Crombie greatcoat and officers' cap. "My God, sir, it's you Flight Lieutenant Zopolowski!"

"Indeed it is, Flight Cadet Higgins. You don't always know who you'll meet at rendezvous when you pass down the escape line. Corporal Davies here you do know of course. He tells me you've suffered a bereavement. My condolences. They're dangerous these transnational unions. It was bad enough for me when 303 lost Jan Frantisek our top scoring fearless Czech pilot at the end of October 1940 when the Battle of Britain was coming to an end but then the next month I lost my English girlfriend Edith in the blitz. So I do know what it's like. I am sorry. I've come here to enjoy pleasanter thoughts. The scent of the pinewoods reminds me of the Masurian Lakes and happy boyhood holidays with my family before the war. Listen now you two. Corporal Davies will give you your next rendezvous."

"Come in here, gentlemen," said Corporal Davies and ushered them into the logger's hut where there was not only a roughly hewn wooden table but rustic wooden benches beside it – ideal for map reading by torchlight. "Sit down, please and report your intelligence," he requested.

"We have very little, Corporal," replied Carl. "Soon after drop off we saw in total six sections of infantry deploy from lorries down the main road. They fanned out into line abreast and searched the wheat fields in a southerly direction. Two Austers passed overhead without spotting us and a pair of Skeeters were co-operating with the infantry along the road inserting their observers into the neighbouring pinewoods until one suffered a fatal accident colliding with a high tension cable."

"Yes, I heard about that from the Flight Lieutenant," answered Corporal Davies. "He told me that it was pilot error."

"I agree," Carl replied. "I witnessed the whole dreadful episode."

"Well unless one of the soldiers did also you may have to submit evidence to the Board of Inquiry. Study the map gentlemen and you will see that your next rendezvous by some cruel coincidence, is at the end of the same pinewood pool jetty, which has such tragic memories for you and me Mr Higgins. It's in twenty-four hours time – 0300 hours tomorrow night. From there if you arrive punctually transport will be available to run you back to camp. Now move on gentlemen. You've been here five minutes already."

Jamie and Carl decided to press on for a couple of hours before lying up. The night was cool and clear; the going underfoot reasonable though uphill. Just before dawn they came across an area of felling with numerous pine trunks piled up ready to be taken away. It was Sunday morning. They felt sure that no logger would come so they decided to use one parachute canopy as a roof to keep off the strong sun and the other as a ground sheet to sleep on. If the cadet on sentry duty noticed a search party approaching he would pull down the covering parachute, rouse his friend and they could lie very low between the piles of tree trunks hoping not to be seen. For an early breakfast they tucked into chocolate and an oatmeal bar and began talking till dawn.

"You never told me about this bereavement of yours, Carl," protested Jamie. "I would have expected that as one of your better friends and now as your crewman you could at least have confided in me. What happened and why keep it to yourself?"

"You know, Jamie, how at the College they go on at us about sharing key information only on a need to know basis on grounds of security," replied Carl, "and I felt that if I told anyone the news could be out that I had been seeing a girlfriend on my daily trips to Brilon, which had been specifically authorised for provisioning purposes only and I could then have got chopped."

"True, but Corporal Davies who used to drive you there has clearly blurted out the story to Polzol and for all we know," Jamie pointed out, "the whole directing staff is now talking about it."

"I doubt it. Polzol is not like that. I trust him but I acknowledge that Corporal Davies should not have let on. I regard it as a trust betrayed," said Carl emphatically, "but I could hardly keep the terrible truth from him because he tried to revive poor Angela from drowning. However, he clearly has no sense of honour."

"What do you expect?" How naïve can you get?" Jamie protested. "He's an NCO not officer material like us. Anyway if he was involved as you describe perhaps the German authorities came to take evidence from him."

"I doubt it," answered Carl. "He didn't see her drown, nor did I. We didn't even rescue her. I wish I had arrived much earlier. Corporal Davies merely tried to put his First Aid skills to good effect at my desperate request but he failed. I think dear Angela was probably unconscious from the time she hit the rocks on her fatal dive off the jetty. Anyway I'll show it to you when we rendezvous there tomorrow night."

"What a macabre coincidence, Carl," said Jamie, "but more important what was she like and how did you meet?"

"We met at a café in town and then she showed me this same woodland lagoon as our next rendezvous where we bathed, lay in the sun, picnicked, and then went off to make love in the forest. I truly had a fleeting glimpse of paradise," Carl answered. "To me she represented all that is best in Germany. You know I have a thing about this country. You'd call it an infatuation, I'm sure, but I'm almost overwhelmed by the contrasts – the magnificent music, glorious baroque architecture, fine literature, stirring Lutheran chorales and profound philosophy on the one hand and Nazism, Communism, Militarism and the inhuman Stalinist edifices of East Germany not to mention the despicable regime which spawns them on the other."

"You always were prone to get carried away on flights of spiritual fancy, Carl. You ought to get yourself a good steady local girlfriend like mine," suggested Jamie.

"I know you've been lucky with Jane," Carl acknowledged, "but Angela was not a spiritual fancy to me but very warm hearted, passionate flesh and blood allied to an intense sensibility that few possess. Her death merely magnified a hundredfold what was to me an extraordinarily profound experience, which I am sure will have changed me for life."

"That may be so, Carl," said Jamie, "but we have practicalities to attend to right away. If you want to be an Under Officer in your last term and pass out well we must not be captured so I suggest you now keep careful watch for an hour whilst I sleep."

Carl and Jamie suffered little disturbance during the day. A couple more Austers flew inoffensively overhead. A group of cheery German ramblers dressed much as Angela had described their stereotype skirted the clearing before disappearing once more into the forest. In mid afternoon there was a more sinister development. Jamie picked up the thwack thwack sound of rotor blades of an approaching helicopter.

"Wake up, Carl," Jamie exclaimed, "there's a Skeeter coming. Help me pack up the top parachute. Quick." They seized handfuls of parachute fabric and folded it beneath them pulling some loose branches over their heads. The Skeeter passed right above the clearing and then they heard the engine and rotor note change as the helicopter hovered and then descended to land on the far side of the wood.

"Hurry up, Carl. We must cover ourselves very quickly in case the crewman passes this way," demanded Jamie. The observer's intention to do so became evident as the helicopter powered up again and lifted off passing back over the top of them in the reverse direction before hovering and landing on the other side of the copse. Both cadets rushed round the clearing grabbing more sawn off pine branches, which they heaped on top of themselves none too soon.

They had hardly burrowed into their newly improvised hiding place before they heard measured footsteps getting louder and surprisingly a gentle whistling. The pongo airman is hardly moving tactically thought Carl and the loss of his friend did not seem to have depressed his spirits. He must regard his woodland walk as a relaxing interlude during his duties.

Jamie wondered how the Army Air Corps could possibly imagine that this drop off and walk through tactic could actually enable evaders to be caught. The arrival of the Skeeter gave them ample warning and clearly two resolute aircrew on the run could well overpower a solitary observer even if armed if they acted boldly. He could not understand why the Army Air Corps had not deployed its helicopters more clandestinely to establish observation posts, which would scan the ground for evaders from concealed positions and radio through to snatch squads of infantry whom they would direct to capture the fugitives. As it was the cadets watched the crewman pass nonchalantly on his way still softly whistling and not even bothering to investigate the piles of tree trunks, a young slender seemingly carefree individual in pale blue beret, jungle green overalls and black flying boots very dissimilar to the muscular hairy armed and hobnailed booted Army aviator of their imagining.

As dusk drew on Jamie and Carl consumed the last of their escape rations – two desiccated biscuits each, an oatmeal bar, a handful of raisins and a chunk of hard chocolate keeping the final half dozen boiled sweets for the march ahead. As before they gathered up and packed their parachutes wrapping their parkas about the waist. They had many miles to cover over harsh terrain, which would be tough sweaty work especially if they were ambushed and had to run their way out of trouble.

All went well till just before midnight when the cadets reached a long strip of open space about half a mile wide between two large tracts of forest. The moon, which had waxed fractionally since the beginning of the exercise, was shining from a clear sky. Anyone crossing the open ground would be very visible and exposed. Carl and Jamie stopped at the edge of the pine trees and decided to wait, watch and listen in case any of the Irish Guards revealed themselves. They planned to make a nonstop sprint for the other side in ten minutes' time if the coast remained clear.

They were about to dash for it when far to their left they heard sounds of surreptitious movement. Twigs were being snapped and footfalls muffled by the carpet of pine needles were just audible. This must be another Flight Cadet crew coming through or soldiers getting carefully into position to monitor any attempted crossings of the open strip thought Carl. Sure enough two shadowy figures broke into a run and started to race across the stretch of open country.

Suddenly a fearsomely furious yelping broke out and at the same time the silhouette of a figure with the unmistakable outline of a peaked cap on his head emerged from the forest shouting, "Go to it, Bonzo! Seize them and grab them!" Carl and Jamie could just make out a lupine shape bounding over the scrubland towards two fast disappearing figures. Suddenly an unmistakably subcontinental accent exclaimed, "Get down you damned creature! Stop biting my arm you bloody dog! Let go, damn you!" Then another higher pitched voice undoubtedly from an extremely excited China Chu interrupted, "Kill him with your dinghy, knife, Yousuf."

Then came another shout from the peak capped man, "If you dare do that, sir, you'll be on a charge at once and I mean it'll be the glasshouse for you straight away."

"All right you've got me," cried Flight Cadet Ahmed as the peak capped soldier, probably a Military Policeman thought Carl, walked towards the still cursing figure with a writhing Alsatian hanging on his arm.

"Now is our moment, Carl," whispered Jamie. "It'll take quite a time for the Redcap to disengage the fangs of his hound of the Valkyries from poor old Ahmed's biceps and I didn't see any other soldiers or dogs for that matter." Carl and Jamie then raced across the strip of open ground feeling as vulnerable as a night patrol in No Man's Land on the Western Front in the Great War waiting for a flare to illuminate them fatally.

Once safely across Carl and Jamie feared that their breathless panting could be heard far away. As it happened a green Verey was soon diagonally set off way out to their right, which the cadets assumed must have been fired by soldiers to indicate the line of escape of another crew. However, they heard no more dogs and saw nothing untoward on reaching Angela's woodland lagoon a full hour early and installed themselves at the edge of the trees to wait and watch.

Carl felt as if he had attained hallowed ground. "This is definitely the place, Jamie," he whispered. "Look there's the jetty with the rowing boat moored alongside. Over there was Angela's secret path to her private sanctuary of the inner forest pool. That's the stretch of grass where we used to picnic and sunbathe. When we are separated from someone we love or are bereaved I believe that an element of that person's spirit does remain within its familiar former surroundings. It is one of life's mysteries how the human personality can imprint itself on a place. Take the voie sacrée from Bar le Duc to Verdun in France. I know there are helmets of dead French soldiers all the way along yet it is not the helmets which made it a sacred road but the fateful steps of all those doomed poilus' feet on their final route march to eternity."

"You can be very profound, Carl," said Jamie sucking his last boiled sweet. "I agree that the physical loss of separation and bereavement are not so different. I'm sure that if we were back in Lincolnshire and Janey were not there each treasured feature of the local scene we know would receive the consecration of our love. I miss her here of course but not as much as I would there. Hold on! I see a light around the corner. It's a vehicle coming. Do you think the Army has seen our arrival and is now going to unleash its dogs of war upon us and round us up?"

"Don't be alarmist, Jamie," Carl answered. "Look the vehicle's stopping by the boathouse. One man has got out to light a fag and the other is walking to the end of the jetty. My God, that's where dear Angela took her fatal plunge. He's sitting down now and dangling his legs over the edge. It must be our contact for the rendezvous."

"He's very calm about it all and shows no desire whatsoever to hide himself from the enemy. He could so easily get himself, his driver and us all caught – most thoughtless," said Jamie.

"I think you're over-dramatising things, Jamie," Carl replied. "I don't believe the Army can be bothered to try and catch us now. When we've clocked off at the rendezvous and delivered our verbal report that's it, we've finished and I expect we'll be driven back to camp. Time to move."

It was 0255 hours and they ran in a low crouch across Angela's now sacred grass reaching the seated figure at the end of the jetty at precisely 0259 hours. "Flight Cadets Jamieson and Higgins reporting as instructed, sir," said Carl to the evidently rotund officer who still had his back to them and gazed out across the glassy moonlit waters of the lagoon. He turned and as he did so the cadets detected a sour odour of whisky fumes blended with cigarette smoke. They instantly recognised the Camp Commander, Wing Commander Jolly and snapped to attention saluting vigorously.

"Stand easy. Now give me your debrief," ordered the Wing Commander as he cumbersomely raised himself to hear them give an account of their actions en route and successful evasion. "It went remarkably smoothly, sir," Jamie began. "We have seen very little of the enemy over the past twenty-four hours."

"I don't believe it, Jamieson," expostulated the Wing Commander. "The training area has been crawling with soldiers. A dozen crews have been captured. Three cadets have come in on their own and now you tell me that the Army were not much in evidence. Didn't you notice what's been going on around you? Perhaps you've been skiving and cadged a lift with a local resident."

The whisky sodden Wing Commander was warming to his diatribe. "I'm told, Flight Cadet Higgins," he went on, "that you've been fraternising with the German girls when you should have been concentrating on shopping for me and my officers. If that's how you've been using your German language skills this past fortnight I don't doubt that you used them again on this exercise to scrounge lifts."

"I did nothing of the kind, sir, and Flight Cadet Jamieson will testify that I'm telling the truth," Carl insisted.

"Well he would, wouldn't he?" replied the Wing Commander brusquely.

"We saw Flight Cadet Ahmed being seized by a Royal Military Police dog and Flight Cadet Chu his crewman escape on his own," reported Higgins. "That surely proves I'm telling the truth, sir?"

"It doesn't to me, Flight Cadet," answered the Camp Commander coldly. "Chu has not arrived and we have no reports yet of Flight Cadet Ahmed either. So in case my theory about your behaviour is right my driver is not going to give you a ride back to camp. You're going on foot. You know the way don't you Flight Cadet Higgins because this is where you used to come for your secret trysts with the Fräuleins."

"Our life is indeed full of contrasts," remarked Jamie as they tramped off down the dusty track. "Some officers like dear old Polzol are the salt of the earth and we have others like Wingco Jolly who are such complete bastards that they defy all description."

"I would not worry about it too much," Carl replied. "It's no big deal in the overall scheme of things. This track back to camp is my voie sacreé, my penitential road from Angela's forest shrine, which I'll never now retrace but which will be etched forever on my soul."

CHAPTER 10

On return to Cranwell after the summer leave at the beginning of September, life changed for Jamie and his Entry in only one material respect. They now lived in single bedroomed two storied barrack blocks around the parade ground instead of the multi-occupied hutted South Brick Lines behind the hangars. The regular pattern of drill, academics, ground defence training and still more drill especially for those on restrictions continued as before.

The fortnightly navigation exercises were now conducted in greater comfort and style in Varsities and more demands were placed on the cadets to navigate by dead reckoning, gee and radio bearings rather than visual pinpointing. Individuals continued to be chopped but at a lesser rate and the Entry's roll call was down by only a further three cadets by the time the pre-Christmas Passing Out Parade was held in freezing fog so thick that the flypast was cancelled and there was serious concern whether girlfriends and fiancées would manage to get to the Graduation Ball. They did. Low visibility and black ice on the High Dyke were not going to spoil their fun.

The second part of the long and dreary Cranwell winter brought an element of fresh drama and excitement to the Entry's lives. Pilot Training on Piston Provosts began for three days a week at Barkston Heath. On the second day back in the New Year the cadets were presented to their personal flying instructors after an introductory briefing from the Officer Commanding Basic Flying, Wing Commander Roland Baker. He was flanked by his two Squadron Commanders, Squadron Leader Henry Hickox and Squadron Leader James Travers in the familiar briefing room where the legendary Polzol had effortlessly held sway before the dozen navexes by Pig and half dozen by Superpig which the cadets had undertaken the previous year.

Wingco Baker, a stocky greying figure in early middle age had the reputation of being exacting, unsentimental and a stickler for detail. Unlike his two Squadron Commanders one a university graduate, the other an Old Cranwellian, both hoping for an operational squadron command on promotion next tour, Baker could hardly be described as upwardly mobile.

Conscientious to a fault the opportunity for combat flying had passed him by. His pair of World War Two ribbons of the 1939-1945 Star and the Defence Medal had come round with the rations to many like him whose aspirations to take part in hostilities were denied by the end of the war. Many supernumerary aircrew opted for civilian life to escape the frustrations of a severely contracting peacetime Service but Baker's go anywhere do anything attitude secured for himself a posting on Tempests retired piston engined fighters as a target towing pilot.

Then the expansion for the Korean War called for more flying instructors. Baker once more volunteered his services and his stint in Flying Training Command began first on the humble Prentice, next the more vicious Balliol. Ever dutiful and studious with the bookwork he soon qualified as an AI instructor, was talent spotted by the Central Flying School to train new instructors and performed so well that he became a "Trapper", a member of the select Examining Wing setting Service-wide basic training standards. It was said he could narrate verbatim the Flying Training Manual of the Piston Provost.

Finally had come his ideal reward, responsibility for all Basic Flying Training at the Royal Air Force College with promotion to Wing Commander – a dream posting for a perfectionist whom the jet age had somehow overlooked and who felt himself very much a senior officer even if he had no front line experience whatsoever. Roland Baker was determined that no procedural laxity, technical incompetence, poor airmanship or operational misjudgement should prejudice a faultlessly accident free flying regime at Barkston Heath.

Below standard Flight Cadets would be eliminated from training early on before they could endanger themselves or put at risk Baker's impeccable record. His counterpart Commanding the Advanced Flying Training component of Flying Wing at Cranwell on Vampires and Meteors would have no cause to complain that Baker had needlessly and expensively passed onto him low grade Flight Cadets who would never cope with jet aircraft.

It was said that on a chop ride Wingco Baker could decide in just fifteen minutes of flight whether a Cadet would make the grade. It was best to avoid such a fearful fate and the most certain way of doing so was as much a matter of luck with the allocation of personal instructors as of flying aptitude. A really bad instructor could turn the most gifted pupil pilot into an under-confident, nervous, hapless, gibbering wreck of an incompetent in just a few sorties. A good one could create a safe and reliable pilot from very unpromising material.

"Sit down, gentlemen, please," began Wing Commander Baker. "You have waited a year to begin your pilot training and you may have wondered what the intensive programme of academic study, continual emphasis on discipline and regular navigational exercises have had to do with your becoming qualified pilots. I can assure you it was time well spent and the more you progress with your training the more clearly you'll realise why.

"Flying an aeroplane," continued the Wing Commander earnestly and warming to his theme, "is not like riding a bicycle. It requires intelligence and precision; the ability to anticipate what is going to happen and to react in advance. It combines technical understanding with physical co-ordination. Flight safety is fundamental to all we do in the air and that is why the objective I am setting you now is nothing less than perfection. It is an elusive goal and it is the standard which with the help of your instructors you will be constantly seeking to achieve.

"In the pursuit of this aim I have the support of Squadron Leader Hickox Commanding A Squadron and of Squadron Leader Travers Commanding B Squadron. They will introduce you to your Flight Commanders and most importantly to your instructors. Each Squadron Commander will read out his list of cadets and give you the name of your own particular flying instructor whom you will go and meet in the crew room. Carry on." And so Wing Commander Baker concluded what he felt sure was another of his AI grade introductory briefings.

The boss' homily over Squadron Leader Henry Hickox strode to the lectern first. He and his counterpart Jimmy Travers were remarkably contrasting characters to fulfil the same role. Hickox was tall, slim and well groomed in immaculate battledress and spoke precisely in clipped laconic phrases, not a word more than necessary. Travers' expanding frame was only just contained by his heavily creased and well worn best blue uniform. His drawling instructions in the purest Queen's English were languid in the extreme.

The hut 150 fraternity came under the aegis of Squadron Leader Hickox, the Old Cranwellian of the two. Although marginally younger at thirty-three he had more front line experience in his case on Meteors and Javelins than the thirty-five year old Oxford educated ex Canberra pilot Jimmy Travers.

Despite his scruffy appearance Travers was said to be an incomparable instructor. His natural patience and psychologically sensitive sympathy thoroughly permeated B Squadron. Henry Hickox was a harder task master. A former aerobatic trophy winner at the Central Flying School he expected others less gifted than himself to reach his own high standards. In the process many more cadets in A Squadron were suspended than in B but those who passed out with the highest marks for flying usually spent their formative first year of pilot training in A Squadron.

Once Squadron membership was established and Qualified Flying Instructors (QFIs) assigned each cadet went to the QFIs' crew room with some trepidation to introduce himself. Taffy Jones was allocated another Welshman the bald headed pipe smoking handlebar moustachioed Master Pilot Tom Benyon who had been instructing for longer than anyone could remember. Seemingly genial on the ground he had the reputation of a holy terror capable of turning the most self-confident and apparently competent pupil to indecisive jelly in the air.

Jamie Jamieson's instructor was at the other extreme end of the age spectrum, a so called 'creamed off' QFI called Tim O'Connor now a Flying Officer who had graduated from Cranwell less than a year before Jamie arrived. Bright and efficient he could still remember what learning to fly was like and got on well with his pupils accordingly.

Garrity was assigned the big jovial Flight Lieutenant Norman Levinson who for all his years in the transport force flying Hastings was a remarkably good aerobatic pilot and enjoyed formation and low flying as much as the former fighter boys. Levinson had a rare ability to sort out the difficulties of the problem pupils. He was more of a remedial uncle to the Flight Cadets than a figure of authority and it was to him they usually turned if they needed a change of QFI.

Carl Higgins' instructor was a naval Lieutenant Mike Morrison on exchange from the Fleet Air Arm where he had distinguished himself as a member of 800 Squadron's formation aerobatic team on Sea Hawks. Tall, good looking with long fair hair, his dark blue flying overalls with golden rings of rank and long calf length zipped black leather boots were much envied. He had a laid back attitude to the chain of command which perhaps derived from a failed catapult launch, which had resulted in HMS Eagle's passing right over his sinking Sea Hawk before he ejected safely from underwater in the great ship's wake. He was more successful on the dance floor and bedroom than as a QFI and reputedly was always partnered by the most beautiful women at the Graduation Ball. Nevertheless his relaxed attitude had a settling effect on Honkers' stomach, which caused him less and less problems as the course progressed.

The cadets did not realise it at the time but the selection of their flying instructor was probably the most fateful decision that the College could make towards a cadet's destiny. Of course the choice was actually done by the QFIs bidding informally between themselves in the crew room but the cadets did not realise this. Their future could either be made or broken by their QFIs and although a cadet could seek a change if his flying went badly, cadets usually picked up the courage to make the necessary request of the Flight Commander too late by which time the fatal loss of self-confidence had become irreversible.

Two days later the Entry began their flying training. Typically it had snowed the day before but without drifting and by the time that their slush flecked bus arrived at Barkston Heath the snow ploughing bowsers had been busy clearing the runways, taxi tracks and hard standing in front of the low wooden Squadron huts where the dumpy Piston Provosts were parked. Resplendent in vivid orange anti-collision paint and with a pale blue Royal Air Force College stripe around the rear fuselage they stood out proudly against the windswept featureless snowfield behind.

All that was not snowbound on the aerodrome was black – black tarmac, black hangars, black huts, black fire and motor transport sections, black control tower – apart from three bright orange windsocks extended stiffly south westwards towards Grantham by the traditional Siberian tradewind off the North Sea.

The initial flying syllabus proceeded as per established schedule – local familiarisation, effects of controls, straight and level flight, climbing and descending, turning, stalling and spinning and then circuits and landings either at Barkston Heath or its grass runwayed satellite of Spitalgate. The cadets' spirits rose or fell according to their progress and to how the relationship with their QFI developed.

Those who already had private pilot's licences from flying scholarships went solo a little earlier than the rest but not much. So Peter Carrick under the larger than life tutelage of a burly Australian Flight Lieutenant QFI called 'Aussie' Arthur achieved it in eight hours. Most including Jamie did it in just under ten and even Honkers Higgins began to master his unruly stomach thanks to his naturally lazy QFI, who let Carl do as much of the flying as possible and sent him solo after eleven hours. Thereafter Carl's airsickness returned only briefly during spinning and the early aerobatic exercises. He found that total concentration was the best antidote to nausea.

Confidence grew among most cadets although not universally. Flight Cadet Blackham who had been so self-assured on arrival at the College became increasingly quiet and introverted. A change of instructor was soon followed by a check ride with the punctilious Squadron Leader Hickox. Blackham still had not gone solo after fifteen hours of instruction. "Good landings begin with good approaches" both his instructors had insisted but his approaches never were good. Always too high or too low, too fast or too slow, with too much power or too little, to the left of the centreline or to the right and with an incorrect flap setting as often as not Blackham never did achieve a smooth three point landing and keep straight after touchdown.

His assessment flight with the stern silent Squadron Leader Hickox could not have gone worse. He forgot half the pre take off checks at the end of the runway, climbed away from the circuit on the wrong heading, overshot the height to level off, failed to look out before his first turn and then through a tardy heavy handed stall recovery almost entered an inadvertent spin whereupon his Squadron Commander uttered the fatal three words, "I have control" and the wretched Blackham knew that his flying career was effectively over.

Thereafter things got steadily worse. By the time it came to circuits and bumps Blackham was drenched in sweat, his feet quivered on the rudder bar and he held the stick and throttle in a vice-like grip. After Blackham made three abortive attempts to land Hickox said simply: "It's time to call it a day. I'll land." Blackham marvelled how anyone could make such an ungainly mulish brute of an aeroplane kiss the ground so sweetly rolling impeccably straight astride the centreline of the runway.

"You taxi in and park," said Hickox once they were clear and on the taxi track. Then Blackham's foot tremors started again. He always hated taxiing. He had never mastered swinging the nose to clear the view in front and as for parking the beastly aeroplane it terrified him. Sure enough he came into dispersal hopelessly crooked. The marshaller waved at him frantically to straighten up but Blackham hurriedly shut down in despair with his aircraft the only one parked ignominiously way out of line. The alternative had been to wave the marshaller away and to go round the pan once more and try again which would have been even worse.

Hickox flipped of his straps, heaved his parachute out of the seatpan and over his shoulder striding off across the hardstanding. "I'll sign in, Blackham. Come and see me in my office when you've made yourself a coffee," he called to the woeful Blackham as he trailed in behind. In the crewroom his friends were solicitous: "How did it go?" "Good luck." "Don't worry it's not the end of the world."

Everyone dreaded an unscheduled check ride with the Flight or Squadron Commander. Few survived such an awesome experience and Blackham feared, as he poured boiling water on his Nescafe, that his chances of bucking the fateful odds were nil. He knocked diffidently on the Squadron Leader's door. He knew that the next two minutes would spell the end of his youthful dreams of pilot's wings and a Pilot Officer's stripe, proud ambitions faithfully nurtured through all the hardships of the past year.

"Come in Blackham, sit down." Hickox had already hung up his overalls, stowing his bone dome and Mae West in the corner locker on the top of which rested his subtly moulded peaked cap. He was authoritatively seated at his Perspex covered table in immaculately tailored battle dress with no hair out of place and the brown covered RAF student pilot's progress report form lay open before him. Blackham could see that Hickox's Parker pen had already written in capital letters SQUADRON COMMANDER'S SPECIAL ASSESSMENT FLIGHT doubly underlined in black ink.

Hickox stopped writing, looked up at Blackham and asked, "How do you think that went?"

"Not very well I'm afraid, sir," Blackham confessed meekly.

"I agree," replied Squadron Leader Hickox. "Your pre flight checks both inside and outside the aeroplane were incomplete; likewise the pre take off checks. Once airborne, and I feared we might even swing off the runway on take off, you made a series of errors in basic airmanship too numerous to relate. Your flying was inaccurate and poorly co-ordinated. On rejoining the circuit you forgot your downwind radio call. You showed no sign of being able to land the aircraft safely and you never gave the impression of being fully in control when you taxi. I feared for the marshaller when you came rushing into dispersal.

"What have you to say, Blackham?" Hickox inquired.

"It's sadly all too true, sir," Blackham answered meekly.

"You've had ten hours of dual with one instructor and five with another. It is my opinion that even if you were given a further fifteen hours of tuition I could not guarantee you'd go solo. It is better for you and the Service if we recognise that you are not just cut out for flying, and by that I include navigation also, as you don't seem particularly happy in the air and performed poorly in the navexes last year.

"I note, however," Hickox went on, "that you have made reasonable progress in academics and that your Cadet Wing Flight Commander believes you have good officer qualities. I am prepared, therefore, to recommend that you remuster in a

Ground Branch, but not that you be commissioned at the RAF College from a subsequent Entry, only from an Officer Cadet Training Unit on a short service commission.

"I believe," the Squadron Commander concluded, "that you have not only set your sights unrealistically high in seeking to become a Royal Air Force pilot but that also you would not wish to serve in a ground branch in which case you will return your kit to stores and be issued with a rail warrant to go home tomorrow. What is your decision?"

"I'd rather leave the Air Force, sir. Now," replied Blackham with new found conviction.

"I thought you'd say that," Hickox replied. "Best of luck in your new career."

Each suspension from the course or chop as the cadets less elegantly described it made the experience of flying training all the more intense for the remainder. There was no lack of application among them. Indeed the more fervent the desire to succeed the more likely that the pupil pilot would become tense, ham fisted in the air and so excessively self-critical that a fatal decline in confidence could ensue especially if a personal rapport with the QFI was lacking. Passing out depended almost as much on the qualities of the instructor as on those of the cadet and on a good understanding between them.

Peter Lascelles the scholarly Wykehamist had the notoriously sardonic, tall and skinny Cockney Flying Officer Dave Peters for QFI known as 'pull through' Peters in the crew room whether because his lanky figure brought to mind the weighted cord with which .303 rifles were cleaned or whether it was from his memorable injunction to pupils in inverted flight "to pull through mate", nobody knew, but he and Lascelles got on famously. Never a man to use a polysyllabic word when a four letter one would do some might have wondered how he ever got into the Officers' Mess, but in the air he simply inspired affection and boundless confidence. Peter Lascelles was flick rolling and Porteous looping over the Fens long before the others could even master a straightforward stall turn or simple barrel roll.

Flight Lieutenant John Edwards and the laconic China Chu maintained a respectful relationship of almost total mutual incomprehension. Edwards had a model career behind him. Winner of the Kinkhead Trophy at Cranwell for flying, he had done a tour in Singapore as a day fighter pilot on Hunters before doing another in Germany on Swifts with 79 Squadron. 'Nil nos obstare potest' was their motto – 'Nothing can stand in our way', very apt for a fighter reconnaissance squadron.

At the Central Flying School he was top of his instructor's course yet he often wondered if any of his impeccable and fluent QFI's patter ever got through to the inscrutably mute 'China' Chu whose sole response to any instruction or advice was "vely well sir". Yet by a process of remarkable osmosis and meticulous imitation China flew with almost faultless precision, which always impressed the Flying Wing executives who did his periodic checks.

Flight Cadet Yousuf Ahmed was much more mercurial and prone to anguished self-doubt whenever his flying did not go well. Luckily he was paired with Flight Lieutenant 'Zog' Oldham. Quite how Zog had acquired such an incongruous nickname was a mystery unless it referred to an erstwhile Balkan King and his regal manner. Zog was a smooth man with silkily groomed black hair "the last of the Brylcreem boys", according to Taffy Jones.

Everybody recognised him by his unique shortie Crombie greatcoat with its black leather buttons. Only he and Polzol wore Crombies, but in Polzol's case

Central European style long and full flowing down below the knees to the top of the flying boot. Oldham should have been an ADC to the Queen whilst still in his twenties. His accent would have given a Guards Officer an inferiority complex, but not Ahmed whose English, drawn straight from the Sindh Club in Karachi, was perfectly matched to Zog's albeit with a lilting Urdu intonation. Oldham's unfailing steadiness and genial generosity of spirit calmed Ahmed down and inspired Yousuf's private conviction that he would, God willing, fulfil his Islamic destiny of occupying a Sabre interceptor's cockpit at Peshawar, in Ahmed's view the most beautiful airbase in the world.

How Carrick had gone solo quite so fast nobody understood, although he himself did. It was the legacy of the benign, wise, moustachioed fifty-five year old ex Blenheim pilot, Mr Shipman, who had instructed him at Yeadon during his pre-Cranwell flying scholarship. An interwar Regular with Wapitis, Siskins, Audaxes and Harts in his logbook Shipman's wartime flying had lasted less than a year and was terminated by flak during a low level attack on invasion barges at Antwerp followed by almost five years in a prisoner of war camp. Unlike Aussie Arthur, Mr Shipman spoke little. When he did it was always kindly and encouraging, and it brought good results.

The warmest words Arthur ever uttered to Carrick were, "With all that time on Cessnas you damned well ought to cope. I'm getting out." Without Aussie's constant pitiless nagging beside him Carrick's first solo was the best circuit and landing of his life. Thereafter the merciless monologue of Flight Lieutenant Arthur resumed: "Your height… your speed… don't forget the power… raise the flaps man… you're sideslipping, keep the ball in the centre… look out you idiot, didn't you see him?... for God's sake, Carrick, hold her straight… can't you feel it, you're going to stall… gently man, don't pull the wings off… do you want to kill me?" It was said that some bad instructors used the crash crowbar between the seats to bash a point home upon the hapless pupil's bonedome. Aussie Arthur was not quite in that category of shame but Carrick's purgatory in the air continued.

When he confessed to Jamie Jamieson that he emerged from each flight with Arthur sweat soaked and uncontrollably shaking Jamie could not believe it. Everybody knew old Aussie. He was one of Cranwell's best loved characters. Irreverent of all Pommie senior officers his lewd jokes in Mess and crew room were legendary and at Guest Night dinners he really came into his own out-drinking College staff and Flight Cadets alike.

How could a jovial exuberant extrovert get the dour phlegmatic Carrick into such a state? Jamie advised Carrick to go and see Squadron Leader Hickox and request a change of instructor, but he knew he would not dare. Yorkshire grit and fatal pride would combine to prolong the agony and perhaps to hasten his suspension one sad day.

The merciless winter merged almost imperceptibly into a grey and windy spring at Barkston Heath. From the College bus the ground elder could be seen now growing in hedges spiked green with the first blackthorn leaves. The cadets' confidence grew as the sap rose.

The unnatural rejection of the sensory world, which instrument flying required in favour of the message of the dials on the blind flying panel became through perseverance second nature to most cadets. The total concentration entailed in instrument flying also demanded sympathy and forbearance from the instructor, which Aussie Arthur utterly lacked. The harder Carrick tried to get needles on the dials pointing the right way the more Aussie shouted, the tighter Carrick's fist tight grip on stick and throttle became and the more his feet quivered on the rudder bar.

Was it for this that he had given up a university place and a normal home life? Had flying to be so hateful? His friends spoke of practising forced landings over the tulip fields of Spalding with the flower pickers waving up at them in their deliberately opened cockpits; of carefree cloud chasing among the cumulus tufts over Folkingham and of ecclesiastical sightseeing by air to Lincoln Cathdral, Southwell Minster, Boston Stump and Crowland Abbey. Even aerobatics, which offered uninhibited joy and welcome release from the pilot poet John Magee's 'surly bonds of earth' to so many on his course yielded no solace for Carrick. He hammerheaded abruptly and ignominiously out of stall turns and swooped inelegantly downwards from slow rolls to a stream of unrestricted Down Under invective from his strap hanging Aussie QFI.

No passing out parade marked the conclusion of the Spring Term. Perhaps it was appropriate. Apart from added greenness to the countryside around Cranwell early May felt little different from early March. All too often Easter fell in term time and there was less Easter joy in the College than at home so to compensate big Guest Night dinners in both College Hall and Junior mess preceded the beginning of a short Spring Leave.

For the Senior Entries these were impressive affairs. The mahogany tables were resplendent with silver mementoes donated by Flight Cadets and Officers of generations past, many of them biplane models from the earliest days of military aviation. The College band's string orchestra up in the minstrel gallery performed its traditional repertoire opening with the Roast Beef of Old England, then onto a medley from the latest Broadway shows, culminating inevitably in the Lincolnshire Poacher and the final Huntman's Gallop rendered on an outsized hunting horn to the accompaniment of a hundred spoons thumping on table tops. Late into the night the serious Mess games would begin like anteroom American football and shoulder riding jousting on bicycles on the marble floored corridors with dustbin lids for shields, broomsticks for lances and bonedomes for helmets.

The Junior Mess could not match such style. Only the officers wore mess dress. There was no music and apart from the Assistant Commandant fewer of the directing staff attended. Nevertheless it gave them on unofficial chance to see how well the cadets held their liquor, what social skills if any they possessed and to judge them in a less formal context than that of classroom, cockpit and parade ground.

Jamie found himself sitting next to his Chief Flying Instructor, Wing Commander Roland Baker on one side, with the Junior Ground Defence Officer Flight Lieutenant Perkins on the other with Flight Lieutenant Frost an ex Shackleton Vampire QFI and Wing Commander Jolly of Survival Camp fame opposite. Jamie nervously broke the ice with Nigel Perkins, "What did you think of Survival Camp, sir? Did we do better than previous Entries?" he inquired hopefully.

"Actually, you did, but perhaps that was because I was closer to the action being part of an evading crew this time," Perkins replied. "Anyway it was better than Scotland the year before... all drizzle and midges as I recall with no possible escape to civilisation unlike to beautiful Brilon. Ask my crewmate Meteor Matthews. He'll agree."

"You misjudge Scotland totally, Nigel," interjected Frost who had just spent six happy years at Kinloss.

"Of course it looks nice letting down over the Moray Firth as dawn breaks with a fried breakfast awaiting you after twelve long hours of night over the heaving North Atlantic, but you Coastal boys always were detached from the real world," answered Perkins, "if you really want to understand what's going on in the service on the ground, at station level, you should be in the RAF Regiment."

"What do you think Wing Commander Baker, sir?" asked Jamie, keen not to leave his Wing Co Flying out of the conversation.

"I have no views really, but I do think QFIs should attend Survival Camp to get to know cadets other than their own pupils. I think we would understand Flight Cadets better in the cockpit if we knew them better on the ground. What do you feel Wing Commander Jolly? You're the Survival Camp expert round here," Baker enquired.

"We could certainly do with more QFIs attending to relieve some of the burdens of our overworked staff from the Regiment," the Wing Commander answered somewhat ungraciously.

"It must be difficult for you Wing Commander Baker, sir, really to get to know the cadets who come through Barkston Heath," Jamie went on. "You will see some of their progress reports and do an assessment flight with a few but unless there's some problem or dramatic incident, which brings a particular individual to your attention, the most you see of the average Flight Cadet is an initial photograph and his final report when you come to sign him off at the end of his basic Flying Training."

"You're being too harsh, Jamieson. More cadets than you imagine whom we put up for suspension are actually reintegrated into the course after a check ride with me," Baker retorted. "What's more I give myself a continuation training sortie once a week to keep my hand in and I often take any cadet who volunteers along with me. Also I insist on leading formations from time to time. Again I take Flight Cadets as passengers who much enjoy the experience and I can soon judge how their friends are progressing with their formation flying."

"I'm pleased to hear it, sir," replied Jamie. "You must get to meet some of the real flying enthusiasts that way, but it is the more diffident ones I'm concerned about. I've got a great friend Peter Carrick who went solo faster than anyone in our Entry and now seems to have become more and more introverted and to have lost all his love of flying. It's not for me to say, sir, but I don't think his confidence is being helped by his QFI. Would he be able to go up with you some day soon? I could tell him that it's definitely not a chop ride but as they say that you've got more hours on Piston Provosts than almost anyone in the Service, I'm sure you could help him."

"I'd be only too delighted to do so, Jamieson," Baker answered. "I'll speak to Squadron Leader Hickox tomorrow morning who I'm sure would be glad to lay it on."

Thereafter Jamie did not want to test Baker's goodwill with courteous but contrived and gratuitous observations.

As for the Ground Defence Supremo Wing Co Jolly Jamie could not bring himself to speak to him, after his notorious rants at Brilon. He was keen to talk to Perkins, a kindred spirit he felt sure, but too obviously public school banter would put off his neighbours so he addressed himself to ex Shackleton Frost, "Did you opt for Coastal, or were you talent spotted, sir?"

"Both of course, Jamieson," Frost responded defensively.

"At least I've contributed to the successful salvage of a sinking tanker off the Outer Hebrides and without our timely precision drop of life rafts to a ditched Canberra crew in the North Sea they'd be in Davy Jones' locker now rather than on the staff of the Conversion Unit at Bassingbourn. I've not just spent my time boring holes in the sky like the fighter boys."

"Of course not, sir," Jamieson replied humbly, but unconvinced of Frost's true feelings since he had heard that Frosty was a keen aerobaticist who had actually put in for the Command's Wright Jubilee aerobatic trophy. Luckily Jamie was saved by the trumpetings of the Posthorn Gallop from having to take the unreal conversation further.

After a week's visit to the Army in Germany for the first week of leave the cadets went their separate ways. Taffy Jones took Natasha down to Wales staying at the Worms Head Hotel in the village where his family used to live, which was still more home to him than Oxwich. They climbed the down overlooking the wide sweep of Rhossili bay and clambered all over the cliffs at Burry Holmes looking for gulls' nests. Janey came down to Devon and pleased Jamie's parents by declaring that Bideford Vicarage felt like a second home.

Sylvia the trainee teacher accompanied Peter Carrick back to Pudsey and was a knowledgeable companion on their Bronte pilgrimage to Thornton and the Parsonage at Haworth. She even professed to have enjoyed a comedy at the Alhambra Theatre in Bradford, which played to a full but singularly unresponsive house. Ever attentive she noticed that Peter's sense of humour had unusually left him, too. "Is something wrong, Peter?" she enquired as they emerged from the theatre into the grimy black soot stained city centre.

"These bloody Bradford audiences must make any comic actor want to cry."

"That's not it, Peter," Sylvia replied. "You did not even stop the car on our night-time drive across the moors, which isn't like you at all. Have I upset you?"

"Certainly not," Peter answered abruptly. "The fault is entirely mine. I think I'm going to be chopped. I'm quite good at drill, always smart and seldom on restrictions. The academics are a doddle. Remember I was all set to go to university from Leeds Grammar till I got the flying bug. The trouble is I no longer enjoy flying. In fact I hate it."

"I can't believe it. I remember that when we met at the College hop in Retford you told me how proud you were to have a private pilot's licence and that you had got it before you even drove a car," Sylvia retorted.

"Maybe, Sylvia, but that seems a long time ago and you don't know Aussie Arthur my instructor."

"Just because you've got a bad teacher doesn't mean to say the subject's uninteresting. Forget your feelings for him and just concentrate. Show him you can cope," she continued.

"I'll do my best," he insisted. "I could never admit to my father I had failed and anyway I couldn't bear to go to a crammer now to study for University."

Prepared and enthusiastic the cadets returned for the Summer term excited at the prospect of more and more aerobatics; the introduction to low flying; landing away cross countries and the first formation exercises. Night flying would come the following term when the evenings began to draw in. Carrick for all Sylvia's encouragement found Arthur as impossible as ever. "Have you thought about nothing I told you over the Easter leave?" he began his debrief after their first sortie. "You're going to have to make a big improvement and fast, Carrick, if you're going to meet the standard required. I think you're bright enough. I know you are. I've seen your academic reports but that brain of yours switches off when you get in an aeroplane. How could you continue your approach to land today without clearance from the tower and with an aircraft still on the runway? Now wake up!"

Disconsolately Carrick made himself a coffee in the crew room. His friends full of confidence and enthusiasm exchanged experiences, "I did my first roll off the top today... We went to Shawbury for our cross-country and they gave us a super lunch in the Mess... I'm sure I severed some tulip heads with my wheels after a practice forced landing... Hickox let me come with him on a formation trip. He's got nerves of steel staying absolutely steady whilst you lot try to knock his wings off."

Carrick flicked desultorily through the magazine Air Clues. Even the 'I learned about flying from that' section failed to stir him beyond wondering if he could start a similar column entitled 'I learned nothing from him' about bad instructors and the misery they cause their pupils.

Suddenly the intervening window to the QFIs' crew room slid back. An anonymous voice demanded for all to hear, "Carrick. To the Squadron Commander's office at once, please."

"Oh dear, Peter it's a chop, chop, boyo," said Jones.

"Don't worry Peter," Lascelles tried to reassure him. "Hickox is demanding, but human. He doesn't fail everybody you know."

Carrick felt oppressed by impending disaster as he walked down the brown linoleum floored corridor to Squadron Leader Hickox's office. He knocked twice, nervously. "Come in, Carrick." Peter who had taken the precaution of wearing his beret stamped to attention and saluted – a bit too formal for Flying Wing he felt but he did not wish to betray any laxity to his punctilious Commanding Officer. "Stand easy, this is not an interview," Hickox began. "I've just had a phone call from the Chief Instructor asking to fly with you tomorrow. He would like you to do a General Handling sortie with him at 09.00 hours. May I suggest you mug up on the Provost's Pilot Notes and keep out of the bar tonight? Enjoy your flight."

"Thank you, sir. I'm sure I shall," answered Carrick trying to lift his spirits. Then he came to attention once more, saluted, turned about and marched briskly out returning to the cadets' crew room, his mind in turmoil.

"Well, Peter, what was that all about?" enquired Jamie disingenuously.

"The CFI wants to fly with me tomorrow."

"Why don't we get the privilege of a ride with the Wing Co?" asked Garrity provocatively.

"I'm sure old Uncle Arthur will miss you," observed Lascelles.

"In that case the feeling will not be mutual," said Carrick over his shoulder as he went to the locker room to get into battledress for the bus ride back to the College.

Next day dawned gloriously fine. Carrick was up at 06.30, ate a big breakfast to steady his stomach for spinning and aerobatics and was onto the bus by 07.30. Celandines along the High Dyke were open wide to the early Spring sunshine. The blackthorn was in full bloom. He had read his Pilot's Notes several times before turning in and had memorised every check, every speed, every pressure, every airframe and engine limitation. Que sera sera he thought to himself as he admired the soaring skylarks on stepping down from the bus. God will decide. I'm at one with the world.

Cunimb Jim's deputy a tweed skirted lady in unseasonable libido deadening woollen stockings whose sagging curves betrayed a premature middle age cheerfully proclaimed the good news of the early advent of the Azores High. For once it was well placed and she could confidently promise no industrial haze, no wind off the North Sea to bring an unwelcome Springtime haar but eight eighths blue, outstanding visibility and a gentle breeze down the main runway. I certainly won't get lost and am spared the wholly insufferable challenge of cross wind landings thought Carrick hopefully.

Before Peter had time for a coffee or even to marshal his thoughts, Wing Commander Baker was in the crew room inviting him to come to the briefing cubicles. Peter noticed immediately how well dressed the Chief Instructor was in starched collar and tie, not polo necked pullover or scarf, shiny black shoes not scuffed unpolished flying boots and with a shield on each sleeve just below the shoulder – on the right arm the three white cranes of the Royal Air Force College against a blue background, and on the left a blood red pelican of the Central Flying School against a black. His pale blue overalls were stain free and looked almost tailor made. By contrast Aussie Arthur's appearance was 'gash' the epitome of casual aircrew flightline dressing. Peter feared Baker's impeccable appearance belied an airborne martinet unforgiving of even the smallest departure from operational procedures or the performance data stipulated in the Provost's Pilot's Notes.

The Wing Commander's briefing could not have been clearer: "You verify the Form 700 entries, Carrick, and proceed to the aircraft. Check it outside and in. Start up, taxi out and take off making all the radio calls yourself. Climb out South Eastwards from the circuit till we get to the Market Deeping area. Do a couple of steep level turns through 360° each way one immediately after the other and when you are sure it is clear below spin the aeroplane recovering after three complete rotations. Make sure you know where you are then climb up to 8000 feet again and show me your aerobatic repertoire. At some stage I shall cut the throttle to simulate an engine failure. Go through your emergency drills, pick a good field aiming to land a third of the way in, but overshoot at 200 feet and climb back to 2500 feet. Finally take me home to Barkston. Do a standard rejoin of the circuit then three approaches and touch and go landings, normal flapless and short but landing for good on the fourth. I may give you a practice engine failure at any stage. Once you've taken the necessary action resume your circuit work and after the last landing taxi back to dispersal where you will shut the aeroplane down and complete the paperwork for me to sign. Then bring me a black coffee to my office and we'll go through the sortie together. Any questions?"

The Chief Instructor's briefing was so clear and concise that Peter felt tempted to ask "Is that all?" but for once he knew exactly what his instructor wanted. With Aussie Arthur the briefings were either so long and formless that Carrick could remember very little especially once in the air and Arthur's shouting had begun or Aussie would forego a proper briefing altogether, saying "Don't worry, Carrick, I'll brief you on the way out to the aircraft" which was a recipe for ignorant despair on Peter's part at his instructor's unexpected demands.

When they got to the flight hut at dispersal Carrick pointed out that the aeroplane had been snagged on the previous flight for a wandering directional gyro but that the instrument fitter had rectified it and that it had been signed off by the Flight Sergeant. "Well spotted, Carrick," said Baker. "We'll see how the instrument performs especially after your steep turns." Carrick's spirits lifted and rose further when the Wing Commander made no comments about any of Carrick's checks, which he had memorised the night before so that he did not need the flight reference card at all.

In fact Baker sat impassive with his hands folded throughout almost the whole flight. His sole observations were – "Don't pull quite so hard at the start of the loop, you'll kill your speed leaving you little margin of manoeuvre when you come to roll off the top.

"Clear your engine regularly on the way down for the forced landing next time or it might turn out to be the real thing" and "in future don't land at the end of the runway for your short landing practice, but on the threshold stripes. If there were any windshear you could end up in the undershoot."

When he unstrapped, Carrick noticed that they had only been away forty minutes and not for the full hour as scheduled. He had not had to repeat any aspect of the flight and had particularly enjoyed the aerobatics, the sequence of which was entirely of his own choosing with one manoeuvre leading smoothly into the next. He confirmed to the CFI that the aeroplane was fully serviceable and that Baker could sign the form 700 accordingly. He felt confident enough to ask him, "How would like your black coffee, sir?"

"Standard NATO black decaf, Carrick," was the reply, "but no sugar please."

Once they were in the office Baker asked Carrick to sit down and enjoy his coffee, then said simply, "I can see no problems at all with your flying. I found it quite a promising performance. From now on you fly with Flight Lieutenant Levinson. Good day." Carrick emerged renewed, almost a different person, confident that he was on a par with all his colleagues and that he might even secure one of those two or three coveted postings onto Hunters.

CHAPTER 11

The cadets' second summer term saw them familiar enough with their surroundings and the Cranwell system for them to compartmentalise their lives and find contentment in almost everything that was not drill, the drearier academic subjects like thermodynamics, aerodynamics and structures and of course restrictions parades, which for a few unfortunates were extremely time consuming. Yet even restrictions inculcated a philosophic fatalism combined with an inured ability to tolerate seemingly endless verbal humiliations and microscopic inspections in a daily routine dominated in summer time by the sweaty dusty heat of the parade ground. Carrick and Jones spent much time together on restrictions as did Yousuf Ahmed for no particular reason other than once charged repeat complaints meant that it was almost impossible to get off them.

Flying by contrast brought incomparable satisfaction. To be a participant in the celestial marvels of sun and sky, cloud and rain, moon and stars was a privilege beyond most ordinary mortals' experience. Yet the cadets were paid for what others could only wonder at and their personal progress was demonstrable in growing ability to operate the Piston Provost with confidence and safely in more and more of the regimes of flight – at low level, in all the basic aerobatic manoeuvres, in cross country exercises landing at strange and exciting places, and in formation for which only complete subordination of the fear of collision to an exclusive determination to follow the leader and maintain perfect station keeping brought success. Equally in instrument flying the 'discipline of the dials' required a total suppression of the deceptive senses of balance and equilibrium an achievement which also enhanced confidence and self-esteem. All felt that the transition to jets next year was now envisageable and, if their courses on Vampires or Meteors went well, their life's ambitions could be fulfilled.

Most understood that survival as well as successful graduation demanded discipline. The most notorious exception was 'gormless' Garrity. How he had not been removed from training early on surprised everyone who knew his fecklessness. They simply assumed that because his father was a distinguished Air Marshal 'Gormless' enjoyed a special dispensation from the rules.

However, one afternoon in early June he was seen by Flight Cadets and QFIs alike to emerge from his aeroplane after a solo sortie, rush to the nose and to stuff enough hay into his pockets from the air intake "to build a bloody haystake" as Carrick put it. He assured his instructor that the aperture had filled with hay from natural causes – it was after all the haymaking season, he insisted. But both his QFI and Squadron Leader Travers as well as everyone else knew that unauthorised low flying was to blame and a rail warrant home to his illustrious Daddy was issued for him the next day.

Many of the more exciting skills, which would feature so importantly in the advanced training on jets like stream and formation take offs and tail chasing, were developed in the basic stage. Already the temptation to emulate the fighter boys was strong, especially to participate in what the legendary Free French writer and fighter pilot Pierre Clostermann called 'Le Grand Cirque', the big circus of the aerial dogfight. All too often cadets' solo general handling sorties turned into a whirling swirling group of Piston Provosts in mock combat in what they hoped were QFI free zones of Fenland airspace.

"Meet you near Folkingham at eight thousand feet, Taffy, and I'll be on your tail before you can even see me," challenged Carrick.

"What about the cloud cover, Peter?" Jones replied.

"No problem, boyo. The Met girl said the stratocumulus though thick today was between four and five thousand feet and should have some gaps through which we can climb. It'll also protect us from the prying eyes of mischievous spoil sports on the ground or from QFIs proceeding on their way unawares below the cloud layer."

"Okay, you're on, Peter," Jones answered. "I warn you that my instructor is very pleased with my aerobatics, but if I waggle my wings you must call it off because I need to go home or actually to carry out some of my briefed lesson."

Off they went towards the Northern edge of the Fens at about a five minute interval, both transiting out below cloud till the unmistakable broad High Street of Folkingham with its big red Georgian pub at the end came into view. Up they went through a well placed gap. Taffy certainly had not reached eight thousand feet when he saw a Provost – Peter no doubt bearing down on him out of the sun. Jones just had time to put the nose down and slam the throttle forward to get more speed before turning upward into his attacker who fearing a collision broke sharply downwards to escape. This was wonderful they felt... the stuff of dreams and all those World War II paperbacks – the bone squeezing g-forces in the violent turns, the roaring engine on full boost, the clever cutting of corners, the pounding heart and wild imagination.

Suddenly Taffy had a tactical brainwave. He remembered the stories of the fighter aces of the Great War and how the legendary Captain Immelmann of the German Air Service had developed a new manoeuvre to catch out unwary pilots of the Royal Flying Corps, essentially a roll off the top of a loop to gain height and reverse direction. "Immelmann turn it will be," thought Taffy. The trouble was that he was not flying very fast – the tight turns had killed off much of his speed and he had steadily lost height and was now at six thousand feet not eight. Too bad.

Down with the nose, maximum power and pull – "gently", his QFI had always reminded him. "Or you might stall." Up up up! Wings level, head back... look for the horizon... there it's coming... wait a second and now push to level the aeroplane... what's this?... it feels sort of mushy and unresponsive... quick glance at the airspeed... not surprising its down to forty knots you fool... I'd better get out of this... push even harder to stop the nose falling... Peter will laugh if I don't complete the roll... and now full left rudder and stick hard over. Oh my God! What's this? The aircraft flicked totally round and pitched violently downward oscillating fiercely, much more fiercely than Jones had ever experienced.

Peter just behind and beneath was almost hit as his friend began to descend vertically just past him rotating rapidly with the cockpit unusually on the outside of the rotation. Peter had never seen this before but knew the Provost must be in an inverted spin. Would Taffy recognise it? If he did would he have the height to recover and would he know that he would have to do the opposite of what he had been taught to get out of a normal erect spin – full opposite rudder and stick hard back. But could he diagnose the direction of yaw?

Peter watched in horror as Jones' Provost plunged still spinning furiously into a big gray clump of stratocumulus. "Look at the ball on the turn and slip... oppose the yaw, boyo and pull… quick. If you're not out of it by four thousand feet you'd better get that canopy back undo your straps and jump hard to avoid the tail." But the altimeter must be unwinding very fast and surely Taffy must be totally disorientated. There was no call on the radio. "Of course not," Peter thought to himself. "Taff will have switched to 121.5 for a MAYDAY if he could compose his thoughts sufficiently,", which he doubted.

Peter felt sick. His knees were shaking. At least the stratocumulus was dispersing but it brought no cheer, only the sight he least wanted to see – a red blotch in a field with a trail of black smoke just west of Folkingham. He set course for home and as he approached the Barkston circuit the tower radioed asking all call signs to acknowledge. "Call in Bravo Tango… Bravo Tango do you read me?" Silence. Peter unstrapped. The flightline crewman was more solicitous than usual. "There's been an accident, Mr Carrick, and I'm afraid Mr Jones has not returned. The local firebrigade has rung in saying there's a report of a big oil fire near Folkingham. Our fire tender and the crash crew have gone to investigate."

When Carrick got back to the crewroom Jamie came up to him at the coca cola machine, put his arm comfortingly on Peter's shoulder and inquired, "I expect you know about Taffy? I'm so sorry, Peter. I realise he was a particular friend of yours and always appreciated the way in which unlike most of us you took him seriously."

"Thank you, Jamie," Carrick replied. "My ground crewman told me when I shut down that Taffy was missing and that the crash tender had gone out to a suspicious oil fire near Folkingham. It sounds grim doesn't it unless anyone thinks he could have baled out?"

"Unlikely I'm afraid," answered Jamieson.

"Apparently there was no MAYDAY call or indeed radio transmission of any kind from Taffy and no one saw a parachute."

"What's more the Basic Flying Wing Adjutant has been to Taffy's locker and removed all his clothes and possessions. He must know something we don't."

"You're right," observed Carrick dejectedly. "It's always the brightest and best and funniest who go first – the ones who make our life worth living. I hope his parents don't hear it from the national news. Who'll inform poor Natasha?"

"Her father will I suppose," suggested Jamie. "He's based here at Barkston. Old Polzol must be all too used to doing it by now, but not to having to break such terrible news to his own daughter. What an awful tragedy."

By the time the coach came to take the cadets back to the College the rumours and theories were abundant. On board the bus Lascelles was holding forth like a flight safety investigator. "Apparently Taffy just span in. A local farmer saw a Provost spin into one of his fields without any apparent attempt at recovery. Perhaps he was doing low level aerobatics, was too slow and too low and just flicked into a fatal spin."

"That must be nonsense," said Jamie. "It would not be in character for Taffy to flout flying regulations like that and what's more nobody saw him doing aerobatics did they? If he had any height at all he knew how to neutralise an incipient flick or failing that how to get out of the resultant spin. The point is that other people say that Taffy's Provost broke cloud already spinning, but this raises a similar objection. He was too responsible to do aerobatics less than the required three thousand feet above cloud and he would have noted the height of the cloud tops on his way up. What do you think, Peter? You knew him really well."

This was the moment Carrick had dreaded. To profess ignorance would be to betray Taffy's memory, but yet he knew Taffy would not have wished him to jeopardise his own graduation with needless candour about their clandestine and fatal dogfight especially after successfully coming through a Wingco Flying's chop ride and a change of instructor. It had been after all, Peter rationalised to himself, a shared decision to flout flying regulations and both, Peter reassured himself, had understood that the consequences of such an escapade could be injury or death or if discovered grounding at the very least. Why face the unnecessary sanction of suspension from training and why should the admirable Flight Lieutenant Levinson find out that his new star pupil had let him down so badly?

Enough lessons had been learned by Peter to last his entire flying career so he decided that the Board of Inquiry would have to do without any self-incriminating witness statement from him and he would not reveal his knowledge to a single soul. Peter then replied to Jamie disingenuously but convincingly: "I always thought that Taffy was too conscientious ever to omit his pre-stalling, spinning and aerobatic checks, so I would have expected him to keep well clear of cloud. I don't expect any of us will be able to help the Board of Inquiry very much but I imagine they'll select very experienced officers to sit on it who will discover the cause. The Air Force does not like unsolved mysteries particularly if they're fatal."

Next morning dawned poignantly beautiful and cloudless with only a light haze eastward over the Fens to dim the azure intensity of the sky. Wild roses were flowering in pink profusion along the High Dyke and small patches of royal blue of the first cornflowers were discernible in fields beyond the limestone walls. Taffy Jones' final plunge to earth was not mentioned in the bus to Barkston Heath although it was on everybody's mind. Emotions had been too drained from an evening in the bar of excessive speculation about what had happened and the account from Jamie and Peter Lascelles of their condolence call on the Zopoloskis was harrowing to recall.

Natasha had seemed numbed and stricken into silence. Her father was clearly shaken. "This is worse for me than anything in the Battle of Britain," Polzol lamented. "I know I lost many close friends in 303 Squadron but we were so busy then we did not have time to think and after what the Nazis had done to Poland we didn't care what happened to us. But David was so very young and innocent of the evils of the world compared to us. It seems so unnecessary. Did no one tell him about inverted spins? Poor dear Natasha."

"Poor us," interjected his rather gruff Yorkshire wife. "It's the bloody Air Force again. Natasha should have been with normal young men who lead secure normal lives."

Lascelles and Jamieson felt they had intruded awkwardly on private grief but Natasha sensing their unease interrupted her mother, "I could not have had a better boyfriend than David. He was so generous, such fun to be with. Don't blame the Air Force, mother. Some of the people in it are just wonderful, but it heightens the pain when we lose them, that's all. Would you agree father?"

"Yes I would, dearest Natasha," he replied. "I think the visit of Jamie and Peter this evening shows what really good friends Jonesey had. Let's all drink to his memory!" Whereupon Polzol poured out five glasses of vodka, lifted his own and exclaimed: "To David, one of the very best!"

Thereafter there was no more to be said. Again Natasha anticipated their potential embarrassment. "It was so good of you to come round, Peter and Jamie.

Let me see you to the door. I just don't know what I'll do without David. I'll probably go abroad for a job this summer vacation – teaching English to foreigners perhaps. I don't want to forget him you understand. I never will of course but Lincolnshire would be too painfully beautiful at this time of year, too full of memory filled landmarks. I need to get away from the wide heathland skies, the barley fields rippling in the wind and cry of the jets, which David loved so much."

"Of course, Natasha, but we'll see you before you go away," Peter answered. "Half term leave starts tomorrow afternoon and I'm sure David's funeral will be down at Rhossili. We'll be there with you to give him a rousing send off."

The day before half term finished was the day of Taffy's funeral. Most of the Entry were there in best blue uniforms. Even friends from the past like Garrity and Blackham came. The little crenellated church on the cliff top would be full. Jamieson had the job of bringing the Flight Cadet pallbearers and of picking up Janey who would come down from London to Temple Meads station at Bristol. He borrowed his parents' big black Wolseley and set off on the long drive round the Bristol Channel and Severn Estuary to Gloucester, across the river Severn, through the Forest of Dean and down to Swansea station where the rest of the group was due. After a Le Mans type drive they got to Swansea on time but then a crisis struck. One of the pallbearers, Carl Higgins had not arrived. Honkers must have missed his train thought Jamie, but mercifully he soon appeared running sweatily having come by coach instead.

Hurriedly they set off not at a funereal pace but in motor rally style, seven passengers in a five seater car, past the old wartime Typhoon base of Fairwood Common where Taffy had flown Austers as a boy, then along the southern peninsula road avoiding the dead end of Port Eynon village and screeching to a halt in front of the Worm's Head Hotel, five minutes before the service was due to start. Conscious that unlike brides at weddings the deceased should not arrive late for his funeral they ran into the churchyard past the sailors' corner where nameless shipwrecked seafarers are buried in search of Jones' coffin. At least Taffy would have a proper headstone, like the standard war grave ones in Cranwell village churchyard, Jamie thought. But where was the hearse? Luckily Lascelles spotted flowers on top of a vehicle in another car park, so off they sprinted to join up with Taffy's coffin.

Famous for another son of Rhossili, Chief Petty Officer Edgar Evans, who perished returning with Captain Scott from the south pole, the village looked down on the wide sweep of the bay from Worms Head at one end to Burry Holmes at the other end and across the Burry inlet to Pembrey airfield home to the Vampires and Hunters of Taffy's youth. What better place to be buried, thought Lascelles.

The diminutive church dedicated to the Blessed Virgin Mary was full. Wing Commander Baker was there, nearly all the Entry and unbelievably chain smoking in the back row in complete irreverence Taffy's Cadet Wing Flight Commander Flight Lieutenant Bracewell. The village had turned out in force in support of Jones' parents and his sister Doris a schoolgirl who sat with her arm linked to her mother's whose face was invisible behind a black Spanish veil.

As the pallbearers processed into the church Jamie felt that stories of coffins of incinerated aviators weighted with sand bags must be true. In death Taffy seemed no lighter than in life. The pallbearing cadets slow marched up the aisle to Handel's March from Saul as they had so often done in happier days on the parade ground before lowering the coffin cautiously onto the trestle table before the altar. Carl Higgins noticed Natasha had come with Polzol who sat imperiously behind the

Jones family with a black band of mourning on his sleeve and a dozen shiny medals on his chest. Natasha's mother had felt she need not go all the way to west Wales for "another bloody Air Force funeral. I know how you must feel, Natasha, but David wasn't even a flying pupil of your father" were her parting words as Zopoloski and his grieving daughter had set off for the Fosse Way and the long cross country drive to the Gower Peninsula.

Jamie could remember little of the service. The traditional hymns were sung lustily – Abide with Me, The Lord is my Shepherd and Cwm Rhondda – Guide Me O Thou Great Redeemer, with the villagers' voices in perfect natural Welsh harmony. The Rector told the congregation of Taffy's youth: swimming off the rocks at Mewslade; the night he got marooned by the tide at Worm's Head; of surfing in Rhossili Bay; of picnics beside the Celtic church's shrine on Burry Island; the family's move to Oxwich; how much the Rhosilli folk had missed them and how much more David would now be missed in death; that the village would keep him in its heart – he had touched the hearts of so many with his cheerfulness and humour; how proud they had all been when he joined the Air Force, which had always been David's dream; how few of us manage to fulfil our own dreams but David had done so with distinction; we should never forget the example he set us.

Then came the recessional hymn – God Be In My Head to the Walford Davies, music sung by the choir in the Black Hangar at Cranwell at so many Sunday services. Jamie felt the tears trickle uncontrollably down his face onto his service sheet.

Then the six Flight Cadets lifted Taffy up for the last time to take him outside for burial, but what was that? As they emerged from the porch into the summer sun they heard it. Jamie's mind flashed back to Stowe "Steals on the ear the distant triumph song" they belted out to the Vaughan Williams tune in chapel every All Saints Day. This was it now – the cry of the jets. He looked out towards the Bristol Channel and then he saw them, four Hunters in wide finger four battle formation winging in from the sea before plunging into the hills of Mid-Wales at low level. Jamie's arms began to shake visibly as the tears ran even faster down his face. He glimpsed across the front of the coffin at Peter Carrick who seemed totally unmoved with stone faced features. How strange thought Jamie. Carrick had been so close to Taffy. Perhaps the loss must just have numbed Peter and deprived him of all feeling.

Soon the pallbearers were stepping over the Californian style artificial grass, which fringed the open grave and manoeuvred into position to Peter Lascelles' instructions. The canvas tapes held firm and Taffy was safely lowered by his friends neither nose down nor tail heavy in precisely the correct horizontal attitude to his last resting place. His unpretentious father and mother were the first to cast Gower dust upon their son's oak clad ashes. Then followed the College executives culminating in Polzol who supplemented his handful of earth with an imperious salute and his daughter Natasha, tearful and agonisingly beautiful in delicate black hat, pale mauve suit and black silk blouse. After her came the cadets in no particular order – Lascelles, Higgins, Jamieson, Carrick, Ahmed, Chu and the rest with finally the villagers and Blackham and Garrity the last to pay their graveside respects.

CHAPTER 12

After half term and the loss of Taffy Jones summer passed swiftly by. The flying became almost routine and the cycle of bus rides to Barkston Heath, marches in shirt sleeve order to academic lectures, daily drill with the constant possibility of restrictions parades, ground defence and physical training became a habit. Cricket matches, swimming, tennis and athletic competitions offered opportunities to get away from Cranwell at least once a week. Natasha, Lascelles learned from Polzol at a Guest Night, had gone to the Isle of Wight as soon as the university long vacation began to work as an English Teacher at a summer school for foreign students in Shanklin. Sylvia was looking for a job in a school up North after graduation, which pleased Peter Carrick. Janey was home most weekends and maintained the county social round with Jamie unabated, although he became increasingly preoccupied with what she did in London during the week.

The winter term, however, brought change and the long awaited challenge of night flying. It would demand all the cadets' hard won airmanship – their skill in instrument flying, ability to navigate and orientate themselves and above all to land safely on the blackest night in the centre of the flarepath.

Flarepath it was because Barkston Heath was shut for runway resurfacing so the Pig family had been transferred to Cranwell South and the Piston Provosts to the all grass aerodrome of Spitalgate whose landing strip was delineated not by electric lighting but by gooseneck flares, which consisted of spurting flames from the necks of oil cans along the undulating runway. Small blue battery powered glim lights indicated the taxiing path between the ends of the runway and dispersal with a black and white checked caravan at the holding point for take off. The goosenecks really concentrated the cadets' minds as a swing off the centre line on take off or landing could become a seriously incendiary event of which their imaginations were all too well aware.

With night flying much of the excitement of the course returned. None of the trainee pilots could be unmoved by the experience: to sit in a pool of diffused pink light in the cockpit with the dark outside; to roar off into the night wondering where to force land if the engine stopped; the rapid transition to instruments and then the blend of instrument flying with exterior lookout; the exquisite beauty of the panoply of lights below against the blackness of the earth – like diamonds on a black satin dress as Levinson put it to Carrick one moonless night; and above all the daunting challenge of landing with the feeling of dropping into a dark pit as with stick hard back and nose high after a carefully flown approach but ultimately with faith the pilot sought the smooth security of a three point landing.

Surprisingly nobody was chopped on night flying. The cadets would not have been put up to it by their QFIs had they not felt their charges safe. The risks were too great but the rewards for competence exhilarating. To land away was a thrill and to navigate by the blotches on the cloud sheets from the big towns below, by mental dead reckoning, pundit beacons and radio bearings brought great satisfaction. Even when the radiation fog came early one night and blotted out both Spitalgate and Cranwell, China Chu and Lascelles who were still airborne solo diverted successfully to Waddington and Syerston, which proved that their training had gone well.

The Passing Out Parade just before Christmas was held on a cold and frosty day, ideal for the thunderous fly past. As usual the withdrawal in slow time to Auld Lang Syne at the end brought back wistful memories of their half dozen predecessors of the last two years whose lives were cut short before even reaching the rank of Flying Officer. Between Senior Under Officer and Sword of Honour winners to the most anonymous Senior Flight Cadet the grim reaper had made no distinction of College rank or record. To whom among the new Pilot Officers passing out would he accord priority this time?

Away with such baleful thoughts! Next month Jamieson and his Entry would move into the main College building, begin their training on jets, diminish the weekly drill sessions they had to perform and lead an altogether more civilised life. More immediately another Graduation Ball had to be celebrated that evening. Gooseneck flares and glim lights were set out around the Orange. The College was floodlit and both College and Royal Air Force standards usually struck at sunset flew illuminated from the topmost pinnacles of College hall. Fiancées and girlfriends were summoned from all the corners of the kingdom. It was a night of excitement and expectation.

Early in the festivities the cadets concentrated more on drinking and conviviality than they did on music and dancing. Those would come later. Polzol and his grumpy Yorkshire wife appeared but sadly not Natasha and came over to the Hut 150 table. "I have news for you, gentlemen," he began. "I won't see you pass out this time next year, sad to say. I've just been posted. I'm off to Chivenor in the New Year. You see I'm fifty-five now and the Air Secretary's office, which controls our destiny think I should stop flying, but at least I've persuaded them to let me be a Training Officer on the simulator at the Hunter Conversion Unit. What's more I've wangled myself a month's familiarisation on the aeroplane before I start the job and pack away my bonedome for good.

"Apparently no other pilot wants this chairborne occupation," he went on, "so I've negotiated myself an extension of my commission till I'm sixty, which will give us plenty of time to renew our friendship before I retire. I'm sure I'll see some of you down in sunny Devon for the course within little more than a year with any luck."

"We'll miss you, sir," Lascelles replied for them all. "You brought refreshing individuality and the wisdom of your great experience to Barkston, which enriched our lives so much in the bleak early days of our navigation training. You came to Brilon, too."

"Don't exaggerate," interrupted his wife Ethel. "You should see him at home. These Polish men are still in the last century and expect their women folk to do everything for them."

"I wouldn't know about that, but how's Natasha, by the way?" Lascelles retorted. "We all miss her. Send her our Christmas greetings."

"She's happily installed in digs in Nottingham, far from the Air Force I'm glad to say," Ethel replied.

"Forgive us gentlemen," Polzol began, "we must be off. A Merry Christmas and successful New Year to you all."

"Why is it that the best men seen to attract such cows for wives? I just don't understand it," commented Carrick.

"I fear it works both ways," Lascelles retorted. "Look at that doll over there with Senior Under Officer Hendricks. How he got promoted I don't know. At least I do. He's the most nauseating creep of a sycophant the College has ever produced. He even used to flatter the acidic nicotine stained Flight Lieutenant Bracewell."

Peter Carrick had brought a teacher colleague of Sylvia's called Juliet as a blind date for Higgins. Sadly Carl found the evening heavy going and conversation was flagging. He hoped they could continue drinking and not have to dance. A Graduation Ball should not be so wearisome. Surely something must happen to lift his spirits.

To his great surprise he saw Yousuf Ahmed actually socialising. Usually Yousuf avoided drinking and dancing and kept himself very much to himself but on this occasion he had invited his family to the Passing Out Parade and Graduation Ball. His father, a Wing Commander in the Pakistan Air Force had just taken up the post of Deputy Air Advisor at the Pakistan High Commission in London. Tall, lean and tough looking with well chiselled features he cut an imposing figure in a high collared mess kit jacket reminiscent of the dress uniforms of the Cranwell Commandants of the 1920s in the portraits around the walls.

Yousuf ushered his father across to greet the Hut 150 crowd, leaving his mother and sister at the family table. "Papa," Yousuf began, "I want you to meet some special friends from my Entry. They were in Hut 150 together when we started off as crows almost two years ago." Before he had time to introduce them individually his father interjected.

"Good show, gentlemen. It was a first rate parade. It reminded me of our own Academy at Risalpur with the cadets' white banded ceremonial caps and the formation flypast in the shape of the number of the Entry passing out. The Begum and Yasmin Bibi – my wife and daughter were also very impressed with the excellent drill and turnout."

"Were you a cadet yourself, once sir?" asked Carl Higgins.

"Yes indeed," the Wing Commander answered. "I was one of the first cadets to pass out of the Academy soon after partition. We still had a number of British officers on the staff. Of course in the old days before the war the Royal Air Force used the Risalpur air base to bomb and strafe dissident tribesmen when there was trouble on the Frontier. The Academy still maintains a Royal Air Force QFI on an exchange posting. I had one on my squadron when I went back to instruct. Flight Lieutenant Duncan his name was. Perhaps you know him."

"Actually not," Carl replied, "but I know Pakistan, sir. My family spent three years in Karachi when the British High Commission was still in the city. My father was First Secretary and we lived in Clifton. We had some wonderful leaves up in the hills at Abbotabad, Nagatali and Muree."

"I tell you what," the Wingco responded. "You chaps will have to come down to our High Commission in Lowndes Square. We always have a reception for the Quaid-i-Azam's birthday. He was born on Christmas Day so for general convenience we hold it two days earlier. You will find the Muree beer is good, likewise the mango juice to which you can always add a surreptitious splash of Scotch and so are the kebabs and samozas. If you want a night out afterwards the High Commission is in the middle of Knightsbridge."

"That sounds fine sir," Higgins exclaimed eagerly.

"You lay it on Yousuf," said the Wing Commander. "Just tell me how many invitations you need." The courtesies of introduction completed Yousuf and his father returned to the family table.

Carl's eyes followed them and fell upon Yousuf's sister Yasmin. Slim necked and slender waisted with almost translucently pale skin she was in desultory conversation with her slightly henna haired mother. Yasmin's dark magenta silk shalwar kameez was surprisingly tight fitting and accentuated the line of her long legs without risking any immodesty. He wondered if she had the dark green eyes so common in the upper echelons of Pakistani society.

China Chu, Higgins enviously noticed, was much better placed than him to find out. He had been invited by Yousuf to install himself at the Ahmeds' table with Mary Wong his new kimono clad girlfriend from Soho's Chinatown. She was soon in animated discussion with Yasmin about where the best silk in London was to be found whilst Yasmin's father smoking a long cigarette looked out across the centre of the dining room where the dancing had just begun.

Although the Ahmeds were still on the main course of the dinner Carl sensed that the plates would soon be cleared away and that the family would be off all too quickly to the George Hotel in Grantham where Yousuf said they were staying. He would have to move fast. Fortune favoured the brave he thought so he excused himself from Juliet for a moment and approached the Ahmeds' table.

Yasmin looked up in surprise when Carl Higgins opened the conversation with his introductory gambit "ek kana bohat acha he" – "the food is very good," he declared. He really wanted to say that Yasmin was "bohat hjubsurat" – "very beautiful," but it would never do.

"So you speak Urdu then?" Yasmin asked turning her almond eyes towards him. "Yousuf never told me."

"I lived in Karachi once," he answered, "but perhaps I ought to speak Cantonese, too. Chu you haven't introduced me to your guest."

"I am sorry Carl. Perhaps I was at the bar. This is my friend Carl Higgins, Mary," China responded. "Like the Ahmeds Mary has come all the way from London. It's her first time at Cranwell."

"Well I hope it's not the last for any of you," Carl replied. "If you'll excuse me I must get back to our party or the Hut 150 group will think I'm a very neglectful host."

"Before you go," interrupted Yasmin, her hazel eyes looking up at him invitingly again, "Papa said that you and your friends are all to get an invitation to the reception in a week's time at the High Commission to commemorate the birthday of our first President and Founder of the Nation, Mohammed Ali Jinnah. We all hope you will be able to come, don't we Mama?"

"Of course my dear," Begum Ahmed responded somewhat coolly.

Once dinner was over most cadets were busy putting to the test Shakespeare's dictum that alcohol provokes desire but inhibits performance. The only way for Carl Higgins to banish Yasmin from his mind and to build up Dutch courage strong enough to face Juliet was by imbibing liberally. Lascelles was under no such boozy imperative. Elizabeth had become even more glamorous during the past year. She had escaped from her bossy mother and the constraints of life in an officer's married quarter to the freedom of a flat of her own in Nottingham where she had resumed her modelling career.

Lizzie was now earning five times as much as Peter even with his flying pay, shortly to increase when he started on jets. It looked as if this differential could well widen. Elizabeth's willowy figure and slinky pale blue dress attracted much attention among the cadets and no little envy of Peter. Her ability to arouse intense desire and passion in him was not always matched by an appreciation of the 'exigencies of the Service'; in other words that he could not always drop everything and come over to Nottingham at her whim and certainly not on four days a week. Peter found Lizzie's attitude surprising for the daughter of a Squadron Leader.

As for Jane and Jamie they had become a fixture in Cranwell terms, a seemingly permanent feature of cadet life. Much of the communal social activity of the Entry revolved around them so it was natural that as a year ago the Hut 150's former inmates all went to Natasha's home in Barkston after the Ball, so this time they should agree with alacrity to Janey's suggestion to give a miss again to Harry Ramsden's Fish and Chips on the A1 near Newark and to enjoy her proffered country house breakfast instead.

Jane's home was romantically set amidst bare towering elm trees through whose gaunt branches glinted a wintry moon half obscured by scurrying clouds. As they passed through the wide iron gates following her Land Rover, Janey slowed and leaned out shouting to Lascelles driving behind, "Just follow us and park beside me. Ignore the dogs, they look and sound much fiercer than they are."

As they made their way along the crunchy gravel drive the imposing silhouette of a vast edifice loomed up in front of them. Lizzie turned to Peter and observed, "This is just the sort of house which would suit me. I could not bear to live in a little matchbox married quarter for the rest of my working life, I've had enough of that already. Of course it would be necessary to have a flat in London as well. Otherwise I'm sure I would get very bored."

"I had not really thought about it," Peter replied truthfully. His sole preoccupation for the last two years had been to avoid getting chopped and to gain his pilot's wings and the Queen's Commission in one more year. Beyond that he just longed for no more restrictions and lots and lots of wonderful carefree flying.

As they entered the house a couple of overweight black Labradors milled around whilst a big Alsatian stood barking menacingly outside. "Don't worry about him," Jane insisted. "He never bites and he's not going to wake anybody up. My parents have gone on their annual pilgrimage to their favourite hotel in County Clare. Daddy's idea of a perfect holiday is to pursue snipe and woodcock through bogs and bramble bushes and to wildfowl along the river Shannon. My brother Henry's away trying to make his millions stockbroking in the City, so we've got the place to ourselves."

The group pushed past the usual paraphernalia of country life in the lobby – hacking jackets, riding caps, thigh boots, croquet mallets, landing nets, cartridge bags and fishing rods – and into the ill lit entrance hall. It was dominated by a massive iron bound wooden chest and a vast Victorian landscape painting of a misty Caledonian loch and glen. There ascended from the hall a wide portrait lined heavily balustraded staircase to the darkly mysterious upper floors.

"Install yourselves in the kitchen and I'll make you a cup of tea," Jane called out. "Then I'll revive the fire in the drawing room, put on some records and we can raid the drinks cabinet for something stronger." The kitchen was homely and warm from the inevitable Aga. "You don't mind Earl Grey in mugs, I hope?" asked Jane. "I'm afraid it's all we've got and there's no milk either. However, I do have plenty of my coconut cookies. I bake them myself and always take a supply back to London with me after the weekend. Tuck in."

Jane inserted a couple of firelighters and the ash logs in the huge grate were soon blazing away. She heaped a pile of 45 records onto the record player – Bill Haley, The Platters, Cliff Richard and much else besides, rolled up the Persian and Afghan carpets from the wooden floor and offered drinks all round. "I'm afraid Daddy and Mummy are very conservative. Glenfiddich is Dad's personal fuel. He says it keeps his blood flowing and Mama just sticks to her gin and bitter lemon, there's plenty of beer in the fridge. Just help yourselves."

Once their glasses were full, the music belted out invitingly and the dancing began, soon intimately except for Carl and Juliet who went briefly through the motions, then resumed their drinks and perfunctory conversation before the blazing fire. Higgins' thoughts just kept wandering to Yasmin and her exciting tight ankled shalwar, so redolent of silk pyjama bottoms, so deliciously smooth to the touch. Jane made the first move to break up the party. "Jamie and I are going up now. It's four-thirty in the morning and I've had a hellish week in the office. Lizzie and Peter, you follow me and I'll show you Henry's bedroom. The rest of you, don't hesitate to sleep on the sofas. It's far too late for you to get back into your hotel in Sleaford. Good night!"

Peter Lascelles felt himself an exceptionally lucky man. In the wan and wintry moonlight he could see that Henry's bedroom had a fine view out over the park towards the Trent Valley. It was still adorned with the mementos of boyhood, school and university – rosettes from riding competitions, a framed photo of a boy proudly holding up a salmon almost as big as himself, cups for athletics and gymnastics above the hearth, a group photograph of his House at Harrow and a miniature oar with the names of the second eight at Jesus College, Cambridge.

Quickly Lizzie and Peter put on the electric fire, drew the curtains and plunged naked beneath the eiderdown. Could anyone else provoke such bliss, Peter wondered. Whether Lizzie had enjoyed some maestro instructor in Düsseldorf or just had exceptionally ardent heredity, which endued her with an insatiable amorous stamina he could only guess, but certainly Lizzie's passion consumed him mind, body and soul.

The others had long since breakfasted when Lizzie fully dressed and packed woke Lascelles at noon. "What a super Ball, Peter. I won't forget it, but I've got to be on the catwalk looking my best over in Nottingham at three, so I've loved you and now I'm leaving you till we meet for the Pakistani reception in a week's time. I'm going up to London with Mum and Dad. They'll be staying at the RAF Club. Mum's determined to do some last minute shopping in Oxford Street and I've accepted Janey's invitation to stay at her flat in Chelsea. It should be quite a party, a great start to the festive season!" She stooped down to kiss him goodbye but got seized by Peter and pulled down by the buttocks onto the bed for an embrace, which he hoped was passionate enough to last for a week.

While Janey looked after Lizzie in her shared apartment in Old Church Street, Higgins was putting up Peter Lascelles and Jamie in his parents' large late Victorian flat in Morpeth Mansions beside Westminster Cathedral. When they arrived the gaslight street lamps were illuminating the wet pavements in a ghostly gleam accentuated by the wintry mist over the old churchyard in front of the entrance to the block. Inside the hallway a wooden panelled, brass handrailed, wall mirrored museum piece of a lift took them to the third floor where Carl's mother answered the door and welcomed them.

"Come in Peter and Jamie," she began, "Carl's told me so much about you. Isn't it amazing that you're all going to the Pakistani High Commissioner's reception tonight? Normally we'd be there ourselves but as ill luck would have it the Chief Clerk is holding his Christmas party at the Office tonight, which must have prior claim on my husband and myself, so Carl will have to represent us. Usually the Pakistani do is as much fun as these supposedly dry social events ever can be. We'll have to meet your friend Yousuf and his parents on another occasion. Let me now show you to your rooms. Then please come through to the sitting room and I'll offer you tea and mince pies."

The flat was much larger than Jamie and Peter had expected. The drawing room was especially spacious and was dominated by a dark Broadwood grand piano on which was arrayed a display of silver framed family photographs as well as of personally signed ones of royalty and leading foreign political personalities. "Who's the pianist?" asked Jamie.

"Well actually I am," Carl's mother replied. "I try to practise everyday. That's why we loved Bonn so much. There was a concert or recital to go to most nights for inspiration. Karachi was very different, wasn't it Carl?"

"Yes indeed, mother," Carl answered, "but I enjoyed the cricket matches and there was that incredible expedition into the Sindhi desert at dawn for a partridge and sand grouse shoot to which we were invited. I remember so well being taken from drive to drive by camel, the exuberance of the beaters and the wonderful hot breakfast they cooked for us after the first two drives."

"Didn't Winston Churchill live for a time in Morpeth Mansions?" asked Peter to stop the conversation flagging.

"Yes indeed," Mrs Higgins confirmed, "and many other MPs and Ministers, too. If we didn't turn it off we'd have to endure the Division Bell, which was fitted by a Tory Frontbencher ringing for votes in the Commons till the small hours of the morning."

"It must be exciting to live in the centre of things," Peter persisted.

"I'm not so sure. My husband seems to work much harder and longer hours in Whitehall than ever he did in any Embassy or High Commission overseas," Carl's mother explained. "I'm quite certain that he envies you all your active outdoor lives. Carl said that your experiences on Survival Camp in the Sauerland were particularly exciting."

"They certainly were for him," Jamie insisted, "because as a fluent German speaker he was allowed off camp most days, which none of the rest of us were."

"Time we were away," interjected Carl before the discussion could get round to the still painful subject of poor Angela's fate.

They rushed round to Victoria Station, jumped into a cab and were among the earlier arrivals at the High Commission over in Knightsbridge. It was clearly not an ordinary diplomatic reception owing to the large numbers of overseas Pakistanis pushing and jostling to get in at the imposing flakily painted tall pillared entrance with the national green and white Islamic flag on top. From the animated arguments with High Commission staff it seemed that many had invited themselves. Carl imperiously uttered a couple of words in Urdu to a harassed official at the door, waved his invitation card on high and swept with Jamie and Peter past the altercating and gesticulating masses.

As soon as they entered Yousuf together with his father in the same Mess dress that he had worn at the Graduation Ball came forward to greet them. "Gentlemen, welcome!"

"Let me introduce you to His Excellency," declared the Wing Commander. High Commissioner Mushtaq Ali, a pensioned off former Muslim League Minister, in a high collared black suit and his diminutive wife were doing the honours as a long line of guests filed past. "High Commissioner," Wing Commander Ahmed began, "you know my son Flight Cadet Yousuf. He's the first Pakistani to train at the Royal Air Force College. I'd like you now, sir, to meet three of his fellow cadets Jamieson, Lascelles and Higgins."

"Did you say Higgins?" their genial bespectacled host inquired.

"Yes Your Excellency," Carl replied. "I think you know my father from his time at the UK High Commission in Karachi. He and my mother asked me to express personally their apologies for their absence tonight owing to a prior engagement and to wish you and Begum Mushtaq Ali a happy Quaid-i-Azam's birthday."

"How very thoughtful," the High Commissioner replied. "Tell them that I wish them a very happy New Year in return. Now you chaps go and make your number with the Defence Advisor. You'll see he's got some Pakistani cadets from Sandhurst and a midshipman from Dartmouth with him."

"I'll take you over," suggested Wing Commander Ahmed. A short and rather stocky four ringed Eurasian Naval Officer seemingly straight from the wardroom in black bow tie and dark blue gold buttoned dress uniform came forward arm extended.

"My name is Captain Harry Engineer," he declared in hearty tones redolent of the British Raj. "Don't get me wrong but I'm actually not an engineer, nor a purser but the very unofficial purveyor of a rum ration to selected officers of the Pakistan Fleet. What can I offer you gentlemen – Murree beer, lime or mango juice, a Scotch perhaps?" Soon they were introduced to their Pakistani opposite numbers, the Sandhurst trio and the sole mariner among them, but where was Yasmin?

Carl searched the room in vain and then he saw her in the middle of a group of some dozen Pakistani ladies in the corner opposite conversing with her mother. Yasmin stood out as taller than the rest, fairer of face and untypically dressed to attract male attention. The small talk was all very well he thought discussing with his Pakistani counterparts the music of Baluch pipe bands; the heroic actions of the Punjabis at Kohima, of the Piffers (Frontier Force) in Waziristan before the war; how the British could not have achieved victory in Burma without the Indian Army; how Kashmir had been treacherously assigned by Mountbatten to India on partition; the tragedy of the 1948 war for Pakistan; which was the best cantonment today and so on. Carl's preoccupation was not the subcontinent but how he was going to get Yasmin across. He would have to enlist Yousuf's help urgently before the opportunity passed.

Carl manoeuvred himself into the animated group of Pakistani cadets with whom Yousuf was earnestly talking shop and describing the demise of Gormless Gerrity for unauthorised low flying. "Has Yousuf told you of his miraculous solo forced landing at Langar when his engine failed?" Carl butted in. "Well it's as true as his tale about the hay up Gerrity's air intake. You're getting modest Yousuf. I bet your parents and sister don't even know."

"They don't actually," Yousuf replied.

"In that case," Carl insisted, "it's perhaps better not to worry your mother and to keep her in the dark at least until you pass out, but I think you could let on to your sister. After all she's been to Cranwell and has met Zog Oldham your QFI at the Ball. When the reception is over why don't you bring her along to join us for a meal afterwards. We were planning on a quick curry. Your father probably knows a suitable restaurant close to the High Commission. Square it away with him. If he approves your mother can hardly object and I'm sure Yasmin would enjoy our company."

Yousuf duly extricated himself from the group and returned to his Cranwell friends. They were still consuming mango scotches with Captain Engineer who was by now holding forth loudly and indiscreetly. "I can't tell you, gentlemen, how happy I am to be posted to London. I feel as if I've come home. You see I can never become an Admiral in the Pakistan Navy, the Quaid-i-Azam's body, God have mercy on his soul, would turn in his mausoleum. If I'm very lucky I could become a Commodore running the Karachi Naval Dockyard, but a Christian Admiral would never be accepted."

Before the Naval Advisor had time to unburden himself of more subversive thoughts, Yousuf was back. "Papa suggests that we go to Shezzan, Yasmin, too. Apparently it's a very pukkha place off Montpelier Square across the road from Harrods. The Pakistani cuisine is four star at least. I'll fetch Yasmin and let's go now so we get a table. Goodbye, Captain Engineer, sir. Have a happy Christmas."

Dinner at Shezzan was a success. Janey and Jamie put the others at their ease. Lizzie was looking particularly glamorous and was clearly in her element in fashionable Knightsbridge. "Jane has suggested that I come and stay for longer next time," she declared confidently. "Why don't you spend more time in London, Peter?" she inquired. He regarded it as a rhetorical question. Yousuf was obviously proud at being at the heart of the Entry's social circle and Carl was simply entranced by Yasmin. After Captain Engineer's well disguised whiskies the cadets stuck to beer and tucked into the kebabs and chicken Tikkas with relish culminating the dinner with a delicious halwa pudding.

"What do you do all day, Yasmin?" asked Janey. "You can't keep your mother company the whole time and I'm sure you have help in the home."

"We do indeed and Mama would soon get fed up with me. I've enrolled at the School of Oriental and African Studies in October and I'm reading for a diploma in Sanskrit. If it goes well I may put in for a degree course in Farsi or Arabic next academic year. I haven't decided yet. I want to be a diplomat. It is time that Pakistan took more ladies into public service."

While making her little speech Carl felt the warm silk of Yasmin's lower leg against his calf. He did not move and Yasmin retained her composure whilst insinuating her whole leg between his own. The effect was electrifying. He felt the blood course up the back of his neck and looked across the candle lit table at Yasmin's pale calm features and into her intense huge almond eyes. "We'll have to do this more often, Yousuf," she said without so much as a quiver in her voice. "I like your friends."

"So do I," said Janey hopefully. "You have to come, Yasmin, to the hen party I'm having in my flat on 5 January – the day before they all go back to Cranwell."

"You'll have to fix it for me with Mama and Papa, Yousuf," pleaded Yasmin. "Explain to them carefully that it's an all ladies affair – a late tea party really."

"I'll do my best, but I must get you back home now," answered Yousuf, "otherwise you haven't a chance."

They got up to catch their taxis in Knightsbridge. Before the first could be hailed Yasmin exclaimed, "Silly me, I've left my umbrella at Shezzan. I'll have to go and get it. Make sure the taxi's waiting when I return, Yousuf."

"I'll keep you company," said Carl as they darted back to Shezzan. "I think, Yasmin that you're making a good choice of career," Carl observed.

"My father's work in the diplomatic service has taken us to so many exciting places and till then you've got SOAS."

Once the umbrella was retrieved from the restaurant Carl and Yasmin lingered outside. "I'm glad you're in Yousuf's entry, Carl," she said. "You can help look after him. Keep him safe. We had so many crashes when the Pakistan Air Force converted to jets. Papa must have lost half a dozen friends in the first year. If I give you a little kiss you will promise me to do that won't you?" She leant forward and Carl slipped his arms behind her and drew her close. That kiss was warmer, fuller and more satisfying than he could believe possible. Perhaps Yasmin brought some oriental magic or perhaps it was because the embrace was so unexpected and excitingly surreptitious. "We must hurry now," she declared. "Do try and organise a meeting after Janey's party on 5 January, otherwise I'll be very lonely especially as you're going back to Cranwell the next day."

"Don't worry, I'll do my best, Yasmin. We must see more of each other," Carl replied.

CHAPTER 13

Janey's hen party in Chelsea was a great success, although it hardly lived up to its name. She did not get back from work till six. By then Lizzie had just returned from a whole day of concentrated clothes shopping as only a fashion professional knows how and looked stunning as a result. Soon the first men arrived – Yousuf dutifully accompanying Yasmin and shortly afterwards Jamie emerged from the bedroom almost immediately followed by insistent bell ringing on the outside door, presaging the eager arrival of Carl Higgins and Peter Lascelles, one carrying a crate of wine bottles and the other a crate of beer.

Janey's flatmate, a leggy horsey blonde from Rutland called Samantha readily entered into the spirit of things distributing glasses, pouring drinks and dispensing chips, nuts and quiche. Janey assumed the role of disc jockey and soon Samantha was taking the diffident Yousuf in her stride as nonchalantly as she would a new obstacle in the hunting field back home in Cottesmore country.

Samantha's lack of inhibition was as novel and thrilling to Yousuf as the intense bewitchment in the mysteries of sense and soul, which Yasmin personified to Carl. Her sublime scent and the rose petal delicacy of touch to her skin electrified him. Yasmin's exotic novelty and originality of mind consumed Carl's spirit with a longing to drink deep of the well of total fulfilment she represented.

At ten thirty sharp Yousuf left to take Yasmin home. Before she went she promised Carl she would not forget him and Samantha obligingly insisted that Yousuf must make sure that Yasmin could come to further hen parties, which she and Janey had planned for the months ahead. Realistically Yasmin wondered how it would be possible to see more of Carl. True her course at SOAS would give her relative freedom, which most Pakistani young ladies lacked and a permanent excuse to get out of the house. However, all too soon her parents would be lining up a husband for her in Pakistan. Names had already been mentioned and Yousuf had given his opinion on each. How long could he be relied upon to play a double game on her behalf? Her best hope lay in the active connivance of Janey and Samantha and a great deal of luck.

Each midwinter return to Cranwell was less cruel than the last. The huts of the South Brick Lines were a distant memory as the cadets of the penultimate entry settled into the comparative comfort of their individual rooms in the main College. Gold buttons on the white gorgettes upon their collars indicated the special status of Flight Cadets now training on jets.

At their first visit to the Flight Lines of Cranwell South a hectic timetable of flying every day was unveiled. The mostly young and evidently keen QFIs were clearly more operationally orientated than their counterparts at Barkston Heath. The Flight and Squadron Commanders, too, seemed more youthful and less remote.

Of Jamie's group only Peter Lascelles was deemed too tall to train on Vampires. His thigh length would have precluded a safe ejection in emergency so he was assigned to the more claustrophobic Meteor 7. The so called Meat Box with its heavy side hinged metal framed cockpit canopy and lack of ejection seat or pressurisation was rightly judged more challenging than the Vampire. This was especially so on one engine when the asymmetric force on the rudder pedal to keep a Meteor straight could become fearsomely strong. At least Peter had a companion trainee in Ronald Anderson, a lanky easy going and benign cadet who had been demoted from the previous entry for lack of academic progress, especially in Maths.

Jamie was lucky with his instructor. Pierre Du Toit was a quiet, reserved and immensely powerful rugby playing South African who exuded an infectious confidence. Leader of the College's four ship formation aerobatic team, the Poachers, he encouraged Jamie to excel at all the key skills of fighter pilot.

After only a couple of hours of dual instruction Jamie was off solo, and to him the mystery and beauty of jet flight never lost their semi-spiritual quality. He marvelled that ordinary people could be so preoccupied with their mundane ambitions, the routine hopes and disappointments of daily terrestrial life when from forty thousand feet the insignificance of man and all his works was so readily apparent.

At times in flight his thoughts verged on the metaphysical. Often he gazed across at his friends' aircraft wheeling beside him in close formation suspended seemingly motionless against the azure sky and wondered how the little pinhead of a bonedome in the cockpit alongside could be the receptacle of a human soul – on the ground an individual personality, the source of laughter and tears, compassion, kindness or cruelty; in the air the source of competence and trust or extreme danger. A fraction of a second of error could lead to a fatal plunge to oblivion. Likewise the ground crew who before flight so dutifully wiped clean the cockpit canopies and closed them carefully upon departure waving cheerily their white gloved charges on their way from dispersal, could never know if they would return and if they would actually marshal home the young pilots who by faith had so readily entrusted both soul and body to the sky an hour before.

By and large the course did well in spite of some tense episodes. Peter Carrick horrified himself on solo aerobatics and his instructor at the debrief afterwards, by losing control after experimenting to see how high a high level loop in a Vampire could be flown. He went gingerly over the top at over 42,000 feet but next thing he knew he was hurtling vertically downwards totally out of control, way beyond the critical Mach Number although throttled fully back and with airbrakes extended. He had either to eject immediately or ride it down and hope the wings would stay on long enough to reach a lesser Mach Number in the denser warmer lower layers where the elevator should begin to work again. They did stay on and he eased out of the dive with shaking legs at less than five thousand feet.

Spinning the Vampire was nearly always to experience the unexpected, so much so that an amended standard spin recovery technique was pasted into pilot's notes nearly every week. China Chu, normally the flying rule book's most loyal adherent, but inspired by an instructor's flick roll at the top of a loop during his early morning beat up of the airfield and mindless of Taffy Jones' tragic fate, tried a Porteous loop in emulation. He counted the aircraft flick about its axis three times in level flight and then it descended rapidly still furiously spinning. The latest spin recovery actions proving totally ineffective and fearing complete disorientation China withdrew his feet from the rudder bar and raised his hands from the control column to the face blind to eject whereupon the rotations abruptly stopped and he was finally able to recover just two thousand feet above the ground. No one on the course deliberately flick rolled the Vampire again.

Night flying as previously at Barkston Heath was particularly challenging. Jamie who had experienced a difficult first solo when the fenland mist moved in early faced a worse challenge on his second, which would have tested a veteran fighter pilot with a dozen years' flying in his logbook. At Met Briefing the imminent arrival of a cold front was announced by Cunimb Jim in dismal tones but the Chief Flying Instructor confidently declared that all the solo students should be safely down well before it reached Cranwell.

They indeed were bar one, since Jamie's aircraft went unserviceable with a hydraulic leak and another Vampire had to be retrieved from the back of the hangar to replace it and be given the customary pre-flight inspection. By the time he took off it was already raining and he had to bury his head in the instruments as the aircraft plunged into thick cloud as soon as it left the ground.

As he climbed the rain turned to hail and hammered fiercely on the canopy. His navigation and collision warning lights reflected an eerie glow from the impenetrable cloud. The aeroplane tossed and bucked. Jamie prayed that the engine would not flame out from an ingestion of liquid ice and that he could faithfully carry out Pierre Du Toit's injunction always to trust to the indications of the flight instruments and not to the siren voices of his senses. He headed for home concentrating for dear life on his blind flying skills determined not to let his revered instructor down.

As he did so he was ordered to hold off from Cranwell as four Valiant V bombers were approaching the airfield and had priority to land. Air Traffic Control seemed oblivious of the fact that it was only Jamie's second solo in a Vampire by night, that his endurance was very limited and that the already atrocious weather was deteriorating fast. By the time that he was finally permitted to descend his fuel was so low as to allow only one attempt to land. Furthermore the precipitation was so severe that the Ground Control radars could not see him either at Cranwell or at Waddington the Master Diversion Airfield nearby.

The choice was either to eject into the storm or to let down prayerfully towards base on a series of cathode ray direction finding radio bearings with no measure of height or distance on the approach. Jamie decided to stay with the aeroplane and mercifully hit no obstacle finding himself on breaking cloud perfectly lined up with the flare path with just enough time to slam the wheels and flaps down and land. The appearance of the runway lights through seemingly impenetrable cloud and rain when Jamie was down to his last fifty feet of height seemed to him as miraculous as the parting of the waters of the Red Sea for the Israelites.

Jamie taxied back to the pan along flooded taxiways. To his astonishment as he followed the marshaller's luminous batons he spotted the Chief Flying Instructor who had rushed out in the pouring rain to dispersal in order to greet him when he shut down clearly relieved that there would be no accident inquiry to attend, telling Jamie that he was proud of him – a rare statement indeed to any Flight Cadet. In the instructor's crewroom debrief over coffee Pierre Du Toit also told Jamie how well he had done. Thereafter Jamie himself always believed that Almighty God had guided him safely home only because he must have reserved some special work for him to do.

Although the Entry spent so much more of their lives flying that it dominated the timetable, the familiar College routine continued but in a subtly modified form. Restrictions parades became a bad memory now that the Senior Entry were friends and shared the same crewroom with the flying instructors. As there was less time for

Academics the lectures were more focused on technical subjects directly relevant to flying. Regular drill of course persisted as did occasional ceremonial parades. The parade ground remained at the heart of Cranwell life.

The patterns of social activity were well established with Jamie and Peter both whipping in for the Per Ardua beagles. After the meet Peter would slip off to Nottingham to be with Elizabeth whilst Jamie joined Janey to spend house party weekends. Peter Carrick continued with Sylvia more out of habit than mutual delight. Janey confirmed that Yousuf saw Samantha at half term at her well timed hen party at the flat which also brought Yasmin and Carl together, who met up with China Chu and Mary Wong for dinner in Soho afterwards.

The penultimate passing out parade was much like that at Christmas except that the Reviewing Officer was not a senior serving office but the Secretary of State for Air, a pin stripe suited rotund Conservative politician who had fought a courageous Second World War in the Brigade of Guards, wore a bowler hat for the parade and delivered the longest passing out speech in memory. He upset Yousuf Ahmed during his inspection when he came along the rank to him by observing how welcome Yousuf would be in the Indian Air Force which he claimed "showed great promise in the Burma campaign but still lacked sufficiently trained senior officers", to which Yousuf remains stoically silent. He upset China Chu as well by telling him to his inscrutably impassive parade ground face that, "I expect you'll be looking forward to getting back soon to Hong Kong?" and then still audibly to the sword carrying Senior Under Officer at his elbow, "actually I didn't know the colony had an Air Force." Chu like Ahmed rightly judged that it was not the role of Commonwealth Flight Cadets to correct one of her Majesty's Secretaries of State, especially at a ceremonial event and simply replied, "Sir".

The Ball in the evening was the last occasion when the Entry would wear their interim Mess dress of best blue uniform, winged collar and bow tie. The graduating Entry with newly earned wings on their lapel and thin single Pilot Officer's stripes on their sleeve were enviable, but the new Senior Entry had its proud members, too. Jamie had been promoted to Senior Under Officer and wore a thick V shaped Flying Officer's stripe on his sleeve; Lascelles, Carrick and Ahmed similarly a narrower V shaped Pilot Officer's stripe to denote their promotion to Under Officer for the final term.

For Carl Higgins overlooked for promotion but nonchalant about it, of much greater excitement was that the Ahmed family was present again. Yousuf must have exercised some quiet diplomacy because Carl to his surprise and delight was allowed to dance with Yasmin who after a year at SOAS seemed more sophisticated and seductive than ever. Her greater maturity emboldened her to slip past the ladies lavatory and out of the back door to the College, making her way with Carl through the pine tees and a back door of the lower west wing into his room, an immediate suspension offence for a Flight Cadet if caught, but treasured moments of illicit bliss for Carl.

Yasmin soon vouchsafed some thrilling intelligence. Her father was due to attend a meeting between key Service attachés from countries both of the Central Treaty Organisation like Pakistan and of the North Atlantic Treaty Organisation in Washington in a week's time. He was inviting his wife and his daughter Yasmin to accompany him for a holiday in America's capital and Virginia. "The timing is perfect," Carl observed exultantly. "Early tomorrow morning, as Yousuf will have told you dear Yasmin, the Entry is due to fly via Newfoundland to visit the United

States Air Force Academy at Colorado springs returning a few days later via a call at the United States Naval Academy at Annapolis, and to Washington for a short programme of briefings and activities at the Pentagon and State Department."

Carl could see a look of wide eyed interest on Yasmin's face. "I'm sure we could manage to meet out there if we're clever about it," Carl went on excitedly. "I don't know where we're being put up in DC but the previous Entry stayed in a hotel somewhere near Du Pont circle. Where are you going to be, Yasmin?" Carl asked.

"Papa mentioned the Washington Hilton on Connecticut Avenue," she replied.

"That's very good," answered Carl with impassioned expectation rising in his chest, "I'll do everything I can to make a meeting out there possible. How you elude your mother and father I leave to you. Perhaps you're going to have to depend on your brother Yousuf again to provide the cover. I'm sure he will. After all I doubt if he would like your parents to know too much about Samantha either."

After in some instances only two hours' sleep the Entry were assembled in battle dress and berets punctually on parade outside Flying Wing Headquarters on the Flight Lines at Cranwell South. Their standard issue grey blue holdalls were packed with Number One uniforms including black tie and winged collar, sports kit for matches against the American cadets and a set of plain clothes for any free time.

The accompanying party of the Deputy Commandant, Head of Academic Training, Chief Advanced Flying Instructor, and two Cadet Wing Squadron Commanders was a high level one. The cadets knew they would have to be on their best behaviour at all times. Carl realised that he would have to be cautious and extremely clever about Yasmin. No cadet could afford to put up a black before the College's top executives. To do so could be fatal.

At eight o'clock sharp the heavy headed Flight Cadets boarded the whispering giant of a four engined Britannia Transport of Number 10 squadron, which would be their exclusive transport for the next ten days. The aeroplane eased itself off the two thousand yards of concrete of Cranwell's main runway and once through the patchy cumulus over Lincolnshire was soon into clear arctic air beyond the Hebrides, passing Keflavik, Iceland, and the many fjorded ice capped coast of Greenland down to Gander in Newfoundland where immense towing tractors and hooded ground crew in fur lined parkas attended to their refuelling before the long flight to Colorado across North America's central plains and prairies.

To their surprise the Britannia landed not at Colorado Springs but at a nearby air base. Unlike Cranwell the United States Air Force Academy had no airfield of its own whereas the Royal Air Force College had four. The American officer cadets did not fly but were committed to four years of intensive service and academic training seven thousand feet up in the remote foothills of the Rockies far from aircraft and aerodromes. Only after graduation and commissioning did their flying training begin. To most Flight Cadets flying was the principal compensation for the rigours of the Cranwell course. Furthermore three years to passing out seemed ample preparation to reach wings standard in flying and to qualify for the Queen's Commission.

The Cranwell party was warmly welcomed on arrival at the ultra modern architecturally imposing buildings of the Air Academy. The splendour of the mountain backdrop and the fierce clarity of the North American sunlight heightened the daunting first impression of Colorado Springs upon the Flight Cadets. The hospitality could not have been warmer but the visiting British officers and cadets found the rigidities of the Academy's system of discipline harsh and unimaginative.

Likewise what seemed to their hosts the more relaxed easy going attitudes of the Flight Cadets masked a tough disciplinary regime at Cranwell, which whilst less outwardly apparent was felt by the Flight Cadets to be more than equally effective.

The sense of being alien allies was intensified in the Dining Hall. The diet of ultra white bread, hamburgers and ketchup washed down with iced water was bad enough, but the Flight Cadets thought the stipulated eating of square meals, that is using knife, fork and spoon only in rectilinear movements simply ridiculous. Likewise they expressed total incomprehension at the Honour Code whereby it was the duty of every American cadet to inform the Academy's directing staff of any misdemeanour perpetrated by a fellow cadet, even by a friend. At Cranwell if authority could be kept in the dark about a Flight Cadet's misbehaviour or disciplinary lapses this was held to be to the credit of the perpetrator and his cadet accomplices alike.

The sporting programme was literally a walkover for the home teams who were fully acclimatised to playing the three competed sports of soccer, American football and basketball at an altitude only three thousand feet less than that at which oxygen masks are required for flying. Even so Cranwell lost the soccer by only one goal.

Senior Under Officer Jamieson gave a fluent presentation without notes or visual aids on the Cranwell Officer Training system indicating to his fellow Flight Cadets his front runner status to win the Sword of Honour on graduation. In contrast the merits of the Academy's unique way of educating and developing the future leaders of the United States Air Force was described in clipped authoritative tones by the straight necked, bullet headed, bristle haired Brigadier General Commandant himself, flanked by a posse of the Academy's executive officers who would be asked by the Commandant to reply to each question according to their specialist expertise, whereas Jamie when asked responded equally effectively completely spontaneously across a wide range of subjects.

The next day after a quick tour of the North American Air Defence Command and Control facilities deep in a mountainside, nearby, the Cranwell party were transferred to the airfield where their Britannia awaited them for the flight across the Great Plains and Appalachian Mountains to Andrews Air Force base outside Washington. From there it was another short coach trip to the Du Pont circle hotel, an unwonted luxury for the cadets.

The following day spent at the Naval Academy at Annapolis was a long and full one. The by now familiar rigidities of the American Services' approach to discipline were as apparent as at Colorado Springs. However, the British colonial appearance of the town and the historic atmosphere of the Academy itself made the visit to Annapolis less of a cultural shock for the Cranwell cadets.

The final stage of the American study tour culminated in morning briefings at the State Department and across the Potomac at the Pentagon. The State Department officials emphasised the importance of the Free World's Alliance system to contain communism – NATO, CENTO and SEATO and the need for military strength to underpin western diplomacy. The Pentagon stressed the necessity for the United States and Britain to maintain an effective nuclear deterrent to offset the numerical superiority of the Soviet and Warsaw Pact forces especially on the Central Front in Europe. An Admiral warned also of the global threat posed by the rise of Soviet sea power. The afternoon was devoted to educational tourism first at the Capitol with a guided tour of both Houses of Congress, followed by another informative guided tour of the White House.

Carl Higgins returned with his friends to the Du Point circle hotel, his spirits exuberant with excited anticipation for the free weekend ahead. Yousuf had confirmed to Carl that morning that his parents were going to spend Saturday over in Virginia visiting Mount Vernon, Alexandria and the Arlington cemetery. He already had their permission to explore picturesque historic Georgetown with Yasmin and then to go with her to the National Gallery of Art finishing with the Phillips collection in Du Pont circle.

For the first time he confided in Carl and asked him a favour. "Carl, my old friend," he requested, "could you very kindly and discreetly take Yasmin off my back tomorrow? I want to spend the day visiting a bar or two with my school friend Mumtaz Qureshi. He's studying International Relations at Georgetown University."

"I'll go down with Yasmin from our hotel to Georgetown telling Papa and Mama that we're off sightseeing in that delightfully English looking part of town. Could you then, Carl," asked Yousuf, "please make your way to the entrance of Georgetown University by 11.00 where I am due to meet up with Mumtaz. We can then go our separate ways," he went on. "Only make sure you bring Yasmin back to the Washington Hilton by six thirty sharp. All hell will break loose if my parents don't find Yasmin in the hotel when they return."

"I'll be more than happy to oblige, Yousuf," Carl replied. "If I can provide a similar service for you in the future, I'd be delighted to do so."

Outside the university Yousuf and Mumtaz bear hugged as if they had not seen each other for years. Carl was cursorily introduced to Mumtaz then Yousuf and his friend ambled away in animated conversation to enjoy the bars and restaurants of Georgetown together. Yasmin and Carl moved off more restrainedly so as not to betray their feelings, but as soon as her brother was out of sight Yasmin plunged her soft warm hand into his asking him as they walked leisurely all the way back to Du Pont circle about his experiences on the visit, how he liked the food in the United States and what he felt about the glimpses of American life the tour had offered.

"You'll be amazed my dearest Yasmin," Carl observed, "but I actually like life in Pakistan, Germany and England more than I do here."

"So do I, Carl," Yasmin replied. "I love London but I still miss the smells and sounds of Pakistan – the scents that arouse the senses in the early morning, the squarking of the ever-present crows, the groaning of the laden ox carts on the Great Trunk road, the bustling crowds in the bazaars and the sight of intrepid passengers clinging to the roofs of the gaudily decorated buses coming down to Rawalpindi from Peshawar."

"You should pursue poetry not diplomacy," Carl joked.

"I would love to actually," said Yasmin, "but it's just about acceptable for a lady in Pakistan to take up a public career in politics, the law or Government service, but poetry would be just not on – who would support her?"

Du Pont circle came in sight and they followed the signs to the Phillips collection of classic pictures set in a small Victorian family sized house.

"If I had money, Yasmin," Carl remarked, "I would not buy cars, houses, yachts or horses. I'd buy pictures. My choice would express my personality and like good books pictures become almost as familiar best friends to whom one returns repeatedly, always with delight."

"Whatever happens to us," Yasmin retorted, "I hope we'll do the same."

"I expect we will," replied Carl presciently, "if not in body because fate sometimes decrees otherwise, but always in spirit."

Once they had viewed the collection Carl and Yasmin strolled gently up the hill and into the entrance at the front of the wide gently curved façade of the hotel. Over a lunchtime salad and looking out over the broad expanse of the swimming pool they mused about the future. "When I get back Yasmin," Carl explained "I'll be plunged straight away into the intensive final stages of the course. Whatever happens I must not foul up my chances of passing out now. My future thereafter is entirely in the hands of the posting people. I am like a pawn in chess. There are some standard moves at the beginning of the game but thereafter it's a question of chance and error. There are few of us indeed who reach the final row and who can crown their career by being elevated to Air Marshal. We are all expendable on the way – vulnerable to our superior officers' operational gambits and the oversights, which bring sudden disaster. What about you, Yasmin?"

"My first degree course should end at SOAS more or less when Papa's tour of duty at the High Commission expires. I can't see myself going back to Pakistan then. I expect I'll go for a higher degree first, probably in America. It should be a challenge in itself and perhaps when accomplished help dispel some of the anti female prejudice of those who select entrants to our Foreign Service," she replied.

"This has been all too serious," said Carl. "Let us enjoy what's left of this precious day. Tomorrow the whispering giant will be winging me back to black windswept Newfoundland and then onward through the night to Cranwell. Thereafter we should be able to meet at least for half term and then at the Graduation Ball before I pass out. I'll try to arrange for a friend to bring his sister ostensibly as my partner because I'm sure your parents still could not accept that we are so close."

"That sounds exciting," Yasmin replied.

"Why don't we now have a swim in this magnificent swimming pool?" Carl suggested. "It would be good to cool down after our long walk. I wisely put my trunks on under my trousers before I came out. Run upstairs, Yasmin, and get your swimming costume on and we'll do a few lengths together." When she changed Yasmin was even more enticing with her silky black hair extending down her back below her smooth shoulders, long legs, willowy figure and fabulous pale olive skin.

Yasmin's front crawl was immaculate; economical and seemingly effortless with impeccable regular breathing. "I've just witnessed another of your many talents, darling Yasmin," said Carl. "Not many Pakistanis swim so well, especially women."

"I suppose it's the Islamic shyness complex," Yasmin replied, "but Mama always insisted that I should have swimming lessons and train regularly at the club. It is one of the things I'm most grateful for."

"So am I," remarked Carl emphatically. "You vouchsafed a vision of great beauty to me this afternoon. Let's go upstairs to celebrate."

Yasmin's room was spacious with a huge television set, capacious drinks cabinet and vast double bed, which seemed as wide as it was long. Yasmin poured Carl and herself a coca cola and then emerged from the bathroom in a white towelled robe with another towel wrapping her hair turban-like around her head.

Carl could only believe that God or indeed Allah had been especially good to him. He felt blessed beyond his wildest dreams as they pulled back the coverlet and fell upon each other longitudinally and latitudinally and indeed facing all points of the compass which the ample bed so indulgently permitted. Passion gratefully spent, the bedside alarm was set for six and well before half past Carl had showered and dressed. Yasmin slumbered on as he made his way dreamily down the hill to Du Pont circle to rejoin his friends and confront the realities of Cranwell life again.

CHAPTER 14

When the cadets touched down at Cranwell late the next morning, the Lincolnshire countryside looked small scale and very green. The American interlude had affected Carl's soul but all he could do now, obedient to his destiny was to devote himself to his duties. He envied Jamie and the two Peters with their girlfriends nearby both so accessible socially and physically. In every sense there was a great divide between him and Yasmin except in spirit and in the almost sacred mystery of sex.

Fate had brought them together. They would remain its playthings in the months and years ahead. Carl determined that he must savour each joyful moment with Yasmin, learn the gift of acceptance and not to fret for the future. Jamie was lucky with his religious upbringing, Carl thought. Perhaps he had learned from it the virtues of patience and resignation to a higher will although with Janey so close at hand he doubted that Jamie had ever actually been tested in the same way as he had.

The last weeks of the course seemed to race by. It was believed that following a recent Defence White Paper the age of the manned aircraft was supposedly over. If so there would be a lesser requirement for fighter pilots in the Service, but the cadets hoped that at least the Transport force would grow, and perhaps those of helicopters and maritime reconnaissance aircraft as well.

Yet they still spent much time on the fighter pilot's routines of aerobatics, formation flying, tail chasing and low flying. How exhilarating the final exercises were. With more experience and growing confidence the four ship flights of soon to graduate cadets broke ever more exuberantly into the circuit after their tail chasing and formation sorties. The cadets returned to the crew room exhilarated and dripping with sweat. A coca cola to cool down was essential before more briefings and then off airborne again two or three times a day.

Half term was celebrated in London with Janey and Samantha's now traditional hen party. This time there was an important difference. Janey and Jamie announced their engagement to the delighted guests. Jamie had proposed to her at the Belvoir Hunt Ball, a thrilling colourful affair in Belvoir Castle two weeks before. Janey's acceptance had been immediate and they decided to keep it secret until the appropriate moment for an announcement in front of their best friends. They hoped to get married in about a year's time either immediately after Jamie's conversion to his operational aircraft or soon after he joined his first squadron.

Janey and Samantha had never hosted a better party. Jamie unsurprisingly was the first of the entry to get engaged. Janey offered him all he desired – deep roots in one of England's few unspoilt counties, a dutiful companion born and bred to unostentatious public service with a united loving family behind her and boundless support in his chosen career. She already could have been the role model for a perfect Station Commander's wife. As a hostess she was incomparable being tolerant of the rumbustuous bibulous habits of Jamie's fellow cadets, always attractive and never stuffy.

Peter Lascelles and Elizabeth were close and might soon have followed the example of Janey and Jamie but Peter was less sure of himself and their future whilst Elizabeth was still fixated on her modelling work, which brought her more and more money and ushered her into a glamorous world of which Peter only had glimpses. His compensation for Lizzie's lack of intellectual stimulus and spiritual empathy lay increasingly in his by now firm friendship with Ronald Anderson his fellow student down at the Meteor Flight. Ron who had been brought up in Rhodesia was easy going and unlike Lizzie made no demands but always provided a ready ear to hear out Peter's woes. He was the ideal companion for trips to local pubs.

Their experiences on the Meteor 7, which they shared with no other cadets, brought them closer together. Both were progressing well in flying even though their instructors were markedly different. Peter had the fastidious Old Cranwellian Flight Lieutenant James Buchan who with two tours on Meteor night fighters – the NF 12 and NF 14 – behind him was obssessive about accuracy in instrument flying. Ron had the wrinkly faced old Master Pilot Jack Simpson who had flown nearly every twin engined fighter from piston engined Mosquitoes and Hornets to Meteor and Javelin jets. To him aerobatics were a supreme art form to be executed as smoothly as perfect parallel ski turns in powdered snow. In James Buchan Peter had a QFI who matched his professional ambition and spurred him on to a standard where he was in contention for the course instrument flying prize. In Mr Jack Simpson, Ron had a mentor who effectively inspired in himself confidence and a calm cool response to all the demands of flying.

Ronald became very much part of the group. He had brought his blonde South African girlfriend Alice Van Meer, a student at Bedford College, London, to Janey's hen party who immediately fell into animated conversation with Yasmin about student life at London University.

Peter Lascelles and Lizzie were soon drawn into the discussion when it became clear that a whole new party circuit among London University undergraduates could open up to them. Lizzie, however, was not keen. The company of scruffy students was not something that she craved. Likewise Yasmin had her reservations. "You know, Carl," she observed critically. "I don't think our going to SOAS or even Bedford College parties would work. I'm certainly too well known at SOAS and word might get back to my parents from Bedford College, too. If they found out that I was partying with you what little freedom I do have would be drastically curtailed. Let's go on meeting through Janey and Samantha at least until you pass out or are posted overseas."

"I agree of course Yasmin," Carl replied. "Peter, Ron and I have already decided to come down to London in a month's time on a special 48-hour weekend pass to get our officer uniforms fitted in readiness for graduation. I'm sure Janey and Samantha can be prevailed upon to host a final pre-commissioning party for us. Romance blossoms intensely when you're amongst friends."

"How right you are Carl," Yasmin answered. "There would be nothing worse for us now than for me to have an unnecessary row with Papa and Mama. You and I have tempted providence long enough and I want so much to be able to attend the passing out ceremonies at Cranwell, to see you and Yousuf get your wings and slow march off parade together as Pilot Officers up the steps and into College Hall to the strains of Auld Lang Syne."

"Not many cadets have the support of a girl as special as you Yasmin," Carl responded.

"More's the pity for them," said Yasmin, "but you happen to be my first and only love and I have just one brother, Yousuf, so you've both had to take pride of place in my heart. The Air Force, too, is in my blood remember. We Pakistanis are a martial race."

When the cadets got back to Cranwell preparations began for the final great adventure – the Advanced Flying Wing's international cross country to Germany. It would be led by one of the Vampire Squadron Commanders, William Parsons and involved sixteen Vampires and two Meteors. The pair of Meteors under Flight Lieutenant Buchan was to fly out ahead at first light to Gütersloh on a preliminary route and destination weather reconnaissance. Upon receipt of the go ahead from Buchan the Vampires would follow in two flights.

Ron Anderson did the flight planning for the Meteors and Peter Carrick for the Vampires under the kindly supervision of Squadron Leader Ashley in almost his last instructional duty at the College before being posted as Navigation Leader to a recently formed Valiant Squadron. He could not resist the parting observation, "Now you realise, gentlemen, that all those navexes your first year over at Barkston were worthwhile." Ron and Peter could only agree.

"They were fun, too," added Peter as they computed headings and timings, plotted the track to circumvent active airfields and danger areas, scrutinised the weather forecasts for en route winds and for possible diversion airfields, noted radio frequencies for airway crossings and arrival at destination, and studied terminal approach procedures for Gütersloh. All these tasks they had happily left to the redoubtable Polzol and his Varsity crew on their last memorable German visit, which already seemed to them now as much ancient history as the first flight of the Wright Brothers.

The morning of the international cross country navex dawned rain-washed and fine. A deep frontal system had passed through in the night leaving Cranwell in the clear. Flight briefing at 06.30 was an hour earlier than usual and began to the throaty background hum of the two Meteors starting up and taxiing out. Cunimb Jim had to interrupt his delivery in mid sentence just as his forecast warm front was approaching the Netherlands whilst Peter Lascelles and Ron Anderson roared off on their early bird departure with their QFIs for Gütersloh.

If the Meteor pair could pass back quickly a favourable weather report the Vampires should arrive overhead Gütersloh just as the approaching warm front would be bringing the first low cloud and drizzle. However, Cunimb Jim had warned that the RAF clutch of airfields at Laarbruch, Brüggen and Wildenrath would all be black by then, that is below flying minima. Only Celle out East near the inner Germany border would remain a reliable diversion.

If the expected weather deterioration set in early or the Vampires arrived late a decision would have to be taken in the cruise at high level to head back to the by then clearing bases in Belgium. Once descended and committed to an instrument approach into Gütersloh it would be marginal in the extreme even to try and reach Celle; to return to the clutch stations West of the Rhine, if open, would probably be impossible; to Belgium still further to the north-west out of the question.

Squadron Leader Parsons who was keen to go and not to reschedule the navex made an interim decision. "Place your overnight bags in the noses of your aircraft, gentlemen. Complete your external and internal pre-flight checks and strap in ready to depart," he instructed. "If Flight Lieutenant Buchan and Mr Simpson report positively on the met conditions, you'll see me give the wind up hand signal to start engines, which will be relayed to you by the marshallers.

"My two sections of four will do a formation take off with an interval of thirty seconds between them. Once airborne I will pull high and the second section keep low. A flight will join up in an Eastbound clearing turn to port. Once up through the stratocumulus layer we shall ease out to battle formation reverting to close formation only for the approach and landing at Gütersloh. Flight Lieutenant Du Toit leading B Flight will follow exactly the same procedure with his two sections a minute later."

Jamie felt he was lucky to share a cockpit with the Flight Commander for what was for the cadets an epic sortie. Peter Carrick was even luckier. He was with Squadron Leader Parsons witnessing all the principle decisions.

Soon Peter's inner helmet earphones were crackling, "Cranwell tower to Bluebird formation; clear to start up and taxi to runway 26 left, wind $270°$ fifteen knots." Instantaneously Squadron Leader Parsons was giving the wind up signal with his white kid leather gloved right hand whilst placing his left on the throttle and the engine igniter button.

Almost at once the first eight aeroplanes were advancing down the perimeter track towards the duty runway with the cadets unusually doing the pre-flight checks on the move to save time and fuel whilst their QFIs taxied the aircraft. Suddenly an anguished radio call went out in the unmistakably Pakistani intonation of Yousuf Ahmed. "Bluebird Leader from Red Three I've left my oxygen tube behind."

"I can't believe it," expostulated Parsons on the intercom to Carrick. "How on earth do you go through all the checks and arrive almost at the runway threshold only to find you have no oxygen tube?" Calmly Parsons transmitted, "Roger, Red Three," in reply and then, "Cranwell tower expedite delivery of oxygen tube to Red Three with his canopy open in section astern."

"The CFI will hear about this," Parsons muttered testily into his mask and began to look at his watch. It seemed like an eternity before the duty Land Rover arrived with the grey elephant trunk like oxygen tube for Yousuf. It had only taken five minutes, not quite long enough to abort the sortie but certainly sufficient time to make a weather induced diversion even more problematical.

How Jamie loved formation take offs – the chop sign of the leader as he called "rolling rolling go" and eased the throttle progressively forward to almost full power, with his friends latched on either side; the smooth raising of the undercarriage and flaps so as not to induce oscillation and then as on this occasion the corner cutting at low level as Du Toit wheeled his section hard to port to join up with Parsons' lead flight, which was now boring into the first thin layer of stratus south-east of the field.

Out over East Anglia the patchy stratus broke completely. Jamie could clearly pick out the big American air base of Lakenheath. This landscape below of fine churches and wide horizons was United States Army Air Force country in World War II Jamie recollected. Condensation trails now marked out the peaceful flight to Germany of his friends; then the onward march to flame and battle of high Flying Fortresses and Liberator bombers, for all too many young American crews a one way mission to wounds, captivity or death.

Once past the English coast and out of sight of land Jamie immediately sensed a change of engine note. Normally the de Havilland Goblin was reliable and unobtrusive emitting an unmistakable whine outside but very little noise within the cockpit. It was so reliable that Jamie verged on the perfunctory in his engine monitoring except in the circuit where a ham fisted forward throttle movement on the approach to check an undershoot on landing would lead to an ugly groaning sound, a possible surge and even compressor stall. Otherwise its performance was unnoteworthy.

Now over the sea Jamie's awakened senses detected suspicious grinding and rasping noises emanating from the single engine beneath him. His normally quiescent imagination kicked in. Had a surge on a previous sortie fatally overheated the turbine blades? Did an ingested stone, bird or undetected foreign object damage the compressor? Were the combustion chambers cracking? All the engine instruments indicated normal readings. The airspeed was unaffected and no one in the formation warned of smoke or flames from his jetpipe so all must be well, but why the persistent and most disturbing noises?

Hyperanxiety was soon replaced by calming practical considerations. Du Toit was in radio contact with Gütersloh and requesting its present weather. The cloud below was unbroken and seemed almost to reach their cruising altitude of thirty-six thousand feet. Gütersloh's response though prosaically phrased was disquieting, "Two eighths stratus at two hundred feet, six eighths at three hundred feet, visibility five hundred yards in moderate to heavy precipitation."

"Thank you Gütersloh approach. Data copied. Request diversion met," called back Du Toit.

"Wildenrath and Brüggen black flag. Laarbruch has just reopened with eight eighths cloud at two hundred feet in persistent light drizzle; visibility four hundred yards. Celle is reporting one eighth at three hundred feet and eight eighths starting at four hundred feet with visibility of six hundred yards in moderate drizzle. For your information Bluebird Leader's Flight is established in descent into Gütersloh."

"Roger, Gütersloh approach we shall follow them down in turn," Du Toit replied, then: "Bluebird Green and Yellow sections prepare for pairs QGH descent into GCA approach to Gütersloh." Jamie was impressed by Du Toit's absorption of crucial information in little more than sixty seconds and almost instantaneous decisions. The reality was, however, that as Leader of the second Flight he had been preparing mentally for complications on arrival for the whole second half of the navex.

He had noted en route that Cunimb Jim's prognostications on the weather were largely correct. His fuel state was already down to nine hundred pounds. Others in the Flight would have less. The Leader always had the most. To return to Laarbruch against the strong upper level winds to an airfield with conditions even more marginal than Gütersloh would have spelt disaster if the met there had worsened or a pair had missed their approach and had to go round again. Celle's weather looked likely to get worse and Parsons' sections were already committed to Gütersloh. Du Toit decided his Flight would follow his Squadron Commander down.

Jamie and the other cadets would experience for themselves the challenge of recovering a fighter squadron to base in bad weather with the usual low fuel state, an operation which required impeccable airmanship, correctly executed procedures and supremely accurate instrument flying. Otherwise as had happened in the past aircraft would be scattered all over West Germany with pilots ejecting in despair or pressing on with potentially fatal consequences to attempted landings at inappropriate air bases in weather far below their minima.

Soon Du Toit and Jamie were overhead the field. His Number Two with China Chu on board was latched tightly onto his wingtip as they entered into the descent plunging with throttle back and airbrakes out into cloud as thick and dark as London peasouper fog. As they turned inbound Jamie saw to his consternation that Du Toit had wildly overbanked. His wingman would never notice and just follow him into any attitude however extreme. Perhaps Du Toit's preoccupations had uncharacteristically interrupted his scanning of the instruments. "Watch your bank, sir," Jamie exclaimed, the first time he had cause to correct his QFI. It was well that he did so and Du Toit was grateful.

"Good for you, Jamieson," he replied. "I've got her now."

Soon they were handed over to the Ground Controlled Approach and the melifluously reassuring instructions of the WAAF talk down radar controller began, "Green One and Two established on the glidepath. Maintain. Right two degrees, 272°. Hold it. Heading is good. Slightly above the glidepath, adjust your rate of descent. Back on the glidepath. Maintain. Left left three degrees, 269°. Slipping just a little low. Adjust your rate of descent. Approaching decision height. Heading and glidepath are good. Maintain. Like the best of wives this anonymous disembodied siren voiced lady with the purest English diction was wooing her errant man home thought Jamie.

"We're at two fifty feet, do you have the lights?" called Du Toit with his head down in total concentration on the blind flying instruments, snapping Jamieson out of his reverie.

"Not yet, sir."

"Three more seconds and we go round again."

"There they are! Left a bit, sir."

"Green Leader visual," called Du Toit as Jamie glanced to his right to see China waving cheerfully from his Vampire still about a mere foot and a half from Du Toit's green starboard wingtip navigation light.

Almost at once they were across the red threshold lights and past the two Hunters on Quick Reaction Alert on the Operational Readiness Platform. Du Toit flared just slightly putting the aircraft firmly down on the puddle lined runway and braking gently so as to turn off at the very end of the runway to allow maximum space for Green Three and Four coming along closely behind.

Jamie took over control from Du Toit who did the after landing checks and radio calls. An RAF Land Rover with a yellow Follow Me Sign on its tailboard appeared out of the murk and led them to a distant dispersal where already eight Vampires and two Meteors were aligned. Within five minutes the whole pan was full with all sixteen Vampires. Soon Jamie and his friends were sharing coffee, Kit Kats and experiences in the crewroom with the pilots of 14 Squadron's Hunters of whom a quarter were familiar faces from earlier Cranwell Entries.

That night the Officers' Mess laid on an informal Guest Night for the visiting party from Cranwell. It was a memorable occasion with an American Football match between the home team and the visitors in the anteroom. Sofas and armchairs were left in position to add an obstacle course to the game, which had no rules other than that only the man with the ball could be tackled. The College's superior fitness prevailed and miraculously there were no casualties. Few cadets got to bed before three with Met. Briefing at seven in the morning. It was lucky that they had their QFIs with them to captain the aeroplanes on the way back.

As Higgins and Jamieson walked down to the briefing hall in crisp wintry sunshine Carl could not let the Gütersloh visit pass without sharing his melancholy thoughts about Angela. "I don't think I'll ever be able to set foot in Germany without thinking of Angela, Jamie," he said.

"I remember well that you were very fond of her, Carl," Jamie replied.

"It was much more than that, Jamie. I felt part of her body and soul. Do you remember La Bruyère's comment? We love well but once, it's the first time: the loves that follow are less involuntary," responded Jamie. "But aren't you just as involuntarily involved with Yasmin?" Jamie insisted.

"It may be so, Jamie, but there's a certain unspoken and inherent reticence between us. At one level it increases the intensity because both of us know in our inner heart that we could never marry. The barriers of family, religion and custom are just too great so there is a cathartic quality, an urgency to our love while it lasts. However, with Angela although I knew her only very briefly it felt like a 'till death do us part' relationship. I could just never imagine that death would part us quite so soon," Carl explained.

"But you got over her loss remarkably well, if I may say so," observed Jamie. "You never seemed too distressed or unutterably bereft at the College and then the exotic Yasmin wafted into your life."

"You're right in a way, Jamie," responded Carl. "Whilst I was actually flying I was completely all right and on the ground the intense daily pressures of Cranwell life helped, too, but now I'm over here my innate identification with Germany and the feel of the country where I spent such happy years as a boy cause my feelings for her to come flooding back."

"It's amazing Carl," Jamie answered, "how the products of two home countries of your boyhood of Germany and Pakistan, Angela and Yasmin should have meant so much to you. My Janey is a Lincolnshire lass through and through albeit with a debby veneer but I'd had nothing to do with the county in my life. Indeed like Henry VIII I imagined it the most brutish in the Kingdom, although I appreciate it very much now."

"True but Janey represents all that to which you subliminally aspired when you joined the Service," Carl objected; "the role of a country gentleman in the making via an honourable career in the Royal Air Force, which has Lincolnshire as its spiritual home."

The en route and arrival weather forecasts could not have been better for the return flight – eight eighths blue all over north-west Europe with outstanding visibility and no excessive headwinds. Squadron Leader Parsons and Peter Carrick led the two flights out as one formation. Peter Lascelles and Ronald Anderson who followed in the two Meteors had a wonderful view from the holding point at the end of the runway as their Vampire friends took off in formation in four sections of four aircraft.

As the high altitude wind was less adverse further North they left the continent over the Zuider Zee and inbound passed the Wash danger area with its bombing ranges well to the South coasting in over Strubby's runway leaving Mablethorpe's serial ranks of caravan parks to starboard overflying Manby and Louth's prominent church spire and skirting the long East-West runway of Coningsby beside Tattershall castle.

Parsons called his flights into echelon starboard for the run in as they continued their fast descent towards base lining up over the greenhouses at Ruskington past the white tombstone flecked churchyard at Cranwell village, and then along the main runway at Cranwell south for a level break at the end onto the downward leg.

CHAPTER 15

All at the College would know that the Vampires were back. Then just as Jamie and Pierre Du Toit had stepped from the cockpit and taken off their helmets there could be heard the unique 'blue note' of two Meteors at high speed and low level as they hurtled along the pan little higher than the upraised canopies of the parked Vampires before breaking upwards to port into the circuit pattern to complete the dramatic homecoming of eighteen elated and soon to graduate Flight Cadets and their proud QFIs.

On return from the navex to Germany little remained to be done to complete the course other than rehearsals for the Passing Out Parade and a couple of solo practices for the Final Handling Test with the Chief Flying Instructor. Failure at this stage was almost unknown, not because the CFI was lax or lenient with errors but because the whole three years of training had been uncompromisingly demanding. No one would be put up for the FHT by his QFI unless he was certain that the cadet would pass. Flight Cadets could now with confidence invite family and friends to their graduation.

Jamie's parents were particularly keen to attend. His father had hardly been back to Lincolnshire since his days on Lancasters at Ludford Magna during the war. Jamie would try to dissuade him from undertaking a depressing pilgrimage to the county's disused bomber bases with their dilapidated hangars, cracked runways, windowless control towers and hardstandings overgrown with weeds. Nevertheless he was to stay at the Petwood Hotel in Woodall Spa, the Dambusters' old Officers Mess.

Sylvia would dutifully as ever accompany Peter Carrick to the Ball. For Elizabeth this would be her last function at Cranwell as her father had been posted to Kinloss in Morayshire in the New Year – Polarbear country in her terminology. The Ahmeds were definitely coming, which gladdened Carl Higgins' heart. Ronald Anderson, an only child, had invited his elderly widowed mother from Bulawayo in Rhodesia. She had her flight to London booked and he had made a reservation for her in the George at Stamford, which he regarded as the epitome of an English country hotel. They had not seen each other for almost three years. At the Ball he would have to trawl the bars for a dancing partner, as Alice had exams at Bedford College that day.

Peter Lascelles was the first to take his Final Handling Test. It went so well that he was informed that he was in the running for the Kinkhead Trophy for flying. Ronald Anderson was delighted for him. "You should be able now to get your pick of the postings, Peter," he suggested optimistically after Peter's post FHT debriefing. "What will it be?"

"Canberras actually," Peter replied. "I've come to appreciate after a year on Meteors the sense of security you get from two engines and I'd enjoy having a crew. A fighter pilot's life is an egocentric one by comparison. What about you, Ron?" Peter enquired.

"It may surprise you, Peter, but I don't really mind," Ronald responded. "After being put down an Entry I just want to pass out. I'm still quite nervous about my FHT and I've only got one more practice left."

With just a week remaining till the Passing Out Parade Cunimb Jim's synoptic charts were studied extremely carefully at Met Briefing for clues as to the likely weather on the great day. It would be too miserable if the guests could not get to Cranwell for graduation because of snow or ice and those cadets like Ronald Anderson who needed more flying practice before the FHT were apprehensive lest bad weather should preclude it.

The sixth day before Passing Out dawned clear but very windy. Jamie was detailed to take command of the early morning Passing Out Parade rehearsal which went perfectly. His award of the Sword of Honour was seen now as a virtual certainty. Afterwards those cadets who had scrounged a lift with their QFI on the practice passing out formation fly past plus a handful who still had some flying hours to complete bicycled cheerfully down to the Flight Lines.

"This will be my last flight in England," cried Yousuf Ahmed to Ronald Anderson. "Pakistan here I come! Pakistan Zindabad! I just want to see for myself before I go what it feels like to be in the flypast. What brings you down here, Ron?"

"My last trip on my own before the CFI puts me to the test," answered Ronald. "I confess I'm a bit anxious. I should be more confident by now but I'm terrified I'll make some terrible balls up and fall at the last hurdle."

"Don't worry Ronald old boy," Yousuf responded encouragingly. "I'll be the first to buy you a congratulatory drink when it's all over."

"That assurance does my morale the power of good," Ron called back. "I suppose I'm lucky actually because I've got my final solo practice later this morning and my test in the afternoon. So with any luck I'll be in the bar when it opens this evening to accept your beer."

Apart from Ronald Anderson there were only three other Flight Cadets – China Chu, Peter Carrick and Jamieson who needed one last practice before their test. They set off once the aeroplanes from the flypast were down and refuelled, immediately after Ronald who was the first away as no Meteors were required for the flypast. Jamie headed off north-east for some upper air work whilst China and Peter remained in the circuit doing touch and go landings – normal, flapless and short. Suddenly their practices were interrupted by the tower, "Cranwell call signs please clear circuit for a practice forced landing. Will call you back on completion."

Both Vampires went over to the Fulbeck satellite airfield nearby to continue their circuit work. Ronald Anderson at about ten thousand feet over Lincoln had brought his starboard engine back to idling power calling: "Cranwell Approach Tango Four Zero passing Waddington inbound to you. Flight Level One Zero for practice forced landing. Airfield in sight, to Cranwell Tower."

Jamie who was over the disused airfield of East Kirkby doing aerobatics clearly heard Ronald's transmission and thought no more of it. He was enjoying himself and was particularly proud of his Derry Turns whereby he converted a tight turn in one direction into one in the other by means of a hundred and eighty degree roll through the inverted attitude without losing any height. He earnestly hoped that the CFI would be impressed with his now smooth uninterrupted sequence of aerobatic manoeuvres, which he reckoned was at the heart of his fighter pilot credentials.

China and Peter who were dutifully flogging the circuit at Fulbeck heard Ronald call, "Tango Four Zero finals. Three Greens. Roller." Then almost immediately, "I can't hold her. Mayday Mayday." By then Jamie who was back overhead Cranwell at three thousand feet waiting to rejoin the circuit saw a spurt of flame just North of the runway threshold followed by billowing black smoke.

Almost immediately he spotted a red fire tender and blue ambulance leave their parking place beside the control tower and advance across the grass to the scene of the blaze, followed by a couple of Land Rovers – probably belonging to the CFI and Air Traffic Control thought Jamie. Cranwell Tower called up forthwith, "We have an emergency. All call signs diverted to Waddington." There much shaken by what had clearly fatally befallen Anderson they refuelled. On rejoining the Cranwell circuit a couple of hours later the full horror became apparent on landing as they rolled past an inchoate foam smothered heap of wreckage beside the main runway piled up at the end of a long black scorch mark gouged out of the grass.

Back in the crewroom Jamie, China and Peter ascertained from the QFIs what horrific tragedy had overtaken their Rhodesian friend. According to Pierre Du Toit, Jamie's instructor and unofficial South African mentor to Ronald, he had hopelessly underestimated the effect of the strong wind on the approach, got on the wrong side of the drag curve putting down full flap much too early and began to sink stone like towards the wooded undershoot area.

In his eagerness to replicate faithfully a real forced landing he had not opened up his idling simulated dead engine to correct the dangerous situation but the good one to full power. Being far too slow the consequent asymmetric torque was uncontrollable and to the horror of all who saw it Ron's aeroplane yawed violently to starboard. Then the port wing went up, the nose dropped further to the right and it almost cart-wheeled into the grass beside the runway virtually inverted.

The death of Ron Anderson only six days before the passing out parade which was reported on radio and television and in all the newspapers hit the Entry hard. Peter Lascelles his fellow pupil on Meteors was particularly distraught. Ron had told him that he had secured a special twenty-four hour pass to go and greet his mother on arrival at Heathrow next day. Who would meet her now and who would break to her the dreadful news?

Peter bicycled down to see the Meteor Flight's Commanding Officer Flight Lieutenant Buchan as soon as he heard of the accident. David Buchan and Peter Lascelles had become very close over the past year. Lascelles was undoubtedly the best pupil Buchan ever had. When it came to flying Peter's application was total. He had admitted that passing out well and securing the posting of his choice was his sole ambition.

Anderson, however, had been more relaxed. Mr Simpson his instructor had felt that he was doing well without undue effort. He had been especially pleased that Ron shared his almost artistic love of aerobatics. He judged that for all Anderson's bad academic reports he had the makings of a natural pilot.

The loss was a harbinger of the end of Master Pilot Simpson's long flying career. He had already rashly promised his wife Madge to hang up his aircrew overalls at the end of the following year. When he got home to the married patch she would doubtless be on at him to bring forward his retirement. He would just have to point out that he already had a new pupil on the Entry below and that he would have to see his course through which should at least give him another four months in the cockpit.

The death of such a thoroughly likeable kid just before graduation was bad enough in itself but it was too depressing to have Madge endlessly repeating her wearisome demand that he provide more security for the family; her tiresome question why at his age he stayed in a job, which always entailed such ghastly episodes; and that he had to be responsible now and realise that flying was a young man's game and that he was not as young as he had been.

At least Mr Simpson could console himself by reflecting that the cause of Anderson's demise was classic pilot error and that as his QFI he was in no way to blame whatever his wife might imagine. He and Ron had done countless practice forced landings together and he had always reminded Ronald to maintain sufficient height and to keep a margin of speed in hand because once you got low and slow on one engine the outcome was all too often disastrous.

David Buchan was at his office desk in the Meteor hangar next to the QFIs crewroom when Peter knocked on the door, entered and saluted. "You'll get your wings the day after tomorrow, Peter," Buchan observed as he raised his eyes from the letter of condolence he was writing in long hand to Ronald Anderson's mother, "but I expect that normally happy event is the last thing on your mind today."

"We're all shocked by Ron's accident," the Flight Lieutenant continued, "and I expect you want to talk to me about it. We'll miss him very much and I am sure his death will have left a big hole in your life."

"It certainly has, sir, but I've come to see you about some important practicalities," Peter replied. "I could not help but notice that you're writing to his mother and I'm sure she'll be glad to know how much her son was appreciated by everyone at the College. However, she's widowed and Ron was her only son. He never spoke to me of any relatives but her. She'll be flying in from Rhodesia tomorrow. She must be en route now so someone will have to break the awful news to her on arrival and what happens to her then?"

"I've thought about all this already, Peter, and I've discussed the situation with the Assistant Commandant," the Flight Commander answered. "First of all," he went on, "I don't want any blame attached to poor old Anderson. There's an official inquiry to come. Of course he should have thrown away his practice forced landing as soon as he realised he could not make the airfield. Never let pride, Peter, induce you to carry through an exercise or a manoeuvre which has gone dangerously wrong."

"Nevertheless," Buchan insisted, "not a word of criticism against Ron must get to his mother's ears. I shall go to Heathrow to meet her myself and drive her back to the College where she will stay in our home in North Hykeham for the duration. Ron's funeral will take place with full military honours in Cranwell village church. I shall invite her to the graduation parade and the CFI hopes to entertain her to lunch."

"If I may say so as your former pupil, sir, you always had the reputation of being a most caring officer even though you were very strict in the air. What you have proposed seems to me to represent Cranwell at its best. We will all be able to celebrate Ron's life in the way in which the College excels, that is on parade. Mrs Anderson will rightly feel great pride in her son and it is good that she should attend the passing out parade and that the CFI should host a special lunch for her. A final suggestion if I may, sir. Could we not send over three Meteors in salute as Ronald is lowered into his grave," Peter suggested.

"I agree, Peter, it shall be done," David Buchan responded. "Now can you let me get on with my letter writing. Could you tell your friends in Cadet Wing what has been decided?"

"I shall, sir. I cannot thank you enough," Peter answered.

"Think no more of it, Peter. What we propose is the least the College could do. We like to honour our own," the Flight Commander explained.

Next day the few outstanding Final Handling Tests were completed. The Senior Entry began to clear their rooms and to pack their belongings. Peter Lascelles, Carl Higgins and Jamie telephoned Mrs Buchan and invited themselves to her home to express their condolences to Mrs Anderson. "I know David will be pleased to see you" she replied. "I'm sure that Mrs Anderson, too, will be very glad to meet Ron's best friends. Your presence for tea will take some of the pressure off all of us. With luck David should be back by six. Come then between six thirty and seven. It'll be good to meet you all. I've heard so much about you. I only wish the circumstances were happier."

Peter, Carl and Jamie jumped into Peter's Morris Minor and headed off to North Hykeham. The Buchans' hiring was at the far end of the village – a converted farmhouse which was usually let out to professional people who commuted to Lincoln or Sleaford but now the Buchans rented it for David's three year tour. When they arrived Mrs Buchan was preparing tea in the kitchen for her two young daughters, Priscilla and Katie. "Welcome all of you!" she exclaimed opening the heavy front door. "Come through to the kitchen. David's not back yet and I'm in the middle of giving the girls their tea."

"What a lovely home," Jamie remarked warmly.

"Well we're very happy here," Mrs Buchan responded eagerly. "We've been so lucky. We had a very pretty place in Oakham when David was at North Luffenham and a comfortable bungalow on the outskirts of Huntingdon when he was at Waterbeach. So far we've managed to avoid Married Quarters, but I imagine that may be difficult if he gets his own squadron."

"Yes I fear it's an occupational hazard," Peter commented, "but eventually you should be able to put down roots later in David's career." At this the cocker spaniel snoozing in front of the fire started to whistle.

"That'll be David," interjected Mrs Buchan. "Bruno's got a sixth sense for the arrival of the Cortina. Come on through to the sitting room and I'll go and greet them."

"Claire, this is Mrs Anderson," Jamie heard Buchan say. "We've had a very smooth journey up the A1 and stopped for a late lunch at the George in Stamford. Mrs Anderson wanted so badly to see it."

"Of course," Claire Buchan replied. "It's typically English. You are very welcome here, Mrs Anderson," she went on. "We were all deeply shocked by Ron's tragic death. Please accept our profound sympathy. Now do make yourself thoroughly at home. Just instal yourself by the fire and I'll go and make you a cup of tea and bring you some cakes and scones. Before I do so I want to introduce three of Ron's best friends to you, Jamie, Peter and Carl."

For a little while the austerely impassive tall white haired and imposing Mrs Anderson hesitated in the doorway. She then moved towards the group at the fireside with her arm outstretched. The three Flight Cadets stood up, shook her hand and awkwardly mumbled words of condolence.

"I am so sorry about your loss," said Jamie directly. "Please accept my heartfelt condolences," added Carl and finally Peter declared more emotionally than the rest, "I shall miss Ron terribly, Mrs Anderson. He became my best friend. You should be very proud of him."

"I am indeed," Mrs Anderson replied simply.

"Aren't you Peter Lascelles, Ronald's fellow Meteor pupil?" she enquired. "Ron always wrote so warmly about you and about what fun it was to fly with you down at your own special Meteor flight. I am fortunate that your Flight Commander and Mrs Buchan are looking after me like this. I could not have a better memorial of Ronald than the company of his friends."

"I always felt that we were in good hands under Flight Lieutenant Buchan's strict but benign supervision, Mrs Anderson," Lascelles responded. "Another of Ron's close friends Peter Carrick will be coming over shortly just as soon as his final interview with his Cadet Wing Squadron Commander is finished. He has spoken to a further friend Yousuf Ahmed about the arrangements for you who I'm afraid can't be here for the same reason as Peter Carrick but sends you his deepest sympathy."

Just then the door bell rang and Carrick was ushered in and introduced. "What a terrible thing, Mrs Anderson," he began. "Ron will be utterly irreplaceable for all of us. He was a great guy to be with and spread such happiness all around him."

"I know," said Mrs Anderson. "He always wrote home most positively about the Air Force. He never wanted to do anything else but be a pilot in the RAF. His late father encouraged him by taking him to the flying club in Bulawayo. He was thrilled beyond measure when he was accepted for a cadetship at Cranwell."

"I'm sure he must have written to you about his lovely girlfriend Alice Van Meer, Mrs Anderson," Carrick went on. "You'll be relieved to hear that his friend Yousuf Ahmed's sister Yasmin has broken the awful news to Alice. She says that Alice is heartbroken of course – they were very close – but wants to come here and to be with you for a while. She's due at Cranwell tomorrow and the Buchans have agreed she can stay with them, too. She'll accompany you to Ron's funeral, to the passing out parade and the Chief Flying Instructor's lunch afterwards. She has got special dispensation from her exams to be with you."

"You are all so thoughtful," Mrs Anderson answered.

"It's the least we can do," Peter Lascelles replied. "Ron was a friend to all of us and set us an example we can never forget. Now if you'll forgive us we must be on our way. The postings are due out tonight as is the list of the prize winners. Tomorrow is the prize giving and wings ceremony in College Hall. We'll see you and Alice there. Thank you again, Mrs Buchan. You're in good hands now, Mrs Anderson."

The next day was the penultimate Passing Out Parade rehearsal under the command of Senior Under Office Jamieson who carried a natural authority for the role. His orders were always calmly delivered and perfectly timed to keep the ranks of Flight Cadets within the appropriate confines of the Parade Square. "That'll do very nicely, Mr Jamieson," the College Warrant Officer grunted to him afterwards which was rare praise indeed. Cadets used the rest of the day for graduation interviews with Cadet Wing Flight and Squadron Commanders.

Yousuf Ahmed who had time to spare slipped down to Flights for a nostalgic final sortie in a Vampire in the last formation practice for the Passing Out Parade. Squadron Leader Parsons who was always sympathetic to enthusiastic cadets took Ahmed with him with alacrity and led off the second wave of a formation twice as large as that which had gone to Gütersloh. This time it was a true "Wing Ding" thought Yousuf the like of which he would probably never experience till, God willing, he was an operational fighter pilot in Pakistan.

Section after section followed Parsons down the runway – high, low, high, low and after take off once airborne swung round hard to port straining to catch up in the climb with the distant shapes of the CFI's squadron already over Sleaford heading purposefully north-east towards the Wolds. On such a brilliant frosty morning Ahmed could see right across the county of his temporary home from the spires of Lincoln Cathedral to the West to Boston Stump to the East. The other landmarks were mostly airfields, active and disused – Coningsby and Binbrook, East Kirkby and Spilsby, Metheringham, Manby and Woodhall Spa. Yousuf felt he was undertaking a farewell tour of these by now familiar reassuring places before the formation made a thrilling low level overpass of Spilsby and then from Heckington and Ruskington villages the concluding run in for the flyby of the College.

Yousuf wondered if he would ever live so intensely as he had at Cranwell. He glanced at the gently undulating sections of twin boomed Cambridge blue striped Royal Air Force College Vampires latched on to Parsons at either side and glimpsed down to the Parade Square below where would come the great culmination in forty-eight hours time in front of his proud parents and his wonderful glamorous sister Yasmin. Certainly there would be no lack of intensity to life if he had to to go war as he felt was likely with the belligerent Indians always keen to seize Azad Kashmir, which had eluded them in 1948.

He emerged from his reverie to note that they were climbing hard towards Fulbeck. The CFI's squadron had by now detached itself to return to base and Parsons' lot were starting a wide arc of a turn past Barkston Heath, in his memory the scene of carefree "Good Old Days" of summer on the venerable Piston Provost. In another minute and a half Parsons had called his QFIs alongside into echelon starboard as they concluded their positioning turn over Cranwell village where Yousuf recalled they had a solemn duty to perform for poor old Ronald Anderson in the churchyard tomorrow.

"Breaking, breaking, go," called Parsons over the far end of the runway easing back on the throttle, extending the airbrake and curving round onto the downward leg. "You have her now, Yousuf. Do the radio calls and make this final landing your best."

"I will sir," replied Yousuf as he popped in the airbrake, dropped the undercarriage and concluded his downwind checks initiating a curved approach opposite the runway caravan, lining up precisely at three hundred and fifty feet and kissing the numbers on the threshold with the gentle delicacy of a first date. "That'll do nicely, maestro," joked Parsons as they turned off down the taxiway for Ahmed's last shutdown on English soil.

After tea everyone rushed to the notice board outside College Hall. In official black typescript on pale blue Royal Air Force College paper was marked out the destiny of the Entry – Beverley and Hastings Transports, Shackleton Maritime reconnaissance aircraft, Valiant and Canberra bombers, Hunter fighters, and helicopters and for creamed off instructors of the future, the Central Flying School. Ahmed topped the list in a special category – Commonwealth Air Forces (Pakistan). Then came Senior Under Officer Jamieson – Hunters, Chivenor followed by Under Officer Lascelles – Canberras, Bassingbourn. Senior Flight Cadet Carl Higgins – Central Flying School, Little Rissington, SFC Peter Carrick – Beverleys, Abingdon and SFC Chu also Central Flying School.

All assembled in the bar to discuss their future. There had been few surprises. Jamie was continuing on his charmed way with the most desirable posting of all.

Lascelles had always wanted to stay on twins. Carrick as a sturdy Yorkshireman was well suited to the Beverley. Even the aircraft's name was redolent of the county. "Who knows," joked Carl, "you might well be posted back to Yorkshire. Dishforth would suit you fine. I'm sure Sylvia would be happy there."

"Don't be surprised if the last laugh is on me," retorted Peter. "There's a really good chance that you'll be the Yorkshire lad, Carl, struck at Linton on Ouse in the foggy Vale of York and still on Vampires. At least you'll be ideal for instructing on the use of the sick bag, won't you Honkers? What's more I'll see the world on Beverleys, even if it's mostly the sands of Arabia and those four Centaurus engines make me prematurely deaf."

"It's been an incredible three years," mused Peter Lascelles aloud. "Remember the inimitable Taffy Jones. Such a shame. I wonder what posting he would have got or my poor old chum Ronald Anderson whom we've got to bury tomorrow."

"Didn't his QFI Mr Simpson ever let on?" asked Jamie.

"Not really," Peter replied, "except that Ron was a man after his own heart, a most accomplished aerobaticist. So he might have gone onto Hunters. Perhaps you're just his substitute, Jamie."

"You may not believe it but I shall miss Cranwell," said Carl. "After what we've been through we know each other very well. I'm sure we'll be able to rely on each other till the end of our days. You'll think me sentimental," he went on, "but I'll miss the roses round the Orange in summer, the cowslips on the North Airfield in spring, the nightingales in the copse at the far end, skylarks on the High Dyke and wild roses in the hedges on the way to the Houblon Arms at Oasby."

"Don't forget those glacial grey days in May," interjected Carrick, "with North Easterlies from the Siberian Tundra sweeping in to Cranwell from the North Sea."

"I prefer to be more positive," insisted Jamie. "For me it's the autumn mist rising in the Trent Valley at early evening after a hard afternoon's beagling and the thought of tea in a farmhouse kitchen to come."

"For me," said Lascelles, "it's morning parade and the strains of the Lincolnshire Poacher on the air with the distant wail of the Goblins starting down on the Flightline. The cry of the jets will summon us all until our days are done."

The final Passing Out Parade rehearsal was in everyone's mind more an overture for the Service funeral for Ron Anderson immediately to come then preparation for next day's graduation. Hardly had the parade rehearsal's ranks been dismissed than the Flight Cadets were forming up outside the East Wing with Ronald's Union Flag draped coffin on a gun carriage in their midst. The black arm banded escort party flanked the cortege with arms reversed as the procession left the College to Chopin's funeral march. Beyond the station Post Office a big bass drum took over from the band. Mrs Anderson and the Buchans came behind in a black limousine, followed by the Commandant, Assistant Commandant, Flying and Cadet Wing executives and their wives all in their own Service vehicles with their bonnet pennants at half mast.

On reaching Cranwell village the band struck up funeral marches again and the procession wheeled into the tiny churchyard. It was the wish of Mrs Anderson that her son should have the simplest of graveside services for which the Church of England liturgy for the Burial of the Dead was well suited.

"Man that is born of woman has but a short time to live," intoned the Padre. Jamie looked across at Alice with her blonde locks tumbling around her shaking shoulders and at Mrs Anderson in her long black overcoat, veiled black hat, black gloves, black stockings and shoes standing erect with one arm firmly in that of Claire Buchan and the other held tremblingly by Alice.

What pride. What unutterable grief. "He cometh up and is cut down like a flower; he fleeth as it were a shadow. In the midst of life we are in death," the Padre's recitation continued. Doesn't every aviator know it thought Lascelles, "but spare us Lord most mighty," the Padre went on. How earnestly would each cadet be praying this. Peter's thoughts were interrupted by a sound too painful to bear of six Derwent engines of three overflying Meteors at full power. His tears now flowed silently and freely.

After the committal the escort party's shots rang out over the grave. Then one by one following Mrs Anderson's brave example the Commandant, the Assistant Commandant, all the executives of the College, Flight Lieutenant Buchan, Master Pilot Simpson, Alice and the whole of the Entry cast their handfuls of earth upon Ronald's coffin top. This final homage done the Flight Cadets formed up and marched off briskly to the Royal Air Force march past, turning to Old Comrades and finally the Lincolnshire Poacher as they came up to the College.

That evening the Senior Entry, their parents, fiancées, girlfriends and close relations, the College directing staff and Chief Executives met in College Hall for the wings ceremony and prize giving. The College band's string quartet discreetly played popular tunes from the musicals at the back of the stage. At the arrival of the Commandant, Assistant Commandant and the platform party the quartet began a chamber music rendition of the Royal Air Force march past.

The Commandant, a daunting but supremely laconic Air Commodore with a fearsome moustache promptly opened the proceedings with no speech of introduction. "I now award Flying Badges to the graduating Entry in alphabetical order," he began; "Under Officer Ahmed." Yousuf led his friends up one by one to have their flying brevets pinned to the breast of their Flight Cadet's uniform – the culmination of all their ambitions, so long awaited; in the event so routine an action.

Next equally simply came the prize giving. "Sword of Honour awarded to the best all round cadet, Senior Under Officer Jamieson. Philip Sassoon Memorial Prize to the runner up to the Sword of Honour winner, Senior Under Officer McIntyre, Queen's Medal for the cadet who has most excelled in academics, Under Officer Ellington, Kinkhead Trophy for the Flight Cadet adjudged to have displayed the highest aptitude as a pilot, Under Officer Lascelles… Ecole de l'Air Trophy for French studies. There being no cadet in this Entry who studied French I have decided to use my discretion to award this prize to Senior Flight Cadet Higgins for German studies." As he descended from the platform Carl noticed a blush suffusing the normally olive palor of Yasmin's face and that Mrs Anderson and Alice were clapping as vigorously as the happy families all around them. Carrick who won no prizes felt that the Air Commodore should have made more of the accomplishments of his friends and told Sylvia so.

The morning of graduation day dawned freezing and fogbound. There could be no hope of a flypast. Luckily the Reviewing Officer the Chief of Air staff had arrived at the Lodge the previous night. The parade turned out no different from all the others. The cadets had done it all so many times before. Jamie felt pride certainly at being Parade Commander but this special responsibility was no more than he had come to expect.

As they marched past the saluting base Lascelles caught Mrs Anderson's eye. He could never let Ronald's memory down he vowed. Carl looked for Yasmin but could not see her. Lascelles, however, certainly also saw Lizzie or at least her hat of exquisitely delicate eye catching pink, a most noticeably haute couture creation, which out glamorised all the other ladies' hats by far but which seemed singularly out of place in the freezing fog.

The ceremony only really came to life for two events – Jamie's receipt of the Sword of Honour from the Chief of Air Staff and then the Marshal of the Royal Air Force's address to the Flight Cadets. He praised them for their turnout and bearing but regretted that the bad weather had precluded a flypast, which he was sure would have been of the same high standard as the ceremonial drill which he had witnessed.

"Remember, gentlemen," he concluded, "that in air warfare no systems operator on the ground is as flexible, full of initiative and adaptability as a man in the cockpit of an aeroplane. Although this is increasingly the missile age manned aircraft will have a vital role in the future as far ahead as I can foresee, certainly throughout the careers of you on parade today. Pilots and Navigators be of good cheer you will be needed in the defence of our country just as much as your gallant predecessors who helped win the Battles of Britain, the Atlantic, the Air Offensive against Germany and countless other campaigns in Europe and around the globe."

All too soon Jamie was requesting permission of the Reviewing Officer to march off the Flight Cadets and Auld Lang Syne's melancholy melody percolated through the icy mist from the College Band's vantage point on the College steps to the assembled spectators. Huddled under their rugs, muffled up in their greatcoats and scarves few could fail to be affected to witness the ceremonial passing of another generation of cadets.

The Entry turned inwards and began the slow march towards and up the steps leaving their successor cadets in sole possession of the Parade Square. How eagerly Taffy Jones and Ron Anderson had awaited this moment thought Carl. How was it that this supreme experience should be vouchsafed to him and so cruelly denied to them. Anyway a wonderful day lay ahead. Yasmin had spoken of her anticipation for these moments. Now she had witnessed them. She felt her brother would bring great credit to the Pakistan Air Force as for himself. There was the Ball to enjoy and Yasmin's delicious company to be fully savoured. He entered the atrium beneath the cupola, threw his cap in the air and shouted in triumph and joy.

The Ball was less exhilarating than most of the graduating Entry expected. The experience of passing out was more exciting in anticipation than in its accomplishment. True it was good to wear well earned wings on the chest and to have a Pilot Officer's stripe on the sleeve but it was hard not to feel melancholy at the imminent scattering of such close knit friends. Also Ronald's funeral the day before could not be easily forgotten. Certainly the old Hut 150 group and the circle around them had got good postings but others were very disappointed. If you were headed for Hastings Transports ambitions to be a member of a formation aerobatic team would have to be foregone; likewise if you were designated to helicopters you had to dismiss any idea of commanding a fighter squadron.

Probably the happiest member of the Entry was Yousuf Ahmed. He knew that when he returned to Pakistan shortly he would have celebrity status as the first Cranwell graduate of the Pakistani Air Force; inevitably judged, he told himself as the prime candidate for the higher appointments. His Wing Commander father would be even more respected at the High Commission in London and the heightened esteem would be pleasurably shared by his mother and Yasmin as well.

From the moment that the first chords of the orchestra struck up Carl was invited to the Ahmeds' table and revelled in the euphoric atmosphere around it. The warmth of Yasmin's approbation of Carl's commissioning and selection as a potential creamed off QFI made her affection for him all too apparent to any perceptive observer, but her Air Adviser father was clearly putting away such large scotch whiskies and her mother was too engrossed in earnest conversation with Mary Wong about activities on the social circuit of Service attaches' wives in London to notice. Yousuf, too, was in high spirits. He had spotted Samantha in a clinging dress order herself gin and tonics at the bar, not exactly ladylike for an ex-debutante he thought but nevertheless decidedly promising for the evening ahead.

Jamie and Janey were the inevitable stars of the Ball. Although historically winners of the Sword of Honour had rarely risen to become Chiefs of the Air Staff his award was an eye turning success for everyone and would be a personal triumph to dine out on all over Lincolnshire during the short Christmas and New Year leave before Jamie went to Chivenor. As for Janey she had effortlessly dressed up for the occasion in a long silk duck egg blue dress and wore a spectacular pearl studied choker around her neck held in place in the front with a large emerald, which caught everyone's attention.

Lizzie, never one to conform readily to Air Force conventions was the sole guest in a short dress but she was the only girl present with the perfect long glamorous legs to carry it off. Peter admired her panache and was swept along with her social ambitions. With her parents due to be "marched out" of their quarter by the end of the week she had already quit her modelling job and got rid of her flat in Nottingham. "Peter's posting to Bassingbourn is perfect for me," she declared to Janey. "I'll be able to live in London and enjoy Peter's company much more frequently than when he was at Cranwell. All he will have to do is hop on a commuter train and within the hour he'll be in central London. I've got myself on the books of a West End model agency. Who knows Peter will soon get posted to Germany and I'll be back on the catwalks of Düsseldorf and Cologne by the end of next year."

Sylvia was too clinging for comfort thought Peter Carrick as they plodded their way through the slow dances and she confided to him, "I do hope you won't stay at Abingdon too long, Peter. You know Dishforth would be ideal for us. I'm sure I could get a job teaching in a village school or in Ripon perhaps. I love the city and I'm told there are plenty of Married Quarters available on the station. I trust that you won't have to do too many long flights down to Cyprus, Aden, Bahrain and so on."

"Please do remember, Sylvia dear, that the overseas trips are what make a posting onto Beverleys worthwhile," he responded. "It's certainly not the flying, that's like piloting a block of flats and the noise of those four huge piston engines at full power especially with water methanol injection is stupefying."

"Don't get me wrong, Peter," Sylvia responded. "I want you to enjoy your work, but I want us to enjoy each other's company, too." Peter's thoughts wandered to the mysterious Alice Van Meer, a blonde bombshell in his imagination. What a shame she could not be with them tonight. He would have to call round to the Buchans tomorrow to say goodbye to Mrs Anderson. Perhaps he could get Alice's phone number then somehow.

Once the Ball was over it was time for one last fling in the big house by courtesy of Janey. As was traditional her parents were away on their pre-Christmas shooting holiday in Ireland. Yousuf had cleverly booked his parents into the

Petwood at Woodhall Spa. "You'll love the half timbered old World War Two Bomber Mess, papa," he had argued. It was at least an hour and a half away in the thick fog, which gave him the time to enjoy Samantha's charms. Carl and Yasmin frolicked in a vast, seemingly medieval four poster bed upstairs. Lizzie gave a demonstration of modelling lingerie in front of the fire whilst Peter Carrick who was excluded from such fun and games drove Sylvia back to her hotel in Newark with a disc slipping interlude of sexual contortions in the back seat of his mini in a layby en route.

Next day the Entry were all quickly away from Lincolnshire except for Peter who headed home to Yorkshire via North Hykeham. Mrs Buchan was touched to see him again, "How good of you to call, Peter," she said in welcome. "You're the only one to have come round after the Ball. I'm sure Mrs Anderson will appreciate it enormously. I'll go upstairs and tell her you're here. Meanwhile Alice will make you a cup of coffee, won't you Alice?"

At least they had met properly and Alice was even lovelier than he imagined with a slightly tanned face, a definite South Africa twang to her voice and irresistible blonde hair, which cascaded down to her shoulders. "It is wonderful to meet one of Ron's real friends," she began. "It is so thoughtful of you to call on his mother once more before she goes."

"I just hope we can meet again, Alice, so that I can tell you more about him," Peter replied.

"That would be really nice," she said reassuringly.

"I could do it on my way to my new posting at Abingdon perhaps," he went on.

"That seems like a good idea to me," Alice answered encouragingly. "Here's my phone number." She slipped a piece of paper into his hand just as Mrs Anderson's footsteps rang out from the top of the staircase.

"I think it is wonderful of you to come round to see me again after the Parade and all the excitement of the Ball," Mrs Anderson exclaimed.

"I just wanted to wish you a safe journey back Mrs Anderson," Peter said, "and to tell you that you and Ronald will never be forgotten by us. If I find myself in Rhodesia on a Beverley flight I'll come and look you up."

"Please do that if you can Peter, it would make me so happy," responded the lovely old lady. "I won't forget Ron's friends either."

CHAPTER 16

Extraordinarily although Jamie's family home was so close to Royal Air Force Chivenor he had not actually visited the station before. Even if he had looked intently across the Taw estuary he would not have seen it. The wooden hutted encampment nestled virtually invisible on the flatlands behind Braunton Burrows between the Taw estuary and the railway line from nearby Barnstaple whose closest station was aptly named Wrafton. Here three years after his first day at Cranwell there began for Jamie a love affair with an aeroplane the Hawker Hunter which would mark him for life.

This time there was no snow on the ground on arrival. Instead the warm wet wind from the British Channel greeted him, which he had missed so much in the more bracing climates of Stowe and Cranwell. No ferocious Warrant Officer was waiting to confront him and he came in his own car and not the Collegiate blue grey bus.

The Officers' Mess Steward was polite and showed him to his hut carrying his suitcase and explained that showers and lavatories were to be found in another hut some thirty yards away. He reassured Jamie that his coal scuttle would be filled every other day and explained that flying clothes were not to be worn in the Mess. If he needed a snack between sorties during the lunch hour he would find a toaster to make hot cheese or ham sandwiches down at flights. Jamie felt that the South Brick Lines had prepared him well for his new existence as a fighter pilot in embryo.

From the moment that he presented himself to the Wing Commander Flying George Gillespie in his totally spartan office to the conclusion of the course in mid summer Jamie was never happier. Gillespie who sported an old-fashioned World War Two handlebar moustache and an Air Force Cross explained the Chivenor ethos to him very simply, in a gentle Scottish lilt, which belied his universal nickname of Grunt.

"Our job here is not to teach you to fly, Jamieson," he began. "We take that for granted. You are here to convert to the Hunter certainly but above all to operate the aeroplane and its systems in the day fighter role. You will learn air combat tactics and gunnery. However, to be frank you'll need another six months on a squadron to get fully operational and I doubt if you'll be able to get the best out of this fantastic aircraft until you've completed your first tour or at least logged over a thousand hours. Now present yourself to your Squadron Commander and then report to the simulator section to practise the cockpit drills and emergency procedures."

Jamie's Commanding Officer Squadron Leader Moxon, a quiet and well spoken Old Cranwellian was relaxed and welcoming and invited him to walk over to the pan so he could introduce him to the aeroplane. A special smell characterised the cockpit of a Hunter. It was indefinable, exhilarating and lodged in the brain of those who had known it like the smells of boyhood, which return to haunt the aging in later life with a sense of lost happiness.

"Install yourself in the office, Jamie," Moxon began, "and I'll show you the taps, knobs, dials and switches. You'll be happy to learn," he continued, "that this is the most pleasant aeroplane to fly that I have ever known. It is rugged and reliable with no real vices, responsive to the controls but not oversensitive although the stick forces are very high when engine or hydraulic failures entail a reversion from powered to manual controls. As you see the cockpit is spacious and not quite as luxuriously large as that of the F86 Sabre – but with good all round visibility. The Martin Barker Mark Four ejection seat is fully automatic. After you've pulled the face blind handle or the one between your legs you don't need to do a thing. The seat should extricate you from most predicaments so long as you have good forward speed when you bale out and a trajectory and attitude on departure from the aircraft of at least level flight.

"The Hunter is both a stable gunnery and instrument flying platform. Although the control column is long it does not excessively obscure the blind flying instruments and I personally prefer the brake lever to be on the stick as it is here and as on the dear old Vampire than on the rudder but where it is always possible with clumsy feet and heavy boots to overdo the braking. To me Hawker's have got it right.

"You will have noticed the dog tooth on the leading edge. Pitch up in tight manoeuvres was a bit of a problem with the Mark 1s, 2s and 4s but the dogtooth reduces spanwise air flow on the wing and you'll be able to pull more 'g' at altitude as a result. Also the Mark 6 version of the aeroplane has the more powerful series 200 of the faithful Avon engine to get you to where the action is much faster. Three thousand feet a minute faster initially.

"We allow you a week to learn all the aircraft's systems and to pass the ground school exam. During that time you'll have some sessions in the procedures trainer with the inimitable Polzol, an old acquaintance of yours I believe. He'll get you up to scratch on the emergency drills, requisite speeds, power settings and so on so that when you buckle a check list to your knee and we pat you a fond goodbye on the shoulder you can roar off into the wide blue yonder with complete confidence. Any questions Jamie?"

Max Moxon had the rare quality of innate empathic leadership. Questions did not much come to Jamieson's mind, more a feeling of deeply fulfilling acceptance. He knew that Moxon trusted him from the start; that he had complete confidence in his maturity, ability and training so that his rightful place in a man's world was naturally assumed before he had even strapped into a Hunter or taken a single ground school examination.

This sense of belonging was accentuated when he reported to the simulator section after breakfast next day. The simulator did not so much replicate the aeroplane in flight as provide a standard Hunter cockpit in which all the necessary actions could be practised from start up to shut down, and most importantly vital drills rehearsed for the most common emergencies like fire, engine flameout and mechanical failure, hydraulic, electrical, instrument oxygen and pressurisation problems.

It was drizzling hard, the kind of Atlantic warm frontal clamp for which all Western Approaches airfields from St Mawgan to Macrihanish were notorious. Even the normally vociferous curlew along the Taw estuary were muted by the clinging sea mist which shrouded the tops of the tin hangars and the orange windsock – just the day for a spell in the simulator which was located in a modest felt roofed hut behind the Met Office.

Jamieson knocked diffidently on the door. "Come in, Jamie, my boy," a familiar East European voice responded. "I knew you'd be the first of the new course to pay respects to your old friend Polzol," he continued. Jamieson crossed the threshold and entered the legendary Polish fighter ace's dusky domain of flashing lights and whirring machinery at the heart of which resided the bulky black contraption of the simulator and associated instrument console at the instructor's table, which assured Polzol continued gainful Air Force employment now his flying days were officially over.

"I never congratulated you on winning the Sword of Honour," Polzol began. "Actually I'd tipped you to do so since Barkston days but obviously could not let on. We had a book on it down at Pig flights. I won £10 on you. Squadron Leader Ashley thought you'd only get the Philip Sassoon prize. Now its not just the up and coming new generation like you, Jamie, who visit this Aladdin's cave of wondrous delights in search of skill and enlightenment but venerable retreads and Hunter squadron and station executives as well. I am host to the cream of RAF society in these simple surroundings.

"By the beginning of next week," he went on, "when they let you loose on the real aeroplane you'd be able to fly it blindfold and more importantly get it safely back if as all too often happens the unexpected befalls you. Now settle into the cockpit and I'll put you through your paces." At first it was easy enough. "Start up, Jamie," Polzol began. "Take off, climb to 35,000 feet on a heading of 330° and level out at cruising power."

Then the pressure mounted with a stream of instructions. "Do a couple of rate one turns, one in each direction through 360°. Now tighten it up to rate two and do the same. Hold your height and head 150°, airbrake out and throttle back for a max rate descent towards base. Remember to reset your altimeter and join the circuit. Don't forget your radio call; into the landing pattern. Onto final approach. What about your landing checks? Increase your rate of descent. Steady. Left 2°. Hold it. Up a bit. At three hundred feet I want you to overshoot and go round again. That's it, good, but remember power on and make sure you're definitely climbing before you raise the undercarriage and flaps. Back on the throttle now or you'll never reduce speed enough to lower the wheels downwind. You have to be ahead of the aeroplane all the time! Well done. Down in one piece. Don't forget to call when clear of the runway. Full shut down checks now please. A morning well spent, Jamie. I see you're sweating. That's as it should be. You've been working. Tomorrow afternoon I want you back again to do emergency drills. See you then."

The groundschool was totally practical and relevant to the Hunter. There were no abstruse mathematical calculations as at Cranwell and most of the final examination was multiple choice. Jamie had no difficulty in easily exceeding the pass mark of 90%. Likewise Jamieson's last session in the simulator also went well. Polzol's flying abilities and outlook were developed in an earlier age and he had the merit of regarding the procedures trainer simply as an adjunct to competence in the air. As an instructor he never viewed simulator skill as an end in itself.

Jamie did not forget Polzol's concluding remarks on engine failure. "Although the Hunter is built like a brick, it does not fly like one. It actually glides very well and being so aerodynamically clean it'll go a long way without an engine. If yours stops and cannot be restarted you don't have to bale out. You may eventually decide to do so but the aeroplane should glide about a nautical mile in still air for every thousand feet of height lost. That should give you in many circumstances quite a wide range of options. We call it a one in one. Wise Hunter pilots practise it regularly. We'll do so soon.

"However, remember that without your hydraulics controlling the aircraft is strong man's work and requires careful anticipation of height and heading to fly accurately. For a forced landing keep plenty of height in reserve. Aim for a high key point just upwind of the downwind leg of some five thousand feet to reach your low key at the end of downwind by three thousand feet especially allowing for wind. Don't put your gear down until you're absolutely sure you can make it and do watch out for a crosswind on finals. If then she begins to roll it'll be very difficult to get her back and if you cannot do so get out before it's too late. Let's get some practice in now. You'll be off solo next week."

The weekend was restful for Jamie. He expected to go solo on the Monday morning so a relaxed couple of days at home in Bideford was ideal. Janey came down by train to join him. To please his father they attended Matins in the parish church. As so often in days of depression at Stowe the Psalms gave him inspiration, "He maketh the clouds his chariot and walketh upon the wings of the wind." This is exactly what Jamie would be doing tomorrow – wind walking in his cloud piercing Avon powered chariot. Even more reassuring were the verses: "Whither shall I go then from thy spirit, or whither shall I go then from thy presence. If I climb up into heaven thou art there... If I take the wings of the morning and remain in the uttermost parts of the sea; Even there also shall thy hand lead me and thy right hand shall hold me."

The rest of the time was devoted to lazing by the fire and to long walks in the country lanes. The dog violets were already out and in the sheltered sunny spots the first celendines and primroses were visible. Jamie reckoned that the early signs of spring arrived in Devon six weeks before they did at Cranwell. On the way back to the vicarage Janey announced that her father had spoken to the Dean of Lincoln Cathedral who agreed that her wedding could be held there, "Mid summer would probably be best," responded Jamie. "The course here will definitely be finished. I should have settled into my first squadron by then and be due some leave."

"I am very glad you're happy with the idea," Janey replied. "We can have the reception in a marquee in the garden. Whilst I think the Dean will want to officiate at the service, I would hope that your father will lead some of the prayers."

"Let's put it to him at tea and we can start drawing up the guest list," Jamie responded. "I'm sure I'll be able to persuade some of my colleagues on the new squadron and fellow Old Cranwellians from my Entry, too, to hold their swords over our heads as we leave the west door."

Jamieson dropped Janey off in Barnstaple to catch her train to London on his way to Chivenor. The thought of marriage brought him deep contentment. On his own Sunday evenings were particularly bleak. He wondered if bachelor officers ever got over a sense of solitude on return to the Mess after a weekend or leave away. Air Force life was such an unnatural existence only made tolerable by the Mess bar, which once back on the station was usually their first port of call.

In flight, however, all melancholy was dispelled. It was as if the realms of air were truly home. He felt sure that the many specialist aircrew passed over for any promotion and the scores of aging Master Pilots and Flight Sergeants felt that way. The sky had become their faithful mistress to whom they would invariably seek to return. It was airborne that they enjoyed total acceptance and where they were always welcome.

Monday morning dawned in pure perfection. A cold front had gone through in the night. The flight line looked well washed after the rain and the visibility was almost limitless. At briefing the Met man warned that the strong north-west breeze would bring in some heavy showers by afternoon. The crosswind was not excessive now but later the wind would veer and strengthen markedly. All the diversions were open – Brawdy and St Athan in South Wales; St Mawgan and Yeovilton in the west country. As the pilots wandered back to flights Max Moxon intercepted Jamie and invited him to his office for an individual briefing.

"This morning is ideal for your first solo, Jamie," he began. "If you look at the flight details on the crewroom board you'll see that I've chinagraphed you in for an hour's sortie between 10.00 and 11.00 hours. Make it simple general handling. I suggest that you climb out north over Baggy Point, past Lundy Island levelling out at 40,000 feet. Do a couple of turns to get the hang of her and when cleared by Air Traffic point her downhill due west at 45° nose down on full power. You may feel a slight twitch on the ailerons as you go through Mach One. Hold her transonic for fifteen seconds or so, then throttle back and airbrake out and head back eastwards doing some medium level aerobatics as you go. Run in over Barnstaple to join the circuit for one roller landing and then a full stop. If you still have plenty of fuel and feel happy you can even make it two touch and goes. Enjoy yourself, Jamie. Very soon the real work will begin when you get on to the gunnery, air combat and tactical formation flying."

Jamie was surprised to find Polzol in the locker room with a pile of flying clothing beside him on the bench. "What are you doing here, Polzol?" asked Jamie. "Are you playing truant from the procedures trainer already?"

"Half the course like you have finished their initial simulator sessions and groundschool, the other half are doing their exams today," Polzol answered mischievously. "This is what gives old Polzol his opportunity to wind the clock back and go flying. You forget that I have friends everywhere, Jamie. The Station Commander Group Captain Prendergast was on my Spitfire squadron at Wunstorf soon after the war. We always got on well and when I explained that I'd have much more credibility as a simulator instructor if I'd flown the aircraft he agreed, so here I am at the beginning of a special short course for odd bods, Air Marshals, retreads, old hands and has beens like me.

"Help me on with my Godforsaken immersion suit, Jamie my friend," Polzol pleaded. "My tummy, which was as flat as a board when I was on 303, has enlarged somewhat over the beery years and makes it very hard to get this hideous suiting, all zips and rubberised fabric, up over my chest and head. Pull, Jamie, pull!" Jamie had rather less trouble with his own, but even so the rubber waterproof seal at the top chafed his neck and he had a struggle to get the connector hose of his anti 'g' suit out through the slender aperture at his right hip. This done he bade Polzol farewell and waddled somewhat self-consciously out to the aeroplane with helmet and gloves in one hand, his strapped kneepad checklist in the other.

CHAPTER 17

Jamie could not believe the start up, taxiing and take off would be so easy. Once airborne he quickly cleaned up the aircraft and climbed out over Braunton Sands. He concentrated hard on relaxed precise flying. The control column was sensitive and he did not wish any involuntary wing waggle to betray to those on the ground that he was a novice. Then he swung right to head north-west past Baggy Point. It seemed that he was overhead Lundy Island in seconds rather than four minutes and equally quickly he found himself at 40,000 feet.

The coast of west Wales stood out to starboard against Homer's wine dark sea below – Tenby, Caldy Island and St Govan's Head beyond. Jamie verified his oxygen – connected and flowing. The black and white indicator ball was blinking reassuringly on the instrument panel. All temperatures and pressures and fuel seemed fine. He set her up on 270° and checked his height – easily sufficient; airframe – clean with everything in the cockpit secure including straps and seat; engine – performance normal; location – appropriate to the exercise. He executed a quick 180° degree turn each way to look for traffic below. He saw none – clear for dive.

Radio clearance to boom was soon obtained and then down she went. Breaking the sound barrier was exactly as Moxon had briefed so Jamie headed towards base for aerobatics on the way home. He did more cockpit and exterior lookout checks. Still the sky was clear so he applied full power, eased the stick forward and pulled up into a loop. Gently does it, he thought and it was definitely harder to keep straight with swept wings than in the Vampire. The Hunter's wings are far back but the line of the cockpit coaming helped him to keep them parallel with the horizon over the top. Now down the other side. Time to ease out. The anti 'g' suit began to inflate and squeeze his legs and stomach. It made Jamie want to cough.

Let's keep this smooth he decided. Maintain the speed he said to himself... up into a wingover to port and let it flow straight into a barrel roll to starboard. Hold it. Now a slow roll, easy but not a really slow roll, check her level and into a four point hesitation roll – much easier, too, with powered controls to hold each 90° point exactly. Time to go home. Down we go. Over to Chivenor Tower and a gentle run in from Barnstaple parallel to the river and the runway. Flick the airbrake, ease back the throttle. Radio call. Down with the wheels... three green lights, they've locked. Hurry that's the end of downwind. Checks are done. Less power and round onto finals... keep it tight, check gear and flaps down... maintain the descent, nice and steady, faintest flare and then rumble rumble, I'm down. Now full power on. Keep straight, wheels up, round onto downwind and same again. Down once more. No need to turn off at the intersection. There's no one behind. On to the end. Call runway clear and there are the friendly groundcrew already marshalling me in.

Jamie's lifetime ambition had been fulfilled at the age of twenty-one. Squadron Leader Moxon came out from his office and joined him for a crewroom coffee. "I'm sure it went just fine, Jamie," he began. "In time you'll learn to tighten up your approaches. You're at your most vulnerable to enemy action in the circuit. So you'll have to be able to get down fast, but for now you can be pleased with a most satisfactory sortie."

Jamie was exceptionally happy at Chivenor. The flying caused him no real problems. When Samantha was away in the country he used to spend weekends in the London flat with Janey. If not, Janey came gladly down to Devon. Midweek he was never bored since meeting up with Mark Driscoll a humorous, easy going and strikingly good looking Ampleforth educated Old Cranwellian, who was the former Hunter display pilot for Royal Air Force Germany.

Professionally Mark was at Chivenor to become a Pilot Attack Instructor. Psychologically the course enabled him to distance himself conveniently from his wife Elaine who had returned from Gütersloh to her mother in Norwich with their three year old daughter Susie rather than continue as she disdainfully described it "as an Air Force camp follower". He was expecting to receive divorce papers any day.

For Mark the pain of separation from his dearly loved Susie could only be assuaged in the cockpit, or at the bar or in the company of the many girls who found his relaxed charm irresistible. In Jamie he had discovered the ideal companion – amusing, intelligent, socially acceptable and above all owing to his devotion to Janey most definitely not a competitor for any female favours which could be found. During the week their routine was to reconnoitre at least a couple of pubs a night, a pattern which was invariably entertaining for Jamie and very often physically and emotionally rewarding for Mark.

The end to this short idyll was clearly imminent by late March when both Jamie and Mark had received good news. Jamie was posted to join 43 Squadron the famous Fighting Cocks at Leuchars in Fife after Easter and Mark was to become a Flight Commander on his squadron, Number 14 back at Gütersloh. Not that Elaine had congratulated him on his impending elevation.

Indeed when he briefly mentioned it in his last phone call to inquire whether she had managed to get Susie into a nursery school, her response was dismissive. "Why should her education interest you? Now you're a Flight Commander you'll have even more excuses to be away. I'm sure you'll be organising lots of weapon firing camps at faraway seaside stations, just as when you were the display pilot you had the alibi of an airshow at a different place in Germany every summer weekend."

Polzol, too, had reason to be happy. He found the short conversion course reinforced his appetite for flying. Once in a real Hunter cockpit he felt as if the years simply rolled back. All aeroplanes were basically the same and the principles of fighter tactics had not essentially changed since his Spitfire days.

He reassured himself with the knowledge that in the Korean War so many of the highest scoring American fighter pilots in those first dogfights of the jet age in Mig Alley along the Yalu river were old hands. They were perhaps not quite such very old hands as himself but nevertheless battle hardened veterans with greying temples like his own who had also honed their combat skills against the Luftwaffe in World War Two.

He was in good company now that he, too, was back in a fighter cockpit. His obliging friend Group Captain Prendergast the Station Commander had succumbed to Polzol's plea to allow him a sortie a fortnight of continuation training to keep his hand in. "It is absolutely essential for my job," he insisted to the Groupie, "for me to stay in touch with the latest procedures and tactics."

"This is all a bit irregular," Prendergast conceded, but mused to himself that friends are better than money in the bank, especially in the Air Force where others control one's destiny so much. Perhaps Polzol would now give him an easier ride when he came to renew his simulator currency next month.

It was a perfect bright and blustery day; Chivenor at its early springtime best. Both Mark and Jamie had been flying that morning and were relaxing soft drinks in hand with Max Moxon on a bench in front of the Mess looking out across the airfield, listening to the redshank calling in the estuary beyond and watching the flocks of migrating whimbrel high overhead, which with staccato piping were beating their way northward against the wind. They were planning a pub exploration in Ilfracombe that evening when suddenly the crash alarm sounded.

Moxon leapt to his feet and dashed for the phone on the bar. "Give me Air Traffic," they heard him demand. "What's up?" … "Tell him to get out NOW," he bellowed into the mouthpiece. "We'll have the helo airborne for him in three minutes so he'll hardly get his feet wet." … "He's bringing it in here? That's mad. Give him the wind, I mean the crosswind component. I bet its gusting thirty knots." … "He won't listen? I'm off to the tower."

"Its Polzol," Max shouted over his shoulder as he ran to his car. "Engine blew up west of Lundy. Thinks he can get back here off a one in one. It's not the bloody simulator or 1940. We don't even really need the aeroplane. It's expendable." The two firetenders and the ambulance moved into position on the grass about a third of the way along the runway.

"You know, Mark," said Jamie, "I don't think Polzol's ever done any single dinghy drill for years. It's very different from the procedure for a ditched Varsity or Valetta. Shedding the parachute harness, inflating the dinghy and getting in with a Mae West and immersion suit on is not like stepping off the wing of a ditched Pig or Superpig into an inflated liferaft."

"I suspect he knows that all too well," Mark answered, hence his decision to stay with it."

"Don't forget his pride either," Jamie observed. "I'm sure that Polzol reckons that a good deadstick landing back at base in front of the home crowd will demonstrate to everyone that the old Polish warhorse is not past it."

"There he is," shouted Mark as a black silhouette could be seen silently coasting in high over Woolacombe. "Ease it out a bit, you'll be very tight with this wind."

"At least he's managed to get his wheels down," Jamie remarked.

"True, but watch how she starts to drop now," Mark responded. "He's very close in downwind. Lucky he's got some height in hand." The nose was perceptively lower as the aircraft banked briefly left and continued awhile towards Barnstaple presumably to eliminate the excess height.

"Round he goes," said Jamie as the stricken Hunter could be seen initiating a steep gliding turn onto finals. "He's obviously keeping the speed up."

"Yes, but I don't like the look of this at all," warned Mark. "With all that bank on he'll be blown off the centreline. He was in far too tight downwind and is now descending rapidly. Why did he go halfway to Barnstaple?"

"I fear you're right, Mark," Jamie responded. "He's certainly got the nose up now; must be trying to stretch the glide and he's still not lined up."

"God this is awful," Mark exclaimed. "He's going down fast and any slower she'll really start to drop. Get out, Polzol. Get out NOW!"

"Mark look," cried Jamie. "The right wing's come up. It must be the crosswind… a sudden gust or windshear perhaps…" He did not have time to finish the sentence before they saw Polzol's canopy fly off followed by two bangs. A black shape shot sideways from the cockpit for some fifty yards before slamming into a grass field and bouncing over and over along its surface towards the far hedge.

The aeroplane continued its uncontrolled roll and plunged inverted into a ploughed area in amongst the approach lights with a muffled explosion and a burst of flame. The ambulance and one crash tender raced off towards the still object before the hedgerow. The other approached the conflagration and started dousing it with its roof mounted foam cannon.

"That's it then, Jamie," was Mark's melancholy response. "Gravity is no respecter of age or person. Defied so long it got him in the end."

"How terrible," said Jamie sombrely. "He didn't even detach from the seat and I never saw any drogue come out."

"It couldn't," Mark replied. "Too low and a sideways ejection with a strong downward component. It could hardly have been worse. One in ones are only for the sharpest and most current and best reserved for ideal conditions. Otherwise, Jamie my friend, get out in good time if you want to see your grandchildren."

"Seems that we face another of those grim Service funerals if that's what the family wants. Will you be going?" Jamie asked.

"I doubt it," Mark replied. "You were at Barkston Heath much more recently than I was and from what I hear Polzol's delectable daughter Natasha was the main point of contact if that's the right expression for your contemporaries," said Mark.

"True but that all ended in tears when her boyfriend David Jones was killed when his Piston Provost span in," Jamie answered.

"Poor Ethel and poor Natasha," he continued. "Ethel must have hoped when he got his simulator job that they could finally look forward to retirement with confidence. Polzol told me they'd sold the house in Barkston village and bought a bungalow in Ilkley. They liked the north and it is close to his brothers who work together in Bradford in the wool trade. After my next sortie I'll have to go round to their quarter to pay Ethel my condolences – 3 Lysander Close, Polzol said it was. Weeks ago he had asked me over for a beer one evening after flying but typically I hadn't got round to it. Now it's too late."

"Don't fret about that, Jamie," Mark replied. "My own superhighway to hell is paved with scores of such dishonoured commitments. I'm afraid, though, that I definitely won't be able to go to the funeral. Let the dead bury their dead, the Bible says. I must see Susie before I return to Germany next week, but at least I can give you moral support by going with you to see his widow this evening."

"How long will your trip last?" Mark enquired.

"Quite a time," Jamie explained. "In fact I should be flight planning it now. It's a pairs low level recce of West Freugh airfield. Were going in to mid-Wales over Burry Port, between Pembrey and Fairwood Common aerodromes. Navy Sea Hawks from Brawdy have been detailed to bounce us en route. We coast out at the Great Orme's head, skirt RAF Jurby on the Isle of Man, take our holiday snaps of West Freugh and come back high level over the top of Green One airway."

"Sounds like a standard pre-graduation navigation milk run to me," joked Mark. "I hope your number two knows that it'll be a case of the blind leading the blind. Don't worry about the opposition. Those fishheads from Brawdy won't even see you. Just hug the contours and trust your wingman to keep your tail clear. If they do make contact you'll find that in those Crab versus Fishhead encounters the Crabs win every time."

With West Freugh duly photographed and the Fleet Air Arm nowhere to be seen Jamie and his retread companion who had already done a tour on photoreconnaissance Swifts returned to base content. As they walked thoughtfully across the pan to sign in Jamie felt sure he would put in a good report to Squadron Leader Moxon. He was pleased that he had performed well in all aspects of his flying but the dream return to the dear Devon of his youth had been fatally marred by Polzol's horrifying demise.

Overhead in the calm of the spring evening the station's aerobatic star was working on his sequence for the summer season's flying displays. Normally Jamie would have stopped appreciatively to enjoy and criticise each manoeuvre, the performance was so elegantly flown and beautiful to watch but today he headed straight for the Mess where Mark was waiting.

Mark had stepped outside to watch the show and offered his comments at once. "He'll have to tighten it up a lot… keep it right in front of the crowd. Vertical eights are a waste of time in a Hunter. Its lack of reheat and insufficient power turn then into cubans. More rolling manoeuvres along the crowd line with crisp Derby turns or wingover reversals at each end would be my recommendation."

"How can you be so cool and detached, Mark?" Jamie enquired. "I just don't understand you."

"I'm not really," Mark bridled somewhat. "I've simply become fatalistic over the years. What happened to Polzol like so many of these ghastly events was totally unnecessary. Perhaps, however, he preferred to end his days suddenly and violently like that than suffer the indignities of old age. My poor old father has been in a wheelchair with multiple sclerosis for a year and a half now. It's pitiful. He suffers and my mother suffers. We all do. He was such a brilliant athlete which makes it worse. Polzol has just followed in the footsteps of sacrifice of so many of his friends in World War Two. Poland is still not free remember."

As they headed off on foot to the married patch the individual display Hunter skimmed past the controller's caravan. It soared airbrake extended up and round onto downwind. Then curving tightly with wheels and flaps down over the lights where Polzol's aeroplane had burned it sailed serenely on to a perfect touchdown. "A young man's salute to a brave old warrior," commented Jamie. "Now let's face the widow Ethel. Natasha won't have got here yet from Nottingham University. I wonder who broke the news to her. I wish Janey could have done it. She and Natasha got on so well."

A group of cars was parked outside the simple brick built service dwelling, an identical Married Quarter to that of Lizzie's parents at Cranwell. One of the vehicles was an RAF blue staff car with a somnolent driver at the wheel and an RAF ensign on the bonnet. It had to be Prendergast. A service Land Rover was doubtless that of the Wing Commander Flying.

They knocked diffidently on the door. A businesslike but friendly and elegant Mrs Moxon opened it and ushered them in. "Ethel's had a lot of visitors," she said. "As you can see Group Captain and Mrs Prendergast are still here; the Gillespies too, but I know that Ethel will particularly welcome friends from Cranwell like yourselves. They were so happy at Cranwell. Natasha also I gather."

Jamie glanced around quickly. All the furnishings were standard Royal Air Force issue. Unlike the cottage at Barkston there were no decorations, mementoes, pictures or family photographs; none of the memorabilia from Krakow, wartime squadrons, Roman Catholic church or Natasha's schooling were visible. It was clear that the Zopoloskis just camped here. Home must already have been in Ilkley.

How much Ethel must have looked forward to being there permanently with Polzol and not to have to share him with the Air Force. He would no doubt have loved to see more of his brothers and Natasha of her cousins. Ethel was sitting almost expressionless by the gas fire. "Natasha will soon be here, dear," a robust tartan skirted lady, probably Mrs Gillespie, was saying in a broad Scottish accent.

Meanwhile the Station Commander was insisting that Polzol died carrying out his duty as ever and doing the job he loved. He would have not wished it any other way. He could personally assure Ethel of that since only a few days before Polzol had told him how happy he was to be flying again.

The Group Captain and his wife excused themselves. "Duty calls, my dear. I'm sure you'll understand," said Mrs Prendergast to the sad figure of Ethel slumped in a worn armchair beside the flickering flames of the dreary gas fire.

"Good to see you here Driscoll and Jamieson," barked the Groupie on his way out. "They don't make them like Zopoloski any more. Quite irreplaceable. I learned a lot from him at Wunstorf in those early days after the war."

"So did we at Cranwell, sir, and here for that matter," Jamie replied. "He really loved the Service."

"He certainly did," agreed Prendergast. "It was his life and I suppose you could say that he died for it, too. Good evening, gentleman."

Without the Prendergasts the room seemed less crowded. Ethel reopened the conversation turning to the two senior officers' wives. "Make some more tea please someone and while you're at it bring us another packet of biscuits." Mrs Moxon and Mrs Gillespie dutifully disappeared into the kitchen.

Then addressing Mark and Jamie as if to reassure herself she began: "I'm sure you must have known my husband well. So many people have told me they had cause to thank him, but I think those last five years at Cranwell were the best."

"I don't believe that any former Flight Cadet will ever forget him," Jamie answered. "Although his job as a staff pilot was out at Barkston Heath he threw himself body and soul into the activities of the College – Guest Nights, sports, receptions and of course he even came out to Germany to help with survival camp."

"So I well remember and I'm sure that Natasha does, too," Ethel responded bitterly. "We lost our family summer holiday that year because of his trip with the cadets to the Sauerland."

"I knew him rather less well," said Mark. "We only overlapped for one term of navigation training at Barkston but I still recall the effect he had when he arrived. He brought flair, humour, imagination and a huge sense of enjoyment to what everyone else thought was a very routine activity."

"I'm sure," Ethel answered simply. "He was always a great enthusiast for Air Force life. I hope Natasha comes before too long. She rang to say that she expected to be here by 10.00 pm. She'll have her views of course but I think we'll hold my husband's funeral near our new home – in Bradford probably. We spent two happy tours in Yorkshire at Church Fenton and Leconfield so it was right that we should finally settle there.

"Anyway," she went on, "I'll discuss it with Natasha and his two brothers but my husband always insisted he wanted his funeral to be a happy occasion; a party even. If they agree we'll make sure that the Polish ex-combatants and the Polish Parish Club organise something special after the Funeral Mass. I'm sure they will."

"Whatever you decide my fiancée Janey and I will be there," answered Jamie. "Do give our deepest condolences to Natasha and always remember that your husband was not just a gifted pilot and a gallant officer – he was an inspiration to all of us. We must be off now. So many others will want to come and offer their sympathy. Goodbye Mrs Zopoloski."

Next day Mark and Jamie went their separate ways after a last lunch together in the Mess. "I've had no complaints from the Wingco," Mark declared proudly over the soup. "Indeed that moustachioed old walrus Grunt Gillespie was quite effusive at my final interview this morning. He actually said that I had all the qualities of a first rate fighter leader; would set standards of accuracy in gunnery, which he felt sure that few in my flight or even squadron could match and so on. But life is full of contrasts. Elaine will not be so complimentary tomorrow. I just hope she doesn't cut up rough and lets me see Susie. Elaine may enjoy being bloody but I know that Susie at any rate likes my company."

"If it's any consolation I've certainly appreciated having you around during my conversion," Jamie responded. "I think we've had a lot of uncomplicated fun here – spoilt at the end by dear old Polzol's dreadful death – but even so we've passed our respective courses. You're obviously on your way up professionally and I've got not only 43 and Leuchars to look forward to but the Big Wedding in June. You must come back, Mark. I'm sure that as Flight Commander you'll be able to borrow an aircraft for the weekend and fly across."

"I'll do my best to be there, Jamie," Mark replied, "even if I have to take the Hook of Holland ferry. If I do, just get your father-in-law to send his driver to Harwich to pick me up. Anyway work hard at bonny Leuchars. Who knows I might even be your Squadron Commander before too long. Stranger things than that have happened."

"See you in Lincoln then in June, if not before," Jamie answered.

"I must dash down to Flights," Jamie continued as he to got up to leave. "I've got one more qualifying squirt at the flag. I'll try not to shoot down the Meteor Tug before I go."

"Don't do that," Mark warned jocularly. "Gillespie for all his bonhomie with me this morning can be quite unforgiving. A grunting walrus if provoked is a dangerous beast. Goodbye my friend. See you at your wedding. I can't wait to meet the lucky Janey." With this Mark jumped into his battered blue MGA sports car and waving cheerily sped off towards Barnstaple. Jamie walked pensively down to the flightline. He would not change it but already he knew that a fighter pilot's life is full of deep unspoken if transient emotions.

Next day Jamie set off on the long drive to Kensington. Wing Commander Gillespie had been summoned to Group for a first discussion about Polzol's crash before the Board of Inquiry was established so Squadron Leader Moxon had given Jamie his farewell interview. "Not much to say is there, Jamie?" he began. "I'm satisfied and I'm sure you're satisfied, too, with your performance on this course.

"My only parting advice to you," Moxon continued, "is never to stop learning and never ever to become complacent in the air. Therein lies disaster. Have a good journey to London and then I'll doubtless see you at Polzol's funeral. Thereafter I'll follow your progress in Fighter Command with benevolent interest."

"Thank you, sir," Jamie replied. "It's been a privilege to convert on your squadron."

Janey welcomed Jamie with kisses and hugs back at the flat and ushered him solicitously upstairs where Samantha was just finishing to lay the dinner table. "You two would like a quiet dinner together, I'm sure," Samantha said. "It's a long tiring drive from Devon and arriving in London at rush hour must have made it worse. You'll want to relax. I'm going to eat out with friends after the cinema. I know you'll have a lot to discuss now that your course has finished, Jamie, and that you're off to Scotland so soon. I was shocked to read of a crash at Chivenor in the paper. No doubt the pilot was a friend of yours."

"Yes he was, but more than that Samantha," Jamie replied. "He was an icon to us, a role model for our generation."

"All the more reason for me to be off," she insisted, "so you can talk about happier subjects tête-a-tête – like your wedding for example. Good night. I'll be back late and will try to be quiet."

Now that they were together Jamie knew that he had not sufficiently realised how much he missed Janey. He could indeed totally relax at last, be entirely himself and be accepted as such. Weekends from Chivenor were not the same. They were very welcome but intense whilst they lasted. There was always the fear that the following week he would somehow mess up the course and be sent off deeply disappointed to learn to fly helicopters or to become a second pilot on Shackletons. Weekday evenings had been tolerable only thanks to Mark whose capacity for entertainment and fun was remarkable in even the most unpromising surroundings. Jamie was sure that if Mark went for a walk in the desert he would find a pretty girl behind the nearest sand dune.

"You must be very cut up about poor old Polzol," Janey began. "He really should have retired at Cranwell when he got to fifty-five."

"I disagree, Janey my dear," Jamie answered. "What would he have done? It would have been a living death for him. He knew no other life than the Air Force and flying. Anyway there may have been other reasons for staying on. Perhaps he wanted to see Natasha through university and then there was the smart new bungalow in Ilkley to be paid for as well. It's quite an up market place, full of well to do wool trade barons from Bradford, clothing kings and money men from Leeds."

"Let's make the best of a thoroughly bad job," said Janey. "I suggest we drive home to Fulbeck after my work on Friday afternoon. My parents will be thrilled to see you again. We can make more plans for the wedding and then set off to Bradford after breakfast. We'll stay Saturday night in Harrogate and I can easily get the train back to London from York next day. If we're feeling devout we could to go a service in the Minster or if we're nursing hangovers a brisk walk round the city walls should help. They'll be beautiful now the daffodils are out."

"As usual, Janey," Jamie responded, "you've got it right in all respects. I've got something right, too. Here's a bottle of burgundy Mark Driscoll gave me to celebrate passing the conversion course." With candles lit they tucked into Janey's cottage pie followed by her best trifle. Thereafter well content it was time to renew the heart warming intimacy, which with all too brief weekend interludes he had sorely missed in the green clapboard felt roofed huts of the Officer's Mess at Chivenor.

The following afternoon Jamie's faithful little Austin A35 set off like a homing pigeon up the A1 past RAF Wittering and the fateful George Hotel in multi-spired Stamford, past the ghostly disused bomber base of Woolfox Lodge, heading right soon afterwards onto the High Dyke with its many emotion inducing landmarks along the way. There were Spitalgate aerodrome as grassy as ever, Barkston Heath just as bleak and windswept as before, and the mysteriously named Byards Leap Garage nestling in sight of the College in its hollow beside the Roman road.

Then hard left they went as if towards Newark before leaving the main road for the Hetherington Lane just down from the Lincoln Edge. As they arrived the big house stood out starkly against the mist swathed sun now setting over the Trent Valley behind the familiar curtain of tall immemorial elms.

It was a traditional English homecoming of leaping dogs, a crackling log fire and mellow lamplight; of welcoming parents courteous with controlled emotion. "Do let me take your case." "Had a good week, Janey?" "Hope the London traffic wasn't too bad – Finchley Road can be terrible." "When did you last eat?" "Your room is just as you left it Janey. I've put Jamie next door." "I expect a drink would go down well." "The Paynes from Wellingore are joining us for dinner. Not to worry. Nothing formal. You don't need to change. Relax."

"Tell me, Jamie, what's it like with Chivenor behind you?" asked the ever benign Colonel Hetherington. "I still remember well my time at the School of Infantry. Useful certainly but I only really learned proper soldiering with the battalion and I was lucky – pulled off to Waziristan to deal with the Faqir of Ipi almost at once. I think the Pathans on the frontier were more instructive to us than any course laid on by the British Army."

"I'm sure, Colonel," replied Jamie politely and briefly not because he did not believe Colonel Hetherington but because his wife was always less than appreciative of the Colonel's familiar Indian stories which Jamie actually found fascinating.

Dinner took its traditional course. "Mrs Langworthy has prepared her normal fare. Lincolnshire hot pot I call it," declared Janey's mother. "You'll find bits of most things in there. To my knowledge there were pheasant's breast, two legs of a partridge, two dismembered woodcock, some pigeon wings, and the greater part of a hare." Then afterwards was served a premature summer pudding composed of last year's frozen raspberries and blackcurrants from the kitchen garden topped with dollops of clotted cream. Finally an exceedingly mature stilton arrived.

"Do keep me company with the port, Jamie," insisted the Colonel, "or if you're more abstemious like my admirable friends the Paynes just stick to the claret. The cellar's full of it."

Jamie felt suffused with a warm contentment. He felt deep down that Janey was the right choice for him. If destiny spared him the fate shared by Polzol and so many of the Senior Entries whom he had seen graduate from Cranwell, anything was possible. He had no desire to emulate the cockpit confined existence of crinkly faced Master Pilots or paunchy specialist aircrew officers any more than an aging athlete would wish to try to recapture the triumphs of his youth. He did not want to fly forever. He knew there was a time for everything in life.

He and Janey would buy a house in the country whilst he was still young and then if he got on in the Air Force and they lived in good service accommodation like the Commandant's Lodge at Cranwell or a Commander in Chief's residence elsewhere they would then let out their home. They could put money aside for a really big house on retirement like Janey's parents – preferably in Lincolnshire, too, with elms, lawns, herbaceous borders, a paddock, tennis court and perhaps even a bit of a park. After all Janey deserved it. She had been brought up to nothing less.

CHAPTER 18

The contrast between Kesteven and Bradford was stark. Polzol's funeral was to be held in the Polish Parish church near the heart of town. The city centre was dominated by fine soot stained Victorian buildings whilst up the hill extended street upon cobbled street of stone built terraced houses. Many corner shops and local businesses were clearly Pakistani with signs over the premises in Urdu script and not a word of English to be seen on the shop fronts. It was another world from hyper English Kesteven county.

The lofty Victorian neo Gothic Polish parish church was packed. It seemed as if half of Poland in exile was present and clearly outnumbered the large number of uniformed Royal Air Force personnel scattered throughout the pews. Jamie and Janey were among the last to arrive and installed themselves towards the back. Glancing curiously around they spotted Peter Carrick without Sylvia and Peter Lascelles, also on his own.

To their surprise they noticed a headscarfed Yasmin with an incongruous looking Pakistani couple. She had persuaded her parents to let her go to support her friend Natasha with the promise that she would stay with her aunt and uncle in the city. He was a doctor originally from Rawalpindi. They lived conveniently nearby in Heaton where he had developed a thriving practice caring for the growing Pakistani and Azad Kashmiri community in Manningham around Lumb Lane.

They were equally surprised to see the Polish Air Attaché arrive. He was an undistinguished looking Colonel with what were clearly not British but Russian medals on his chest who in normal circumstances would not have been very welcome, but for diplomatic reasons could not be seen to miss the occasion.

The organ boomed out Chopin's Funeral March. Then in came the coffin draped with the Union Flag of Polzol's country of adoption and topped by his medals, original Polish officer's cap and a wreath of Polish red and white roses and two profuse sprays of white lilies doubtless from Ethel and Natasha. Unusually the pall bearers were mostly senior officers – Squadron Leaders Moxon and Ashley and Wing Commanders Gillespie and Baker. They were assisted by two late middle-aged heavily bemedalled citizens, clearly Polzol's brothers. Ethel and Natasha both veiled in black and in sombre suits walked behind followed by a large cortege of fellow family members.

This is going to be hard to bear thought Jamie but the Requiem Mass was preceded by a sublime Polish anthem sung by local schoolchildren from the church's Sunday school, which lifted his spirits. The liturgy that followed was half in Latin half in Polish except for an address delivered from the pulpit in a clear demure voice by Natasha. "It was my father's wish," she began in English, "that this should be an occasion of celebration for his life and that there should be no sermon or eulogy.

"Many of his dearest friends were lost without trace and received no burial so my mother and I decided that in honour of him and them I should read a few special verses. They come in the form of the poem Per Ardua written by John Gillespie Magee a British born Canadian Spitfire pilot from RAF Wellingore who was killed in a collision with an aeroplane from Cranwell on 11 December 1941.

"In a letter to his parents in America shortly before he died John Magee enclosed the poem explaining that 'to those who gave their lives to England during the Battle of Britain and left such a shining example to us who follow these lines are dedicated'.

"They that have climbed the white mists of the morning;
They that have soared, before the world's awake;
To herald up their foemen to them, scorning
The thin dawn's rest their weary folk might take;
"Some that have left other mouths to tell the story
Of high, blue battle – quite young limbs that bled;
How they had thundered up the clouds to glory
Or fallen to an English field stained red;
"Because my faltering feet would fail I find them
Laughing behind me, steadying the hand
That seeks their deadly courage – yet behind them
The cold light dies in that once brilliant land…
"Do these, who help the quickened pulse run slowly,
Whose stern remembered image cools the brow –
Till the far dawn of Victory know only
Night's darkness, and Valhalla's silence now?"

As Natasha descended diffidently from the pulpit Jamie marvelled at her very personal tribute to her fallen father. It was clearly the choice of a university student of English but more movingly the almost mystic quality of the poem was so appropriate to Polzol's personality and achievements.

He had indeed left other mouths than his to tell the story of his front line part in the Battle of Britain. His own life's work had constantly entailed thundering up the clouds to glory. Had not the light of freedom died in the once brilliant land of Poland and had not Mark and himself witnessed Polzol's final fall to an English field stained red?

A final libation of holy water on the coffin and the national anthems of Britain and also of Poland presaged its measured departure down the aisle to the flower topped hearse outside and to its interment in the vast civic cemetery on the edge of the city overlooking a townscape of smoke stacks, blackened mills, cobbled streets and back to back houses to the moors beyond. Polzol's burial place would be anything but special, but his official British war grave headstone of Portland stone with its chiselled Polish eagle and the carved post-nominals of DFM, DFC and VM to his singular name and rank would still in death distinguish him from the departed Bradford citizenry around him.

To fill in the time between Polzol's interral and the gathering back at the Polish ex-combatants' club Jamie and Janey took themselves on a brief excursion to the Bronte sisters' home villages of Thornton and Haworth nearby to clear their thoughts before facing a social event, which could further drain them emotionally after the Funeral Mass. They returned uplifted by their visit to the Haworth Parsonage the scent of the moors and fine forbidding sweep of the landscape.

Ethel and Natasha with Polzol's brothers and their wives together with a much medalled President of the club and a remarkably young Polish priest were greeting the guests in a line at the door. "You have been so good to come all the way from Chivenor to support us," said Ethel. "I'll never forget how you and your fellow officers called round to see me on the day my husband died. Now I understand why the Air Force was like a family to him. He certainly had wonderful friends."

Before Jamie or Janey could respond Natasha added, "What marvellous days we all had at Barkston, even though they weren't without their sorrows even then, especially for me. Looking back now I would not have changed anything."

"Your dear father made it all possible," Jamie responded.

"I was so glad to see Yasmin," Natasha cut in. "Do take care of her. I don't think she knows many people here except you both. She told me that her aunt and uncle would not be coming to the reception, but that she particularly hoped to catch up with you, Janey. She said you both used to get on so well in London."

The ever solicitous Natasha need not have worried. Yasmin was already being very well looked after by Peter Carrick and Peter Lascelles and two blonde girls who introduced themselves in flat Yorkshire accents as Polzol's nieces. An unattached Carl Higgins was hovering on the edge of the group hoping to break in and re-establish romantic contact with Yasmin.

Once all the guests had arrived and been welcomed by the family both of Polzol's brothers called for a toast. First the elder raised his large vodka filled glass and proposed a toast, "To the memory of my dear gallant brother Squadron Leader Zopolowski." The younger one proposed a toast, "To our beloved Poland – may she soon be free." The final toast of the club President given whilst looking fixedly at the Polish Air Attaché was to "Her Majesty's Royal Air Force, the proud guardian of freedom". Immediately accordions struck up God Save the Queen, the Polish National Anthem and then the Royal Air Force march past which mutated into a miscellany of waltzes, polkas and tangos.

Tables were swiftly moved to the side of the hall to give space for dancing. Girls in gaudily embroidered blouses brought food of all kinds and the vodka flowed ever more freely. Soon the floor was filled with whirling couples amongst whom in addition to Jamie and Janey were Peter Lascelles with one Polzol niece, Peter Carrick with Natasha and Carl with Yasmin who looked striking, the belle of the impromptu ball, in an all white narrow trousered silken outfit of Islamic mourning.

"My father always insisted that his funeral should be happy not sad," declared Natasha to Peter Carrick forcefully above the dance music.

"I still would call it sad, Natasha," Peter confided, "but with decidedly happy potential. This is certainly no wake, more a commemorative party. It takes me back to the good old days when we were cadets and you and your ever hospitable parents were at Barkston."

"Yes, but don't forget, Peter, that David Jones' death ruined the Cranwell experience for me," Natasha retorted.

This was the subject Peter Carrick did not want her to raise. Taffy's fatal crash had nearly wrecked his career, too. He had lived with his guilty secret ever since and now Taffy's girlfriend was in his arms. What could he say? His lips uttered what seemed to him an unconvincing automatic response. "His loss was a terrible blow to all of us you know."

"The understatement of the year, if I may say so," Natasha replied.

"It wasn't meant to be," Peter answered. "I think we can only come to terms with these awful events by understating them. If we didn't they'd be too painful to bear. Such defence mechanisms are necessary. Otherwise we would not be dancing now."

"I take your point," said Natasha quickly. "We can talk about these deeper insights afterwards. Let's just get on with the dancing." What did she mean by afterwards Peter wondered? Natasha was certainly more sensitive than Sylvia and emitted a chemistry which Sylvia for all her virtues had never possessed, at least not with him.

Carl and Yasmin were sharing a table with Jamie and Janey. "If it had not been for poor old Polzol's death we would never have been brought together again so soon," Yasmin began, "although by no means all of us are here. I see Mary Wong from time to time in London. China Chu comes to visit her from Little Rissington most weekends, but he'll be going back to Malaysia to instruct before long and it'll be decision time for her."

"How's Samantha?" Carl asked.

"She's fine," Janey replied, "but I think you'd agree, Yasmin, that she misses Yousuf very much. By the way what news do you have of him?"

"He could not be happier," Yasmin answered. "He converting onto Sabres as he always wanted to do."

Peter Lascelles wandered across from the bar having relinquished Polzol's niece to her local friends. "When do you go to Laarbruch, Peter?" Jamie enquired.

"Just after you and Janey get married, I hope," Peter answered. "Lizzie has already declared that she's putting the clock back and is determined to re-establish herself in Düsseldorf even though it's quite a long way from the base."

"That's not nearly as bad as if she'd gone back to Mum on the Moray Firth," Jamie replied. "You'll be enjoying something new and exciting when you join 16 Squadron. The role should take you around a bit, at least in Europe, and you'll be able to spend amorous weekends in Düsseldorf."

"In a way I envy your Canberras, Peter," Carl interjected. "I'll be instructing on our familiar friend the Vampire just down the road from here at Linton on Ouse. What's worse my dear Yasmin is off to Washington in September – not to Georgetown University actually, but to George Washington University in Foggy Bottom – funny name isn't it – to read for another degree this time in international relations. I reckon they could best she studied in my arms. What do you think Yasmin?"

A definite blush suffused her olive cheeks, "The practical perhaps, Carl, but GWU will still be necessary for the theory," Yasmin replied.

Jamie and Janey were the first to slip away. The luxury suite they had booked at the Hydro Hotel in Harrogate beckoned. Carl wanted to savour the last minutes of Yasmin's company before Polzol's family took her back to her aunt and uncle.

Peter Carrick, too, would linger as long as he decently could with Natasha until her mother clearly wanted to go home after a physically and emotionally exhausting day. "Don't just disappear, Natasha, when you get back to Nottingham University. I've been thrilled to be with you this evening. Even though you must have been suffering you made me happy and I would not want this evening together to be an isolated event," Peter pleaded.

"Nor would I," Natasha retorted. "The fact that David said you were one of his closest friends somehow made it right for me that you should be my dancing partner on the day of my own father's funeral." Luckily Peter did not feel he had to answer, but he knew where his future now lay and it was certainly no longer with Sylvia.

CHAPTER 19

Polzol's funeral rather than graduation from the College marked the end of the initiation and training of Jamie's Cranwell generation. Thereafter they went their several ways – Jamie himself to Leuchars in Fife, Peter Lascelles to Laarbruch, Peter Carrick to Dishforth and Carl Higgins to Linton on Ouse. China Chu like Yousuf Ahmed before him went back to his homeland.

The grand county wedding in Lincoln Minster of Jamie and Janey was all that it should have been and more, but the bride's side of the cathedral was much fuller than Jamie's. His father with his medals on the stole around his neck gave the final blessing, but the Dean took the service and Padre Cinderton now Chaplain in Chief of the Royal Air Force preached the sermon.

He chose as his text the verse from the Deus Misereatur which the choir had beautifully sung, "Then shall the earth bring forth her increase and God even our own God shall give us his blessing." Praise God and by your exemplary lives seek to ensure as the psalm said, "that His way may be known upon earth". Be fruitful and multiply. These were his principal themes.

Of Jamie's contemporaries only Peter Lascelles, Carl Higgins and Peter Carrick were there. Lizzie was down from Scotland for the occasion but Yasmin pleaded end of term examinations rather than parental obstruction as the reason to stay in London to Carl's deepest regret. Natasha came across from Nottingham, which thrilled Peter Carrick beyond measure.

Jamie's friend Mark Driscoll, Flight Commander of 14 Squadron at Gütersloh made up the sword bearing party of four in Number One officers' uniforms with gold and bright blue ceremonial belts, who with gleaming blades extended framed the bridal couple's emergence from the cathedral's west door.

The reception to which all the great and good of Lincolnshire seemed to have been invited filled the ample Marquee on the wide lawns of Janey's family home in Fulbeck. Peter Lascelles and Elizabeth knew this would be the last wedding they would attend before their own in the station church at RAF Kinloss the following month.

"I'm afraid I can't offer you such glamorous nuptials, Peter," Lizzie confided to him wistfully. "Nor can the lawns of the Officers' Mess at Kinloss be compared with this glorious setting, but we'll enjoy our due share of glamour later on, won't we Peter? I know," she went on, "that I'll be able to earn twice as much as before when I return to the catwalks of Düsseldorf. What's more as a fully fledged Canberra pilot on full flying pay and soon to be promoted to Flying Officer you'll be able to take me to the finest resorts in Europe – the Italian Lakes, Sorrento, Biarritz and the French Riviera – not to mention Garmisch for the skiing."

Lizzie's excited anticipation did not vouchsafe so much as a second's pause to allow Peter to express his opinion. "I'm greatly looking forward to skiing there when you go off on your alpine survival course at Bal Kohlgrub next winter," she enthused. "I've just spoken to Jamie's friend Mark Driscoll who tells me that the last time members of 14 Squadron went down to Bavaria for winter survival training at least half of them brought their wives with them who took themselves off to

Garmisch Partenkirchen to ski. Anyway half of Germany will be on our doorstep – West Berlin, Hamburg, Baden Baden, Oberammergau and all the other wonderful places."

"Not exactly on our doorstep if I may say so, Lizzie," Peter retorted. "We'll actually be infinitely nearer to Holland than anywhere else, but who am I to stand in the way of such evidently entertaining ambitions," Peter asserted confidently trying to mask his growing apprehension that as far as Lizzie was concerned she would construe her signature in the marriage register as simply the counterfoil to a blank cheque made out and signed by him in her favour.

After an idyllic honeymoon in Deauville – Normandy's mild Atlantic weather was not much different from that of his home county of Devon – Jamie and Janey installed themselves in a modest bungalow at the edge of St Andrews within easy reach of Leuchars. Jamie took to squadron life and a junior officer's responsibilities like a proverbial duck to water. Janey soon built up her circle of friends among the other pilots' wives, both the town and gown communities of St Andrews as well as within the wider network of Fife's landed gentry.

Meanwhile Carl had been happy learning to instruct at the Central Flying School. From Little Rissington on the top of the Cotswolds Yasmin remained within relatively easy reach. Samantha perhaps honouring Yousuf's increasingly distant memory continued to provide a cover and a venue for their clandestine assignations as Yasmin's parents remained as vigilant of her activities as ever.

Carl's final weeks of the course on the Vampire were especially fulfilling. He loved the cross country bus rides to and from the Advanced Flying Wing's detached home from home at RAF Kemble. The spring and summertime walks over the flower strewn grass of the airfield to lunch at the diminutive Officers' Mess were a joy.

Furthermore the reassuring familiarity of a well liked aeroplane with which he was thoroughly at home gave him confidence. This made it easier for Carl to master the QFI's art of patter whereby demonstrations of control techniques in the air were given a fluent logical step by step verbal accompaniment. In addition he learned much from the mutual sorties with his vastly more experienced colleagues with whom he alternately played the role of pupil and instructor. Each such exercise was preceded by one with his own instructor to whom he had to repeat it satisfactorily after the mutual practice.

Linton in Ouse by contrast was an anticlimax for Carl. He enjoyed the flying, but unlike Cranwell he found the Advanced Flying Training School more of a sausage machine. Most of the trainee pilots were on short service commissions and although he got on well with his pupils none stood out as a real character or a star. Station life was briefly cheered by an influx of French speaking Lebanese Christian officers being groomed on the Vampire en route to Chivenor in preparation for flying their Air Force's newly acquired Hunters. They livened up the Mess with their exotic parties, large American cars and elegant girlfriends but their irrepressible charm and sense of fun only accentuated Carl's yearning for Yasmin.

As the late summer nights drew in she informed him that she was soon off to Washington to begin her international relations programme at GWU but promised him that she would visit her aunt and uncle in Bradford before she went. Could they meet she asked and could not her old friend Natasha come over, too. That way the doctor and his wife's anxieties would be allayed and perhaps Peter Carrick could be induced to come down to the city from Dishforth to make up the party for a foursome for old time's sake.

They met up at the gaunt oversized Victoria Hotel beside the railway station where Carl had optimistically installed himself in the bridal suite. Peter and Natasha duly arrived and Natasha was promptly despatched in his car, street map in hand, to go and collect Yasmin from her doctor uncle's house in Heaton. Her departure on a mission vital for the success of the weekend gave Carl and Peter time to reminisce.

"Whatever happened to Alice Van Meer?" Carl began. "You were much smitten by her when she came to Cranwell for poor old Ron Anderson's funeral as I recall. I think she impressed everybody actually but the rest of us were too diffident in those woeful circumstances to make the first move."

"Sad to say she turned out to be a passing fancy; not for want of trying on my part but I discovered that she already had a man waiting in the wings," Peter admitted. "I would not go quite so far as to suggest that she had been two-timing Ron but I soon found out that a South African working for De Beers in London had first call on her affections. I could not really compete, not from Dishforth and even less from the distant routes south and eastwards which the lumbering Beverley flies. Anyway diamonds are a girl's best friend, as Marilyn Monroe made so memorably clear," he explained.

"However, since ill winds seem to bring me luck," Peter went on, "Natasha and I hit it off at her father Polzol's funeral as you know. What you were not aware of, Carl, is that since then we've seen each other most weekends when I'm not off on route. She has wisely not mentioned me to her mother Ethel yet and I'm not sure she's keen to do so for a while.

"You would have thought that losing Taffy Jones and her seemingly indestructible father in the space of two years would have inoculated her against the Air Force for life but I suspect the bug is actually too deeply established in her bloodstream. Anyway we just get on so well. She's bubbly, vivacious and funny. Life with her is never boring."

"In short," Carl interjected, "she's the perfect antidote to a dour unsmiling Yorkshireman like you."

Natasha was soon back with Yasmin who looked radiant in a canary yellow shalwar kameez with a delicate silk scarf draped casually over her shoulder. Oblivious of the group of Friday evening drinkers she gave Carl a hug and a lingering kiss before the four sat down for a pre-dinner round of drinks.

"What's the news then, Yasmin?" Natasha began.

"For once I haven't much," Yasmin replied somewhat disconsolately. "Since the summer term ended at SOAS life has seemed rather empty. That's why I have been looking forward to this weekend so much. Yousuf, however, could not be happier now he's on Sabres at Sargoda. I still see Samantha from time to time, but you Carl have seemed a very long way away," she confided. "It was such a shame you were not able to get a posting nearer to London. Couldn't you have pulled some strings, Carl?"

"Sorry Yasmin. Exigencies of the Service," Carl responded simply. "I think you Peter and Natasha have shown us how we should have organised our lives. Peter tells me that you, Natasha, are going to begin a teacher's diploma course at Leeds in October and with your mother's home in Otley nearby you will be in easy access from Dishforth on Peter's all too brief interludes from long distance flying."

"How is your mother bearing up?" Carl asked solicitously.

"Reasonably well," Natasha answered reassuringly. "I don't think Mama misses the Air Force much and my uncles and aunts have rallied round. Hardly a week goes by without an invitation for her to go to one or other of the Polish clubs."

"Does anybody know how Jamie and Janey are getting on?" Peter Carrick enquired.

"Well, Janey rang me on return from honeymoon to thank me for my wedding present," Natasha replied. "They apparently loved Normandy and back at Leuchars Jamie has achieved his first live interception, of a Russian Bear reconnaissance bomber north of the Shetlands, which he and his Flight Commander escorted out of British airspace."

"No doubt our esteemed Sword of Honour star is well on the way to his first Air Force Cross by now. I bet he's a Squadron Leader before he's thirty," Peter responded.

"Deservedly so," interjected Carl. "Anyway this is neither the time nor the place for talking shop. We have an important decision to make. Do we go to Abdul Qureshi's curry house on the junction of Lumb Lane with the Circular Road which you recommended, Yasmin, as the best in the city, or do we rely on room service for our dinner and perhaps postpone the curry till lunch tomorrow? Do we take a vote or do we have a consensus for my preference for room service?" he asked.

"Most definitely," responded Yasmin in favour of Friday night intimacy as the precious hours of her last romantic weekend before departure for Washington ticked away.

A pre-autumnal evening chill comes early to the West Riding and especially to the eastern fringes of the Pennines so Carl and Yasmin were thrilled to find the chambermaid had anticipated their desire for comfort by lighting the gas fire. Very soon an elderly retainer who must have been on the hotel staff for decades was discreetly knocking on the door to bring in their dinner of chicken tikka and pilau rice followed by mango ice cream washed down with Tetley's beer.

"I hope you enjoy your dinner," he began. "It's a long time since we had a honeymoon couple occupy this suite. I trust you'll accept this little box of chocolates with the compliments of the hotel to go with your Jasmin tea or as a souvenir perhaps."

"Most thoughtful," said Yasmin.

"Thank you, indeed," replied Carl conscious of this delightfully unexpected consequence of his signature for them both as Mr and Mrs Higgins in the hotel register on arrival.

Perhaps the poignancy of the occasion and the painful awareness that true bliss is so ephemeral intensified their desire. The heady scent of Yasmin's olive skin and the proud firmness of her lissom body were more bewitching than ever. The repressed anticipation of the anguish of imminent parting inspired her not to resigned passivity but to heightened passion – beyond any they had experienced in the Hetherington mansion at Fulbeck, Samantha and Janey's flat or the Washington Hilton for that matter.

The knowledge that this would be their last night in each other's arms for an infinity of time made the blending of sensual bliss with inward pain almost too hard to bear. Tomorrow Yasmin would have to go back to her aunt and uncle's house. She was only in the hotel with Carl by deceit through her having told them she would spend the night at Natasha's mother's home in Otley. There was an ever present danger that they could ring her there but it was a risk well worth taking, which only served to fan the flames of her all consuming desire.

Passion consummated Carl sank back into the deep pillows and wondered whether such transient happiness was the fruit of love or purely lust. Yasmin he felt at heart gave herself so totally only in the knowledge that they owed each other no more than themselves. Marriage was beyond question and they did not need to broach the subject. They were not boyfriend and girlfriend either. They were free of such a status even in the estimation of their family and friends.

Rather they had met by divine intervention, were one but that same divinity called them now to different directions. Anyway it was inconceivable that a spirit as free as Yasmin's could be set in bonds as constraining as Air Force Married Quarters or a Service hiring in the local town provided by the station accommodation office.

Even his dear parents with their happy years in Karachi behind them would not be able to comprehend Yasmin and himself as an entity. It was her defiance of conventional definition which thrilled him so profoundly. Pray God that their destinies would bring her back to him before his days were done but in his heart he knew he could not count on it.

Next day Natasha's melancholy duty was to drive Yasmin back to her aunt and uncle's house before saying goodbye to Peter who had to return to Dishforth to fly to Aden that night. Carl and Yasmin's parting was brief and seemingly undemonstrative. Their love of the night before had already fully expressed the sum of all their feelings.

"Ring me before you finally take flight for Washington," Carl entreated.

"I will. The exigencies of the Service as you so dispassionately and phlegmatically call them will never erase you from my heart. You know that darling Carl," Yasmin replied before enfolding him in a final embrace.

"Come on you two," Peter interrupted. "I've got flight planning to do this afternoon and Natasha should have dropped you off, Yasmin, in Heaton hours ago."

"All right, all right. Don't be so impatient, Peter," Carl responded firmly. "Just allow us one last farewell kiss." This time Yasmin did not linger but slipped a little lapis lazuli box into his palm.

"This is for your cuff links, collar and Mess dress shirt studs, things which you can't afford to lose before Dining In nights or ceremonial parades. It'll be a memento of me wherever the exigencies of the Service take you. God speed as you British say, my love."

"God willing destiny will bring us together again," answered Carl.

"I'm sure it will," said Yasmin with confidence stepping delicately into Peter's Austin A40 saloon with tears flowing freely down her pallid cheeks.

CHAPTER 20

Back at Linton on Ouse the Mess was bleak as only an RAF Officers' Mess at the weekend can be. The emptiness of the dining room and corridors was accentuated by late August block leave, which took the Acting Pilot Officers of the Senior Vampire course and many QFIs away. Officers who commuted weekends to their families in far flung permanent homes had left long since as soon as they could decently escape on Friday afternoon.

Just a handful of hardened bachelors and bruised casualties of divorce or separation remained, some in the anteroom thumbing through glossy magazines with glazed unseeing eyes their minds fixed on the happiness of times past or contemplating a dreadful future of an infinity of such emptiness.

Only a foursome of Lebanese second lieutenants playing tennis on the court outside evinced any life. Carl was pleased to see his flying student Sammy Haddad among them. With any luck he would come into the bar with his friends for an aperitif before they all dashed off to York for a Saturday night out.

Carl had come to like Sam Haddad very much. He was always respectful, alert and eager to please. Sam was much more overtly enthusiastic than Carl's other pupil Acting Pilot Officer Trevor Edwards who seemed more focussed on the gratuity to be had on leaving the Air Force after eight or twelve years' service than on flying as a vocation. Sammy Haddad was always knocking on the QFIs' partition window in the crewroom begging to be allowed to join a formation lead sortie or an airtest.

At six pm sharp Carl was in the bar just as it opened. Soon afterwards showered and relaxed after their tennis the four Lebanese officers entered in animated conversation already anticipating eagerly their forthcoming night out. A couple of the Mess' more permanent bachelor drinkers were perched on stools in the corner. Carl was just preparing to order himself his first pint of beer of the evening. "Let me get this drink, sir," Sammy Haddad insisted detaching himself from his group of Lebanese friends. "I owe you one. You saw me off solo very early on and I've enjoyed every moment of the course ever since. What have you got in store for me on Monday, sir?" he enquired.

"I'm going to introduce you to high level aerobatics, Sam," Carl replied. "They'll require sensitivity and a light touch on the controls but should pose no problem. Just before we return to base we'll do a bit of spinning revision to liven things up and stop you getting bored."

"Sounds like a trip I can really look forward to," Haddad answered confidently.

"Let's, not anticipate Monday morning now," Carl responded. "You've still got most of the weekend ahead of you, Sammy." How ironic it was that his Lebanese pupil Sam at the same age of twenty-one and the same lowly rank as himself should be having such fun at Linton whilst he, his British instructor with all the responsibility and standing of a QFI and full flying pay should following Yasmin's departure be facing a totally empty social life.

"Excuse me, sir, I must rush," Sam interjected. "My friend Joseph Haroun's girlfriend Patricia is introducing us to all her friends from the secretarial college and we can't keep them waiting."

Monday dawned gloriously clear. Carl always enjoyed his early morning walk from the Officers' Mess across the dewy grass to Met briefing in the Operations building. The QFIs sat in front and the student pilots behind. The station meteorologist confirmed that visibility would remain excellent throughout the day with a moderate wind more or less down the runway. There would be no problem with the weather Carl thought to himself for Sam Haddad's solo practice later on.

The Chief Instructor Wing Commander Chivvers, Carl's former cadet wing squadron commander at Cranwell, issued the flying orders of the day, gave particulars of the diversion airfields of Leeming and Waddington and confirmed that there were no Royal Flights or other notifiable air movements, which would interrupt the normal flying schedule.

Chivvers' appointment pleased Carl because he had always been benevolently disposed towards him at the College and was universally recognised there as fair minded. His primarily front line background on fighters gave him a practical outlook to set against the fastidiousness verging on pedantry of some of the longer serving QFIs, especially those who had served down on the 'waterfront' at Rissington on the staff of the Central Flying School whether as instructors of would be QFIs or as 'trappers' as the members of its feared but respected Examining Wing, which maintained flying standards throughout the service, were called.

Briefing had been expeditiously conducted, another admirable characteristic of Chivvers' style and by 08.00 hours Carl and Sam Haddad were together in the briefing cubicle. High level aerobatics were not a difficult exercise to explain. It was a case of ensuring there was no cloud about, maintaining good lookout and orientation and above all avoiding brusque control movements, which could precipitate a stall or subsequent departure into an inadvertent spin.

Sam had always been smooth and sensitive on the controls – an ideal candidate for graduation to the Hunter, thought Carl. He did not anticipate any problems for him. Sam had no questions and they were soon airborne heading westwards towards the Pennines before turning north-east into clear airspace above the Yorkshire moors.

At twenty-eight thousand feet over Helmsley Carl began his first demonstration of a high level loop pattering away fluently to Sam throughout with an easy running commentary as he swung the aircraft into a tight turn first one way then the other looking hard into the direction of turn, then above and especially below to make quite sure the sky was clear.

He then smoothly applied full power, lowered the nose to build up speed and eased the control column steadily back watching his wings carefully to make sure they were level with the horizon all the way round. Over the top he inched the throttle back a bit to help the nose to drop and progressively brought the stick back to maintain plenty of 'g' on exit to complete the loop at precisely the same height as he had entered into it. "You have control," said Carl. "Now Sam, you repeat the exercise exactly as demonstrated please."

Sam began well conscientiously clearing the sky around the aircraft but initially pulled too hard on the stick so that they juddered into an incipient stall on the way up. "Just relax the pressure," advised Carl calmly. "Now the juddering's stopped continue the manoeuvre. Look back for the horizon over the top. There it is, now back a bit with the throttle. Look out still for your wing tips and keep straight on the way down. Start pulling. Not enough 'g' there, Sam, and you left the pull out a bit late so we've lost a couple of thousand feet. Otherwise quite promising." Up they went again to regain the altitude lost.

"Now try again, Sam," breathed Carl over the R/T. "That was okay for a first attempt, but let's just repeat the performance." This time Sam was too gentle with the stick on the way up and had lost flying speed before the apogee of the loop was reached. The aircraft wallowed inverted, the nose plunged earthwards and the left wing flicked up. "Just hold the controls firmly central," advised Carl. The aeroplane regained speed and was easily righted by Sam. So up they climbed once more to twenty-eight thousand feet where Sam then performed the manoeuvre to perfection.

Sam to the accompaniment of Carl's calm unhurried commentary had got the hang of rolls off the top of loops, vertical rolls through one rotation only at such high altitude, barrel rolls and aileron turns vertically downward with airbrakes out and throttled fully back again through just one turn to prevent an excess build up of speed.

Before returning to Linton Carl instructed Sam to show him a full spin with a standard recovery for the minimum loss of height. Sam performed the introductory checks to perfection, cleared the sky well, throttled back and applied full rudder just at the point of stall. "There she goes," explained Carl as the aeroplane flicked one and a half times, then plunged vertically down with a vicious rotation.

"Check the slip indicator," he continued. "Oppose the yaw – that means the ball with full rudder then stick centrally forward. See the spin is stopping. Hold it. Wings level. Ease out of the dive. There's the horizon. On with the power. Now up again to twenty-seven thousand feet and do the same again, but with wheels and flaps down. I want to see you clean up the aeroplane as soon as she departs."

This time the departure was quite violent with the right wing flicking down. However, by quickly raising the undercarriage and flaps, with a check forward on the control column and a smooth application of power Sam demonstrated to Carl that he could act fast and reliably in potentially difficult and dangerous situations. He was more than happy to send his pupil off solo to practise high level aerobatics.

So confident was Carl that he forwent formal debriefing in a cubicle in favour of a more relaxed chat with Sam over coffee at the crewroom bar. He signed Sam away on his forthcoming sortie, finished his coffee and Kit Kat whilst reading the accident reports in the latest Air Clues magazine and then set off on foot across the apron to the Met office at the base of the control tower to check the latest weather for the afternoon's cross country to St Mawgan in Cornwall with Edwards.

Carl was only halfway there and watching a Vampire climb out when he heard a hollow grinding sound as of an imminent compressor stall. He thought no more of it at first. It was normally caused by some ham fisted student's applying power too abruptly when he got low on the approach. However, this time was different as the grinding was followed by a muffled explosion. Then the engine noise stopped and the climbing Vampire's sudden descent ended with an audible thump followed almost instantly by the forlorn hooting of the crash alarm.

As he reached the door to the tower it flew open and Wing Commander Chivvers emerged running towards his Land Rover parked outside. "There's been an accident, Carl," he shouted. "I think it's your pupil Haddad." Carl felt the air depart from his lungs as if kicked by a horse.

"Can I come with you, sir?" he asked.

"Jump in," ordered Chivvers setting off at maximum speed across the grass towards the overshoot area upwind of the main runway. "Get ready to open the airfield gate will you Carl," instructed Chivvers.

When they got there it was already open. The crash crew had arrived on the scene first. The fire tender and an ambulance could be seen at the end of a long wheat field where the barely identifiable remains of a Vampire were blazing furiously. The fire tender was dispensing copious foam over the wreck from its roof mounted dousing cannon. A couple of silver asbestos suited and integrally helmeted members of the crash crew were trying to approach the locked cockpit with portable extinguishers in one hand and fireman's axes in the other. However, Carl could mercifully see little detail through the roaring flames and thick black oily smoke.

Then a fierce gust of wind briefly drove back the conflagration and Carl saw again that the canopy was indeed firmly closed. The pilot had clearly not tried to get out and his bone dome was discernible with the outline of a cedar of Lebanon on the top. Chivvers was right. It had to be Sammy. He was the only Lebanese officer to wear the national emblem on his flying helmet and not simply on the right sleeve of his overalls as did the others.

The driver of the fire tender leant out and shouted down to Carl, "I would not get too near if I were you, sir. There could be explosions at any time. Leave it to us, sir. This is our job." It must be hotter than a potters kiln inside the cockpit thought Carl as he glanced again toward the blaze momentarily overcoming his nauseous revulsion. The two intrepid firemen had reached the canopy through the flames and were furiously hacking away at the tough Perspex. Chivvers came over to the fire tender where a third fireman was keeping the rescuers' access path clear with a separate foam hose and a fourth was playing a jet of water on his heroic colleagues to keep them cool with another.

"I'm afraid it was Haddad, Carl. I'm so sorry," confirmed the Chief Instructor to the young QFI. "R/T from the tower to my vehicle has verified it. Apparently he hit a huge flock of lapwings just after take off which put paid to his engine."

"I already knew, sir," Carl replied simply. "I recognised his helmet with the cedar tree on it, but thanks all the same."

At that moment the two firemen who were astride the nose section and cutting away at the pilot's straps extracted an inchoate shape from the cockpit. The ambulance backed up to the wreck and two white coated rubber gloved orderlies helped the rescuers to carry the charred mass from the edge of the flames to a body sized plastic tray, which they covered with plastic sheeting and lifted into the rear of the vehicle. It drove promptly off leaving the firemen to continue dousing the flames.

Chivvers turned to Carl and said, "No one ever gets fully used to such horrors. They afflict even the hardened soul. We must just get on with our job but if you want the afternoon off today you have my permission to take it. Have you any sorties planned?"

"Yes sir, I have one," answered Carl. "I'm due to fly to St Mawgan on a high level landing away cross country with my other pupil, Edwards. I was just going to the Met office to check the weather and do some preliminary flight planning when this happened. I intend to fly the exercise as scheduled, sir."

"I'm sure you're right to do so," the Wing Commander replied, "but remember my office door is always open. If you have any thoughts about Haddad and the accident before the official Board of Inquiry begins please feel free to share them with me. I'll run you back to Flights."

On arrival Chivvers went in to see the Squadron Commander and Carl entered the students' crewroom. Joseph Haroun and his two fellow Lebanese officers were there to meet him. "Don't take it too hard, sir. It was an act of God," said Joseph. "It's extraordinary because only yesterday Sam confided to me that he had recently dreamed of being welcomed by the Blessed Virgin Mary in a Lebanese garden full of cypresses and lofty cedars. It was a beautiful place scented with lavender, thyme and aromatic Mediterranean herbs. I'm sure he's there now."

Haroun went on from his moving depiction of honest faith to more practical matters. "I've already rung the Embassy about the arrangements and we've seen our respective Squadron Commanders. As senior Lebanese officer on the course I have fixed an appointment with the Station Commander at 17.00 hours tonight. We have it in mind to hold a short memorial service in the station chapel the day after tomorrow morning at 11.00 hours, which will leave time for Sam's coffin to be taken to Stansted Airport to be put on a Transmediterranean Airlines cargo aeroplane, which takes off for Beirut at midnight. The funeral will be for the family and Lebanese Air Force to organise obviously."

Carl was deeply impressed with the dignity and calm efficiency of the three young Lebanese officers, who as soon as the cruel tragedy of Sam's death occurred had taken upon themselves to honour their fellow officer by doing everything appropriate on his behalf entirely correctly with thoughtfulness and evident reverence for his memory. The conversation with Haroun over, Carl went to see his Squadron Commander.

Squadron Leader Hew Williams, a balding, stocky, normally ebullient Welshman had spent his early career on Venoms, instructed on Balliols and come to Linton after Staff College and refreshers both at Manby and the Central Flying School. He usually exuded wise benevolence but now he was in untypically sombre mood. "Do take your hat off and have a seat, Carl" he began. "Please don't blame yourself for what happened. The situation Haddad faced was not survivable – engine failure immediately after take off beyond the end of the runway. He knew that ejection so low and slow would have been fatal.

"I've already recommended to the Station Commander that a permanent bird scaring system be installed on the airfield to prevent a repeat of Haddad's collision with the lapwings. Have you got anything to say to me privately about Haddad and the accident or do you want to keep any comments for the Board of Inquiry?" asked Williams.

"No nothing, sir," replied Carl, "except that I did not have time to write up my report on our last sortie together early this morning. Haddad's file has already disappeared from the cabinet."

"Yes I know," answered Williams. "I've got it for safekeeping for the accident inquiry, so I'd be grateful if you could install yourself at the side table here and get it done now before I send it on to Wing Commander Chivvers.

"By the way," he continued. "I'm assuming you'd wish to continue your flying programme this afternoon so I've sent Edwards off to the Met section and then Flight Planning to prepare your navex to St Mawgan. Anything else Higgins?"

"Yes indeed, sir," Carl responded. "Please get me another pupil as soon as you can. I'd be underemployed with just one and I don't want time to brood on the death of Haddad."

"You're lucky there. I think I can help, Carl," the Squadron Leader replied genially. "Acting Pilot Officer Richard Hawtrey has been having problems with his instrument flying. He alleges that his QFI shouts and makes his life a misery. There's a tricky challenge for you young man, to restore Hawtrey's self-confidence and performance in the air or else we'll have to suspend him."

"Thank you, sir," Carl replied, put on his hat, saluted and made his way to his fellow QFIs' crewroom where his instructor colleagues sought to console him with solicitous commiserations.

As soon as Carl got airborne with Edwards his spirits began to lift. He had specially chosen spectacularly beautiful Welsh routings, outbound to St Mawgan and back to base, which did full justice to the incredible visibility. On the way out the turning point was Royal Naval Air Station Brawdy at the farthest extremity of Pembrokeshire and on the return RAF Valley in Anglesey overlooking the Menai strait and Snowdonia.

It was so clear and cloudless that from some seven miles up the country spread out like a map. The only potential ambiguities came at the respective turning points. Edwards to his credit correctly identified Brawdy rather than its satellite of St David's. Over Anglesey on the way back Edwards was right again pinpointing the home of 4 Advanced Flying Training School at Valley rather than the relief landing ground of Mona in the middle of the island.

At St Mawgan they were entertained to crewroom tea and biscuits by Pilot Officer Farquharson who after initial misgivings was enjoying his posting as a co-pilot on the resident Shackleton Squadron. He had already had a detachment for a week to Gibraltar and next month, he informed Carl, he was due to for another this time for a fortnight to the Azores.

As they chatted about Cranwell contemporaries and times past Carl confided to Farquharson how his pupil Sam Haddad had been killed that same morning. "Poor you, Carl," Farquharson responded. "What a dreadful experience. I am so sorry. Did you know that our friend Peter Lascelles was a lot luckier? He had hardly got to Laarbruch before he ejected from his Canberra, which was somehow rammed by a Hunter from Gütersloh. The Hunter pilot went straight in."

"Anyone we know?" asked Carl anxiously.

"I don't think so," answered Farquharson. "A certain Flying Officer Purbrick apparently. He'd only recently joined 14 Squadron and was diverting to Brüggen owing to bad weather at Gütersloh. Peter and his navigator landed in farmland south of Krefeld. Peter suffered no broken bones, only severe bruising."

"I hope his drama makes Lizzie a lot more solicitous about him," observed Carl. "I always felt he was taken for granted by her."

"I doubt it," said Farquharson. "Rumour has it she was back on the catwalk the very next day and didn't even drive up to Laarbruch to see him in the Sick Bay."

"How did you find all this out?" inquired Carl.

"Freddie Parker's also on maritime. We converted together at Kinloss and then he got posted to Ballykelly. His girlfriend Camilla from Nottingham modelled for a bit with Lizzie and they've kept in touch ever since. He rang me with the news last night," Farquharson replied.

"Thanks for the hospitality, Farquie my friend. I'll send Peter a get well card to boost his bruised ego," Carl answered. "We must get airborne now or Linton will be closed down when we arrive. See you about the circuit. Perhaps I'll be your instructor when you go through CFS in years to come. Stranger things have happened."

Next day's memorial service in the station chapel was brief but dignified. All of Flying Wing attended as did the station executives. The padre officiated in English. A bearded black robed Maronite Christian priest said prayers in Arabic. Sammy Haddad's Squadron Commander Hew Williams read the lesson from St John's First Epistle with typically Welsh reverence for its language: "This is the victory that overcometh the world, even our faith… and this is the record that God has given to us eternal life and this life is in his Son."

The funeral message of Psalm 90 was apposite: "Thou turnest man to destruction… as soon as thou scatterest them they are even as a sleep; and fade away suddenly like the grass. In the morning it is green and growth up, but in the evening it is cut down, dried up and withered."

In resurrection hope for Sam two well chosen Easter hymns were lustily sung – "The strife is o'er the battle done, now is the victor's triumph won." The second some twelve centuries old by St John of Damascus could almost have been written for the premature passing of a Levantine soldier of Christ: "The day of resurrection! From death to life eternal, from earth unto the sky. Our Christ has brought us over with hymns of victory."

Wing Commander Chivvers' address was simple and heartfelt. "We have been honoured," he began, "to have had Second Lieutenant Sam Haddad and his fellow student pilots from Lebanon amongst us. It grieves us greatly that with Sam's tragic death the Lebanese Air Force should have lost an officer of such outstanding promise.

"In his short stay at Linton on Ouse" he went on, "Sam Haddad set us a memorable example of cheerful, willing application to every task and duty. He loved flying. His own QFI and those on his squadron who flew with him admired his enthusiasm and eagerness to learn. His untimely death is as profound a sorrow to us as it must be to the Lebanese Air Force. We share the grief of his family and friends back home. By his death we feel part of a single grieving community sorrowful but united in the pursuit of peace and security in our respective countries. We are bound firmly together by the sacrifices which their constant maintenance entails."

The pallbearers readied themselves – Joseph Haroun and his two fellow Lebanese officers, Acting Pilot Officers Edwards and Hawtrey with Carl back right as if in charge of a squad of marching cadets at Cranwell. The organ played the Lebanese National Anthem and then Carl's selected team lifted Sam's flag-draped cedar wood coffin to their shoulders and slow marched to the black hearse waiting outside. They eased it in from the back and Carl stepped forward and reverently removed the Lebanese flag handing it to Joseph Haroun.

The pallbearers took three paces to the rear and saluted. The congregation now assembled on the chapel steps saluted also. The doors of the hearse were shut and the vehicle moved off. It glided past a ceremonial guard of white belted, peak capped airmen at the main gate who crashed to attention and slammed their right hands onto their presented rifles in a parting tribute to the fallen as the long black vehicle set off on its unhurried journey to Stansted and to home.

That very evening Carl had his last telephone conversation with Yasmin before she left for Washington. It had been trying to his fortitude to wait for her calls since their brief idyllic weekend together in Bradford. For him to ring her would still have been unacceptable to her parents. The Begum, her mother had of late become even more pressing, Yasmin reported, that she make a good match soon which would do credit to the family. The Wing Commander was less insistent about their daughter's early marriage and more indulgent towards her plans for academic success in America.

Nevertheless Carl had spent too much time for his peace of mind in recent days hanging around in the bar or re-reading out of date magazines in the anteroom waiting for her to telephone. So when the hall porter with news of Yasmin's call finally interrupted Carl's desultory perusal of the situations vacant in Flight International he was awoken excitingly from his reverie about the well paid boredom of flying for an airline and rushed with tremulous anticipation to the telephone cubicle in the hall. Carl was longing fervently to hear the soft yet stimulating Karachi modulation of Yasmin's enticing voice.

"Dearest Carl," she began, "I'm due to fly out tomorrow. You will write to me won't you. I could not bear to lose you. It is terrible that I have to leave you now just when your own pupil Sam was so tragically killed. It must be God's will to test your courage. These sorrows seem incomprehensible but remember that in a few months we've enjoyed more happiness than most people experience in a lifetime. I cannot and will not believe that it is finished for good."

"Nor can I, darling," Carl agreed, trying to sustain some optimism as he contemplated the desolation of life without her. "How are your family?" he enquired seeking to move the conversation on to positive ground.

"Good news, I'm glad to say, Carl," she replied. "Papa has been promoted Group Captain on the tour expiry of the Air Advisor who has been recalled to Pakistan. Dad is lucky to be appointed as his successor in post, so my parents have to stay in London a good while longer. As for Yousuf he is off to East Pakistan next week. His squadron is going to Dacca on detachment for six months as the resident air defence unit just as the monsoon peters out and the dry season begins. He's thrilled as you can imagine. What about you my love?"

"I've got a new pupil called Hawtrey who's been put in Carl Higgins' remedial class to sort out his IF. I think with patience I'll just about get him up to passing out standard even though after winning his wings he'll still need supervision in the cockpit for a bit. I can't see him in any other role than as a second pilot on transports or maritime reconnaissance.

"As for the future," Carl continued, "I hope that before too long I can be posted to fighters like Jamie and Mark or even Canberras like Peter but preferably the PR9 high level reconnaissance version. If the worst comes to the worst the diminutive agile swept wing Gnats are beginning to take over as advanced trainers from the ageing Vampires at Valley. I would not mind that job, a challenging new aeroplane and plenty of sea air. So that's it, my love. My little ambitions are very parochial compared with yours, preparing yourself at GWU to represent Pakistan on the world stage. But as you've often reminded me it's the seemingly small things in life which really matter. I'll try to appreciate them even without you beside me to keep my eyes open to life's beauties. God bless you and God speed."

"May the Almighty and Merciful One bless you, too, and keep you safe until we meet again," she replied sobbing uncontrollably into the phone.

With Yasmin's departure Carl's life at Linton established itself in an unremarkable routine. He devoted himself wholeheartedly to his flying building up his experience at some thirty-five to forty hours per month. Just as he had forecast Hawtrey graduated successfully. Squadron Leader Hew Williams congratulated Carl on his professionalism, which was confirmed by his elevation to A2 flying instructor status.

Edwards also did well after a slow start. He secured the posting of his choice to helicopters saying he could get operational flying in the Middle or Far East on rotary wing or at least the chance to do something useful for stricken humanity as an air sea rescue pilot.

Before he was even assigned replacement students Carl found himself summoned to the Chief Instructor Wing Commander Chivvers in his office halfway up the control tower overlooking the signals square and the airfield. As usual Chivvers was totally relaxed and immaculately dressed in made to measure battle dress with starched collar and Cranwell cufflinks. On the walls of his office hung pictures of the aircraft to which Linton on Ouse had been home right back to the heavy bombers of World War Two in the days of Leonard Cheshire. Knowing Chivvers' reputation Carl had put on his best blue uniform rather than slopping down in flying overalls. It was a subliminally correct decision for what was to follow.

"Make yourself comfortable, Carl," the Wing Commander instructed. "Like a coffee?" He rang the bell on his desk and the Flying Wing Adjutant a heavily bemedalled aircrew Warrant Officer came around the door.

"Sir you called?"

"Coffee for two please, Mr Harvey – standard NATO."

"Very good, sir."

"Hew Williams tells me you've done an exemplary job getting Hawtrey through," Chivvers began. "I did his final handling check as you know and Hew is right. I think he'll make a perfectly acceptable second dickey on Hastings. As for Edwards he did the best practice flame out landing of the course on his test with me. He impressed me and I'm sure he deserves the posting of his choice and will do well on helicopters. What's more I got a good report from standards flight on your upgrade to an A2 QFI category. Hew says you've been putting in more hours than anyone else in his squadron – standing in for sick instructors or QFIs on leave and courses, doing air tests, positioning flights, leading formations and so on.

"All this must have come to the knowledge of the powers that be, Carl, since I got a phone call from Air Chief Marshal Swallowfield's personal staff officer over in Germany asking for you to go across for an interview the day after tomorrow. The C in C needs a new ADC to see him through his final year. He promises you a month's Hunter conversion course down at Chivenor before you go and a posting onto fighter reconnaissance Hunters in Germany when you finish with him. Or you can keep on instructing afterwards and transfer to Valley on the Gnat. The Air Marshal certainly won't hold it against you if you decide to stay here with your pupils till your tour ends. Not everyone is cut out to be an ADC. What do you think?"

Carl could hardly believe his ears. To return to Germany, his spiritual home with FR the most thrilling job in the Air Force in prospect and an immediate Hunter course on offer was the stuff of fantasy. "Of course I accept, sir," he replied with alacrity. "I just want to thank you for letting my name go forward."

"Don't thank me, Carl," Chivvers answered. "It's for your Squadron Commander that you should be buying a thank you pint. Hew'll miss you.

"Drive over to Dishforth tomorrow," the Chief Instructor continued. "They have a Beverley going across to Wildenrath every Wednesday morning. You'll be met on arrival and taken to Headquarters Royal Air Force, Germany and Second Allied Tactical Air Force at Rheindahlen – the C in C wears two hats as C in C of both. I'm sure the interview will go just fine. I've already been onto Command to get them to come up with a replacement QFI for you. Any questions?"

"None sir and thank you very much."

"Oh one thing, Carl, you're due to report for the short Hunter course at Chivenor at 0800 hours on Monday morning. Give my regards to Group Captain Prendergast. Good day."

Carl arrived at Dishforth in time for breakfast in the fine pre Second World War permanent Mess. Peter Carrick was there to greet him in the hallway as arranged and together they made their way to his squadron, which was located in the southernmost of the large brick built hangars across the runway from the Great North Road A1. "I've managed to organise my flying schedule to take you over to Germany myself," Peter explained proudly. "I got my captaincy on the aeroplane only last week, so I'm still seizing every opportunity to build up hours – even on milk runs like this weekly trip to Wildenrath.

"My next objective is to wangle myself a parachute course," he went on. "It is all very well providing a jumping platform for the Army, but I feel I would be a more effective lift provider for the airborne forces if I knew from personal experience more of what their role entails."

"Admirable sentiments, Peter, and entirely laudable but I do not believe they're worth a crushed vertebra, a broken limb or even putting your aircrew category at risk," Carl replied. "What does Natasha think?"

"I think she now wants to marry me, but seriously she and my Squadron Commander feel I'm mad, but the Wing Commander Flying Richard Day who went to the Army Staff College at Camberley and did a tour at the School of Land Air warfare at Old Sarum sees the point and is all in favour. I pressed him on the idea when he was in his cups at a Mess Guest Night and he promised to take it up with Transport Command. The Senior Air Staff Officer there is an old friend of his from their time on the Berlin Airlift together flying Yorks into Gatow from Hamburg.

"So long as the SASO can be persuaded that I'm not going to act as a precedent the Wingco Flying reckons that I'll be on the course at Abingdon with a bunch of maroon beretted troopers before the end of the year. In the meantime to get fit I run round the perimeter track twice a week and go to the station gym twice a week as well. An ex-parachute jumping instructor down there puts me through my paces rolling on the mats and jumping off the wallbars. He reckons I'm one of the very few aircrew officers he's met who actually wants to jump out of an aeroplane. He claims they've usually got a psychological block against it."

CHAPTER 21

The cavernous rear fuselage of the Beverley was filled with a Land Rover, a light field gun and an assortment of crated vehicle parts. The boom above was fitted out with seats taken up by a squadron of proverbial Rock Apes, denim clad RAF Regiment personnel en route to airfield defence duties at Brüggen.

The Flight Sergeant Despatcher who roamed the vast cargo area wired into the aircraft's intercom at the end of an ultra long lead invited Carl to climb the steep ladder to the flight deck up top. When he got there Peter Carrick who was accompanied by a Flight Lieutenant Second Pilot senior in rank to himself ushered Carl into the rumble seat he swung across between them. A Flight Lieutenant Navigator and a Warrant Officer Flight Engineer addressed themselves to their respective tasks at the plotting tables and crowded instrument displays behind.

As the mighty beast lumbered forth out of dispersal the roar of the four Centaurus engines was almost deafening especially without a bonedome to deaden the sound. How Peter could taxi from so high up without crushing the taxiway lights or straying off onto the grass amazed Carl.

Peter insisted on demonstrating to Carl the short take off technique with water methanol injection for maximum power. Held on the brakes against the straining engines the Beverley emitted a stupefying crescendo of sound. The aircraft vibrated furiously at full boost till brakes unleashed it surged forward and was soon climbing steeply away. Once over the North Sea Peter let Carl fly the aeroplane as far as the continental coastline, which he found uncomplicated though sluggish yet surprisingly satisfying. He could understand now the satisfaction of flying even the largest and most lumbering of transport aircraft.

At Wildenrath a staff car with sergeant driver was on the tarmac to meet Carl and whisk him to Headquarters Royal Air Force Germany, which nestled among trees over a large area near Mönchengladbach. What a strange destiny had brought him so unexpectedly back to Germany Carl mused as he signed into the Mess. As he did so a punctilious civilian attendant handed him a note on official crested blue paper which read: Flying Officer Higgins, You are to report to the Air Officer Commanding in Chief Air Chief Marshal Sir Thomas Swallowfield at 0900 hours tomorrow morning. I shall be at the main door of the Mess to collect you at 0830 hours. Signed John Fowler, Wing Commander, Personal Staff Officer to AO C in C.

Carl did a brief reconnaissance of the bar and anteroom, which contained Army as well as Air Force officers of a variety of nationalities but the Mess was clearly very dead. He decided to make the best of a boring reality and to turn in early so as to respond brightly to the Air Marshal's questioning next morning.

Wing Commander Fowler was short, slim and dapper with prematurely greying hair. Carl noticed a General Service Medal ribbon and one for the Queen's Commendation for Valuable Service in the air on his barrel like chest. His accent was redolent of Douglas Bader or a BBC news reader of the 1930s.

"You're a lucky chap, Higgins," he began. "To be talent spotted by Swallowfield. I reckon he's the best boss in the Air Force. He lets you get on with your job. Of course he expects you to do it properly. Luckily the chances are that you will because you would never wish to let him down. But remember, his standards are of the highest."

"I certainly will, sir," replied Carl sincerely.

They approached the long squat rectangular 1950s style Headquarters building. A large expanse of lawn lay in front leading to a line of national flags of NATO member states and an extra large one of the North Atlantic organisation itself. "One wing belongs to us – the Second Allied Tactical Air Force and Royal Air Force Germany. The other belongs to the British Army of the Rhine and Northern Army Group," Fowler explained. "Two double hatted four star British officers command all four organisations, which are supposed to work together in perfect harmony to keep the Warsaw Pact forces in their place and to deter any aggressive adventuring on their part at our expense."

They parked at the PSO's designated slot and once Carl had received his temporary pass walked up the steps to the top floor – an extensive corridor lined with signed portrait photographs of past Commanders in Chief and scenes of allied aircraft, air and ground crews and bases from every part of the Second Allied Tactical Air Force Command.

"This is my lair, which I will most probably share with you if the AO C in C likes the cut of your jib," declared the Wing Commander as he ushered Carl into the large outer office. It had two big shiny wooden desks, one for the PSO and one for the ADC with another much smaller one of synthetic material tucked away in an adjoining annexe where sat the secretarial sergeant whose task it was as office administrator to deal with the filing and to process the paperwork.

"Sergeant Thompson," said Fowler, "this is Mr Higgins. He may be joining us before too long."

"Very good, sir," the sergeant replied immediately returning his attention to the heaps of files in the tin trays before him.

"Give me the Commander in Chief's papers for today sergeant," instructed the Wing Commander as he led Carl into Swallowfield's own office placing them in the middle of his totally bare, gleaming mahogany desk.

Carl had time to notice gilt framed pictures mostly oils of aircraft and aerial combat, jungle and mountain scenes, interspersed with more portraits of distinguished officers of all three Services. An ample glass faced cabinet contained a collection of cups, crests, trophies, silver models and assorted martial objects d'art. A Japanese Samurai sword lay on a low glass topped table between a chintz sofa and two armchairs in front of his desk.

"The C in C arrives at 0855 hours sharp each morning unless he is away touring squadrons and stations of course," explained the PSO. "If he appoints you he will expect you to receive him at the door of the outer officer, take his coat and cap which should be placed on the stand in the corner and to accompany him to his desk inquiring if he has any special instructions for the day. When he has perused his files he will ring for me to deal with the matters arising. Is that clear?"

"Yes indeed, sir."

"I suggest you sit down at the ADCs desk for now," Fowler concluded. "Fortuitously he's gone flying today. He's over at Gütersloh keeping current on the Hunter. The C in C likes to use the two seater T7 from station flight there as his personal communications aeroplane. Either myself or the ADC acts as his safety pilot."

"Yes I know, sir," Carl responded. "I remember his arrival by T7 to take a passing out parade at the College when I was still a junior Flight Cadet down in the South Brick Lines."

"I'm afraid your Cranwell jargon passes me by, Higgins. I came up the hard way with a short service commission," the PSO answered frostily. "It wasn't made permanent till I was thirty. More importantly how many hours have you got on Hunters?"

"Two and a bit actually, sir. I had three trips in an F4 and a couple in a Canberra down at Kemble at the end of my CFS Course."

"I'm sure Sir Thomas will want you to put that right at the earliest opportunity," Fowler went on. "Certainly before you join him."

"I very much hope so," replied Carl. "My Chief Instructor at Linton intimated that if selected I would have to take the short Hunter conversion course at Chivenor first. I must confess that's in good measure why I'm here apart from the great privilege of the invitation from Sir Thomas of course and the fact that I like the country and speak the language."

"Stress that to the C in C," advised the Wing Commander. "He's desperately trying to integrate the Luftwaffe more fully into the Command's operations. As a relatively recently reformed Service it still lacks modern experience and a good German speaker could help him liaise much more effectively with German officers as well as local civic dignitaries. You could be very welcome here if you play your cards right."

The door to the outer office swung open and in strode Sir Thomas Swallowfield. "Where's the ADC?" he bellowed.

"At Gütersloh doing his continuation training on the Hunter if you recall," explained the PSO.

"Of course, of course," replied the AOC tossing his Air Marshal's cap like a Frisbee in the direction of the distant hat stand.

"Not a very good shot I'm afraid," commented the C in C. "I was a better marksman in my fighter pilot days."

Turning his gaze towards Carl who was standing to attention beside the absent ADC's desk Sir Thomas inquired forcefully, "And what would you be doing here young man?"

"I'm Flying Officer Higgins, sir. I received an invitation to present myself for interview in this office at 0900 hours today," replied Carl.

"Then we'd better get to it," the AOC insisted firmly. Turning to the PSO who was bustling forward behind him he barked; "Forget the paperwork for a while, John. Higgins and I have serious business to attend to. Leave us to it but before you shut the door just ask Sergeant Thompson to bring us coffee and biscuits."

"Certainly, sir."

Carl followed the Air Marshal respectfully into his office. He noticed he had a pronounced stoop and that he was tall and very thin with a sallow complexion and piercing blue eyes. Sir Thomas eased himself into one of the chintz armchairs and beckoning to Carl urged him to do the same. "Why should you abandon your pupils at Linton, Higgins? Don't you care for them?" he began. "Don't you want to fly all the hours God gives?"

"I enjoy instructing, sir, and really I want my students to do well but I think it's time I moved on from the Vampire and broadened my horizons," Carl replied feeling inadequate.

"What makes you think your horizons will be broadened behind a desk at HQ in one of the dreariest flattest parts of Germany?" Sir Thomas inquired testily. "When I was your age I simply wanted to fly nonstop at least until I went to Staff College and enjoy with luck another ten more years or so in the cockpit afterwards."

"So did I," said Carl, "but I could not just ignore your invitation especially as it came with strings attached. The Chief Instructor at Linton assured me that if you accepted me as your new ADC I'd have to do a short Hunter conversion at Chivenor first. Do you remember, sir, that when you came to take the passing out parade at Cranwell some five years ago you urged us in your address to show initiative? What's more when on the inspection beforehand you asked my friend Jamie Jamieson what he wanted to do on graduation he replied fly Hunters in Germany and you approved strongly. Well he's been short toured from Hunters at Leuchars to convert onto Lightnings with 74 squadron at Coltishall. Now if you select me, sir, I would be short toured, too, get a Hunter conversion and be available for consideration for Fighter Reconnaissance on the aeroplane in Germany after you've done with me."

"Quite a speech, Higgins, if I may say so," observed the AOC critically. "What would become of you after you left HQ we can only speculate. I could propose a role for you but the Air Secretary in his wisdom disposes of the postings. What's more do you realise you'll have to act in the office here as a fully professional aide and administrator but your job will be to make my duties easier in every respect? You'd be almost part of the family. Are you for example prepared to help Lady Swallowfield with the official entertaining in the evenings at the residence?"

"I would be more than delighted to do so, sir, particularly if I can use my German," Carl answered excitedly. "I used it as Adjutant of the Flight Cadets' survival camp at Brilon. I have an RAF interpretership qualification in the language and was brought up and educated in Bonn where my father worked in the Embassy."

"Okay, Higgins, I've heard enough. You're on. I'll break the news to your Chief Instructor Wing Commander Chivvers," Sir Thomas declared. "I've taken the precaution to book you on the short Hunter conversion course which starts at Chivenor next Monday. Report there at 0900 hours and to me here at its successful conclusion."

"Thank you, sir."

"Thank you, Higgins. I think you'll miss your instructing but you can always go back to it later on. John Fowler will accompany you out. See you in six weeks time. Oh by the way, you're not married are you? That's a relief because as ADC to a C in C you have to be married to the job and I need you to be available at all times."

"Of course, sir. Fully understood."

"How did that go?" asked Fowler as they made their way to the entrance hall of the HQ.

"I presume all right, sir, as Sir Thomas wants me back in six weeks' time."

"Good. I look forward to working with you but take nothing for granted especially on the Hunter course. FR Squadrons accept only the very best and more importantly I want to know that the AOC will be in safe hands when he flies with you. The security of NATO will depend on it."

The staff car ran Carl back to Wildenrath where he was supposed not to see Peter Carrick in the Mess. "Why are you still here, Peter," he began. "I would have expected you to be at least halfway back to Dishforth by now."

"I should have been and I was due to fly to Bahrain tomorrow but the Beverley sprang a mammoth oil leak and a spare part and engine fitter are being flown out from England. What you are plans?" Peter asked.

"There's no aircraft to fly me back till tomorrow. Either I hope to accompany you Peter, or there's a communications aeroplane – a Devon or Pembroke scheduled to take the Deputy C in C of 2ATAF Lieutenant General Kurt Himmelmann to a conference in Whitehall. Everybody knows him – crinkly faced with a lot of scar tissue from severe burns when his ME262 jet fighter crashed at Riem near Munich at the end of the war. John Fowler, Swallowfield's PSO, says I can go with scarface to Northolt – of course your Beverley would be a lot more fun if you can get it serviceable."

"Much more urgent is what we do tonight," Carl declared. "I refuse to hang around the bar all evening. You must remember, Peter, that since Yasmin left for America I've been leading a monastic existence at Linton. Why don't we ring Peter Lascelles at Laarbruch and ask him to drive down and pick us up if he's not night flying? He could persuade Lizzie to invite out a couple of her model friends on a blind date with us. See if you can get a call through to the 16 Squadron crewroom. We might just be lucky."

Peter Lascelles was delighted to hear his friends whose phone call could not have been better timed as he was about to leave for home in Düsseldorf to begin forty-eight hours' leave before embarking on a week of night flying. Lizzie was unlucky with her modelling companions none of whom was prepared to accept her invitation of an instant blind date of a dinner party with English pilots that very evening. Nevertheless she promised to lay on supper in the flat and overnight accommodation there for Carl and Peter Carrick.

When Lascelles picked them up he was full of news as they sped down the autobahn. He was in expansive form insisting that the Canberra was a joy to fly. As he had hoped he was regularly sent on exercises and detachments way beyond the 2ATAF area of responsibility. He was due to spend next month at Akrotiri in Cyprus and a week after that in Denmark. Lizzie, too, could not be happier with her modelling and was earning good money, which she hoped to spend on a sports car. However, she was becoming more maternally minded since she heard that Janey had moved into a beautiful old rectory outside Norwich following Jamie's posting to Coltishall and was expecting their first baby. Lizzie had suggested that a flat was not ideal for raising a family.

Peter Lascelles' plan he confided to his friends was to put in for the Central Flying School course next tour in the hopes of being selected to instruct on Gnats. With luck they could rent a place in Anglesey by the sea. He had heard of the establishment of a Gnat formation aerobatic team at Valley called the Yellowjacks and its demonstrations had been well received. He was already wondering if he could be chosen for it. Lizzie would enjoy the glamour of the display circuit he felt sure.

Lizzie, in a stunning green silk trouser suit welcomed Peter and his friends effusively at the door of their second floor flat in the tall grey 1930s apartment block, which had miraculously escaped the carpet bombing of the war. Peter and Lizzie had tried imaginatively to achieve with fashion prints and haute couture drawings a cheery light relief to offset the depressing effect of their landlord's massive German furniture, the heavy double glazed windows and sombre curtains.

"I expect you all could do with a beer," she began. "Anything interesting happening at Laarbruch, darling?"

"Nothing unless you consider a forthcoming week of night bombing on the Nordhorn range interesting, my love," Lascelles replied somewhat wearily.

"What about you two?" Lizzie inquired brightly.

"I've found my metier as an aerial truck driver," Peter answered. "A civilised trip like this one to Germany is a pleasant contrast to the more usual shuttle runs to Aden, Masirah island and Bahrain. I have my own crew now and what is truly the icing on the cake is that Natasha's got a job teaching English in Leeds – ideal for her with her mother down the road at Otley and ideal for me of course."

"I'm returning to my second home of Germany via Chivenor," explained Carl as he attacked a plateful of Swabian noodles and spicey meatballs, "unless I put up some awful black which causes the C in C to change his mind about having me as his ADC. I'm going to have to brush up on my social etiquette to humour Lady Swallowfield's dinner guests. I'm happy enough to do the Swallowfields' bidding for a while to earn my passage onto an FR squadron as promised."

"I have news for you, Carl," Lizzie responded. "I got a picture postcard of the Lincoln Memorial from Yasmin last week. She says that the course at GWU is tough and that she misses her friends in London, which I presume means you. Yousuf's spell in East Pakistan was too dramatic for her taste. First he landed wheels up at Cox's Bazaar following a hydraulic failure and then spent a long time in hospital with a nasty bout of malaria. She hoped I might come and see her in Washington – nice thought, but not really practicable."

Next morning Lascelles ran Peter and Carl up to Wildenrath and dropped them at the Operations office. Peter Carrick's crew chief was there to greet him with a tale of woe. "The oil pressure was still low on run up, sir. I hope we can get the aircraft serviceable before the end of the day, but I can't promise it."

"Very good, Chiefy. There goes my trip to Bahrain," and turning to Carl Peter explained, "there goes your lift back to Yorkshire, too. I suggest you cadge a ride with the Deputy C in C. According to the movements board he's due to leave for Northolt in a couple of hours by Pembroke. If you hang around here one of his pilots from the communications squadron is bound to appear. I'm going back to the Mess to put my feet up."

"Goodbye, Peter. Don't forget to ask me to your wedding. A Polish party really would be something to look forward to."

"Who says I'm going to marry Natasha?"

"Nobody, Peter. I just feel your destinies are somehow bound together."

CHAPTER 22

Every seat on the Percival Pembroke was taken by senior officers of the British Army of the Rhine except for four reserved at the front for a Luftwaffe Lieutenant Colonel PSO to General Himmelmann, his ADC a young captain, the Deputy C in C himself and Carl. An obsequious white jacketed Flight Sergeant attendant fussed around them dispensing coffee and biscuits served with fine crested bone china, followed later in the flight by canapés, delicate sandwiches and beer.

From close behind him Carl could see that Himmelmann's burns had been more extensive than he had realised. The General was relaxing in short sleeves as he put away the beers. Carl noticed that apart from his eyes, nose and scalp which had been protected by his oxygen mask, helmet and goggles scar tissue covered most of his face and neck as well as his wrists, which must have been the gap of bare flesh between leather gloves and flying suit vulnerable to the flames. Like a stereotyped German General from a Bateman cartoon he was reading Der Spiegel magazine through a tightly gripped monocle.

Turning to Carl Himmelmann unexpectedly addressed him by name in fluent idiomatic English. "Flight Lieutenant Higgins" – Carl had been promoted that day and Lizzie had sewn on his extra stripe before he left the flat – "congratulations on your appointment. I'm sure you will enjoy working with the Commander in Chief as much as I do. He runs a very happy ship."

Then totally changing the subject, "Have you been to Northolt before? I have in September 1940. My visits are happier now. I was in Adolf Galland's Geschwader (Wing) of Messerschmitt 109s then and when we attacked the airfield the mad Polish pilots gave us a terrible time. They were completely fearless and came at us head on. That was how I lost my best friend Rudi Steinmeier. He turned away at the last moment to avoid a collision and got a belly full of Polish lead. I shall never forget it."

"Isn't that an extraordinary coincidence, sir?" Carl replied trying to bring the conversation onto common ground. "When I went through the Royal Air Force College we had one of the same Poles whom you called mad on the staff, Squadron Leader Zopolowski. Sad to say he was killed only a few months ago flying a Hunter. We could never imagine him retiring. He loved the Air Force too much and of course he wouldn't go back to a communist Poland. Now he's gone the way of your friend and so many of his. It's lucky we can work together now in NATO to deter another war."

"Quite right, Flight Lieutenant Higgins," the General answered. "But remember I can't go home either. In a way it's even worse for us East Prussians than for the Poles. Not only was my birthplace the fine city of Königsberg seized by the Red Army and renamed Kaliningrad but the Soviets took the whole of East Prussia compared to only one third of Poland. They drove out all the Germans and incorporated it into the Soviet Union."

The General called for another beer and warmed to his theme. "My family were unpolitical," he went on. "I only joined the Luftwaffe reserve before the war to get free gliding lessons and then was called up in 1939. For how long must successive generations of Germans be punished for the sins of their fathers by losing their homeland?"

Recalling a similar conversation with Angela, Carl replied simply, "I well understand, sir."

He was relieved to see Harrow on the Hill to starboard as the Pembroke chugged gently over the patchwork of suburban housing on its approach to Northolt and alighted on the main runway. He could see the historic Officers' Mess on a small mound overlooking the airfield and a line of staff cars and drivers on the tarmac awaiting their distinguished passengers. The German Air Attaché was at the aircraft's steps to greet the Deputy C in C. Himmelmann addressed him directly. "Take Flight Lieutenant Higgins to the Embassy with you, Hans. He can change in your office. He has a train to catch to his base up North this afternoon."

"Jawohl, Herr General."

Back at Linton the news of Carl's appointment had spread fast. On arrival at the Mess there was a message in his pigeon hole handwritten on lined white official paper with an RAF crest at the top. It read: "Carl, congratulations. You are excused Met briefing tomorrow. Report to my office at 0830 hours." Signed Hew Williams, Squadron Leader.

Next morning Carl felt strangely adrift without the early routine of Met briefing. The extra half-hour in bed was no solace. The Mess was unusually empty for breakfast. Only a handful of secretarial types from station headquarters lined up at the buffet for their scrambled eggs instead of the eager jostling throng of his flying colleagues.

Carl really missed Met briefing. It was one of the principal social events of the day and the routine was reassuring. The semi theatrical performance was often enlivened by heavy quips from the Met man, audibly whispered cynical interventions from the floor, the self-confident authority attendant upon Service rank and style shown in the instructions from Wing Commander Chivvers and his Squadron Commanders, and the infinite fascination of the ever changing nature of the lower atmosphere wherein all their duties lay and destinies were decided.

At 0830 sharp Carl knocked clearly on Squadron Leader Williams' door. "Come in!" the boss shouted. "Ah Carl. Well done. Congratulations. Have a seat. You must be pleased but we all shall miss you. New job and an extra stripe on your shoulder. Your life is moving on fast."

"Thank you, sir," Carl replied. "I've been happy in your squadron."

"I could tell," Hew Williams responded. "That's why I gave you the job of putting Hawtrey to rights after the cruel loss of Haddad. You obviously enjoy instructing. It requires psychological insight and a natural personal sympathy and you have both so I hope you'll return to it when your time with Swallowfield and Hunter Tour are done. I'm sending you on your way with a good report as is the Chief Instructor. Wing Commander Chivvers has a conference at Command to attend today and asks me to say goodbye to you on his behalf. I suggest you clear the station quickly and get on your way promptly to Chivenor. It's a long drive from the Vale of York."

Indeed it was. Some ten hours later Carl drove cautiously in the all shrouding sea mist through the hutted encampment. The Corporal at the Guard Room had not known who Carl was and after a cursory glance at his Form 1250 confirming that the bewinged head and shoulders image bore some resemblance to Carl had waved him through pointing randomly in the drizzly darkness to where the Mess supposedly lay.

Trial and error brought their reward. The steward at the reception desk knew no more of Carl's programmed arrival than the Corporal on the gate. No accommodation had been prepared for him but then he recalled that a "Mr Rowlands was suspended last week and his room should be available in hut thirteen. Lucky for you it would seem, sir."

Only two inveterate habitués were in the bar. A wet Friday, washed out for flying had induced an early weekend exodus from the station. Dinner was already off and Carl had to make do with a cheese sandwich rustled up by the barman before tramping off in the penetrating light rain to Hut 13. He could not even bother to attempt to light the coke stove but stripped back the coarse damp bedclothes from the tin bed, jumped in, pulled them up to his chin and tried to will himself to sleep with thoughts of happier days.

The vivid contrasts of Air Force life never ceased to amaze him – the intensity of his short ill fated love for Angela, the passion which dear Yasmin aroused, the magical exhilaration of jet flight and the horrors of its concomitant companion the sudden death which stalked them all and had assigned his most likeable and promising of pupils Sam Haddad to an untimely cremation.

Next day dawned crystal clear and fine with a visibility in the pure maritime air of which only the westernmost of British airfields can boast.

Saturday and Sunday in the Mess were more than Carl could endure. He would in Air Force terms undertake two sector reconnaissances by car, one North to Ilfracombe on the Saturday, one South to Bideford on Sunday. Ilfracombe out of season looked forlorn even in the late winter sunshine. Most fish and chip shops and tearooms were closed. The Salter steamers, which plied the Bristol Channel in the summer time were not sailing otherwise he would have taken a day trip to Lundy Island. He settled for fish and chips from a mobile van on the edge of the harbour and a pub crawl through Croyde and Woolacombe on the way home.

When he arrived at Bideford next day he marvelled that so many of Sir Francis Drake's fleet were launched into such a tiny river. As he crossed the bridge church bells were ringing in the morning air. Carl remembered who the vicar was and answered their call to prayer. He felt as he listened to Jamie's father's opening sentences as if he were the prodigal son being summoned home by his conscience. "I will arise and go to my father and say unto him, father I have sinned against heaven and before thee and am no more worthy to be called thy son," he entoned.

Carl recalled the Cranwell church parades and services in the old iron hangar, Taffy Jones' funeral at Rhossili with the Chivenor Hunters tearing past overhead. He would be in one of them soon. He must do his own respectful flypast of Taffy's grave he mused. He had coasted at Cranwell and never really exerted himself then or since. It was time to make his life special. Enough very special people had done their best for him – Angela, Yasmin, Sam Haddad and now Swallowfield was giving him a chance. He would have to take it.

At the church door Carl introduced himself to the kindly vicar with medal ribbons on his stole who was greeting his parishioners as they left. "How's Jamie, padre?" Carl enquired. "I was in his Entry at Cranwell."

"What's your name?"

"Carl Higgins. I'm at Chivenor for a month for the short Hunter conversion."

"Of course. Of course... I've heard about you. You're the German linguist who bought in the market all the fresh fruit and vegetables for the survival camp in Brilon. As luck would have it Jamie and Janey are here from Coltishall for the weekend with our grandson Teddy. You must join us for lunch. We'd be thrilled."

"So would I, vicar. It's a wonderful invitation I could not possibly refuse."

"Hang on while I get this ecclesiastical gear off and I'll run you to the vicarage. You can pick up your car later," the Reverend Jamieson replied. He emerged from the vestry a couple of minutes later and beckoned to his battered Triumph Herald parked just round the corner. The parsonage was a crumbling late Georgian gentleman's residence which had as yet escaped the predatory grasp of the church commissioners. The garden was ample if unkempt with a yellow carpet of aconites and the earliest snowdrops just emerging to the fitful sunshine under the trees.

A ponderous pair of under-exercised Springer Spaniels greeted their master and his guest. Jamie and Janey were lounging beside the blazing log fire in the drawing room with young Teddy crawling around the furniture. They rose as one from the sofa when Carl appeared. "This is the most wonderful surprise," Jamie exclaimed hugging his friend.

"Your father took me by surprise, too, by inviting me here," Carl responded. "Great to see you both, Janey, and to get to know Teddy."

Whereupon a smiling, benign, well rounded apron clad lady appeared from the kitchen in welcome. "I'm so pleased you're here," she enthused. "I know who you are. You're the one who got the Ecole de l'Air Trophy at Cranwell for German not French."

"Good memory but you can do better than that, Mama," Jamie interjected. "This is the famous Carl Higgins whose interpretation made sure that the staff of survival camp received all the local delicacies they needed to keep them in good humour. Not surprisingly he was creamed off and went straight into instructing."

"Delighted to meet you, Mrs Jamieson," Carl responded.

"Call me Patricia please. Anyone in Jamie's Entry counts as one of the family. Weren't you also in his squadron at the College?"

"Yes indeed, Patricia," Carl answered self-consciously. "Good to meet Teddy, too. I wonder if he'll be the third generation of Jamiesons to wear Royal Air Force wings on his chest."

"Give him time," objected Janey. "Let him at least stand on his own two legs before you get him airborne."

Sunday lunch was traditional and convivial washed down with plenty of claret. "To make glad the heart of man," the vicar appropriately observed.

"Happy to learn, Carl, that you're going to Chivenor," Jamie commented. "You'll love it. At least Moxon is still there commanding the odds and sods squadron you'll be on. He's super. Muscle and grunt Gillespie has gone to Wattisham as station master and Prendergast is now an Air Commodore deep in the Ministry. I hope Max Moxon soon goes up like them but didn't the psalm say that 'promotion cometh neither from the East, nor from the West, nor yet from the South'?"

"Quite right Jamie, psalm 75," the old Lancaster hand finished the verse. "And why? God is the Judge: he putteth down one and setteth up another. Dead man's shoes we used to call it. The trouble was that there were always rather a lot of them waiting needlessly to be polished outside the bedroom doors in the Mess at Ludford, but perhaps such divine intervention is at least as fair a means of selection as Buggins' Turn."

"The saddest loss is dear old Polzol from the simulator section," Jamie went on. "I cannot imagine the place without him. His experience and irrepressible banter made the chore of logging hours in the procedures trainer a pleasure. One other thing. I hope you find as good a soul mate on the course as Mark Driscoll was to me. Trailing round the pubs of Barnstaple, Ilfracombe and Woolacombe solo especially in winter won't exactly lift the spirits."

"What about yourselves?" Carl inquired. "I've heard on the grapevine that you've made your home of a magnificent old Rectory just outside Norwich and that the Lightning is getting over its teething trouble well with 74, much better than the early days of the Swift."

"Right on both counts, Carl. So much so that the squadron is looking for an aerobaticist to demonstrate the aeroplane round the display circuit this summer. Everyone sees the Lightning simply as a hot rod Mach two stratospheric interceptor with only forty minutes endurance, but you can actually do a spectacularly tight low level aerobatic sequence with it and you can always throw in a double dose of reheat to keep the crowd awake. I expect they'll choose one of the many old and bold on the squadron. I still haven't got twelve hundred hours in my logbook but if my friend Max Moxon became Wingco flying at Coltishall I might stand a chance. He always believed in giving his protégés plenty of encouragement. You work on it, Carl."

"I will of course but my self-interest will have to have priority and that means passing the course."

"I don't believe an A2 has ever failed, Carl."

"There's always a first time for anything. I wonder if Swallowfield would have me if I did. I must think and act positively because I could not bear to go back to Linton and if I didn't qualify on the Hunter I can't see myself instructing on Gnats either."

"On that cheerful note it's time we got ready for the long drive back to East Anglia," announced Jamie. "Do come and stay with us, Carl, if you find yourself in Norfolk. If I get the demo job I might come across for a display or two in Germany, who knows. By the way any news of Yasmin? Janey says that Samantha got another card from her recently."

"For me nothing, I'm afraid," Carl responded. "She's probably concentrating on her studies and trying to avoid romantic entanglement to show her parents she'll be ready for an appropriate match."

After a mug of tea and slice of cake in the kitchen Carl bade the Jamiesons goodbye. Jamie's parents were most solicitous. "Don't forget you've always got a bolt hole here. If the Mess becomes too claustrophobic the vicarage can be your second home," Patricia insisted.

"You'll love the Hunter, Carl," Jamie commented in farewell. "It's a delight. The cockpit even smells right but it can be a heavy handed brute in manual. Remember what happened to Polzol. When in doubt get out. The Bristol Channel's pretty warm, not like the North Sea off Leuchars."

"Thanks my friend. As ever you've cheered me up a lot."

The course went well for Carl and he certainly loved the aeroplane. Everything about the Hunter was right – its looks, feel, sound, sturdiness and even as Jamie had said its smell. The handling was as honest as its appearance. As was to be expected

Carl and Moxon hit it off, so much so that he authorised Carl to fly more sorties than his short conversion course stipulated introducing him to low level navigation and battle formation.

As a special indulgence Moxon allowed Carl a final trip as a formation leader. "I know you've done plenty of this before up at Linton, Carl," explained the Squadron Leader over a cup of coffee in his office. "You must have countless hours in your logbook instructing advanced students in close formation on the Vampire and then leading them when they try out their technique solo. It will have demanded smooth flying, plenty of anticipation and a cool nerve from you.

"Today," Moxon continued, "because of leave commitments, courses and sickness we find ourselves without a staff pilot weapons instructor or QFI who can give one of our Jordanians, a certain Hussein Ali an additional close formation trip to get him up to scratch. For some reason he still finds formation a bit of a problem and looking through his instructors' reports from Syerston and Swinderby he was rated as below average at it in both the basic and advanced stages. Would you like to help out? The Jordanian Air Attaché is badgering us all the time to get the Jordanians through quickly so that they can go back out and onto aircraft, which have just been delivered."

Carl was more than willing to oblige. "I would love to, sir. Anything to keep me here longer before I take to my desk in Sir Thomas' outer office at Rheindahlen."

"I thought that would be your reaction. It'll be a straightforward exercise. Pairs take off… climb to thirty thousand feet out to sea… formation changes at height between echelon port and starboard, close line astern then long line astern followed by a gentle tailchase… reform into echelon starboard for a pairs descent into the circuit with a one minute level break onto downwind and a stream landing. Any questions?"

"No, sir, but any other information about Hussein Ali?"

"Just one thing," Moxon responded. "He seems to to be a bit tense and taciturn as his Final Handling Test approaches. His QFIs noticed the same thing at a similar stage at Syerston and Swinderby. Probably lives on his nerves. You'll find him solid but very uncommunicative I'm afraid."

Carl came up in the crewroom to Hussein Ali who was drinking black coffee and smoking an evil looking sheroot of foul smelling Egyptian tobacco held in deeply nicotine stained fingers. "I'm leading you today, Hussein," Carl began, "one more close formation practice. Like to come through to the briefing room? Everything's standard, Hussein. You know the form. Diversions are Brawdy, St Mawgan, St Athan and Yeovilton as usual. The weather and vis are good. We're on the westerly runway with a very slight crosswind from starboard. The trip will be identical to your last close formation sortie with Flight Lieutenant Blackmore. He felt you needed a little more practice and I'm here to give it to you." Carl repeated Moxon's briefing almost verbatim. "Any questions Hussein?" His pupil looked blank as if the briefing had passed him by and did not respond. "I take it you're happy with everything then," Carl declared.

All was apparently normal at first. Carl's exceptionally saturnine pupil did his checks, started up, make his radio calls and taxied perfectly well. At the runway threshold Carl called "Red section take off" and on acknowledgement from the tower to line up he aligned himself just left of the centreline with Hussein Ali the other side of it and fractionally back.

"Red section clear to take off," called the tower.

"Red section taking off," Carl replied bringing his white kid leather gloved right hand down three times on the cockpit coaming and easing the throttle very gently forward on the third to about ninety-three per cent power whilst keeping impeccably straight with rudder. He gave a mini-second glance to his right where Hussein Ali was now only just visible. Carl thought no more of it. His number two had obviously been slow to apply power, got behind and would doubtless rectify it, with luck smoothly and safely.

Carl was overoptimistic. He kept his aircraft on three wheels a fraction longer than usual, then smoothly lifted the nosewheel off with a gentle input of back pressure on the stick checking forward to ensure he did not get prematurely airborne to make the transition from take off to flight easier for his number two. His calm concentration was interrupted by a fearsome jolt and grinding sound from his right. The aircraft lurched violently towards the runway lights to port and out of the corner of his eye Carl saw the awesome silhouette of Hussein's Hunter undercarriage still extended seemingly leaping over his starboard wing.

Carl just had time to slam the throttle shut, stopcock the engine and to bellow into the R/T "Barrier, barrier, red leader barrier" and point his nose into a gap between the safety net's vertical strops whilst hurtling onwards notwithstanding his hard braking towards the sand dunes of Braunton Burrows.

In spite of the aircraft's speed of over one hundred knots the top horizontal strand of the barrier went smoothly over the cockpit mercifully not forcing open the canopy. Both wings were firmly enmeshed and the aircraft was halted abruptly but not violently still in the runway's concrete overshoot area. Carl cut the electrical power and waited.

The crash crew were on the scene within a minute, Max Moxon and the Wing Commander Flying within two, the ambulance not till much later. A ladder was soon rustled up and Carl was helped out by strong armed firemen who put the safety pins into his ejection seat and assisted him down the steps and into the Flying Wing Land Rover. "What was that all about, Higgins?" the far from sympathetic Wing Commander Haigh demanded to know of a much shaken Carl whose legs were still quivering though he felt no obvious injury, not even a strained back.

"My wing got clipped by my number two, sir."

"Too right it did Higgins. The starboard aileron's still lying out there on the runway and if you look back at your aeroplane you'll see the wingtip light is smashed and half the trailing edge is lost."

"Did Hussein Ali get airborne okay, sir?" Carl inquired tentatively.

"If doing leapfrog over his leader's aeroplane is considered okay I suppose he did. He's been despatched on diversion to St Mawgan, which has a three thousand yard runway, which should give enough room for him to not to do any further damage. The other aircraft, which were flying at the time, are scattered about between South Wales and the West country."

"I am sorry, sir," Carl responded defensively.

"I prefer no accidents to needless apologies afterwards, Higgins. What's more it'll take a while to disentangle your aeroplane from the safety net and tow it away. The barrier will need to be thoroughly checked and possibly repaired," Haigh's diatribe continued. "Meanwhile, I had a couple of Final Handling Tests to do today, which will now have to wait," he went on. "Report to your Squadron Commander, Higgins. We've had enough damage wrought for one day. I'll be getting a call through to Air Chief Marshal Swallowfield asking him to take you a bit early if he'll still have you. So get ready to clear the station today."

Back in the crewroom there was much sympathy for Carl from his fellow course members. "I think you did well," said one. "I imagine the only damage to your aeroplane came from your number two. If you'd pressed on and got airborne I wonder if the aeroplane would have been controllable without the aileron."

"Have a strong coffee," said another pouring whisky from a hidden flask into Carl's Nescafé.

"How about some cake, sir, to get your blood sugar up and restore your nerves?" suggested a young Jordanian giving Carl a sticky sweet Arabian pastry. "Don't worry, sir," he assured Carl, "St Mawgan's just rung through to say Hussein has landed safely." Whereupon Squadron Leader Moxon strode in looking serious.

"I need you in my office, Higgins, now. First I'm sorry your course ended like this," Moxon began, "but you're not to blame. Wing Commander Haigh rightly demands an impeccable flight safety record to be maintained so he has already made certain decisions. First you are to write a report on the episode right away, then give your flying kit back to the safety equipment section, pay your Mess bill, leave the station and go straight to Headquarters Royal Air Force Germany and report for duty there. For your information Lieutenant Hussein Ali is to return to his unit in Jordan at once without a Hunter qualification."

"Inevitable I suppose, sir," Carl responded.

"What's more, Carl, you may be interested to know," Moxon continued, "that my own next tour has been brought forward and changed. I'm to take up a ground appointment with the Apprentice Training School at Halton immediately and in my current rank. It goes without saying that no more supernumerary hours are going to be flown here especially by people like yourself not on the staff. However, Carl, you will still be going to Rheindahlen qualified on the aeroplane and with a good report from me for what it's worth. I doubt whether the inquiry will attribute any criticism to you for what occurred. It has been a pleasure to have you on what was my squadron. I wish you well. Goodbye."

CHAPTER 23

When Carl appeared at the AOC's office a whole week early he was warmly greeted by his predecessor Jack Clark. Clark was two entries Carl's senior at Cranwell and had won fame among his peers for masterminding the installation of an Austin Seven on the College roof to mark April Fool's day. Since then he had calmed down although he had a reputation on 54 Squadron for high living. He was due to stay in the fighter world beginning a Lightning conversion course in a week's time.

"Welcome Carl. Here already," he exclaimed. "Don't worry my desk's big enough for two. We can start the handover process a week before schedule. It could be very good for you as we're due to go up Berlin next week for the commies' traditional May Day parade the other side of the wall. I'll try and make sure the old man takes you. He'll be here any minute."

Thereupon the door was flung open and Sir Thomas strode in pitching his hat towards the distant hat stand. "My aim is deteriorating, Jack. Pick up my cap and come in will you?" He spotted Carl. "So you've made it here early, Higgins," Sir Thomas commented impassively. "Disentangled yourself successfully from the barrier at Chivenor I see. Harry Haigh was bellyaching over the blower to me about you. In my book anyone who's keen enough to fly extra hours goes up in my estimation and has my full support. Next time pick your wingman more carefully. It's best to give camel bashing Arabs a wide berth. An unreliable lot in my experience."

John Fowler was less welcoming. "I'm glad you've arrived safely, Carl, albeit ahead of time," he began. "I gather you managed to cause quite a stir on your short conversion down at Chivenor. Not only were you sent prematurely packing but you seem to have been the cause of my friend Max Moxon's sudden posting to a ground tour without the promotion he must rightly have expected."

"You could put it like that I suppose, sir, though you've actually omitted the key determinant of it all, the somewhat wayward airmanship of my wingman, a certain Lieutenant Hussein Ali."

"Be that as it may," Fowler went on. "Your chances of any special dispensations will as an ADC here be zero. The grapevine tells me that the last time you were in Germany you acted as interpreter for a survival camp for Cranwell cadets at Brilon and used the freedom it gave you to court the local ladies."

At that point Clark emerged from the AOC's office conveniently absolving Carl of the need to reply to Fowler's provocations. "Sir Thomas wants to see you now, Carl," he interjected. "He's got some ideas about the handover he wants to discuss."

"If you'll excuse me, sir," Carl muttered as he broke off the unpleasant exchange and took refuge in the AOC's office.

Sir Thomas was at his desk already methodically making his way through the stack of files before him. "Draw up a chair, Carl," he began. "I think it's fortuitous that you've arrived a week early. Not only will Jack have more time to complete the handover to you but more importantly I want you to accompany me to the May Day parade in East Berlin next week. Your interpretation could be invaluable. It'll be Jack's last official engagement with me and I've invited your contemporary Peter

Lascelles from Laarbruch to join the party. I always invite one or two outstanding young officers to the event. It gives me a chance to get to know them better and to broaden their outlook making them understand what we're up against in NATO."

"Will the PSO be coming?" Carl inquired.

"No, he'll be minding the shop in my absence. John went up with me last year. This time I want to give you and Jack your chance."

"Thank you, sir."

"Oh, another thing Carl I've decided to grant Jack a forty-eight hour pass to mark the end of his stint with me so he can get home to see his parents before he starts at Coltishall. So when we return from Berlin next Wednesday evening I'll be depending fully and only on you to look after me."

By the end of the week Jack had seemingly introduced Carl to everyone who mattered at both the Air Force and Army Headquarters. General Himmelmann was particularly effusive when Jack and Carl made their courtesy call. He had models of a Sabre and a Starfighter on his desk and photographs of squadron and station groups on the wall but nothing from his wartime Luftwaffe days. Only a faded photograph of the youthful pupils at a pre-war civilian gliding school presumably in East Prussia indicated that the General had a past in aviation before the mid 1950s.

"Kommen Sie ein – alter Kamerad. Come in old comrade," he bellowed to Carl. "Next week we go to Germany's true capital. I think you'll find die Berline Luft, the Berlin air intoxicating. What happens in Berlin decides the destiny of Europe as you'll soon find out. My wife and daughter are coming, too. We're staying with my brother Willi. He's a lecturer in economics at the Free University not to be confused with the Technical University on the other side, which turns out trusty apparatchiks for the DDR."

Quite a convoy of official cars set off for the communications squadron at Wildenrath on the Monday morning where they were joined by Peter Lascelles, tall and distinguished in a perfectly tailored Gieves officer's greatcoat. The select party boarded the Percival Pembroke. "You're lucky, Carl," observed Jack. "The high wing will ensure you have a good view. Now that it's evening and the lights are coming on you should be able to spot the inner German border especially at the lowly altitude of eight thousand feet at which we have to fly down the corridor from Hanover. It's much darker on the DDR side. The difference in candlepower between East and West Berlin is even more marked. The Western sectors are lit up like a Christmas tree compared to the Soviet one."

"I'm looking forward to the happy sound of two Alvis Leonides myself," replied Carl. "The engine never let me or anyone else down in my Entry on Piston Provosts. Taffy Jones' tragic demise was not the engine's fault."

Dusk was deepening as they swung away Eastwards from Wildenrath. The last shower cumulus diminished and died as night came on. Tea and biscuits were served. Himmelmann chose beer. His daughter Heidi in the window seat next to Carl preferred hot chocolate. "I always have it after skiing," she observed. "Do you ski?"

"Not really now though my parents used to take me when we lived in Bonn. Peter here is the real expert. He goes to Bad Kohlgrub every winter to practice his Alpine survival cross country skiing techniques by courtesy of the Air Force. Isn't he lucky?"

"Yes I suppose so if you are prepared to live in an igloo. I prefer a good hotel myself," Heidi replied emphatically.

"Sad to say I will have to stay in the drab old Mess at Gatow on this trip. What about you?"

"We're with uncle Willi in Schöneberg actually."

"To me that's an appropriate place," Carl responded. "Do you remember the operetta 'Es war en Schöneberg im Monat Mai' – it was in Schöneberg in the month of May. Very apt. I went with my parents to see it in Cologne. It was tuneful, romantic and fun as I recall. I think this trip will be fun, too."

Conversation was light and easy. Heidi was effervescent, humorous and had a ready smile. Her complexion was clear, her eyes an almost translucent Prussian blue and her hair athletically close cropped without being severe. "We're almost there," said Carl as he caught a glimpse of Berlin's girdle of lakes in the moonlight and in the distance the illuminations of West Berlin. As they taxied in RAF Gatow seemed a gloomy place, a spacious empty aerodrome too big for its current role. The aeroplane taxied to a halt in front of the control tower.

"See you tomorrow, Carl," said Heidi cheerfully. "My father tells me I've been invited to the Air Marshal's dinner at his official residence."

"That's very good news," Carl responded enthusiastically.

Sir Thomas' and the Commander in Chief of the British Army of the Rhine's motorcades formed up at the Headquarters of the British Berlin brigade, swept through the green open space of the Tiergarden, past the Siegersaüle monument and on to the Invalidenstrasse checkpoint – the only way out of the British and into the Soviet sector.

At the arrival of the two shiny black British staff cars with their four star generals' plates up and official ensigns fluttering from the bonnet tops the duty West Berlin border guards jumped to attention and once across the No Man's land to the East Berlin side the East German soldiers and Volkspolitzisten or Vopos did so even more exaggeratedly coming to a quivering salute once the VIPs' passes had been verified.

The parade itself seemed interminable with much goose-stepping from the massed formations, a surfeit of martial music and a plethora of guns, missiles, tanks and armoured personnel carriers. How the Polituro members sombre hatted and grey suited high up on the reviewing balcony could endure such repetitive tedium year after year Carl found difficult to understand.

"Do we get anything out of this parade watching, Jack?" asked Carl.

"Not as much as from fishing it would seem. Do you remember when a Warsaw Pact Mig went into one of the West Berlin lakes? Our boys had the greatest fun extracting it, taking it to bits and analysing all its systems. Then of course there's the British Military Mission to the Soviet Forces in East Germany, BRIXMIS, but look to your left and you'll see one of Sir Thomas' party a wingless Squadron Leader with dark glasses and binoculars who seems to find the parade fascinating."

"As for me," Peter Lascelles remarked, "I can't get back to West Berlin soon enough. I know Lizzie would love it here but she's a bit less mobile now that she's pregnant so she'll have to wait before she attends any fashion shows on the Kurfurstendamm."

"Great news, Peter," Carl interjected. "I expect you're keen to get back to UK for the delivery."

"Yes indeed although Sir Thomas doesn't yet know that I want to leave his Command and get to CFS to qualify to instruct on the Gnat at Valley. It would be good to bring up our baby in the fresh air of Anglesey."

The AOC's occasional residence in Berlin was much more desirable than his rather dreary permanent one in Rheindahlen. The tranquil wooded location on the extreme Western edge of the city was ideal for entertaining. The guests appreciated the perfect lakeside view for their pre-dinner drinks with the setting sun sinking over the pine encircled dinghy studded waters.

The British Army was well represented by the Commander in Chief of Northern Army Group, the Berlin Brigade Commander and their wives. General Himmelmann looked imposing with his monocle still in place and was accompanied by his dauntingly chic willowy wife Dörthe, the Gräfin as she was nicknamed, who puffed away on a long cigarette in an ivory cigarette holder. Lady Swallowfield by contrast was short and pushy, always bossing the ADCs about to dispense this or that to her guests in an accent clearly refined over many years of elocution classes and studied imitation of those whom she deemd the great and the good.

"I never knew the Deputy C in C was a Count," Carl observed to Jack.

"Keeps it quiet. Uses no title, no von, likes to be the model image of Mr average citizen in uniform, the perfect military representative of modern Germany. His wife's family," Jack continued, "goes back to the pagan bashing Teutonic Knights, lived in a medieval castle and owned an East Prussian estate as big as Rutland."

"Riches to rags and back up again to at least a respected status in the very bourgeois Buundesrepublik," commented Carl.

Heidi was not with her parents but chatting in a corner to two grey suited puffy faced and paunchy middle-aged Germans. One identified himself as the Deputy Burgomeister and the other as Leader of the Social Democratic Party in the city. Heidi who had clearly inherited her mother's glamour and her father's ebullience and wit was holding her own in a heavy conversation.

"Peaceful coexistence is what the city needs," the dogmatic Party boss was insisting. "We should stop the Bonn Government's revanchist provocations."

"Quite right," declared the man from town hall, "if I were in the West German Government I would try to get the Americans to set an example by taking their nuclear weapons out of Europe."

"I would start here by demanding there be no more shootings by the East Germans of escapees at the wall," Heidi interrupted bravely. "That's where peaceful coexistence should begin by the Easterners allowing divided families to reunite."

Carl overheard the tense conversation and came to Heidi's rescue. "Gentlemen please," he exclaimed boldly. "We have a rule. No politics or religion in the Mess. It applies also to our hosts', the Commander in Chief and Lady Swallowfield's residence. Let's look where we're all going to sit for dinner," he continued taking Heidi gladly by the arm to the seating plan, which he and Jack had meticulously drawn up. Carl had placed himself conveniently beside her, far from the German city functionaries who were to sit next to the two senior British Army officers who he felt sure would bore them into quiescence.

On the aeroplane Carl had only been vouchsafed tantalisingly sideways glances at Heidi sitting alongside to his right. He had particularly noticed the fullness of her lips exaggerated by the perspective perhaps but rich with abundant promise. She had been wearing tight blue jeans, which accentuated the athletic firmness of her thighs and a clinging black sweater, which showed that her youthful breasts needed no visible support.

Heidi had the strong teeth of a characterful person, which she revealed readily when she smiled, which was often and heart-warmingly so.

Now in a sequined dark magenta evening dress he could appreciate the whole woman. For one so young, and she was still a political science student at Marburg an der Lahn university, she looked exceptionally distinguished – a real lady of the world as befitted high society in Berlin an erstwhile capital of style and cabaret and fun.

Dinner was a success. Perch from the nearby lakes was washed down with Franken wine. Venison from the adjoining forests was accompanied by a wholesome Kalterer See Austrian red. Carl and Heidi hit it off at once. "Thank you, Carl, for saving me from those fellow travelling bores. How did you guess what they were like?" she asked.

"Having been at least partly brought up in this country I have a kind of sixth sense and perhaps I've inherited my father's professional skill of eavesdropping at cocktail parties."

"I'm not sure we deserve reunification," Heidi went on. "To me our West German politicians are all as bad as each other. I don't trust Willi Brandt. How come he was out of the country throughout the war? You have to admire Konrad Adenauer's longevity but I'm not keen on the Christian Democrats – too drearily dominated by Rhineland Catholics. As for the gummi Löwen (rubber lion) Ludwig Erhard he may have produced an economic miracle but he doesn't raise my political pulse. The Bavarian CSU I find too strident, particularly Franz Josef Strauss. He's developing a personality cult. I suppose I'm a liberal in ethos as in economics, so it's FDP for me but it's not much of a party these days."

"It seems that we're breaking the etiquette of the house, Heidi," Carl responded, "but no one else can hear and anyway these matters are your university studies you're discussing with me." They need not have worried as their earnest conversation was soon halted by Sir Thomas' after dinner speech welcoming his guests. It was a flat affair and overlong, neither funny nor seriously informative; formal and diplomatically correct with John Fowler's fingerprints all over it.

At least it upset nobody though it induced Carl to whisper to Heidi. "It would be better if my new boss Fowler just let the Air Marshal speak from the heart. He's a kindly man, an enthusiastic aviator and must have a rich fund of flying stories."

"Just like Papi," rejoined Heidi. "Everyone thinks he must be very fierce having flown with Galland, Steinhoff and Günther Rall and survived the war but it's really a pose. There's nothing he likes better than to sit down with a few beers and crack jokes."

The Deputy Burgomeister got ponderously to his feet to reply. "Herr General und sehr gnädige Lady Swallowfield, Air Marshal sir and most gracious Lady Swallowfield," he began. "It has been an honour for my party colleague and myself to enjoy your wonderful hospitality in this lovely residence to commemorate May Day as the guests of our friends and allies the British to whom we owe so much.

"We will never forget," he went on, "how the Royal Air Force and many British civil airlines, too, sustained us during the Berlin Airlift…"

"Or their carpet bombing, too," Carl heckled quietly to Heidi.

"It is a relationship of mutual dependence. I know our exports are much valued in England. I saw many Volkswagens the last time I was there and Mercedes, too, may I add.

"Some German exports have been particularly appreciated over the years – Georg Friedrich Händel and dare I say it your monarchy."

"Oh dear," whispered Carl. "A lead balloon of a speech."

"We Germans," the Rathaus deputy chief continued confidently warming to his theme, "enjoy what is best from modern Britain – the Scotch whisky of course and the pop music. Your soldiers help support the economy of West Berlin and I know their qualities are welcomed by the large number of German girls who marry them. During the war you had your GI brides; now we have our Tommy brides."

"Good Lord deliver us," exclaimed Carl to Heidi almost audibly. "What is it that induces pompous middle-aged men to make fools of themselves in after dinner speeches?"

Luckily after the toasts and helping the departing guests on with their coats, Carl and Heidi, Peter and Jack escaped in Heidi's Volkswagen Beetle. "Show us the nightlife, Heidi," the pilots exclaimed as one. She duly obliged taking them to a club of the KuDamm.

"You certainly know your way around. You must come and stay with uncle Willi a lot," Carl observed.

"I do. Marburg is a good place to study, but too gemütlich, (How do you say it – demure, cosy?) for me to live there full time. Berlin is such a vibrant contrast. I feel I'm returning to my roots here. How I long for the damned wall to be broken down and for this wonderful city to be our capital again. I know that committees of the Bundestag come and hold meetings in the old Reichstag building but we the new generation of Germans deserve better than this. Here is the centre of gravity of our country not that sleepy Rhineland village Bonn even if Ludwig van Beethoven was born there."

"A real speech from the heart, Heidi," commented Carl warmly. "I like a woman with feelings and imagination, too. Let's dance. Peter and Jack will be happy at the bar watching the floorshow. They might be lucky and pick up a local souvenir before the night is out."

"They're more likely to have their wallets picked but I agree the sights are impressive," Heidi replied, pointing to a trio of naked dancers insinuating themselves snake-like in the ultra violet light round metal poles in the centre of the floor to a jungle beat rhythm from the band.

The pole dancers' acrobatics alternated with striptease, singing, cabaret and mime in the smoke filled dusky dungeon of a club and the girls readily joined the Royal Air Force table after the performances on stage. Peter Lascelles was undoubtedly the focus of their attention.

When they resumed their gyrations after a particularly far fetched act by a supposedly transvestite dwarf Peter confessed to Jack Clark, "I get into terrible trouble the whole time from Lizzie for eyeing other women but it is they who make a beeline for me. I can't help it that I like feminine company, but I don't actually seek it."

"I do," said Jack, "but I've always been too focused on my flying and rugby and now as an ADC I can't give the time that the excitements of the chase deserve. What's more I'm too proud to pay for my pleasures."

"There's no harm in at least asking what the going rate is, Jack," Peter volunteered. "You might be pleasantly surprised."

"Sorry, but I've got Yorkshire blood. It's not just a question of pride. I'm mean as well."

Heidi left early with Carl for a lingering libido charged drive back to Schöneberg via RAF Gatow and the neighbouring forests. Peter and Jack emerged from the club at five in the morning as dawn was breaking over the Brandenburg

Gate. "You go and get a taxi back, Jack," Peter suggested. "I'm waiting here for Lisl. I can take my time. I've no official duties to perform tomorrow and the aeroplane's not leaving till late afternoon. She's promised to show me the town."

Carl and Jack met up over breakfast in the Mess. "What a night!" commented Jack. "My head's still befuddled with beer."

"Yes, night of a lifetime," Carl responded. "I think I'm falling in love with Berlin."

"With Heidi you mean," interjected Jack.

"Be that as it may she's got to go shopping at KDW with her aunt today but she proposed that we take a trip to the East. She says there's a tourist coach, which goes from the KuDamm to visit Frederick the Great's summer palace Sans Souci at Potsdam. How about it, Jack?"

"I'm game, but what about our passports? Don't we need visas?"

"Not if you go in the tourist bus Heidi says. It's simply waved through at the checkpoint. Anyway I'm just described as a student in mine."

"So am I, let's go!"

It was just as Heidi had described. At checkpoint Charlie the American soldiers on duty showed little interest. On the other side of the wall the Vopos and East German military personnel merely collected all the passports from the driver and after a short wait returned them duly stamped. Once out of the drab confines of the city the countryside looked weed strewn, perfunctorily cultivated and badly neglected. "The obvious result of the Government's system of co-operative farms," Carl commented. The little personal vegetable allotments by contrast were clearly productive and lovingly tended. Most had an immaculate garden shed, often with a window or two and a television aerial – welcome bijou weekend retreats for the dwellers of the vast impersonal Stalinist blocks of flats in East Berlin.

Sans Souci King Frederick II's magnificent palace was imposing though greatly in need of restoration. Jack and Carl with the other western tourists were kept strictly to their guided group. Even for the standardised cream cake and coffee served after the tour in a small separate dining room they were well segregated from the local visitors.

At the modern Cecilienhof villa nearby where the Potsdam agreement was concluded between the four principal wartime allies they were given a homily about its merits and the consequent inviolability of the frontiers of the USSR and DDR. "I'm glad Heidi didn't join us," Carl observed. "Yalta and Potsdam are places of infamy in her historical atlas where Churchill in the first case and Attlee in the second signed away the freedom of millions of her fellow countrymen."

"And of the Poles for that matter," interjected Jack, "as Polzol's decision to pursue his career post war in the Royal Air Force demonstrated."

On the way back the coach stopped briefly at the Museum of German History on the wide boulevard of the Unter den Linden. The display portrayed the workers' struggle against capitalist oppression and the debt of gratitude which the German people owed to its Soviet liberators from Nazism. "We could have done without a call at this propaganda palace," Jack declared, "but what worries me more immediately than the ideological rubbish we saw and the comrades' rewriting of German history is that this unscheduled stop will make it very hard for us to get back to Gatow in time for take off."

Worse was to come at the wall. Vopos crawled all over and under the bus seeking East German stowaways. All the passengers were made to get out and sit in a grim waiting room at the checkpoint whilst their passports were scrutinised and the police looked beneath the seats and in the engine compartment and boot of the coach. Then one by one the tourists were called out by name to receive their passports back and complete their journey to the West. "Here we go, Carl: or at least here we stay," joked Jack.

Sure enough Carl and Jack found themselves left till last. The bus driver and guide were told by the police to proceed on their way with the other passengers. "We are asking Mr Clark and Mr Higgins," it was explained, "to remain with us whilst further formalities are completed. These official matters will take a little time."

"We would ask you to wait here," a young Volksarmee lieutenant insisted to Jack and Carl. "There seem to have been some irregularities in your passports and procedures, which have to be investigated."

"This is the last thing we need. We were already running late," muttered Carl dejectedly.

"Best not to talk in here for obvious reasons," Jack replied firmly.

A good hour passed and then the lieutenant of the guard returned with a senior officer. "My comrade Commanding Officer here wants to address some remarks to you personally. Herr Oberst, bitte schön... Colonel, please." The rotund leather jack booted sallow faced Commander of the East German checkpoint began with menacing civility.

"You clearly enjoyed our celebration on May 1st of the worldwide festival of the workers in this fine capital city of the German workers' own republic of the DDR. We like to make commemoration of May Day memorable for our visitors, but frankly we did not expect you back so soon after the event or to come through this checkpoint and not through the Invalidenstrasse in the British sector.

"It would have been normal," the Colonel went on warming to his theme, "if you wanted to visit the Headquarters of the Soviet Group of Armies at Potsdam to have come in uniform after an application through the usual channels and we would of course have given you every facility. But to disguise yourselves as tourists and to describe yourselves as students when you hold important junior appointments at a key NATO Headquarters could be interpreted in a very sinister manner with serious implications.

"However, I have chosen to take a generous view of your actions. You went to the Cecilienhof where de facto recognition was given by the great powers to what has become the German Democratic Republic. At the Museum of German History you will have seen how the workers of our socialist homeland made it the universally recognised success that it is today and you will have learned of the fraternal spirit which has sustained them throughout this historic enterprise."

Carl and Jack remained very anxious about their fate but there was still more to come from the Colonel. "You will have heard, too, that our respected leader Comrade Walter Ulbricht has repeatedly called for detente in Berlin and on the inner German border. He truly believes in peaceful co-existence between East and West and as evidence of those facts I have decided that you should proceed on your way. Here are your passports gentlemen. You may pass now to the American sector. Good day." Carl vouchsafed a brief: "Vielen Dank, Herr Oberst, many thanks Colonel," and with heart still pounding walked with Jack across the buffer zone to the American side.

Once safely there Carl pulled his identity card, RAF Form 1250, from his back trouser pocket and demanded to see the officer on duty. A black gum chewing gum toting GI ambled over to the office. "There is some urgency soldier," Jack exclaimed unable to restrain his impatience.

Eventually a slightly more attentive and interested young Captain emerged. "Look Captain," Carl began, "we got detained by the East German guards the other side and we're due to be flying out of RAF Gatow with COM2ATAF and Comm Northag in ten minutes. We're the same rank as you and will be in deep trouble if you can't help us. Lend us your jeep and driver to get us to the aerodrome before the VIPs' aircraft departs."

"We'll pay you back with the biggest crate of Budweiser you've ever seen next time we come to Berlin," Jack pleaded.

"Okay, okay. Most irregular, but I got the message. I learned at West Point not to ask permission first but afterwards. I'll explain what happened to my Colonel later. Off you go!"

"My boss the Air Marshal takes the same view," said Carl, "but I doubt if he will still be my boss if your driver doesn't step on it."

The United States Army jeep hurtled through West Berlin siren wailing. It screeched to a halt outside the Officers' Mess at Gatow. "Send the Mess bills for Flight Lieutenants Clark and Higgins to us at Headquarters," Jack shouted to the receptionist. After a thirty-second change into uniform he and Carl were back in the jeep.

"Just drive straight onto the tarmac, Corporal, blue light flashing," Carl instructed the driver. "I'll give Air Traffic a phone call to explain what happened when we get to Wildenrath." Luckily the pan was empty except for the Pembroke, which had started up but still had its chocks in position and rear door open. "Thanks driver," shouted Carl above the din of the engines handing the American Corporal his last D marks. "Have yourself some beer on us tonight. You've shown us that NATO co-operation really works."

On board Sir Thomas and the Generals pretended not to notice the commotion behind them as Carl piled into the seat beside a smiling welcoming Heidi and Jack into the one beside Peter Lascelles. "You should have stuck to the local talent on the Western side of the wall, Jack, as I did," Peter commented grinning broadly. "Much more satisfying I assure you. When Heidi told me you'd both gone East in plain clothes I thought they'd set up some honey trap over there for you, hence your late arrival."

"It wasn't like that at all," Jack explained ruefully as the Alvis Leonides engines roared and the faithful Pembroke climbed out towards the British zone's boundary with East Germany, Potsdam and Hanover down the corridor below.

Back at Headquarters next day the atmosphere was grim. Fowler was at his most obnoxious. First he addressed himself to Jack. "As far as I'm concerned your handover is now complete. You worked okay with me up to now, then Higgins arrives and all sense of responsibility goes out of the window. I want you to take leave of the AO C in C immediately and be on your way to Coltishall tonight.

"As for you Higgins," Fowler went on venomously, "you've got only one more chance. Before you even got here you wangle yourself an extra sortie, which was not part of the Hunter Conversion course you were on and it ends disastrously. Then you've hardly arrived at HQ before you're off into East Germany through the wrong checkpoint, in plain clothes, posing as a student in itself a potential threat to NATO security – not that you know much about anything here yet. You were very lucky. You could easily have been held by the East Germans and it would have been on extremely costly and tiresome business to get you back."

Sir Thomas was firmly disapproving but less unreasonable as he addressed both Carl and Jack in his office. "So the excitements of Berlin got the better of your judgement, Carl. It's a heady place but you nearly landed yourself in an extremely dangerous predicament. I will not tolerate any indiscipline from you again. As for you, Jack, we'll regard it as an aberration. You've served me well but put up no more blacks please when you get to Coltishall. Take the Lightning very seriously. It is not a forgiving aeroplane."

Carl coexisted with John Fowler in an atmosphere of cool correctness, rendered tolerable by Sir Thomas' geniality. The office duties were not onerous and even helping Lady Swallowfield to entertain was paradoxically eased by her insistence that Carl should withdraw once her guests sat down to dinner. Acting as safety pilot of the two seat Hunter for Swallowfield was no hardship either. Sir Thomas had amassed more than five thousand hours over the years, had always kept in current flying practice and often allowed himself a barrel roll or two and a few loops on the way home.

What made the job truly worthwhile were the weekends. It was rare that the Commander in Chief had a Saturday or Sunday engagement so Carl could regularly set off in the Mercedes diesel he had acquired from a taxi driver in Mönchengladbach to see Heidi in Marburg. About once a month she came to Rheindahlen to visit her parents.

Carl occasionally wondered whether his feelings for Heidi were an unwitting auto-compensation for the loss of Angela, but the two girls were very different. In Germanic tribal terms Angela had been of the Alemani with her dark auburn hair and green eyes. Heidi was taller and totally Teutonic. Angela's presence was more electrifying; Heidi's more comforting and reassuring. Angela's mind verged on the poetic and mystical. Heidi was practical, full of good sense, the ever competent companion, indubitably a mother in waiting.

Her parents seemed happy with her choice of English boyfriend. Indeed they kept open house for Carl. Some of his happiest times were weekends with Heidi in the Deputy Commander in Chief's residence. Her mother Dörthe, the Gräfin, probably regretted that Carl's family had no land or friends in common with her, but was realistic about the new social order in Germany within which she had to bring up her children. Carl and Hans Himmelmann became close friends.

Carl listened attentively with real interest to Himmelmann's stories. "It was hell in the Battle of Britain being so often tied to the bombers instead of being able to range free and get at the British fighters. If you got into a serious dogfight over England you had to watch your fuel gauge as closely as your tail. Those of us who did survive learned a lot in a short time. I was sent off to the Eastern front in early 1942 after a year's rest instructing in fighter tactics.

"Out East it was a turkey shoot," and the General reminisced. "The Russian fighter leaders were competent but the rest showed no initiative whatever. Again I was lucky. I flew a wonderful aircraft the Focke Wulf 190. My God how I loved that aeroplane! I was only shot down once, in July '44 and luckily I was sent back to hospital in Germany to recover."

"What were your feelings about the allied bomber offensive against German cities?" Carl asked in one of his bolder fireside moments over the beer.

"It made me hate Hitler even more especially after the July plot failed. People like von Stauffenberg, Von Kleist and the other plotters were our sort of people. Our class if you understand it and this revolting, mad, jumped up Corporal was destroying our country. He should have sued for peace after D Day. How could we win a war on two fronts against the combined might of America and the Soviet Union?

"We might conceivably have stopped the bomber raids – the American daylight ones at any rate – if we'd used the jet ME262 as a fighter from the start as Adolf Galland wanted but the Führer always thought he knew best and we wasted many months trying to turn it into a bomber.

"However, I probably would not be talking to you now if the ME262 had become an interceptor sooner. It wasn't the roving Mustangs and Thunderbolts which did for me. One of my Me 262's Jumo engines spewed its turbine blades out of the jet pipe soon after take off and I could not hold her. She cart-wheeled into the overshoot and burst into flames. Luckily for me I ended up in an American military hospital within a week where they did all the skin grafts, which saved me and made my eventual return to the Luftwaffe possible."

After about six months of Carl's tour Himmelmann was posted away as a full General to the Harthöhe, the hill outside Bonn on top of which lay the Defence Ministry, to become Inspector General of the Luftwaffe. Carl then spent even more time on the road between Rheindahlen and Marburg. He could adjust his arrival almost to the minute but fatefully his journey planning was upset by a trio of disasters on his return early one Monday morning to fly with Sir Thomas to Twenthe in the Netherlands.

First there was an immense traffic jam on the autobahn between Cologne and Düsseldorf. Then the level crossing on the railway line between Mönchengladbach and Rheindahlen was down. Finally the Hunter T7 had gone unserviceable and a much slower Devon had to be pressed into service. When Carl finally arrived at Wildenrath fuming with frustration Sir Thomas had already left with the PSO, John Fowler who was supposed to be off duty that day.

Fowler could hardly bring himself to speak to Carl next morning. "I knew your appointment would end in tears," he admitted. "If I'd had my way I would have cancelled it after the episode at Chivenor. Now you've let Sir Thomas down and my wife Hilda, too, incidentally. I had promised to take her to Cologne for the day. However, your future is not in my hands. Go and hear what Sir Thomas says. He's waiting for you in his office."

Carl entered and saluted. "Relax Carl," Sir Thomas began. "I could have done with your up to date knowledge to talk more authoritatively with the Dutch fighter boys. I'm sure your late arrival at Wildenrath was not intentional but you have always to plan for the unexpected. That's absolutely basic. John Fowler has confirmed my view that you're not cut out to be an ADC. Not all of us are. What do you feel, Carl?"

"I fear you are right, sir, but you ought to know that I am very sorry for what occurred."

"If you're not going to work for me any more it is probably best if you don't return to this Command, certainly so long as I am the AO C in C. That'll mean no fighter reconnaissance for you, at least for a while," declared Swallowfield emphatically. Carl's spirits sank. He had set his heart on FR and the prospect of imminent separation from Heidi was grim.

"However," Sir Thomas went on allowing the trace of a smile to soften his piercing gaze, "I don't see why you should not stay on the Hunter in another role elsewhere. From what I've seen when we've shared the cockpit you like the aeroplane and I have had no doubts about your flying ability. So I'm sending you back to Chivenor for the long course. Would you be happy with that Carl?"

"Indeed I would, sir, but could I just say that if there's a chance to get some operational flying overseas – in Aden perhaps, I am keen to volunteer."

"Good for you Carl, I'll see what I can do."

CHAPTER 24

The Beverley from Abingdon dropped Carl at Khormaksar airbase in the Aden Protectorate after a long haul via Cyprus. During the stopover at Akrotiri Carl asked the young captain of the aircraft what had become of Peter Carrick, "Oh, he's doing fine. He and Natasha have a baby boy Tadeusz and have moved down to Colerne. He's on Hastings there. After his parachuting accident you would not have expected it," the Flying Officer replied.

"What happened?" Carl asked anxiously. "I never knew."

"No paratrooper likes the side exit from a Hastings. The rigging lines so often get twisted in the slipstream. Well that's exactly what happened to poor old Peter. He didn't have time to kick out of his twists and thumped at great speed into the DZ at Weston on the Green. At least he had the sense to lower his weapon container first so he landed on his feet, but he crushed three vertebrae and could not walk for two months," the Flying Officer explained. "He was lucky to get his flying category back. However, everyone's tipping him to become a Flight Commander on his new squadron soon and he dotes on Tadeusz. Natasha's pregnant again, too."

There was more good news on Carl's arrival in Aden. None other than Max Moxon and Mark Driscoll his Commanding Officer and Flight Commander respectively on 8 Squadron were on the tarmac to greet him and welcome him to the crewroom. "From a selfish point of view I'm glad your stint as ADC didn't last too long, Carl," Max commented sardonically. "We've got a serious job on our hands out here and I need proven enthusiasts."

"I expected you to be still at Halton, sir," Carl responded.

"So did I, but my predecessor got taken ill with amoebic dysentery and apparently could not recover properly in this fearsome heat especially with the strain of all the operational flying. Prendergast who now works for the Air Member for Personnel got wind of the problem and put in a good word with the Air Secretary, so here I am in my old rank and still on the trusty Hunter."

"I got talent spotted, too," Driscoll added. "It was suggested, quite wrongly of course, that I was getting too friendly with the Station Commander's wife so I was banished from the UK to the sunny Aden Protectorate to cool off. At least I escaped the instructional tour they had in store for me. I was supposedly earmarked for the Gnat. They need QFIs with lots of swept wing experience and with my aerobatic display background they already had me in mind for the new Yellowjacks formation team at Valley. But here we get to fire our guns and loose off rockets almost every week. There hasn't been an opportunity like this for operational flying since the confrontation in Borneo."

Feminine company was scarce in Aden though Mark Driscoll never seemed to lack female attachments to while away the short off duty hours including two nurses, a teacher, a secretary and even a purser from one of the big merchant ships which staged through. Carl did not mind the emotional solitude. He was still very committed to Heidi. A constant stream of letters kept him in touch and for his first brief leave they met halfway for a week's seaside holiday in Cyprus.

On the ground the security situation deteriorated alarmingly. The revolutionary Front for the Liberation of Southern Yemen (FLOSY) became increasingly active. Trips to the club or to town diminished as terrorist attacks grew bolder and bloodier. British Army units under pressure or beleaguered Firquats of locally recruited tribesmen often had to call in air support. The squadron was required to provide firepower in response most days, which meant an operational sortie for at very least a pair of aircraft.

Moxon was exemplary in leading calmly from the front getting airborne on operations himself whenever he reasonably could. Mark Driscoll kept everyone cheerful however fraught and stressful the situation. He rarely let his flying impede his social life or his active social life impede his flying. Even the tragic loss of the squadron's newest and youngest member Pilot Officer Kevin Reynolds who failed to pull out of a rocket attack on a rebel mountain stronghold in the rugged Radfan only temporarily curtailed Mark's ebullience.

It was not heartlessness on Mark's part, but the natural consequence of a lifestyle, which was completely addictive and which he would never voluntarily give up. He urged Moxon to get onto Headquarters Middle East Air Force and insist that Kevin's replacement should be at least a second tour pilot. "We haven't time to bring him up to speed on the squadron, sir," Mark insisted. "We can't afford any more Kevins."

He was right. The tempo of the conflict was increasing. The Firquats did their best but were unreliable with FLOSY infiltration and subversion of their home villages. More and more of their remote hilltop piquets and isolated mountain outposts had to be reinforced with British troops regularly inserted by helicopters, which needed fighter protection themselves.

One Sunday morning Mark roused Carl from his bed. "Up, up, up my friend. There's a flap on! Down to the squadron forthwith."

"Can't I even have breakfast, Mark?"

"Too late, bedhog. You can snatch a coffee and a Kit Kat in the crewroom. Drink plenty before you get airborne that's all. This is going to be a hot sortie. You'll be sweating buckets."

When Mark and Carl arrived Max was already at the chinagraph board in the briefing hall pointer in hand with an array of maps propped up on easels around him ready to give his situation report and operational instructions. He spoke clearly with a precise diction which could be easily heard above the whirr of the punkah fans overhead.

"Late yesterday afternoon," Moxon began, "a platoon strength firquat on the summit of this hill marked BP designated Bruneval Peak by the Paras who last occupied it to protect the main road out of town, called up for urgent reinforcements. They feared they could not guarantee to hold out overnight.

"We could not pass a relief convoy up the road," Max continued in measured tones. "It is overlooked by the enemy and may be mined. We could not parachute more troops onto the peak either. The terrain is unsuitable. Anyway the enemy is too close and our men would be vulnerable in the descent. No practical DZ exists there. So a pair of Whirlwind helicopters dropped off two sticks of SAS onto Bruneval without loss just as night was falling. A Flight with concentrated cannon and rocket fire kept the enemy's heads down most effectively whilst this delicate operation was accomplished.

"First thing this morning Captain Tawney commanding the Firquat and Lieutenant Jones of the SAS both radioed in reporting losses: in the case of the Arab soldiers three seriously wounded and in the case of the SAS one trooper sadly killed by a sniper and one walking wounded. They report that the enemy growing in number and audacity is encroaching dangerously on their defensive positions advancing from rock to rock. Yet more FLOSY troops are swarming up from the road and although the defenders are still holding out their ammunition cannot last forever. Resupply is urgent. They need water, too, and to evacuate their casualties.

"The Brigadier has been onto the AOC and we are to cover a breakout by our defenders along this ridge to another peak named Rodman's Post (RP on the map) after a celebrated SAS officer who spent a fortnight on top monitoring traffic on the road below. Our squadron sent an aircraft over very fast at first light at extremely low level. His pictures and the debrief of the pilot Flight Lieutenant Jenkins confirmed that Rodman's Peak is unoccupied so the job for B Flight will be to apply cannon fire and rocket projectiles upon targets of opportunity amongst the attackers of Bruneval Peak whilst our men disengage.

"A Flight will then be on the scene to cover the helicopter evacuation of the wounded and of the SAS fatality from Rodman's Peak as B Flight returns to base. I will be leading the first section of B Flight of four aircraft and Flight Lieutenant Driscoll the second. Flight Lieutenant Jenkins will lead a four ship section of A Flight which will take off half an hour later, hold off, and be called in by the SAS Commander as required for the evacuation. Flight Lieutenant Baird with another section of A Flight will remain on base at ten minutes' notice to scramble if further firepower is called for."

The only concession Carl allowed himself to the possibility of being shot down was the insertion of a small rubber water bottle of blackcurrant juice into the map pocket down his right leg and a khaki coloured sunhat into the breast pocket of his overalls. Anyway he was not really anxious. True a number of the squadron's aircraft had returned from strafing sorties with minor damage from small arms fire and occasionally from ricochets of stone splinters thrown up by the rocket projectiles. But on no occasion yet had an aeroplane been seriously at risk. The greater danger, Carl felt was of becoming fixated on the target or inattentive about the terrain as had tragically occurred with Kevin Reynolds.

B Flight lined up on the runway for a pairs take off with Carl leading off his number two Flying Officer Donaldson twenty seconds behind Max Moxon and his wingman Pilot Officer Greenwood. Once airborne the Flight swung north in loose battle formation climbing to ten thousand feet as they left the built up area behind them for the mountainous badlands ahead. Soon the run in point of a fork in the valley road became visible and surprisingly close to it day glow identification strips laid out in the form of an H on the top of Bruneval Peak.

Moxon and Donaldson peeled into a dive as Moxon called "Attack, attack, go", whilst Carl and Greenwood orbited the crossroads. Carl could discern puffs of pebble and debris as the lead pair's weapons struck home quite close to the summit, then Moxon and Donaldson were soaring up again for another run. They strafed four times and then Moxon called "Blue 1 and 2 clear".

Carl who had spotted movement amongst the rocks and the glint of metal probably from a rifle barrel or magazine just over a thousand yards below Bruneval Peak positioned himself and called "Blue 3 and 4 attack, attack, go" as he dived towards his target. He did not believe that any tribesmen could survive the concentrated blitz of his rockets or the follow up stream of 30 millimetre Aden cannon shells.

Carl was feeling well satisfied as he called that Blue 3 and 4 were diving into another strafing run. Rivulets of sweat were trickling down his face below his oxygen mask and the anti 'g' suit squeezed his legs and lower torso reassuringly as he eased out of his third attack. Suddenly the aircraft shook and the blind flying panel shattered before him. He felt a hard bruising blow to his right leg followed by liquid trickling down his shin into his desert boot.

He anxiously scanned the few instruments which still functioned. The jet pipe temperature was rising fast towards the red lined upper limit and the hydraulic pressure was exhausted. The flying controls solidified as they went into manual. Whilst still gaining height he put the aircraft into a gentle wingover to port determined to spot the Arab marksman who had crippled his aircraft and seemingly wounded his leg.

Carl had hardly glimpsed a stooped brown figure scurrying towards the shelter of a big boulder before the fire warning light came on to a clanging of bells in his headphones followed by a terrifying explosion and a total loss of engine power. He slammed the throttle shut, cut the fuel and called, "Blue 3, Blue 3 Mayday Mayday ejecting!" thinking he must get out at the top of the wingover before the nose dropped and he lost control.

However, Carl could still see movement among the rocks just where his downward trajectory would take him. "Vengeance is mine: I will repay, saith the Lord" flashed through his mind. Vowing to get his own back he decided to stay with it for a few more seconds. "I think I can just about line up to give him a blast," he determined. With great effort he did so and allowed himself a two-second burst of cannon shells before heaving on the ejection handle between his legs.

Next thing he knew was the force of the airstream tearing at his helmet and his arms flailing uncontrollably. Then the stabiliser drogue came out with a bang and he was pitched forward out of the seat. The parachute was deploying sideways as he smashed onto the top of a rock as if on the end of a pendulum. His left hip took the full force of the impact and his head whiplashed onto the stony ground below. The world went black but obviously not for long as he could still hear the ripple of cannon fire and the explosion of rockets all around him.

Carl detached his helmet which had somehow come forward over his face, bashed the quick release box of his parachute and pulled on the rigging lines to bring it out of view of the FLOSY troops he knew must be very close. His fate if they got their hands on him did not bear thinking about.

The pain in his pelvic area was excruciating. He wanted to cry out in agony but managed to control himself. He gingerly examined his right leg. A bullet had pierced his flying suit but was obviously deflected by the metal top of his water bottle whose contents had run stickily down into his boot. Miraculously there was no wound. He could move both feet but the hip pain was too great for him to try and walk, which he dared not anyway as his friends from the squadron were still blasting away at the hillside, which was already a densely beaten zone of bullets between the defenders of Bruneval Peak and their attackers.

After a few more minutes the din ceased. All Carl could now hear was the ping of rifle and machine gun rounds against the rocks and far above the cry of a jet as one of his squadron circled the battle area clearly watching over what he hoped would be the extraction of the beleaguered firquat and SAS by helicopter.

In spite of his intense pain Carl certainly did not want to be overlooked. He felt sure the squadron assumed he was dead. They must have imagined that no one could bale out at such low level in such an extreme attitude and survive. He would have to catch the circling Hunter's attention.

Carl pulled himself up onto the rock for the next pass and waved with his white flying gloves. His desperate gesture was met with a hail of fire from the tribesmen below but as he sank onto his back again he noticed that the aeroplane was waggling its wings. He had been spotted but not only from the air. Lieutenant Jones who was scanning the slope below to target advancing FLOSY troops saw Carl's despairing wave.

Jones turned to the six able bodied troopers around him – towel headed, sweaty, dust stained and festooned with bandoliers of cartridges, with grenades at their belts and spare magazines in their chest pockets.

"I need two volunteers to extricate the downed Hunter pilot," he began, "one strong man to carry him if necessary and another to back him up and provide covering fire. We'll try to isolate the FLOSY attackers from the rescuers with mortar fire and the Browning heavy machine gun. The boss of 8 squadron overhead promises me we'll still have four Hunters to protect us whilst we get to our helo lift from Rodman's Peak."

A swarthy Pacific islander weighing at least sixteen stone stepped forward and a small but wiry Geordie trooper volunteered also. The pair immediately began zig zagging down the hill towards Carl. Carl turning onto his better side could see up the slope where he soon detected the two SAS men coming down to him. He heard the Browning open up and the detonation of mortar bombs between himself and the road below. Soon his attention was drawn to a particularly intense burst of automatic fire and looking up towards Bruneval Peak he saw one of the rescuers fall, his burly companion return briefly to his side and then proceed even more rapidly down towards Carl.

As he reached Carl's boulder the ground around them erupted with incoming fire. Carl raised himself with one arm and the immense Fijian trooper gave him a fireman's lift onto his shoulder and began striding towards the distant summit of Bruneval seemingly regardless of Carl's weight or the danger. Carl could not believe such a bulky target as themselves would escape the hostile bullets, but then he detected that the circling Hunter had detached itself from its patrol of the combat zone and was hurtling towards a huddle of rocks further down the slope.

Carl feared the pilot would replicate Kevin Reynolds' plunge to disaster but he soared upwards and repeated weaponless potentially head removing attacks on the tribesmen several times whilst the Fijian made steady progress upwards. He reached Lieutenant Jones' position just as the fearless singleton slipped away to be replaced by four more Hunters, no doubt the rest of A Flight all burdened with a full load of rockets.

"The pilot here Flight Lieutenant Higgins is ready for evacuation, Mr Jones," panted the Fijian trooper. "We've come so far together, sir, I'll carry him along the ridge to Rodman's Peak. Sad to say I lost Geordie Armstrong on the way down. Bullet through the heart. His body's not recoverable, but luckily our covering Hunters have arrived." As he spoke a salvo of rockets struck home more or less where Carl had landed onto a boulder.

By the time the six remaining SAS men, Captain Tawney and his assorted Arabs from the firquat with their casualties, Carl and equipment made their way along the ridge to the lift off point on Rodman's Peak the first Whirlwind had appeared.

The second section of A Flight had already left the area of engagement for Khormaksar and been replaced over the top of Rodman's Peak by the first section of B Flight. Max Moxon's long delayed return to base was dramatic as he ran out of fuel on touchdown and had to be towed back into dispersal.

CHAPTER 25

The Wing Commander Consultant Surgeon at the RAF hospital Wroughton was pessimistic. "Your hip and pelvis are very thoroughly smashed up, Higgins. It's going to take quite a bit of reconstructive surgery including much metalwork – pins and wires etc – to put it all together and then many months of rehabilitation at Headley Court before you're mobile again. I presume you want to resume flying?"

"Most definitely, sir. Fighter reconnaissance in Germany preferably. I fancy the role, love the aeroplane and my fiancée or rather the girl whom I'd like to be my fiancée lives over there."

"You may have to place your heart's desire elsewhere," responded the Wing Commander Surgeon.

"No, sir, she's a really lovely person and she's coming to see me next week," Carl insisted. "Her father's addressing the Royal United Services Institute in Whitehall and he's persuaded my old boss the C in C Germany to grant him one last favour before relinquishing command – a trip across with his wife and daughter by courtesy of the RAF. Now Sir Thomas is returning to the UK to be Air Member for Supply and Organisation I'm sure he'll overlook my past misdemeanours and let the posters send me back to Germany."

"You're not getting my point, Higgins," the consultant replied firmly. "You must prepare yourself for never sitting in a cockpit again. Assuming I do a perfect job sorting out your injuries I still doubt if your pelvis could stand the strain of 5 or 6 g's day after day. Even if you went onto transports or maritime eight or nine hours at a time in an aircraft seat would probably not be tolerable for you.

"Of course," the Wing Commander went on delivering the final blow to Carl's hopes of getting back to flying as gently as he could, "I'll do my very best and so will Headley Court. You have my blessing when it comes to Germany especially with your German fiancée but you're going to have to be realistic and accept a ground tour. What's the girl's name?"

"Heidi, Heidi Himmelmann."

"The Luftwaffe ace of aces' daughter?" inquired the surgeon obviously impressed.

"Indeed so."

"I wish you both well. Meanwhile I'll be operating on you tomorrow evening. I'm glad she's coming."

"So am I," confirmed Carl forcefully, "but not only her, Flight Lieutenant Peter Carrick and his wife Natasha, too. He flew the casualty evacuation Hastings which brought me home. He's an old friend from Flight Cadet days."

"It's amazing how you Old Cranwellians always stick together," observed the surgeon smiling.

Carl's operation was to be a lengthy affair but his spirits were lifted by two welcome visits, one from his parents and the other from Peter Carrick and Natasha. "We saw in the paper that your squadron had lost a pilot, which was worrying enough," Carl's mother began, "but when your friend Peter rang us to explain you'd been shot down and were back in England in hospital we were actually relieved because it could have been so much worse. You're in good hands here at least."

"I'm very glad it's a relief to you both because for me it's my worst nightmare, Mama," Carl replied. "The surgeon has told me I'll have to give up flying and you know I would never have even considered joining the Air Force except to be a pilot."

"Do you have any idea what you'll want to do once you're recovered?" Carl's father inquired.

"Yes, father I'd like to prove the surgeon wrong. If Douglas Bader can be a successful Wing Leader in wartime with only one leg and Cyclops Brown now command a Trials Squadron at Boscombe Down with only one eye I don't see why I should not get my aircrew category back and as a pilot, too."

"Admirable sentiments my dear Carl but it may take a little time to rehabilitate yourself and to persuade the authorities you're fit to fly. I would suspect it will best be done from inside the Service because once you leave the Air Force it may be very hard if not impossible to get back in especially as a pilot."

"What does Heidi think?" Carl's mother asked. "She seems such a sensible girl."

"I don't yet know, Mama. She's due to come and see me tomorrow but I would like to have definite plans for the future to discuss with her. I don't want her to visit a washed up wreck. I did have a thought stemming from our trip to Berlin. I think I'll put in for a job on the staff of BRIXMIS, the British Commander in Chief's Mission to the Soviet Forces in East Germany. I have up to date operational experience and the language skills but I don't quite know how to achieve it."

"String pulling is usually a good bet, Carl," his father suggested. "After what has happened to you I'm sure Swallowfield will be sympathetic and want to help. I can put a word in for you myself when I get back to the office. The firm is not altogether uninterested in the product of BRIXMIS, but what about your friends? Can't they canvass support for you?"

"Yes of course, Papa. Jamie Jamieson and Janey are due to call by en route to a bucket and spade holiday in Devon in a couple of days' time. He got on particularly well with Air Commodore Prendergast his then Station Commander at Chivenor who is now working for the Air Member for Personnel, which I gather partly involves talent spotting for the intelligence staff."

"There you are, Carl. It seems a viable objective to me. We'll be on our way now to let you build up your strength for the op. Lots of love."

Peter and Natasha were Carl's last visitors before the operation. It was cheering to Carl to see such an evidently devoted and united couple who took honest wholeheartedly unalloyed pleasure in simple things. "I insisted on flying the Casevac sortie down to Aden myself," Peter explained. "Now I'm a Flight Commander I have quite an influence on the squadron's flying programme and I was also able to supervise the configuration of the aircraft with all kinds of resuscitation equipment, an appropriate team of nurses and a good Medical Officer on board because we heard you were very bad indeed; critical in fact."

"Service communication is like Grandmother's whispers at a children's party," Carl responded. "No doubt my injuries had worsened ten fold by the time they were reported to Headquarters Middle East Air Force and thence to Colerne and Wroughton, but as you can see I'm fine."

"You're more than that," Peter insisted. "You're officially a hero. You've been gazetted today with the Distinguished Flying Cross. The citation was on the Orders board at Station Headquarters this morning. Moxon's got a DSO, too, for drawing the enemy's fire like Guy Gibson at the Möhne Dam, and Mark Driscoll a mention in dispatches. Warmest congratulations."

"In my case it's come up with the rations as they say," Carl answered. "The one who really deserved a gong was the Fijian SAS man who rescued me."

"He's not been overlooked either. He got the Military Medal."

"We're very lucky," Natasha continued eagerly. "Because Peter's doing so well they gave us the best Flight Lieutenant's quarter on the married patch. Tadeusz is going to a super infant school on the station and he's hoping for a little sister to keep him company. He's got only three and a half months to wait. Tonight we go to a big dinner at the Polish Hearth Club in Kensington for the survivors of the Battle for Monte Casino as the guests of my uncles. My mother's coming, too. It's wonderful that after so many flights to distant places Peter's got a really long weekend at last. Seeing you here, Carl, being properly looked after shows me just how worthwhile Peter's work can be. Not that I didn't really know it already, but your safe evacuation to UK is the best reward Peter could have. You agree don't you, Peter?"

"Of course, my dear."

When Carl gradually regained consciousness after the long operation he still felt decidedly detached from the world. His nether regions ached and owing to his drug induced torpor he doubted if his comments to the nurse made much sense. However, when she asked if he would like to see Flight Lieutenant and Mrs Jamieson he brightened and became much more alert. "Wonderful, nurse; bring them in please," he replied clearly.

As the door swung open Carl tried to lift himself up a bit more on his pillows. "Don't move! Just stay there, Carl," Jamie insisted. "It's great to see you so obviously enjoying the rest. You know you're one of the rare elite with a postwar DFC a very well deserved award and we're delighted that Max and Mark weren't forgotten either."

"I spoke to Natasha last night," Janey began, "and she said you were looking fit and relaxed."

"Relaxed I certainly am after all the dope they've injected into me. Fit, not quite yet and certainly not fit to fly for many many months, I'm afraid."

"How's Teddy?" Carl inquired trying to move the conversation from his injuries to happier domestic topics.

"He's great. We're very lucky with the big garden at the Old Rectory which abuts onto a wood," Janey replied. "He has plenty of space to play and we have wonderful woodland walks at weekends if Jamie's not away on Armaments Practice Camp, a course or detachment somewhere, but that's usually rare. I run Teddy into Norwich for his infants school each morning and we have lots of friends in the city."

"It sounds a marvellous life to me," Carl enthused in all sincerity.

"It normally is," Jamie added, "and of course I've been fortunate enough to find myself on the first squadron of a new aeroplane. With any luck the Lightning should see me through the most intensive part of my flying career but the black hand of a malevolent destiny has touched us hard. Our friend Jack Clark was killed a week ago. You will have missed the news because of your injuries, but it really devastated us."

"How absolutely awful. What on earth happened? Jack was so meticulous and responsible," Carl replied. "It's a terrible loss."

"The cruel thing is that he was doing so well. Everybody liked him. He took to the aeroplane like a veritable duck to water," Jamie explained. "He converted to the aircraft faster and more smoothly than anyone. Nobody was keener or better regarded in the squadron."

"He'd just got a new girlfriend, too," Janey interjected, "a physiotherapist. They were already very fond of each other. She gave him the support and encouragement he needed – a most attractive, funny, lively girl. It's so sad."

"That's an understatement, my love," Jamie continued. "The whole thing could not have been worse. There had been much talk of getting the Lightning better known, its capabilities more widely appreciated to persuade other countries to equip themselves with the aeroplane. It is an exceptional single crew all weather interceptor, climbs like a rocket and yet is remarkably manoeuvrable. Command therefore decided that the Lightning should be shown off in public more and the decree came down for us to select a demonstration pilot who would display the aircraft at major airshows and to potential customer Air Forces.

"When the invitation went out for a competition on the squadron to decide who would have the responsibility and the glory to be Mr Lightning for the season there were three entrants – Ted Halliday a former test pilot on A Squadron at Boscombe Down, the one which evaluates new fighter aircraft for the Service, Simon Rampling a founder member of the CFS Red Pelicans aerobatic team at Little Rissington and Jack. The judges were equally distinguished. The CO and Wingco Ops were on the panel plus an ex-member of the Black Arrows and another of the Blue Diamonds formation aerobatic teams. In the event of a tied verdict the Station Commander would have the casting vote.

"For a whole month they practised," Jamie went on, "gradually bringing their manoeuvres down to a strictly enforced minimum of two hundred feet, the crowd line was never to be crossed and the show kept as much as possible within the airfield boundary. Rehearsals over base were carefully monitored by the Co and Wingco ops.

"I never dreamed of entering," Jamie explained. "I find it hard enough to operate the Lightning effectively especially using the airborne interception radar to fight in cloud or at night without trying to get good enough to demonstrate the aircraft at the limits of its flight envelope in front of hyper critical spectators at hangar top height."

"I'm very glad to hear it," Janey insisted firmly.

"Anyway there was no doubt about it," Jamie explained. "Ted was as precise as you'd expect a former test pilot to be, but his sequence lacked showmanship. Simon's was elegant and smooth but there's all the difference between hanging on your neighbour's wingtip in a formation team and cutting a dash in a Lightning on your own. Cut a dash Jack most certainly did. His hesitation rolls were a delight, so crisp and well defined; his slow rolls so fluently slow. He used reheat to the full. The crowd always likes a good blast and his tight turns with full afterburner to bring the aircraft back on line were amazing – 6g easily, never much higher than the windsock. He was the worthy winner and unanimously so in the view of the judges.

"The first public shows went well," Jamie went on eloquently. "Jack built up a high reputation. He even received quite a fanmail down on the squadron. When the Wingco learned therefore that the NATO Defence College were on a study visit to the UK he was on to Command at once to ask if Jack could demonstrate to the delegation the remarkable performance of what he reckoned was the best interceptor in NATO.

"Jack departed for the display duty accompanied by the boss in a spare aeroplane. The weather was cloudless; the visibility perfect, the local aircrews at the selected bomber station envious and the up and coming senior NATO officers grouped in front of the control tower eagerly expectant for what they hoped would be the flying demonstration of their lives – at least this is what Jack must have intended to give them.

"Off he roared into his routine with a light fuel load and blazing afterburner into a near vertical climb straight from take off winging over into the usual immaculate stuff – inverted flypast, Derry turns, Cuban eights, the lot. Now one of his crowd stoppers had been to approach low and slow with flaps and gear down at a high angle of attack, slam her into full reheat pitch forward and accelerate into a loop half rolling into the reverse direction on the way down.

"This awful day he must have been a little bit too slow on entry, or a little bit too low over the top or both because he never recovered from the loop and just tent pegged as they crudely put it, into the ground leaving a vast smoking crater at the intersection of the two runways right in front of the distinguished spectators. At least Jack's agonised realisation of his error must have been brief but an appalled bunch of NATO visitors had to be shepherded into the bar for some stiff brandies before getting shakily back on the bus. The poor old boss' return to Coltishall must have been the most dismal in his life."

CHAPTER 26

Heidi's visit brought home to Carl just how emotionally dependent he had become on her. How happy he was at Rheindalen. How bereft he had really been at Khormaksar though the intensive flying and especially the operational sorties had assuaged his solitude. It was as if the sky had become his faithful mistress to whom he could always repair; sometimes for extra exhilaration, sometimes for solace in the one place where he would be unquestioningly accepted.

The brief holiday in Paphos had been an interlude of pure perfection because in Heidi his life all came together. There was the intense physical thrill of her long limbed athleticism and wholehearted espousal of life and love. Yet she brought more; the impersonation of his spiritual attachment to Germany and as the ace of ace's daughter an unspoken understanding that her devotion would have to share a place with his irresistible mistress of the sky. Carl's injuries might have forced this mistress out of his life for a while but he knew he would inexorably return as the moth though burned yet seeks the flame.

"Papi and Mutti send their love," Heidi began cheerfully. This benediction showed a generosity of heart Carl had not expected.

"Mine asked to be remember to you, too," he replied simply. It was not strictly true of course and betrayed the traditional British reserve which had perhaps impelled him to seek refuge in the arms of Angela and Yasmin rather than find "a nice English girl" as Jamie had done so successfully and Peter Lascelles had done more stormily.

The orderly withdrew discreetly leaving them to themselves in the officers isolation ward. Heidi put her face tenderly beside his on the pillow and bestowed a lingering küßchen, a little kiss which did not merit its demure diminutive. Then snuggling up closer she slipped her hand deep down inside the sheets. "I see we are wide awake my little treasure. I detect no sign of paralysis I'm glad to say," she declared proudly. "I think the prognosis is very good for us."

"So do I," affirmed Carl. "You know we've been so lucky. I had six whole months as an ADC in Germany. Some people don't last six weeks in that job. It was great – passion in the woods of Berlin, weekend commuting to your snug little bedsit in Marburg, and then a whole magical week together in Paphos. But since I got hurt in Aden I've been thinking. I know I'm going to have to do at least one ground tour. They won't believe however well I rehabilitate myself at Headley Court that I'm fit to fly. So why don't we take advantage of this divine intervention. I'll go all out for a job on BRIXMIS and then we could live together in Berlin as husband and wife."

"Carl darling, I was expecting a shocked and self-pitying patient," Heidi responded. "Instead I see you have grand plans for the future, but you didn't need to explain them so fully. If you just ask me will you marry me, I shall say yes."

"Will you?"

"Marry me?"

"Yes."

"I thought I was supposed to be asking that question."

"I am."

"The answer is definitely... Ja, bestimmt! Most definitely yes!"

"That is just wonderful. My spirits are so high I'm sure I'll be in hospital at least a week less now so we can bring forward the wedding. Will you tell your father when you go home with him?"

"Of course."

"But don't I need to ask him first?"

"I don't think so. My parents sent you their love didn't they?"

"Yes, but if they have any objection I'll gladly go and ask him properly – just as soon as I'm mobile."

"I'm sure that won't be necessary. We Germans are not always as formal as you imagine."

Carl's convalescence went well. He spent six weeks at Headley Court under the care or rather the forceful tutelage of an intimidating squad of physiotherapists, PT instructors, masseurs and orthopaedic specialists. He was confronted by an array of apparatus – weights, pulleys, treadmills, dumb bells, skiing machines, presses, wall bars, gym horses, bean bags, benches and mats. He swam often, not as relaxation but to enhance the mobility of his lower limbs and improve his cardiovascular fitness. At the end of it all he went off to join Heidi in Marburg for a fortnight's leave before returning to the Central Medical Establishment just off Harley Street for a crucial assessment by a Board of three senior Medical Officers.

"Your report from Headley Court is good," the Chairman of the panel confirmed. "The Chief Medical Officer there states that few patients have put in a more impressive sustained effort to rehabilitate themselves with a view to returning to their former duties. However, he has reservations about your taking up a flying appointment at least for a while. You will need full leg movement to operate the rudders properly for example. He doubts whether you have that. We shall conduct a little test."

"I want you to perform six squats before us," the Medical Wing Commander instructed Carl. "Crouch on your haunches and then raise yourself on your toes to full height without using your hands." Carl duly executed the exercise as required though it hurt his hips acutely. "Now do it with this five pound weight in your hands," the Wing Commander insisted. "It is necessary to demonstrate that you could cope with a load on your rudders."

"If you'll excuse me sir that's just too painful," exclaimed Carl giving up reluctantly after the first attempt, "but in a modern jet aircraft you hardly use the rudders."

"You do in some," objected the only winged member of the Board, "the Gnat is a case I know. It has toe brakes."

"Even so the foot pressure must be pretty light, isn't it, sir?" Carl asked the aeromedical Squadron Leader.

"Maybe so but I still have my doubts."

"What we'll do," the Wing Commander resumed, "is we'll send you to Valley for an airborne physical evaluation in a Gnat not only of your leg strength including braking and taxiing but also of your capability to withstand sustained high g loadings. On the outcome of this assessment your flying category will depend. I must warn you it is my considered view that if you fail your condition is not likely to improve and that you should reconcile yourself to changing to a Ground Branch or if that is uncongenial to leaving the Service altogether."

Carl went away dejectedly for a long weekend with his parents in London. They were not as sympathetic to his determination to stay flying as he had hoped. "You've done very well, Carl. You've been an instructor, an ADC to a Commander in Chief, flown on operations, what more do you want especially now you're engaged?" his mother pointed out. "From what I hear life on a fighter squadron is as peripatetic as a travelling circus. You'll soon be wanting to set up home, put down roots. Or at least if you won't, Heidi will."

"I know mother, but Heidi's used to the life you criticise. You never used to be so critical before I went to Aden. I am just at the threshold of the best flying jobs of my life – joining a formation aerobatic team perhaps, getting my own squadron, possibly becoming a test pilot, being Wing Commander Flying of a big base or even station commander."

"I think your mother just wants you not to be too disappointed if you can't return to flying," Carl's father explained.

"This is all hypothetical, Papa, because fate will decide my destiny. On Monday I have to report to Valley for a check ride on the Gnat and if my hip and pelvis can cope with the strain I will still have a chance to get back to flying. Otherwise as everybody seems to be advising me, Mama included, I'll just have to find another job inside or outside the Air Force. If you'll excuse me I'll ring Peter Lascelles and Lizzie to ask if they will put me up. He's instructing at Valley and they have a house overlooking Treardur Bay. It'll be good to see them again and he can give me some good tips before my test."

The drive to Anglesey was long but the welcome on arrival from his friends was warm. The view across the sea to Snowdonia was spectacular and the garden where the Lascelles' baby Veronica was sleeping in her pram was a delight – full of fuchsias, dahlias, mombretia and chrysanthemums. Peter had just returned from his daily swim in the sea. "I hardly notice the cold now, Carl," he boasted. "It's a case of mind over body. My bathes help me stay fit throughout the summer months and keep me at home unlike golf or cricket, so you approve don't you dear?"

"Of your swimming and the beach, yes; of Wales and the Air Force no," Lizzie responded equivocally.

"Tell me about the Gnat, Peter," Carl inquired eagerly.

"It's a delight, you'll love it. Unlike the Vampires we learned on it's a modern aeroplane with sparkling performance. It's unbelievably sensitive. The only drawback is the poor view from the back for the instructor. It's easier side by side as in a Provost or Vampire. You can actually see what the pupil's doing, but perhaps he learns more independence tandem. Being so light it climbs like a fighter which makes conversion to the Hunter or Lightning easier later."

"Well it did start off as a fighter. Indeed the Indians use it as such today," Carl explained.

"They certainly do and I'm afraid I've got more very bad news for you, Carl," Peter replied, "as if the loss of Jack Clark was not enough."

"It is for me," Lizzie interrupted. "At this rate we'll have no friends left."

"Anyway," Peter went on, "the tragedy is that Yousuf Ahmed was killed in the Indo-Pakistan war, shot down by a Gnat apparently as his ill luck would have it. They're so small and agile perhaps he never saw his attacker until it was too late."

"That is just too awful for words," Carl lamented. "Poor, poor Yasmin. Has Lizzie spoken to her?"

"She tried. Rang her in Washington – number unobtainable. Even rang the Pakistan Embassy there. They didn't know anything about her. Her parents had already left London and gone back to Pakistan at the end of last year. I believe Yousuf's father went up to Air Commodore and is in some staff job in Islamabad."

"I feel almost guilty myself," Carl responded bitterly. "Surely we British could have given the Pakistan Air Force tactical advice on how to cope with the Gnats and Hunters. We sold the aircraft to the Indians and it would have offered some kind of balance but Britain has always tilted towards India ever since partition. So our Yousuf was a victim of great power politics in a way. Trained by the British he was destined to be killed by one of the fighters they delivered to his country's enemy. To his family he will be a shahid, a martyr, but that's not much consolation."

Lizzie stylish as ever prepared a delicious dinner starting with oysters, then bass accompanied by a delicate Muscadet, finishing with what she termed a Swiss pudding of locally picked dewberries mulched into porridge oats with double cream. Her model figure had returned and as she made clear she was keen to resume her professional life.

"It's all right for you, Peter," she began over the Madeira. "You've got your Yellowjacks commitments which take you away regularly at weekends and as it's the first Gnat aerobatic team you're quite a celebrity in your way. I'm stuck at home, however, with Veronica. She's georgeous of course but all the people round here are Welsh. We don't know a soul and the only entertainment is the endless round of coffee mornings and the odd charity bazaar on the station. It's quite a contrast from Düsseldorf I can tell you, or even Nottingham for that matter. I have nothing in common with these people. They bore me rigid."

"I understand, my love, but it'll get better," Peter replied ruefully. "I expect to be a Flight Commander on Canberras next tour – in Germany or Cyprus with any luck. That would not be bad. Or I might be on the waterfront of the Central Flying School instructing future instructors on the Gnat. I'm sure you'd like to live in the Cotswolds. It's extremely fashionable.

"There's even talk," Peter continued, "of moving the Yellowjacks to Kemble as part of the CFS and making them the national aerobatic team with a new name, the Red Arrows. That would be great."

"For you perhaps Peter," rejoined Lizzie, "but think again. You've got no guarantee they'll send you anywhere nice and it's time we decided our own future – if only for Veronica's sake. I don't want her to be a poster's pawn, too. I'm going to bed. You and Carl can finish the Madeira between you. Come up quietly please."

"I'm so happy to hear about Heidi," Peter began. "I really liked her. I think you're very lucky and have made a wonderful choice."

"I'm glad you think so, Peter. I regard you as one of my oldest and closest friends. You know her and I trust your judgement."

"I think it makes all the difference," Peter replied, "if like Heidi you've been born into a very senior officer's family and lived well in smart quarters and residences. Lizzie's father, however, is still a Squadron Leader in the Secretarial Branch and quite honestly it's a dog's life. Everybody looks down on you and regardless of how hard you work you get nowhere."

"But in Heidi's case her father was the great roasted war hero who became a top General and one of the chief architects of the new reformed Luftwaffe."

"The war's influence, Peter, was even more significant," Carl insisted. "Heidi's mother lost everything – estates, homes, friends, way of life, money, the lot. After that you come to appreciate all your husband can achieve in a Service career. We've been spoilt by comparison."

"It's time we had a night cap," Peter insisted pouring Carl a generous brandy.

"Remember I've got one of the most important flights of my life tomorrow," Carl remonstrated ineffectually. "I need to keep a clear head."

"So do I. We've got the Yellowjacks' final rehearsal for the Battle of Britain display. This season may be my last, Carl."

"Why on earth? You've only just joined the team."

"I've decided to PVR, to go for premature voluntary release."

"I can't believe it," exclaimed an astonished Carl. "You've got everything going for you."

"Lizzie doesn't see it that way I'm afraid. She says I'm a failure; that all my Winchester contemporaries are earning three or four times as much as me as high fliers in the City and so on with nice permanent homes of their own; that her identity is being suppressed by the Air Force; her personal career ruined."

"But you've done so well," Carl protested.

"That's what you say. However, she goes on and on and on like this late into the night. I get more and more emotionally exhausted, totally drained by it all psychologically and physically. Sometimes I can hardly lift myself into the cockpit in the morning. The fatigue is so great. It's sad because it's very beautiful here and it would make me very happy to see Veronica growing up in this lovely place beside the sea and there would be other lovely places afterwards because Air Force bases are usually in the deepest countryside.

"Yet whatever happens I don't want Veronica to be part of a single parent famly so I've really no choice," Peter concluded.

"Has Lizzie actually given you an ultimatum to choose between the Air Force and your marriage?"

"Not in so many words yet but she will. She's become so abusive of me that she's now almost more my enemy than my friend, which is infinitely sad. I dread coming home, linger in the Mess bar or take an evening detour on my way back via a pub or two.

"I relish the Yellowjacks' displays away from base. It's so refreshing to find that girls actually like me. We had a show at Jurby in the Isle of Man two weeks ago. I stayed in the Castle Mona Hotel a grand grey stone crenellated establishment just back from the seafront in Douglas. After the display we all went to the casino nearby. I didn't win any money but I met a flaxen haired Viking over the green baize tables. There are quite a lot over there.

"The Nordic genes must have stayed pure for a thousand years. Anyway everything proceeded so naturally, without any complications or pressures. She was full of admiration for the hotel and even complimentary towards me as a person. I don't think it was because I am a Yellowjack and we'd given the promenade at Douglas a good flypast on our way North to Jurby. I believe she just fancied me and said so. What's more she was like a gazelle in bed."

"You've let your enthusiasm run away with you, Peter. What will you actually do if you quit the Air Force?"

"Like nearly everyone else of our metier who leaves I'll become an aerial bus driver," Peter explained. "I'll have to get my Airline Pilot's Licence and then flog the routes becoming steadily fatter, living out of a suitcase, with my body clock permanently out of synch, but earning a good salary or compensation as the

Americans appropriately call it. Doubtless we'd have a desirable residence in the suburbs not too far from Heathrow and Gatwick, in Esher or Weybridge perhaps. London would be easily accessible by train for Lizzie and I expect the Surrey schools will be excellent for Veronica."

When Carl reported to the Chief Instructor's office next morning the Wing Commander was solicitous. "I have heard you earned your gong the hard way and now the CME has sent you to us to see if you're fit enough to fly after all your injuries," he began. "This check ride will be very important to you so we've chosen one of our best QFIs to accompany you. He's just been awarded the Air Force Cross for outstanding devotion to duty over many months on your old squadron out in Aden, so he's presumably a friend – Mark Driscoll.

"Apparently he asked to do all the Hunter air tests on top of his heavy operational commitments and Flight Commander duties at Khormaksar," the CFI went on. "He landed a Hunter in perilous circumstances safely back at base with a raging engine fire."

"It seems in character," replied Carl.

"Anyway he's now Deputy Leader of the Yellowjacks and our chief standards officer trying to keep us all up to the mark. Forgive the pun."

Standards Flight had a small office at the base of the Control Tower next to the Met section. "Welcome to my empire, Carl," Mark came to him in greeting with hand outstretched. "It's wonderful to have you back in the old routine evidently in rude good health. When we put you into Peter Carrick's Hastings with a mask on your face and tubes attached to many parts of your body you looked decidedly the worse for wear. We wondered if you could ever regain the AIGI Medical category on which our employability as aviators depends. Now we've got to prove in the air that your health is in fact as good as it looks."

"I've been looking forward to this trip so much, Mark. Doing it with you is an added bonus," Carl responded.

"What better way of confounding those pessimistic medics than having you upside down with nothing on the clock as they say? We'll wind it up a bit, too, putting on plenty of 'gs' to show your heart is still able to pump the blood out of your boots and into that renowned brain of yours and that your nether regions won't crumble under the strain. Lastly I'll ensure you have a lot of rudder work – mostly on the ground but a bit in the air as well to demonstrate that your hips are now problem free."

"I tell you what, Mark, why don't you give me a standard final handling test as you would to a student to qualify for his wings and then if we've still got time you could take me through the Yellowjacks' fair weather airshow sequence?"

"Agreed, but didn't they call you Honkers at Cranwell? Puking is 'streng verboten'. A pupil did it on me last week with his oxygen mask on." He went a bit quiet and then piped up, "Sir, I think I'm going to be… Hurrgh…"

"Beating airsickness is one of the little battles I've won along the way, Mark. As Peter Lascelles says about bathing in the icy sea of Anglesey, 'it's all in the mind' and I've had it licked since Piston Provost days," Carl replied reassuringly, "so I'll be a happy passive participant in your formation display routine."

"Have a seat and read these pilot's notes on the aircraft and then take yourself to the simulator," Mark instructed. "I've warned the Master Pilot in charge to expect you for a demonstration of the cockpit checks, operating procedures and emergency drills. Then have a good lunch to settle your stomach for aerobatics and be back here for a quick briefing at 1400 and take off at 1430 hours."

Mark was special. In his company life was fun and he seemed to do everything effortlessly well. It was paradoxical that someone so unselfish and naturally generous should be the victim of a broken marriage; the perforce absentee father to a devoted young daughter.

On the station his quiet authority and exceptional talent fitted him well for the standards flight. Under his direction it not only kept his fellow instructors graded as QFIs and rated in instrument flying. He turned standards into a remedial section where his perceptive individual attention often restored the proficiency of failing student pilots without the need for them to seek an invidious change of instructor on their squadron. The 'chop rate' or percentage of washouts at Number 4 Flying Training School had begun to decline steadily since Mark's arrival at Valley.

Carl felt almost subliminally as he could only sense not see Mark behind him that Mark was in his natural element. "I feel we're going to enjoy this sortie. She's all yours," was Mark's only comment. Use of the rudder bar and toe braking on leaving dispersal had not even given Carl a twinge in his bad hip.

Carl mused as they positioned to line up on the runway how personality communicated itself in the cockpit. He could not see Mark behind him yet his presence transmitted a sense of mutual well-being and calm contentment. Their diminutive Gnat with its marked anhedral – the down pointing wings above a narrow undercarriage and rather tail down posture looked squat and unremarkable as it sat on the centreline awaiting take off clearance. Then they were away like a dart piercing the heavens leaving Holyhead and Treardur Bay to port as they curved upwards to the north-west over the Skerries towards the broad Irish Sea and the sky.

In the upper air the aircraft danced as on angel's wings. Whereas flying the Vampire had been distinctly physical, the Hunter a classically elegant experience of guiding a sturdy thoroughbred at the touch of a light rein, the Gnat was feather-like to the fingertips. Mark asked for turns at maximum rate and high 'g' breaks into imagined attacks. Carl's pelvis ached a bit but the aeroplane's speed of response and precision in manoeuvre amazed him.

Steeply they dived slipping sweetly and swiftly transonic, reaching 1.1 times the speed of sound between the Calf of Man and the Mountains of Mourne before further descending landward to join the circuit to the mid Anglesey satellite airfield of Mona to practise touch and go landings including emergency procedures. On overshoot in manual control without the powered all moving tailplane Carl found the headstrong aeroplane reared uncontrollably skyward for lack of nose down elevator trim. Mark eased her onto her side and into the downward leg reducing power and speed. "Datum shift, we call it Carl," he explained. "It can be a bit dramatic for the uninitiated. For such a small insect the Gnat can inflict a nasty bite on the unwary." To enhance his view from the back he asked for even more tightly curving approaches than usual but in the light wind it was all routine for Carl whose reactions had not slowed in hospital.

"Time for an impromptu solo rehearsal of what our leader Don White will take us through for the Battle of Britain show," Mark announced into his oxygen mask. "The circuit's clear and will stay that way. The students are on Ground School exams. I have control." They plunged towards the main runway from a wide high orbit and up into a loop easing out into a wingover port calling diamond go at its apogee. Down they swept again in front of the imaginary crowd line into another loop in the reverse direction holding low on exit and climbing higher to hurtle down for a low level pass before the phantom spectators into a vertical climb. "…upward bomburst, bomburst go," called Mark at the top.

The aircraft rotated through ninety degrees, inverted itself and dived steeply. Skirting the hangars it soared skyward once more to rejoin the imaginary formation. "Reform arrowhead, arrowhead go," ordered Mark, looping over into a curving descent to reposition. Then "rolling, rolling go" he called swinging into a barrel roll to starboard followed by a tight turn onto the runway line and with the instructions "line abreast, line abreast go" and "rolling, rolling go" banked into a barrel roll in the opposite direction.

As they emerged they rolled the other way into a wide wingover. Then "extended box extended box go" was the order as they accelerated into a fast descent to two hundred feet at the runway intersection followed by "looping, looping go" with another rotation through ninety degrees this time steeply down for a departure on full power between the hangars at tree top height.

"How's your stomach, Honkers?" Mark asked anxiously.

"Glad of the good lunch Mark, and my pelvis is fine, too." In fact it hurt him a bit but he would never reveal it to anyone.

"Glad to hear it," Mark replied. "I'll just show you the future Grand Finale. I want Don White to introduce a synchro pair into next season's programme particularly if we go to Kemble as the Red Arrows. We'll have to raise our game to shine on the international display circuit."

They orbited Mona gently as Mark went on enthusiastically. "I'll demonstrate you the opposition barrel roll I'm proposing – minimum height 200 feet, maximum 400 feet; my aircraft one side of the runway and my counterpart's aeroplane the other side from the opposing end. A third of the way down I call 'barrel roll, barrel roll go' and we're barrelling outwards as we cross in the middle. Should be safe and spectacular, a welcome addition to the traditional follow my leader routine for the pair."

With a quick positioning manoeuvre and eighty per cent power they were off along the hangar side of the runway at 200 feet, then after calling "rolling, rolling go" with back pressure on the stick and a deflection of aileron they swept up pressed positively into their seats to four hundred and fifty feet at the top recovering smoothly to 200 feet at exit and then way back to Valley.

"Just a bit cautious, Carl," Mark explained. "I prefer to be a little bit high than below datum height."

"So do I, most definitely," Carl replied, "but you're obviously going to have to maintain your respective lines very strictly. It'll be hard to watch your height, line, rate of roll and the other aircraft all at once. You'll have to trust your oppo totally."

"One flight with me and you're talking like a prima donna. Nice landing. Now park on the end of the line as near to standards as you can. If you had been doing a CFS instructor's categorisation ride with me I'd have given you an A1 for handling. Next time I'll want you to patter as you fly. You've passed."

After a welcome iced coca cola Carl and Mark reported to the Chief Flying Instructor, Wing Commander Douglas Archer, who greeted them warmly. Small, dapper, bustling and eager Archer had a reputation for enthusiasm in the air and on the ground. No one could cast doubts on his relevant experience after his recent tours at the Central Fighter Establishment at West Raynham and as a Vampire Squadron Commander at Number 5 Flying Training School, Oakington. The ribbons of the Air Force Cross and Queen's Commendation for Valuable Service in the Air on the breast of his well pressed uniform bore testimony to his competence.

"How did it go, Mark?" he began. "I can't believe that Carl had any difficulties with the flying even if he is new to the aeroplane. But how about the hip when braking and the pelvis under 'g'?"

"As you'd expect, sir, Carl performed as the virtuoso we all on 8 squadron knew him to be," Mark confirmed. "At the end of the test we went through the Yellowjacks' Battle of Britain display sequence over at Mona. I think we should sign Carl up for the team. He complained of no pain at all even in the tightest manoeuvres."

"Just as I thought," Wing Commander Archer replied. "I'm delighted. Whether you will be, Carl, is another matter. I have received an urgent signal from Adastral House. In the event of your fitness being established here, which it has been to my satisfaction by Mark, you are to be a supernumerary pilot on the Air Experience Flight at Cambridge flying Chipmunks for air cadets whilst you undergo specialist training. You are to be posted to BRIXMIS in the New Year and will remain in the General Duties (Pilot) branch. Clearly someone very high up regards you as an extremely talented individual. I suggest you go on a week's leave and await joining instructions from your new unit."

"But I thought the whole point of my check ride here was to see if I am sufficiently recovered to return to fast jets," Carl protested. "I was hoping to complete my tour on 8, or if not to rerole onto Fighter reconnaissance in Germany. Just because I put up a black as an ADC at Headquarters there shouldn't invalidate me now. Or at least couldn't I join my friends Peter and Mark here after recategorising on the Gnat with CFS at Kemble?"

"Laudable sentiments, Carl," the CI responded, "but 'ours not to reason why'. After the latest Berlin crisis they probably need good German specialists more than ever. I bet you didn't realise that BRIXMIS has two Chipmunks at Gatow so you'll be able to keep your flying currency and your flying pay. Didn't Mark mention to me that you've got a German fiancée? I'm sure she won't be disappointed."

CHAPTER 27

Carl and Heidi were delighted to be back in Berlin and soon found a flat in Charlottenburg. Their wedding had been a modest but intensely happy event in Bonn. Carl's mother and father and his in-laws got on well. The music was uplifting with fine chorales in best Lutheran style.

Carl had chosen his favourite hymn – nun danket alle Gott, "now thank we all our God… who from our Mother's arms hath blessed us on our way with countless gifts of love… and still is ours today," to please his parents as the worthy tribute he hoped of a dutiful and grateful son.

Of his contemporaries at Cranwell only Peter Lascelles now a civilian studying for his Airline Transport Pilot's Licence and Peter Carrick were present, both on their own. Lascelles was delighted to be out of the classroom. Three senior officers supported him – Group Captain Chivvers station commander of Gütersloh, John Fowler station commander of Wildenrath and Max Moxon now deservedly Wing Commander Operations at Laarbruch.

On his first morning Carl reported to the Senior British Officer at the BRIXMIS Headquarters at Hitler's old Olympic Stadium complex, Brigadier McPherson formerly of the Argyll and Sutherland Highlanders. Carl and the Brigadier immediately respected each other. McPherson had won a Military Cross in hand to hand fighting against the Chinese on the Imjin river in Korea and a mention in despatches in Aden. A soldier's soldier he had held only one staff appointment in his whole career. At BRIXMIS he drove his teams hard encouraging them to take justifiable risks to obtain key information on the Warsaw Pact forces deployed in East Germany.

Carl then presented himself to McPherson's Royal Air Force deputy Group Captain Tim Hannam, a highly complex and notably intellectual character. Hannam had already served as deputy air attaché in Moscow and done a tour in intelligence in the Ministry of Defence. With an engineering degree from London University and a graduate of the Empire Test Pilots' School at Farnborough the Group Captain was the foremost technical brain in the mission, notwithstanding which he insisted on flying the BRIXMIS Chipmunks at Gatow regularly.

"Glad to have you aboard Carl," he declared in welcome. "I've been studying your file and it makes impressive reading. I trust that you and your wife Heidi have settled in happily. It'll be a great advantage that she already knows Berlin so well, understands its complicated politics and how this divided city fits into the East/West military and ideological confrontation at the heart of Europe.

"After a week of briefing here," he went on, "I suggest you go to our compound at Mission House, Potsdam for a couple of days appraising the local scene. Then we'll send you on your first information gathering tour with Squadron Leader Flanders. He's a navigator, fluent German and Russian speaker and has already been at BRIXMIS for a year and a half so really knows his way round and how to prevent the STASI and KGB cramping your style.

"Flanders is on leave till tomorrow so I suggest we take ourselves to Gatow after lunch. I don't need to introduce you to the Chipmunk. I gather you managed to put in a hundred hours on the aeroplane flying Air Cadets at the weekend from Marshalls Airport in Cambridge. However, I'll take you through the various local operational procedures which are important. If they're not followed you could even get yourself shot down. Once should be enough for you, I'm sure."

When Carl arrived at Gatow that afternoon an instinct informed him that as the base had proved the entry point to what became married life with Heidi so the future within his new field of clandestine operations would have its focus there. He could not believe that the Air Force's decision to let him remain a pilot in spite of the initially negative judgement of the Central Medical Establishment, and subsequent provision for him of a role at Cambridge on the humble Chipmunk primary trainer could have taken place without a special purpose. He felt sure that Group Captain Hannam would introduce him to it now.

The BRIXMIS Chipmunk's Training Sortie constituted the only air movement from Gatow that afternoon. The Group Captain installed himself in the front seat of the aeroplane explaining that it was usual to have the rear one available for a photographer or observer. Hannam made it clear that they were only allowed to fly inside the Berlin Air Traffic control zone, an area within a twenty mile radius of the Berlin Flight Safety Centre.

Their missions could be varied but important. Often they had to fly into East Germany at very low altitude to photograph a target of opportunity such as a new tank park, a recently constructed radar installation or a column of military vehicles. Sometimes they could respond to an imminent crisis more swiftly and less provocatively than personnel on the ground. For example when the Berlin Wall went up on 13 August 1961 a Chipmunk reconnoitred along its length to monitor the scale and nature of the building work in progress.

Carl had enjoyed his weekends Chipmunk flying at Cambridge where he had made friends with the instructors of the university air squadron who invited Heidi and him to their parties in the unit's town headquarters at Chaucer Road. She felt from the start that the Royal Air Force was accepting her socially and endeavouring to make their young married life fun. Carl soon become very proficient on the aircraft which pleased him.

When Hannam asked Carl to demonstrate very short landings and forced landings as well as tight turns at ultra low level for a notional photographer in the back seat to obtain downward pictures unobscured by a wing he had no problems. "I see you're in your element, Carl," Hannam observed. "I'll make sure you get as much airborne time as possible, but our Chipmunks are only an adjunct of limited value to our primary role of obtaining first hand information in the field on Soviet and East German military dispositions."

"Don't worry, sir, I only expected to fly as a bonus on this posting," Carl replied.

"Talking of bonuses," Hannam responded as they drove back to BRIXMIS HQ at Olympic Stadium, "you've proved today, Carl, that you're fit to continue getting your flying pay, but tomorrow we'll introduce you to BRIXMIS' main work which will earn you your real salary. You'll be undertaking a long distance tour with an experienced mentor on your first excursion to the other side."

In the secure briefing room Hannam spelt out the mission to a major Soviet airbase near Cottbus. "We believe," the Group Captain began, "that a full squadron of MIG21 FISHBED aircraft has deployed there from West Ukraine. It has been suggested to us that these aircraft may have a new centre line pod fitted which could indicate a reconnaissance role. On the way back Squadron Leader Flanders will drop you off at the Mission House in Potsdam to meet the staff there, especially the resident senior NCO, and to do your first spell as duty officer. You'd better warn your wife that you could be away for a few days – three at least."

When Carl got home Heidi was distraught. "I went to have tea with my cousin Sabine," she began ruefully and when I get back here I found someone had been through our flat and rummaged in all our papers. Nothing has been stolen and everything has been put back tidily but not always in exactly the same order. There are a couple of dirty footmarks on my prized white sheepskin rug. It could not be you or I as we always take our shoes off when we come home. How on earth did they get past the concierge? The doors and windows were all locked, too."

"If you remember, darling, I warned you that even here in West Berlin we're under regular surveillance. When I did my induction course it was made plain to me that neither we officers nor even our families would be clear of harassment. If you rang Sabine first they'd know you were going to be out. If you think how many thousands of Easterners came over in the months before the wall went up it's not surprising that in that number many agents were inserted. We mustn't let these things get us down. Report any incident to me, my love, and I'll communicate the facts to the security officer. If it's bad remember BRIXMIS can always retaliate by getting Headquarters BAOR to make life more difficult for our Russian counterparts of the SOXMIS in West Germany. We do so regularly."

"Actually Papi warned me before we came, my love. He said that they target the wives looking for ways to blackmail us and so put pressure on our husbands. He feared that for me it would be worse than most as the daughter of the famous warmongering revanchist NATO General, a classic class enemy with deep family landed roots in East Prussia – since the Soviet land-grab part of the USSR of course."

"All the more reason for me to do my job well," Carl tried to calm her. "We provide information on what our forces are up against in Germany the whole time and if we're alert should be able to give our masters good warning of dangerous developments on the other side. By the way I'm off on tour tomorrow, sweetheart. I can't tell you where but I hope to be back in seventy-two hours, though it may be a little longer. Look after yourself. I'm glad you've re-established contact with Sabine."

Next morning after meeting up with his mentor Squadron Leader Joe Flanders at the stadium HQ they drove across to obtain the latest intelligence information from their American counterparts who had been watching the Cottbus airbase only two weeks previously. They confirmed that the perimeter was very secure and amply defended with watchtowers, lights, high barbed wire fences, booby-traps and barriers, but that on the Western side there was heath and scrubland where hides could be prepared for a concealed observation post. The familiar squadron of Mig 19 Farmers was still on the base but there was no sign yet of the Mig 21 Fishbeds whose presence had only been reported through human intelligence and not officially confirmed by any of the three allied missions.

That Joe Flanders was a character was clear from the moment that their modified Opel saloon tour car drew up at the checkpoint into the Soviet zone. "Herzlich wieder willkommen Herr Mayor – a hearty welcome to you again Squadron Leader," declared the Vopo Lieutenant as he checked their passes.

"What was that about?" Carl inquired as they went through promptly. "Why so welcome? Aren't they supposed to make our lives over there as miserable as possible from entry to exit?"

"Yes indeed, and they usually do but I'm always studiously respectful and try to engage them in conversation about the weather, when such hard workers last had any leave, the latest football match – they love to watch Western teams on TV – or any titbit of innocuous news. Even the Grepo border police and ordinary Vopos are human and we all have our weaknesses. Once we cross over our job is not to miss a thing – even down to the morale of the checkpoint guards."

As they left the cleared strip along the wall heading south-east a shiny BMW emerged out of a dingey side street in front of them and an untypically modern Mercedes behind. "I see we have company already Corporal Lee," Flanders remarked to the driver.

"Yes indeed, sir, the usual suspects. It'll be interesting to see if they try to accompany us all the way or more likely hand over to their accomplices as we leave the city."

There was little point in trying to shake off the BRIXMIS Opel's shadows within greater Berlin. They could call up too many colleagues and the BRIXMIS number plates were very conspicuous. Anyway Flanders wanted to press on before losing them so as to get into a covert location in view of the target airfield well before dark, locate an alternative hide for use if bounced and an emergency rendezvous where he and Carl would rejoin Corporal Lee and the vehicle if any of them were compromised.

Surprisingly the dark bespectacled tails in their incongruous Western saloons stayed alongside. Flanders had expected them to disappear at the Brandenburg boundary. He wondered if their destination had leaked. There had been much talk of a Soviet mole at HQ. Normally he would have been shadowed by cross country four by fours but it was as if his shadows knew they were not going far and on good roads.

As usual the ever resourceful Lee suggested a solution. "You remember that forest halfway to the target, sir?" he asked. "I suggest we go for a woodland wander. They won't have four wheel drive and a reinforced bottom like us. Once we've lost them in there we can emerge onto the side roads going South and take the long way round to the airfield."

"You'd better be right, Corporal," Flanders declared firmly. "I want Flight Lieutenant Higgins here to know he can trust you to drive him safely out and safely back on tours in future. Besides we've got a job to accomplish now. Otherwise you'll find yourself back in the Motor Transport section at Macrihanish, which would be no fun at all."

Lee turned off the main highway onto a minor road at the last minute and then accelerated furiously away. The STASI BMW ahead missed his manoeuvre and was lost. Past the next village the expected forest appeared. Corporal Lee took the second loggers' track into the heart of the woods. Still the Mercedes followed tenaciously. The surface of ancient heath land beneath a carpet of pine needles was firmly compacted. Lee engaged four wheel drive and put his foot down smoothly off the track into a stand of widely spread tall mature pines.

The ground became greener, grassier and clearly boggier. A game of slalom around the tree trunks began with the leather jacketed pursuers. A minor stream crossed their path which Lee took at speed. The Opel hit the far bank spine joltingly hard but maintained traction and they sped back towards the track further on. The Mercedes did not even attempt the water jump. The BRIXMIS car eventually emerged from the forest unharassed and from the next village proceeded still on country roads towards Cottbus.

"Is driving over here always so exciting?" Carl inquired.

"That episode was nothing," Flanders replied. "No one shot at us; no dragon's teeth were sown in our way; we encountered no road blocks and we had only a pair of STASI vehicles to evade. We were lucky. It could have been more. It's often easier to get away at night. We switch all our lights off, deactivate our brake lights and drive quite speedily just on night vision goggles. We can also go out by Land Rover to be more mobile across country but the Opels are less conspicuous, more comfortable and faster."

In the gathering dusk Carl noticed that high buildings and tall masts had red anti collision lights on top. They must be nearing a zone of intensive aircraft activity. Sure enough the evening calm was shattered by a roar as a pair of Mig 19 Farmers hurtled past and broke downwind into the circuit of an as yet invisible airfield. Soon they reached warning boards beside the road indicating that they were entering a restricted area.

Lee swung off onto a cart track past an isolated hayrick and barn. There was no farm to be seen nearby but there was always the risk of being spotted by a local labourer who could report their presence to the authorities. Flanders warned of the ever present danger from now on of armed and trigger happy Soviet foot patrols.

They headed uphill across a field towards a tangle of low bushes, bracken and brambles interspersed with silver birches, alders and occasional pines. "You stay here, Corporal, and hide the car well," Joe Flanders instructed. "We'll walk for fifteen hundred yards on a compass bearing of 020° and we should come, if our US friends are right, to the Americans' hide. They say it has a good view over the airfield."

"In case the Soviets have discovered it already," the Squadron Leader continued, "we'll bivouac a bit further on and find another observation post of our own. Luckily the forecast is for rain tonight so I need not ask you to return, Corporal Lee, to brush away tyre marks from the grass. The rain should eliminate them nicely. You're lucky. It will certainly be drier for you in the car than in our bashas. We hope to rendezvous with you here at the vehicle in exactly twenty-four hours at 1900 precisely and drive away in the dark. If we don't appear give us another twenty-four hours. If we still don't show up then we'll meet you by the village pump in the central square of Grossheim some six miles back in seventy-two hours' time. Then if we miss that final emergency rendezvous you must assume that we have been detained and you are to report back to the mission house in Seestrasse accordingly."

Carl followed Flanders up the gentle hill through the damp bracken and tiresome brambles. A fine persistent drizzle had started and Carl silently called out the paces to himself in case Joe Flanders lost count. His compass bearing looked exactly accurate. Progress was slow but there was just enough light left for them to discern the outline of an A frame hide with a birch branch roof reinforced by sods of earth and camouflaged with dead bracken. The entrance was orientated towards the airbase below which was already fully illuminated. Clearly there would be night flying later.

"That's a pity," Flanders observed to Carl. "They may have stood down tomorrow morning just when we need to be photographing Fishbed fuselage pods."

Flanders and Carl traversed round the hill to another viewpoint some way from the American hide. Before they could settle down an armed foot patrol of three fur hatted airfield guards walked along the outside of he perimeter fence oblivious to the BRIXMIS team above them watching their every move. Luckily the Soviets did not have dogs.

The danger past, Carl and Flanders sat on a tree trunk consuming hot soup and coffee from their thermoses and in Carl's case Heidi's lovingly prepared and wrapped sausage and cucumber pumpernickel sandwiches washed down with her best chicken consommé. Their leisurely supper was noisily interrupted as two Mig 19 fighters took off in turn boring into the cloud laden drizzly darkness.

"I wonder if these sorties are wise," Carl commented. "If you remember Met was going in for an occlusion to become virtually static over the East German/Polish border tonight. I bet they get diverted. You can already hardly see the red light on the radio mast in this lowering lurg."

"At least the guards won't bother to come up here in such foul weather, I'm sure," Flanders replied. "I'm going to put my groundsheet down, poncho over my hide and sleep with my clothes, parka and flying boots on. We're too exposed to erect a tent. We may need to get away fast."

"I agree," Carl replied. "I wish I'd practised making an A frame in the dark on Survival Camp."

"There's a first time for everything," Flanders observed. "You'll have a lot of novel experiences on BRIXMIS and learn enough new skills to last you a lifetime."

Carl was just getting off to fitful sleep when one after the other the Soviet fighters returned to base. The pilots are at least competent on instruments he thought to himself. Old hands probably. The cloud base could not be more than two hundred feet at the most. Once they were down the airfield lighting went out. Night flying scrubbed no doubt. Must wake up before dawn to be ready to observe at first light and to make a hurried departure if we get a visitation from Soviet guards.

When Carl awoke damp but refreshed Joe Flanders was already up sipping black tea and chewing an oatmeal bar. The sky was clear and there was a glorious aroma of pines. Down on the airfield camouflaged vehicles moved on the perimeter track and tractors were towing aircraft out of the hangars into a long flightline on the hardstanding outside. The Warsaw Pact is obviously confident that NATO Air Forces are not going to mount a surprise attack Carl noted to himself, although winding taxiways leading to distant hardened aircraft shelters and well dispersed blast pens showed that the Soviets took the possibility seriously.

The first sortie had hardly got airborne before a group of six guards came up the hill towards them turning off onto what was to the BRIXMIS watchers an as yet invisible track to the radio facility above them. Only two returned by the way they came. Sentries had doubtless been posted to protect the mast and would probably be either replaced or withdrawn at nightfall.

At 0800 hours the first four ship formation of Mig 19s roared off in two pairs, followed by two more flights of four from the same Squadron as they came from the same end of the line and had identical code letters on the fuselage. None of the aircraft carried under wing stores. Around midday an Antonov Transport arrived. Some crates were deposited at one of the hangars from which no aircraft had been towed – no doubt a maintenance facility. Its location was duly noted as was that of the hangars, which actually held aircraft.

In the afternoon the heavy lifter departed and Farmer operations resumed this time by the second squadron at the other end of the line. It seemed they were witnessing an average day on a fighter station as spent in any major Air Force.

Carl was beginning to imagine that BRIXMIS life must be a repetitive routine of monitoring Soviet aircraft types and armament, unit designations, sortie lengths, activity levels on base and in the air, airfield security, defences and protection measures. Soon after a sardine and biscuit lunch, however, he was rudely disabused of his complacency.

Joe Flanders and Carl had left their bivouac for a better viewing position higher up the hill obscured to sight from the hut at the foot of the radio mast by a thick thorn hedge. A discreet reconnaissance upward had revealed that there were only two sentries on duty above them. Two were missing. This was sinister.

"I bet their combing the hill for us," Flanders whispered against the thunderous background of more departing Migs. "I expect our arrival was spotted by an unseen local informer and the guards are hoping to catch us out. As a precaution I took all my kit as usual with me. I've learned never to leave anything incriminating at the bivouac site and only to return to use the same one with the utmost caution."

"I was not so wise," Carl admitted. "I left two heavy thermoses full of soup for tonight's supper in my A frame."

"Not very clever, I'm afraid. Don't even go back to look for them," Flanders warned. "The place is probably staked out by the Soviets already. Crawl up to the spur to have a look down by all means and report back to me. We can always brew hot drinks in the car with our water heating element using the cigarette lighter socket."

Carl was surprised by what he saw. Both A frames had been flattened. Two hatless young blonde Soviet soldiers were sitting on the familiar tree trunk with AK47 assault rifles across their knees swigging a steaming drink doubtless hot soup from the two thermoses beside them. During a lull in the aircraft movements he could even hear their conversation. It was certainly not in German, Russian or any Slavonic language like Lithuanian. He reckoned that with their finely cut fair features they were probably Estonian conscripts, unlikely to show much commitment or professionalism as their impromptu picnic whilst on duty clearly showed.

"Two Soviet guards probably Estonian conscripts are lunching at our bivouac site, boss," Carl informed Joe Flanders.

"Let's not hang around," Flanders insisted. "It's time to move on pronto. Anyway the Soviets usually fly on alternate days so I suggest we leave the airfield and go Fishbed hunting on the range instead. I have not visited the Gadow Rossow air to ground facility for a while. It's time I paid it a call. You'll need your tin hat, Carl, because it's definitely a permanently restricted area. Prepare for a long drive North."

They dog legged round their old bivouac site and began a stealthy fifteen hundred yard return to the tour car. The sight which awaited them was not a happy one. Corporal Lee was still on board patiently waiting in his seat, but the driver's and front passenger's windows had been smashed in, and he was sitting at the wheel with a bloody field dressing to his face.

"I had a visitation during the night, sir," he began remarkably calmly. "Two sentries came up to the vehicle and bashed in the front windows with their rifle buts. I got an almighty blow in the face. I think I've lost a couple of teeth and the wound bled quite badly for a while. It's stopped now. They were laughing and joking in Russian and disappeared as suddenly as they came. No officer was summoned; no complaint issued. I think they were looking for bigger fish – yourselves probably gentlemen. Have you had any trouble?"

"None I'm glad to say Corporal. Are you fit to drive or shall we return to Berlin and get your face seen to?" Flanders responded.

"I'm okay, sir."

"Fine; we proceed to Gadow Rossow range. I bet we catch the Fishbeds there."

The drive North started uneventfully. Flanders wondered whether the Soviets might conceivably be apprehensive of an official complaint about the injuries inflicted upon Corporal Lee. He would certainly urge Group Captain Hannam to persuade the Chief to lodge one. After a strongly worded note from McPherson to HQ some kind of sanction would with luck be executed upon SOXMIS. This was the only logical reason why their vehicle had no tail. Yet the airbase security staff would not imagine that Corporal Lee was unaccompanied and must have issued a general alert. Joe Flanders knew from hard earned experience that after one brush with the Soviets more trouble was surely to be expected.

Carl who was up front shared with Corporal Lee the full blast of the icy wind through the shattered windows, but they still had to travel fast to get into good cover on the range well before dawn. Carl concentrated on brewing mugs of hot OXO with the immersion heater which he shared with Flanders. The roots of Lee's smashed teeth were too painful to tolerate hot beef stock and he sucked sweets instead to keep alert. He certainly needed to do so.

Twice trucks swerved across the centreline from the other side of the road trying to force them into the ditch. Thereafter they accelerated and proceeded without lights. Even so a mystery Mercedes overtook them at speed, cut in sharply and was brushed aside by the Opel, which sped away rapidly after the collision. "Don't stop Corporal," Flanders ordered. "BRIXMIS tour cars are meant to be sturdy. You can inspect the damage tomorrow and tape it up if necessary whilst we're scouting around."

At about four in the morning they arrived at the Gadow Rossow range. There was a quarter moon shining wanly through a translucent layer of high cirrus. They had been driving for ten minutes beyond the barbed wire, coil upon unending coil of it stretching as far as the eye could see in the dim moonlight.

"We bale out here, Corporal," Flanders instructed. "You return and hide the car in the same place as last month on the safe side of the Restricted Area sign. Come back and get us here at exactly 1930 hours tomorrow evening. Failing that we'll walk out later and hope to meet you at your vehicle hide at 0530 hours the following morning to give us time to get some miles under our belt before dawn."

Negotiating the barbed wire was not easy, especially with the tiresome encumbrances of binoculars and cameras. By placing their ponchos and parkas on top to blunt the barbs Carl and Flanders made it over the barrier with minimal damage to flesh or uniforms. They pressed on through the tangled scrub and clinging briars to install themselves on a small bush clad knoll from which there was a good all round view from cover, not that Joe and Carl believed that Soviet personnel would enter a live firing zone with the danger of unexploded ordinance, or that a call would be made to interrupt the air to ground weapon delivery exercises that day, just to go searching for them.

It was on their exit that the danger of discovery, physical assault, detention or even shooting was greatest. They earnestly hoped that Lee had hidden their vehicle well out of sight. Soon the tentative rays of the rising sun illuminated the range sufficiently for the day's flying programme to begin.

First a squadron of Mig 19 Farmer fighter bombers swept in low, climbed for height, and curved downward letting rip with rockets and cannon into invisible targets. The detonations could be felt through the ground on which Carl and Flanders lay dutifully photographing each aircraft and noting in confirmation into their tape recorders the armament configuration, squadron designations and other technical details of interest to the intelligence boffins of NATO.

Then they had a visitation from a flight of Ilyushin 28 Beagle twin engine light bombers, the Warsaw Pact's aged and inferior counterparts to the RAF's Canberra force. The four aircraft wheeled distantly overhead and released their practice bombs from medium altitude. The earth shook which was unnerving.

Finally just as Carl and Joe were about to pack up and go home a whole squadron of Fishbeds appeared. The Mig 21 fighters were unmistakable with their sharp delta wing planforms, pointed nose cones and swept back tailplanes. "I think we've struck gold," Flanders commented as he prepared to shoot away with his special long range camera.

The first flight swooped down and fired its fuselage mounted cannon. The second loosed off salvoes of underwing rockets. The third dropped bombs from the racks beneath its wings. Last and most excitingly four Mig 21s with a centreline pod did low level reconnaissance passes, presumably taking target pictures for analysis. "Did you get them all, Carl?" Flanders inquired.

"I think so boss but I found it hard to track the last four at such speed."

"I hope you snapped at least the pods okay because they're what we came for."

As they walked cautiously back in the gathering dusk Flanders insisted on grubbing around in the mud looking for exploded 23 millimetre cannon shell cases, whilst Carl kept a careful lookout for Soviet range personnel. Joe triumphantly found two cases to take back for technical study by the intelligence experts. Once safely over the wire they were heartened by the sight of Corporal Lee approaching in the Opel. They piled in and withdrew the exposed films hiding them in compartments under the carpet. "Back to the Potsdam villa, fastest," Flanders demanded.

Amazingly the journey was initially incident free, although Lee thought they had a distant shadow behind them as they neared the capital. Almost at the edge of Berlin a Vopo police car shot out from a side road bringing them to a halt. Another accelerated up to them from far behind and screeched to a halt alongside.

"We have observed your driving. It has been erratic. We have reason to believe that in contravention of the traffic laws of the German Democratic Republic you have been driving under the influence of alcohol. Notwithstanding your special status you are bound to obey the rules of the road. Step out of the car," the Vopo Lieutenant ordered.

"He will not," Flanders replied firmly.

"I see you have already been involved in an accident," the Vopo officer continued. "Your front left wing is badly damaged and how do you account for the broken windows?"

"We are not moving," Flanders insisted. "We are accredited solely to the Soviet forces in Germany. If you lay a finger on us an official complaint will be lodged.

Get the local Soviet Commander here at once. Otherwise we will remain blocking the road."

For five hours the tour car and its occupants remained immobile. The Vopos returned to their vehicles and began to chain smoke. Eventually a Soviet Army staff car accompanied by two Russian cross country vehicles arrived. "What have we here, major?" the Colonel declared. "A badly damaged vehicle, I see. Our German comrades tell me your Corporal driver was drunk at the wheel and driving dangerously."

"That is nonsense, Colonel. Your comrades of the German People's Police are getting above themselves. Ever since 1946, just after the Great Patriotic War in which your forces and ours were comrades in arms, our Mission has been officially affiliated to your Commander in Chief alone," Flanders insisted.

"We were actually on our way back to the Mission," he continued, "to lodge a complaint about the unprovoked act of vandalism, which our vehicle sustained at the hands of two of your sentries whose lack of discipline and uncontrolled violence led to their seriously injuring my driver Corporal Lee."

"As you can see," Flanders explained, "he is in urgent need of medical attention. If there has been any fault in his driving, which I deny because I have been watching his performance all the way not least for my own safety, it is solely as the result of pain from his injuries.

"In short," Joe Flanders concluded, "if this totally unwarranted and unsubstantiated allegation by these police officers who have no relevant jurisdiction whatsoever is taken any further I assure you that the traditional invitations to you and your staff to the Queen's Birthday reception at the Mission House will not be forthcoming this year. Or if they are out of the magnanimity of my Chief's heart then only orange juice will be served to our Soviet guests. We would not wish them to drive erratically home and experience any difficulty with their comrades of the German People's traffic police."

"Raus, raus," the Colonel bellowed at the Vopos. "Out of the way. Let Major Flanders pass. Can't you see the Corporal needs to get to a doctor quickly?"

"Thank you Colonel," Flanders responded. "I admire officers who are respectful of protocol."

"Oh by the way, Major. Is the reception on the Queen's real or official birthday – in April or June?"

"Don't worry my friend. I'll have a word with the Chief and make sure there are parties on both. One last thing, Colonel. I can prove we have not been drinking. This whisky bottle has not been opened and it's the Famous Grouse. Keep it as a souvenir of your wise intervention to maintain correct fraternal relations between former comrades in arms."

Group Captain Hannam was waiting for Flanders' tour to come in at the Mission House and received them warmly. "Happy to go off on tour solo now?" he inquired of Carl. "I warn you that these expeditions are not usually so fruitful or mercifully so exciting. You certainly struck gold with the Fishbed centreline recce pods on the range – even if it did cost Corporal Lee a couple of teeth and some damage to the vehicle. We'll keep the car here for inspection by the Soviets when we lodge our formal complaint," he declared.

"I suggest you all come back with me," Hannam went on. "The Yanks should be impressed by the Fishbed photos. You'll be glad to debrief fully at our HQ and to get back home quickly. Corporal Lee will want to call on the Medical Officer pronto and to see an orthodontist, too, I'm sure."

The return crossing over the Glienicke bridge was trouble free. The Soviets clearly did not want to sour relations further, especially with Hannam. The Americans were indeed appreciative of Flanders' rolls of Fishbed film. "Gee Joe, we've been trying to get pics of these pods for weeks and you go and do it on your first sortie. One of these days you'll get a bomb on your head out on the range," the United States Air Force analyst exclaimed enthusiastically. "I only hope the beat up of your Corporal is not a prelude to driver bashing against us. I trust you have not stirred up a hornet's nest over there."

In the debrief at the stadium HQ Brigadier McPherson was much exercised about instigating what he called "a proportionate response," to the Soviets' violence against Lee and the wilful damage to the tour car. "You've done well, gentlemen, but I trust not at the expense of normal relations with the Soviet hierarchy," he insisted.

"You were sticking your neck out, Flanders, by photographing their aircraft on a live range. I'm only glad that you obtained your information with no injury to yourself or to Flight Lieutenant Higgins. If you had got hurt we could not necessarily have extracted you, or only at inordinate cost.

"I think you were wise, Flanders, to treat the Soviet Colonel diplomatically on the way back," the Brigadier continued. "However, we will still ask them to the Queen's official birthday reception at the villa in June and to another one we're holding in her honour in April. So that you don't lose face we'll offer them Buck's Fizz to drink and see how they receive it.

"Finally, I'll ask Headquarters BAOR to have one of their SOXMIS tours detained briefly on some pretext, but we won't make any SOXMIS officers personae non gratae. Everybody likes us to maintain a normal relationship with the Soviets – HQ BAOR, NORTHAG, the Foreign Office are insistent about it even if you and I know what our teams face in the field is not pleasant and often very dangerous as Corporal Lee understands more than most. Pass on my commendation to him please, Flanders."

Carl was relieved to get home on time to Heidi's welcoming embraces. The flap over the assault on Corporal Lee and damage to the Opel had meant that Carl was required at the tour debrief with the Chief and excused duty officer responsibilities at the villa. "Everything go all right?" she asked innocently.

"Yes dear. Mission accomplished as they say. I expect to return to more routine operations like train spotting next time."

"I hope so, Carl. Your clothes and boots are filthy. Your trousers are badly torn. Your parka's ripped, too. You look as if you've been living in a muddy ditch these past few days."

"You could say so, sweetheart," Carl replied.

"Aren't you going to be flying again soon?" Heidi asked. "I thought I'd married a pilot and pilots are supposed to live dangerously but well in comfortable Messes and Quarters. But talking to the other wives as I did whilst you were away they say that you'll hardly ever get airborne. I would have thought all the field work they mentioned could better be done by the Army Teams."

"They'd never recognise the kind of kit we're watching out for love, although we do help each other out. Anyway why are you so keen to get me flying again? I've been assured that my flying pay is secure."

"I have my reasons, Carl. I'll share them with you soon," Heidi admitted intriguingly.

"You'd better do so in a secure place, my love. This flat was almost certainly bugged during the burglary. Let's take Würstchen the Dachshund puppy for a walk in the park after supper. I bet he didn't get many walks when I was on tour. We can talk safely then."

"You bought him for me after the burglary to protect me, Carl; not as a canine incentive to take more exercise."

CHAPTER 28

What a joy Heidi's company was. After the transient bliss and attendant agonies of loss and parting with Angela and Yasmin Carl felt he had found true contentment at last. Their little flat really was a delight. Heidi's love and devotion had transformed a modest few rooms just like so many others in the modern block of reborn Berlin into their first true home, which they would never forget and where their hopes for the future would be nurtured.

After dinner they set off for the park with a happy little Würstchen trotting alongside. "You said you were keen that I should start flying again, my love," Carl began. "I explained that I still get my flying pay and I'm sure BRIXMIS will use me just as soon as the need arises. The trouble is that the airborne role is only an adjunct to our primary operations on the ground and anyway we can't fly far from Berlin so won't usually see much from the air."

"I know that my love, but I have a problem," Heidi responded. "My uncle – Sabine's father – is stuck on the other side. He perhaps unwisely went across for a family funeral and got detained by the STASI on some trumped up pretext, disseminating subversive literature I think it was, and we need to get him out. Papi says it's very important we get him back to the West.

"Manfred's not Papi's brother actually," Heidi went on, "but my mother's. He's a brilliant scientist. He worked as a rocket engineer with Werner von Braun at Peenmünde on the Baltic on V weapons during the war and escaped the Red Army afterwards. You know that Von Braun and others went to the USA and are prominent in the American space programme now. Some, however, went or were forced to go East and are currently working for the Russians.

"Even now the Soviets are trying to find such people," Heidi continued emotionally, "and Manfred would be a particular prize. He's working for Messerschmitt Bolkow Blohm in Bavaria at Manching and Ottobrunn on a top secret new aerospace project called the MRCA. It involves not only Germany, but Britain and Italy as well. If we can't get him out Papi says that NATO's deterrent capability could be compromised for a generation. I don't think that Manfred would ever talk but we can't risk it."

"Sweetheart this is all very disturbing, but I don't see how I come into it," Carl replied.

"Well Sabine who assists a clandestine organisation helping to smuggle refugees out of East Germany says that it would be too dangerous for Manfred to swim the Spree, climb the wall, join a tunnelling group or escape in the boot of a car. If he was caught we would never see him again and the STASI's torturing interrogators would make him talk. We need to extract him in a manner, which the Soviets and their East German comrades would not stop. Even if they knew one of our aircraft was involved in such an escapade I don't think they'd dare to shoot it down."

"I would not bet on it, Heidi," Carl warned. "They've killed members of Western Mission Teams on the ground and shot down stray Western military aircraft over the years."

"But the Chipmunk is a primary trainer and carries no armaments," Heidi protested. "You'd be back into West Berlin in five to ten minutes."

"Maybe, but I know the Mission will never authorise it. I could not even ask."

"What did you tell me Swallowfield said in his speech when you passed out at Cranwell? Act first, ask permission later. If you ask beforehand it can only be refused."

"That was all a very long time ago, Heidi dear. The world's moved on. Everyone's now talking about détente, peaceful co-existence and Ostpoktik. Our job is to get the information we need as unprovocatively as possible."

"But people are still being murdered on the wall and the comrades weren't very nice to Corporal Lee either," Heidi insisted.

"It's none of our business I suppose," she went on, "but from what I read in the papers, and from what the fellow BRIXMIS wives tell me as well as my German friends and relations the Warsaw pact is still rapidly modernising its forces: they outnumber NATO by three to one in men and two to one in tanks on the Central Front. I'm informed that they've based much of their equipment well forward to be able to destroy us all within forty-eight hours from a standing start."

"Don't talk shop at me, Heidi. You're my wife!"

"That's not a licence to be stupid, Carl, like most of the other Service wives I've met. I'm supposed to be knowledgeable about what's going on in my own country. Never underestimate me."

"I wouldn't dream of it, don't worry love."

"My family were a force to be reckoned with in the old Germany," Heidi declared proudly. "And we will be again in the new. By the way I've got myself a job to keep me away from the shops and the coffee morning routine whilst you're off on tour. Der Spiegel magazine has taken me on as a stringer under the name Hans Dietmeyer to write stories about events in this great city which will, mark my words, one day be capital of an undivided Germany again. Our job is to make it happen – in our lifetime I hope."

"I thought we were supposed to be enjoying a leisurely evening stroll in the park, Heidi. Instead you talk to me as if you were addressing a rally of East Prussian refugees. You should be a member of the Bundestag."

"If you wind me up enough, Carl, I might just stand. You British are so damned tolerant. Don't rock the boat should be your national motto. So long as you keep muddling through as you put it, you're happy."

"I thought that was what makes us nice to live with, my love," Carl retorted dejectedly. "At least that's what you used to say until this bracing Berlin air got into your lungs."

"Don't take it personally, Carl dear. Look at it professionally. Unless we can get Manfred out," Heidi explained, "you and your Royal Air Force friends will be much more at risk of a surprise attack. You won't be able to keep the Warsaw Pact's forces on their bases if the MRCA's capabilities get to the Soviets. Forget Germany. That's my problem. View it from the perspective of self-preservation."

"Okay my love."

"I just want to be able to tell Sabine that my dearly beloved husband is at heart one of us," she pleaded. "When you've done a few more weeks' touring I'll explain to you what needs to be done. These things have to be planned meticulously and it takes time. Let's go home, Carl dear. The marriage bed has been too long cold and empty without you. You fire me up much more than politics. It's just that my rhetoric gets the better of me sometimes. I care too much about things. Maybe my genes are to blame but you're the love of my life and that's what really matters."

"Now that's the kind of speech I really like to hear dearest Heidi. Perhaps I appreciate it all the more for the long heartfelt preamble. Of course I'm open to suggestions. It's just that whatever we do about Manfred has got to work. The last thing any of us could afford would be a disaster."

"You know I have complete faith in you, Carl. Otherwise I would never have married you."

Next morning instead of preparing for another tour out East, Carl was summoned by Group Captain Hannam to his office. "You've made a promising start Carl," his boss began, "and I know you'll make your mark in this organisation, but after your derring do with Squadron Leader Flanders and the injuries sustained by Corporal Lee the powers that be are keen to see less provocative operating procedures on our part. I am determined that they should not prejudice our capability to give due warning of technical and military developments the other side." The pin striped wets in Whitehall are at it again thought Carl trying to remain impassive.

"This initiative comes from the very top," the Group Captain continued as if reading Higgins' mind, "from the Foreign Office in London no less. They are keen to initiate confidence building measures as they call them; in other words not to upset the Soviets. So a two day NORTHAG-RAFG conference at their Rheindehlen HQ has been organised on all this for the day after tomorrow. I want you to represent the RAF part of BRIXMIS. How do you feel about it, Carl? It's a great opportunity for you."

"But I was just beginning to get stuck into the Fishbed recce pod project, sir," Carl protested. "Squadron Leader Flanders has made a very promising start but there is much additional data on the performance of the system which we badly need."

"That may be so but be realistic, Carl. After what happened with Jo Flanders a low profile is what is called for on your part. At the very least your role for the foreseeable future would be limited to routine train spotting and road traffic monitoring.

"I reckon, however," Hannam continued, "that with your Foreign Office family background, recent operational experience – the DFC on 8 Squadron and all that – you are just the man to go with Brigadier Pearson to the conference. You'd be in elevated company for a junior Flight Lieutenant and Pearson's an old Aden hand like you. Your participation should help your career."

"But my job on the mission is what matters to me, sir," Carl explained. "I don't want to be dragged into politics."

"Anyway it's essential you go, Carl," the Group Captain insisted. "The Foreign Office and Treasury are making a joint bid to take our Chipmunks away. They say that the aircraft upset the Russians and cost too much money to run. You enjoy your flying, Carl, and I'm sure you'll fight to keep them for the good military reasons you'll advance on our behalf at the seminar."

"Very well sir," Carl replied his mind moving rapidly. Maybe I can secure a sufficient stay of execution on the Chipmunks to lift Manfred out of the Russian sector before they are withdrawn, he thought. What is more it would be safer to plan the operation in the Rhineland far away from the ever present Warsaw Pact shadows and eavesdroppers who bugged their conversations and monitored their every move in West Berlin.

"There's just one thing, sir," he pleaded. "Could Heidi come with me, sir? She has not seen her parents for a long time and I'm sure it would be helpful to have the Luftwaffe Inspector General's support for our case behind the scenes. They, too, benefit from our product in the Allied Tactical Air Forces."

"Agreed," Hannam answered decisively. "The Com Squadron Devon leaves for Wildenrath at 1600 hours this afternoon. Heidi can certainly go with you and why not stay the weekend out West while you're at it. The aeroplane is not scheduled to fly back to Gatow till Monday."

Carl raced back to the Charlottenburg flat having grabbed a copy of the operational procedures of the Chipmunk Flight from the mission to study on the aircraft. When he arrived Heidi was working away on a report on Turkish immigration to Berlin she was preparing to send through to Der Spiegel magazine. "Do you have a deadline on that, my dear?" Carl asked anxiously.

"Why do you want to know, Carl? You don't normally seem very interested in my work," Heidi replied brusquely. "What's up?"

"I've got to go to Rheindahlen this afternoon for a two day seminar with a free weekend out West afterwards. Will you come, too?"

"Can we possibly afford it, Carl?"

"I can offer you a lift there and back by courtesy of the Air Force. I'd like you to come obviously."

"I'd be delighted," Heidi responded with enthusiasm. "We could visit my parents who are not so very far away and I can perfectly well finish my piece for Der Spiegel in Bonn. I've already sorted all the material in my head. What's more I have a few social obligations I must fulfil," she added cryptically.

When the staff car dropped them on the apron at Gatow the Com Squadron Devon had just started up. Brigadier Pearson was already installed forward of the prominent main spar and dismissively acknowledged Carl's greeting keeping up an earnest conversation with a grey faced and suited civil servant who Carl had always thought was part of the Berlin brigade's financial department. Carl realised that his duties must be more wide ranging and sensitive than mere number crunching and accountancy.

Carl and Heidi sat in the back ostensibly to get a better view of East Germany on the flight down the corridor to Wildenrath hoping to be able to discuss the uncle Manfred extraction plot out of earshot. They noted with satisfaction that the broad beamed serge skirted and battledress bloused WRAF Corporal Flight attendant dispensed only a plastic cup of coffee and a biscuit to her passengers and would not be solicitously patrolling the aisle on their behalf. This was clearly a working sortie not a VIP flight. Their secret planning would not be overheard above the high pitched buzzing monotone of the Gypsy Queen engines either by the busty Corporal who sat impassively next to the lavatory chewing gum and desultorily perusing an old dog eared copy of the Daily Mirror or by the serious minded loquacious figures sitting up front.

Heidi boldly opened the conversation. "I have arranged for Sabine to take the PANAM flight from Templehof to Cologne on Friday afternoon," she began. "We'll dine together in the city and I'll join you at my parents' home in time for a family nightcap afterwards. Papi is laying on an official car to collect you from Rheindahlen and bring you there as soon as the seminar is over. I'll be hiring a VW in Mönchengladbach to get me around. I have some friends of Sabine to see whilst you're in conference so that by the end of the weekend the outlines of Operation

Uplift as we'll call it from now on should be defined. My father must know nothing about it. I do not want him compromised in any way, although I know he'll be delighted with the result if we pull it off as I know we will thanks to his intrepid son-in-law."

It was a strange detached feeling for Carl to be back in Rheindahlen. The Mess was as dead as ever and nothing had ostensibly changed at Headquarters. Sir Thomas Swallowfield's name stood out clearly in gold letters on the board listing past Commanders in Chief of Royal Air Force, Germany, but Carl had no inclination to retrace his steps and call on the recently promoted Wing Commander Bracewell who was now incongruously Personal Staff Officer to the C in C. Doubtless he was filling the familiar outer office with tobacco smoke and bad language.

Carl followed Brigadier Pearson to the Army end of the HQ where photos of tanks and armoured personnel carriers lined the walls. No old friend from Cranwell or postings past would emerge to greet or cheer him with shared reminiscences of good old days. He was incognito and on arrival at the conference hall clearly on his own, the sole representative of his Service among a dozen or so middle ranking Army officers and senior civil servants.

Brigadier Pearson formally opened the proceedings standing stiffly at the lectern in an immaculate perfectly pressed uniform rendered even more authoritative by his red lapel tabs and the long row of medal ribbons on his chest among which stood out a Korean war campaign medal, one from the United Nations, a yellow and black ribbon from the Mau Mau emergency in Kenya, a General Service Medal and above all the purple and white broad vertical stripes of the Military Cross. His chipped Indian Army style diction and laconic phraseology were those of a fighting soldier.

"We are here, gentlemen," he began, "at the behest of the Ministry of Defence and the Foreign Office. Our aim is to explore ways of conducting the work of BRIXMIS more cost effectively in a manner more conducive to furthering the political process of détente with the countries of the Warsaw Pact upon which the Government is embarked.

"It is our belief in the mission," the Brigadier emphasised, "that our personnel provide an invaluable service for the British Army of the Rhine and Royal Air Force Germany in giving them advance warning of technical and military developments in the Soviet Armed Forces in East Germany thus minimising the possibility of an effective surprise attack against NATO.

"However," Pearson continued, "with the advent of peaceful coexistence and the corresponding confidence building measures now at the heart of the defensive posture of the Western Alliance, our political masters are hopeful that our mission's role can be fulfilled more economically in a manner which accords with these new strategic realities.

"We will therefore review," he went on, "all our operational procedures during these two days with the assistance of expert representatives of the Foreign Office, Ministry of Defence, and Treasury. No aspect of our work will be exempt from scrutiny and we shall examine our information gathering techniques critically with the assistance of our customers in BAOR and RAFG. I suggest that we deal with Army matters today and Air Force ones tomorrow finishing with a final wash up period combining both in the context of a reformed and rationalised BRIXMIS with concrete recommendations. That is if indeed it is the view of this conference that we should retain BRIXMIS at all in the current international environment."

It soon became clear to Carl early on in the Army session that the Treasury and Foreign Office had it in for the mission. Things had changed significantly in the DDR since the bad old days of Walter Ulbricht the sallow and somewhat pudgy faced representative of the Foreign Office asserted. The new Secretary General of the Socialist Unity Party Erich Honecker was humanising the regime behind the Berlin Wall. It would soon move towards the moderate Hungarian model of goulash communism. Mr Davies the pinstriped apparatchik from the Berlin brigade agreed. "I am sure the opening of our Embassy in a prime location on the Unter den Linden in the Russian sector can only accelerate this welcome process of normalisation," he claimed.

A red faced Guards Colonel PSO to the C in C of BAOR, asked what diminution of offensive Soviet military capabilities had actually taken place to which neither the men from Whitehall nor Mr Davies the civil servant from West Berlin had a reply. The man from the Treasury backed his civil service colleagues by claiming that evident cuts in expenditure on BRIXMIS would give a positive signal to the Soviet leadership that our determination to achieve détente was genuine and that Warsaw Pact force reductions would surely follow such an imaginative demarche on our part.

CHAPTER 29

Carl left for the Mess after the first day's proceedings much dejected. He felt that the whole exercise was a classic Treasury driven Whitehall stitch up to save money and out of all correlation with the military dispositions on the ground in East Germany. It was proposed that the Army element in BRIXMIS would lose one officer, two other ranks and two civilians plus half a dozen vehicles.

Carl spent the evening preparing his case for preserving the Chipmunk Flight, which he judged was very vulnerable to disbandment. He earnestly hoped that Royal Air Force Germany would send an officer to the seminar capable of defending the Air Force's interests in the next day's discussion. Without the Chipmunks Operation Uplift could not take place. Heidi would never fully understand in spite of any explanation he might give such was her growing fixation about the division of Germany since she had taken up journalism in Berlin and so great had become the influence of her cousin Sabine with her now that he could only see marital trouble ahead if he did not get uncle Manfred out.

The following morning the senior Foreign Office mandarin present initiated the discussion. "We had a very useful session yesterday and have made progress towards the goal so succinctly expressed by Brigadier Pearson of adapting BRIXMIS to work more cost effectively towards furthering the process of détente. Concrete suggestions were made by the Army representatives for achieving this objective. My colleagues and I look forward to a comparable response from the Air Force element today.

"I would remind you," he went on in uncompromising tones, "of the political parameters before we begin. My colleagues and I wish to see less intrusive information gathering techniques – no unauthorised entries into Soviet airfields and firing ranges or physical dismantling of Soviet weapon systems such as radars and missiles. Above all we look to see a reduction of Air Force manpower in the mission and the elimination of the most provocative operational procedures such as overflights of East German territory by BRIXMIS aircraft.

"After all," he continued with evident relish, "if we now recognise the German Democratic Republic as a sovereign state this sovereignty has to apply to its airspace also. We must ask ourselves therefore whether in current circumstances the retention by BRIXMIS of its own private Air Force can any longer be justified."

Carl went to the rostrum with a heavy heart. In Air Force parlance the case he was about to make faced a strong built in headwind, but the sight of thick plumes of smoke curling up from the back now indicated that his shock support weapon Wing Commander Bracewell was fired up. Over the pre-conference coffee Bracewell had promised Carl to launch a salvo or two against these 'desk jockeys from Whitehall' assuring him that his boss Air Chief Marshal Sir James Broderick would not countenance the emasculation of the Air Force component of BRIXMIS.

Carl had also taken the precaution of informing his boss Group Captain Hannam of the outcome of the seminar so far. Hannam was prepared to follow his Army counterpart's example and accept a cut in manpower and vehicles, but he drew a line at the Chipmunk Flight insisting that if Carl could not prevent its disbandment he would take the matter up with the AOC in C in person.

Once he started to speak Carl began to feel at ease. He knew his subject and the DFC ribbon on his chest gave him a psychological advantage as he was viewed by the participants as an expert on operational matters albeit in a very different theatre. He was certainly not intimidated by the men from the Foreign Office. His family's social circle had been full of them.

He would throw a bone to the pursuing Whitehall wolves at the outset. "Group Captain Hannam authorises me to announce," he declared, "his willingness to implement reductions in the Air element of BRIXMIS exactly commensurate with those already agreed by the Army. I must emphasize, however, the exceptional importance which the mission attaches to the Chipmunk Flight. In some critical episodes like that during the construction of the Berlin Wall it can be invaluable.

"Although it can only penetrate some twenty miles from the Berlin Air Traffic control centre," Carl explained, "this is still a useful distance to spot Soviet military developments, which could jeopardise the security of the Western sectors of Berlin and indeed NATO's defensive dispositions in West Germany. If there are multiple incidents along the wall they can be investigated swiftly by air and the Chipmunks' capability to provide aerial photographic cover facilitates intelligence gathering enormously. At this point I invite Wing Commander Bracewell PSO to Com 2 ATAF and RAFG to give his view from headquarters."

The Wing Commander stubbed out his cigarette, strode to the podium and came straight to the point. "Before the proceedings began I checked every issue which Flight Lieutenant Higgins has raised with my Commander in Chief Air Chief Marshal Broderick", he began, "I can confirm that in all respects Flight Lieutenant Higgins' comments have the support of his headquarters. I would go further and insist that to describe the Chipmunk Flight at Gatow as BRIXMIS' private Air Force is a travesty. In many operational scenarios in and around Berlin air surveillance is less intrusive to use a simplistic adjective than action on the ground and swifter in response."

"In Royal Air Force Germany we always seek to operate to maximum economy compatible with efficiency," he went on uncompromisingly, "so we would concur with the reductions in Air Force personnel and equipment proposed for the mission but any arbitrary curbs on the role of the Chipmunk Flight or even its withdrawal we would regard as an unwelcome degradation of BRIXMIS' capabilities. We should remember, gentlemen, that in the NATO Air Forces we have to face the world as it is and not as we might wish it to be."

The pinstriped front row of the conference looked uneasy at such a blunt exposition of military thinking. "That'll be enough for now," interjected the Brigadier. "Our friends from London and I will briefly adjourn whilst the rest of you have a final cup of tea. We resume at 1600 hours sharp with the conclusions."

"Well spoken, Carl," Bracewell observed reassuringly between long draws on his cigarette. "I remember how articulate you were even as a Cranwell cadet. I also admired you then for getting over your air sickness so bravely. It is a common affliction as back seaters on night fighters like me know all too well."

When the proceedings finally restarted they were surprisingly brief. Brigadier Pearson summarised the conclusions of the conference. "We have a consensus I am glad to say on reductions across the board at BRIXMIS in men and materiel. We have agreement on an overall modus operandi for BRIXMIS personnel, which will reassure our friends from the Ministries in London, be regarded as a sign of our good faith by the Soviets but yet preserve our key ability to give the early warning of developments within the Soviet Group of forces in East Germany, which HQ BAOR and RAFG require. Finally for a trial period of six months the Chipmunk Flight will become non operational. It will of course fulfil its currently programmed tasks till the end of this month but thereafter will be stood down."

Carl was shocked by the outcome of the seminar but not surprised. The Whitehall contingent would not have been satisfied without their pound of flesh. Now they could return to London with agreed token economies at BRIXMIS in their briefcases. Notwithstanding Bracewell's blast of reality they would cite the moratorium on the Chipmunk Flight's operations as the wholly appropriate standing down in the currently less threatening East-West scenario of what they would still describe as BRIXMIS' private Air Force. It could safely now be left to wither on the vine. Royal Air Force Germany was bound to have more pressing issues on its plate than to clamour for the Flight's reactivation in six months' time.

There were therefore only three weeks left within which to implement Operation Uplift which promised to be one of the most difficult and audacious in the heroic blood stained litany of escapes across the wall. At least Manfred was under house arrest not prison; albeit closely watched. His guards would have to be bribed and the Chipmunk's landing ground accessible from the garden where he took his daily supervised outside exercise.

Timing would be crucial as would the weather.

Carl bade Bracewell farewell. "You did your best, Carl," the Wing Commander acknowledged. "I'll send a good report on your contribution to Hannam and speak well of you to the C in C, something which did not always happen last time you were here I gather."

"Well done, Carl," echoed Brigadier Pearson. "We came out of it all as well as could have been expected. Going to visit your in-laws I gather? Enjoy the weekend. See you back at Wildenrath at 0800 Monday."

The field grey Luftwaffe Mercedes saloon and driver awaited Carl and whisked him away from the Rheindalen headquarters of mixed memories to the imposing villa on the edge of Bonn where the Himmelmanns lived. The Gräfin, Heidi's mother was at the door to meet him with Heidi and the family German shepherd alongside. "Hope your conference went well, my love," Heidi began. "Papi's away on a tour of Luftwaffe bases in Bavaria so we won't have a family meal tonight. Sabine and some friends are due to join us for dinner in town instead. They're coming round here for a drink beforehand."

Carl was now irreversibly committed to an undertaking whose chances of success were at best one in four. Even if he got Manfred out the reaction of the powers that be would be less than rapturous. After the conference he realised that the security of the Allied Air Forces and the effectiveness of their equipment counted for little with the men from Whitehall with whom he had had to contend at the conference. MRCA hardly mattered for them against their precariously constructed project of détente. His career was in severe jeopardy.

Heidi drove Carl down to Cologne and parked in a side street near the cathedral. "It should be safer here than in Bonn," she observed. "Bonn's not so bad as Berlin but you can never be sure who's watching you or trying to overhear your conversation."

She had chosen a restaurant with well spaced candlelit tables and installed herself at one with a good view of the door.

Within a few minutes Sabine and a nondescript looking middle-aged man entered. They did not need to look around but went straight to Heidi's table which was obviously pre-booked. Sabine introduced her companion Johann Langfeld to Carl. He was clearly well known to Heidi who greeted him warmly: "How good of you to join us so soon after your latest excursion, which Sabine told me was particularly difficult."

"That's an understatement, Heidi. The STASI must have broken one of the potential refugees under interrogation because they discovered the entrance to our escape tunnel in a previously safe house and captured two of our diggers whom they trapped underground. Far from any détente the border police seem to be getting daily more vicious. They shot one of our charges dead swimming across the Spree only a week ago."

"How come, Johann, that you are allowed to travel freely to and fro?" Carl inquired anxiously wondering if he could trust the so called Johann Langfeld with such a sensitive mission. "Why do they accept you on the other side?"

"That would be a long story," the grey faced enigmatic Langfeld replied. "Suffice it to say that Johann Langfeld is not my real name. I am actually Polish by race and was brought up on the Gräfin's estate in East Prussia where my father was the Deputy Head Forester.

"Just before the war I went to university in Lvov in south-east Poland to study history. Then came the implementation of the infamous Molotov/Ribbentrop pact and Lvov was incorporated into the USSR where it remains to this day within the Ukrainian Soviet Republic.

"I dared not return to East Prussia. My people though divided between Germany and Russia were at war with the Nazis. Many were massacred by the Soviets. So rather than being caught up in the conflict in Ukraine I took myself to Moscow to escape the purges of Polish intellectuals in Lvov ready to sell my soul to the Reds to survive. What do you British say? If you can't beat them join them. With my language skills I was soon talent spotted by the Rote Kapelle. I draw a line under the wartime undercover period of my life. I am not proud of it."

"I expect you earned the Soviets' trust the hard way, but they must have had a few debts to repay you after the war," interjected Carl.

"They did indeed. That's why I was then moved to Potsdam as a political adviser to the Soviet Army in 1949. But I witnessed the workers' uprising against communism in Berlin in 1953 and its cruel suppression.

"I soon managed to obtain a transfer to a newly established travel bureau in the Soviet sector of the city, which was to promote Berlin as a destination for tourists from neutral countries like Sweden, Finland and Yugoslavia. This is still ostensibly my business in East Berlin and I am the boss of the outfit now but since the DDR is becoming increasingly recognised in the West I am allowed to travel to the Federal Republic, Austria and Switzerland as well on promotional visits.

"But since the brutal Soviet crackdowns against the Hungarian uprising in 1956 and the Czech reforms to socialism in the spring of 1968 my existing disillusion with the Soviet system turned to bitter hatred against it. Since 1969 I have been acting as a courier promoting tourism certainly but now clandestinely from East to West also. My network can boast about a hundred successful escapes from East Berlin to the West with only a dozen or so casualties to date with three killed, four wounded and five arrested which is an outstanding record. However, Hans Bloch as we shall call him from now on seems to be a particularly high value client. The risks of operation uplift are great but I gather the rewards will be commensurately high."

"That's right Johann," Sabine explained. "Hans' employers are making available to us five hundred thousand Deutschmarks to facilitate Hans' safe arrival in West Berlin. There is an immense amount at stake technically, militarily and politically over his successful extraction so we have accepted your advice not to risk any of the traditional escape routes but the airlift is very much time constrained.

"We have only till the end of this month to achieve it. After that the light trainer aircraft we intend to use will be withdrawn from service for at least six months, and perhaps permanently.

"Our friend here will fly the mission," Sabine declared authoritatively as one well used to directing such hazardous enterprises, "which will have to be disguised from his authorising officers. If it fails he will be court martialed. If it succeeds NATO will breathe a collective sign of relief but our hero will inevitably be banished from Berlin and possibly demoted in the Service though his audacity, skill and courage will probably ensure his career is safe. Remember he is a decorated veteran already and the Air Force would not wish the bad publicity if he had to resign his commission."

"I have given all this a lot of thought as you'd expect," Carl explained. "The Chipmunk Flight has a very full programme of preplanned sorties till the end of November but I will need to persuade a senior officer to authorise me for one final continuation flight to stay current at night flying. I propose to take off at dusk because night flying begins half an hour after sunset and to slip across the wall while some daylight remains to your landing strip, which you will have paced out and identified to me in advance.

"Herr Bloch must be available to jump on board at the end of the landing run," Carl insisted. "I cannot afford to stop the engine. Then we will return at ultra low level in the gathering gloom. Once into West Berlin I intend to declare an emergency and make a supposedly forced landing on the grass of the Tiergarten, which must be illuminated by car headlights.

"Hans will then have to be driven off immediately in one of those vehicles," Carl declared firmly. "I cannot contemplate landing back at Gatow, or Tegel or Templehof for that matter. Hans would never be able to get off the base. They are very well secured and the Soviets would certainly demand him back. He has to be transferred secretly into West Germany.

"That is the outline of my proposal," Carl concluded. "You must now fill in the details, Johann, and your people make it happen on the ground the other side. I repeat we have a once only chance of success. If agreed this mission cannot be rescheduled my end. Just pray all of you for suitable weather."

The dinner concluded with agreement to go ahead with Operation Uplift on 30 November. Johann Langfeld was to return to his office in East Berlin forthwith. His were the crucial responsibilities of locating a useable landing strip for a light aircraft close to Manfred's detention house, getting him there punctually and undetected for the flight to West Berlin and above all assessing the personalities and duties of his guards and how they could be suborned. He would need every pfennig of the 500,000 Deutschmark escape fund.

Sabine was to organise the reception team of motorised landing path illuminators including the get away driver to spirit Manfred away on arrival in West

Berlin, hide him till the inevitably furious international drama died down and then secure his safe transfer to West Germany. She would also liaise with Langfeld throughout the period of preparation and with Heidi who was to act totally normally maintaining her level of journalistic output but keeping Carl informed of developments.

On arrival back at the mission Carl was called in to see Group Captain Hannam. "Both the Brigadier and Bracewell tell me you did well at the conference, but perhaps not well enough from my point of view," Hannam began. "The AO C in C has already rung through to express his regrets for our imminent loss of the Chipmunk Flight. I don't believe it will be temporary. The Flight will therefore complete all its scheduled tasks by the end of the month, which means that continuation training will have the lowest priority." This was not good news.

"I would only expect that, sir," Carl replied. "As you did not mention them I presume our required cuts in men and vehicles are acceptable. At least they're on a par with the Army's but as for the Chipmunk Flight it was clear that the representatives from The Treasury and Foreign Office wanted to axe something very visible, high profile and emotive. They were not amenable to military logic and I fear as you do that they plan to turn the six month stand down into a permanent disbandment unless a major crisis intervenes."

"I share your judgement," the Group Captain responded. "For the next ten days to a fortnight you'll be off on tour in Mecklenburg, Carl. If you want a final pre stand down Chipmunk Flight on return you'd better make your number with Joe Flanders who is Flight authorising officer this month. I'm getting mine in tomorrow. Thereafter priority will inevitably be given to operational missions. Your sortie will be at the bottom of the list, serviceability permitting."

The fortnight Carl spent monitoring Soviet aircraft movements from air bases in Mecklenburg seemed interminable. He did his job conscientiously but his mind was elsewhere. His perpetual growing anxieties were chiefly focused on Johann Langfeld. Was he reliable or was he a plant? If he was playing a double game he knew enough to blow Carl's career for good. Heidi also would be sent packing from Berlin and the shockwaves of the scandal would reverberate around the Harthöhe in Bonn, too. The position of the Inspector General of the Luftwaffe would be in jeopardy even if he swore truthfully that he was completely ignorant of Operation Uplift.

Similar doubts applied to Sabine. Carl knew really very little about her. He had no reason to doubt her efficiency or trustworthiness but he had been in Berlin long enough to know not to trust anybody. If she was captured by the STASI he had to assume that she would talk. His key role would be revealed. What possible exculpation could he have – that he was acting under duress? This was wholly implausible. Unless that is he betrayed Langfeld and framed him as the author of the most fantastic plot ever to discredit the son-in-law of the Luftwaffe Inspector General by implicating him in the grave misuse of RAF assets to spirit a relative of the Inspector General from detention in East Berlin to the West.

Whichever way you looked at Operation Uplift the prognosis was unpalatable. Success would see Carl posted from BRIXMIS probably to a punitive ground job in the UK. Failure would cause him to be drummed out of the Service by Court Martial. Neither outcome would make for a tranquil married life with Heidi in her beloved Germany. The plaudits of her family for his enterprise, skill and daring would be scant compensation for the inevitably damaging fallout from the biggest professional and personal gamble of his life.

Carl returned from his BRIXMIS fact finding in Mecklenburg a week before the great day. His home coming to Heidi was as warm as usual but he hardly had time to change clothes before she was asking him to take the dog for a walk. "Can't I relax for just one minute?" he protested.

"It's not that my love but it's one of those simple happy things we have so little time to do together these days," she replied.

"All right, all right, I'm coming," Carl relented conscious that she must need a long debrief with him to bring him up to date with all her cousin Sabine's and Langfeld's activities out East. No doubt everything has gone pear shaped he mused sombrely.

It was actually liberating to step out in the gathering dusk with the first lamps of the evening coming on, the damp autumn leaves underfoot and Würstchen the Dachshund trotting contentedly alongside. "You'll be amazed Carl," she began, "how well the preparations are going. I am advised that our friends are confident that they can deliver Hans on time. There remains, however, a problem with one guard who is apparently totally incorruptible. Johann will either have to pay his superior more for the duty roster to be changed so that he is not on duty in the late afternoon of the day in question or if that cannot be achieved more direct action will have to be taken to solve the problem."

"I don't want blood on my hands," Carl insisted. "I have enough on my plate without the possibility of being indicted as an accomplice to murder."

"We have already thought of that. It'll be a case of either doctoring the guard's lunch or if that does not work of delivering a non lethal injection," Heidi sought to reassure him. "These can be totally incapacitating and leave next to no trace. Veterinary surgeons use them all the time."

"That's as may be but it still seems a highly hazardous enterprise to me."

"To you certainly, Carl, but these are familiar methods to intelligence services. It will appear that the guard collapsed from natural causes and by the time an accurate diagnosis of him can be carried out, Hans will be up and away."

"I take your word for it love," Carl answered full of foreboding.

Heidi and Carl resolved that thereafter he was not to be burdened with the details for Operation Uplift from the other side of the wall apart from such matters as affected his ability to undertake the flying element of the escape successfully.

"I will need to receive full information on the location, surface, approaches and layout of Johann's proposed landing ground as far in advance as possible," Carl demanded, "so that I can meticulously plan the routes in and out. I must memorise the danger areas, avoid the worst of them and be able to identify instantaneously every pinpoint along the outbound and inbound tracks.

"I will have to advise Hans in good time whether his designated strip is suitable for landing and take off or if diversionary activities have to be laid on in various locations in the East," Carl explained, "to distract the other side from the passage of a Royal Air Force primary trainer in a manner which is clearly not typical of a normal BRIXMIS mission. We may have to alter Johann's proposals or at the very least adapt them to what a light aircraft is able to perform in such critical circumstances."

"You sound as if you are addressing an Air Force briefing, not chatting to your loving wife on an evening stroll," Heidi replied.

"I can't help that, my dear. I am being asked to risk everything on Operation Uplift. I cannot afford it to fail, so naturally the years of professional training take over and they demand the subordination of all normal gentle emotions to the drive for success," Carl responded.

Two days before the operation Carl was handed by Heidi the full details of the site from which 'Hans Bloch' had to be extracted. Carl had imagined that he would have been detained near the city centre, in the Mitte district close to the very heart of power in the DDR or well south-west of the city in Potsdam near the Soviet Army's headquarters.

Instead he discovered that he was being held in the suburb of Weissensee an area of big gardens, allotments, villas and orchards. A very suitable field had been selected by Langfeld but its location in the north-east extremity of Berlin meant a difficult overflight of a large area of the Soviet sector.

However, there were no obstacles on the approaches. Hedges ran along the sides giving a measure of cover. No fences, water troughs or livestock offered a hazard. The surface which Johann had paced out carefully was flat grass and apparently firm. According to him it was not overlooked by any high rise building and a track skirted the side of the Northern hedge for easy access and getaway by car. Behind the Southern boundary lay warehouses and a storage depot, which seemed seldom in use.

On the eve of Operation Uplift Carl went in to work very early with the exact position of his designated landing field and a mass of precise information on its surroundings to hand. He headed straight for the mission map room and arrived well before the duty Corporal. The heavy door swung open at the insertion of his security card.

Carl extracted from the drawers detailed maps of North and East Berlin on which crucial data about Soviet and East German military, police and governmental establishments were superimposed. Listening carefully for the sound of the Corporal's impending entrance he surreptitiously transcribed all the key material onto a sheet of paper pencilling in the features with the greatest care. He meticulously annotated in red the sensitive sites, which were likely to be protected by armed guards.

Carl then plotted an outbound track Northward initially from Gatow then Eastbound skirting the Northern fringes of the city to Weissensee, which would pass on his starboard side before he turned West to line up for landing with a tall radio mast, which lay just beyond the Western extremity of the field.

Once safely down Carl would taxi rapidly to the other end of the strip where his precious passenger should be waiting for him. Then they would take off immediately Westward turning hard to port onto a south-westerly heading. He determined to return at full throttle at rooftop height right across the centre of the city past the Fernsehturm tower, which dominated the skyline of East Berlin, passing over the wall in the narrow gap between the Brandenburg Gate and the Reichstag building for a straight in approach onto the grass of the Tiergarten.

The weather forecast on the kitchen radio before he left the flat was going in for an incoming belt of rain in the outlook period. The 29 November would remain fair but a band of rain, heavy at times was expected to reach Berlin by mid afternoon the next day with a strengthening wind from the south-west. This news weighed heavily upon Carl. Would Joe Flanders still authorise the sortie if the weather deteriorated badly? Would the visibility hold up or would sheets of nimbostratus come rolling across Gatow from the lakes and pine forests as the rain set in obscuring the pinpoints, which he had carefully planned along the route? Would the landing ground become dangerously soft? On the other hand guards would be less likely to patrol outside in bad weather and he might be able to slip in and out of the stratus layer to avoid hostile fire.

On the final evening before Uplift Heidi and Carl were glad of their customary walk with the dog. It had been one of those crisp clear exhilarating days of early winter for which Berlin was famous. Würstchen the Dachshund seemed oblivious of his masters' mood. Whatever their anxieties his daily escape from the flat was the sum of his ambitions. It was now the same also for Carl. Home no longer bought him calm or respite from his wild speculations.

The physical dangers of strafing rebel tribesmen in Aden had surely been much greater than the risks of Operation Uplift. Then the whole team from headquarters personnel, to operations staff, squadron executives and pilots down to toiling ground crew were striving for the same end. Here it could not have been more different. His superiors and friends alike in the mission would have been aghast at what he proposed to do.

It was true that Johann, Sabine and even his dearest Heidi had all done their utmost to plan a successful operation. But from the landing and pickup in the muddy field at Weissensee the responsibility of delivering Hans Bloch unscathed to West Berlin was entirely his. At least the familiar evening stroll with Heidi dispelled the oppressive foreboding which gripped him in the flat. She seemed almost unaffected by the daunting challenge he faced next day.

"You can relax now, my love," she declared. "I have total faith in you and so does everyone involved in Uplift. I know what you are doing is worthwhile even if it causes some temporary upheaval in our lives. I married a Royal Air Force pilot recognising what it meant. I cannot expect to live in Berlin forever. I became a camp follower when I married you and your job must send us how do your Gunners say it – quo fas et Gloria ducunt – to where duty and glory lead. By tomorrow night you will be famous and our Manfred will be free. No one else could carry out what you are going to achieve."

CHAPTER 30

It was already grey when Carl awoke from a fitful sleep and a stiffening breeze was shaking the last leaves from the gaunt trees in the street outside. As in Aden before an operation he removed anything incriminating from his wallet and left his pocket book at home. He retained a hundred Deutschmarks, a five pound note, his Royal Air Force identity card and BRIXMIS pass. This last was important conferring on him if not diplomatic immunity at least a formal status, which was internationally recognised. It did not make Operation Uplift in any sense legal but rendered it comprehensible even if far beyond his official remit. It offered, too, some potential plea bargaining value and the ultimate possibility if captured of eventual release in a pawn for pawn exchange of agents with the Soviets.

Heidi's stoical upbringing came through on his departure for work. "Home for dinner as usual?" she asked.

"I sincerely hope so," Carl replied. "As you know I like to get home a little earlier than normal on a Friday evening. It looks like rain. I think I'll take my raincoat. It might be a good idea if you give Würstchen his walk in the afternoon today. The forecast is rain for tonight."

"Very wise. Würstchen does not like getting wet any more than I do. Bye, my love. Don't work too hard."

"I won't."

Carl's morning was spent answering a questionnaire of technical details, which required further clarification from his report on the Mecklenburg tour. He took his response to Group Captain Hannam in person to have it signed off promptly so he could get down to Gatow in good time. This was a mistake. The Group Captain was in conference with Brigadier Pearson and only received Carl just before lunch. Carl fervently hoped that on a Friday afternoon the old man was not going to be too critical.

His optimism was misplaced. "I want you to revise items three, six and seven. Your replies are skimpy. Check for additional facts with the rest of the team and leave your final report on my desk before you leave this afternoon," the Group Captain demanded.

"I'm sorry about this. I know you wanted to go flying but it would only have been a sentimental sortie for old times' sake as the Flight is due to stand down this evening."

"Very good, sir," Carl replied simply and saluted closing the door behind him. "Does the Group Captain still play his round of golf on Friday afternoons Sergeant Smithers?" Carl asked the office manager on his way out.

"Indeed he does."

"In that case I'll leave my report with you sergeant to keep in your safe over the weekend for Group Captain Hannam to study first thing on Monday morning."

Carl rang round his colleagues to obtain the missing data and retyped the rejected paragraphs himself. "I'm off to Gatow now, sergeant," he told Smithers as he deposited the revised report in his in-tray. "Keep this secure for the Group Captain."

"I will, sir. Are you going flying in this?" Smithers asked as the first drops of rain ran down the window panes and the frames rattled in the rising wind.

"Indeed I am, sergeant. It'll take a lot more than this to stop me getting airborne. It could be my last sortie with the Chipmunk Flight."

On Carl's arrival at Gatow Joe Flanders was pacing the crew room. "You've made me come all the way out here on a Friday afternoon, Carl, in this vile weather when you can see that flying is soon going to be scrubbed. You know you can't divert out of West Berlin if the cloud base clamps. What's more should the wind strengthen further it will be beyond the Chipmunk's limits and I am not prepared to mark the Flight's temporary disbandment with a bent undercarriage even if the maintainers have six whole months to repair it."

"You've just got to let me go, sir," Carl entreated. "I'm due to go off on leave to Cambridge with Heidi. She was so happy there. So as not to get bored I've arranged to fly with the Air Experience Flight at Teversham again and the boss has told me he needs me to be night rated as he plans to introduce the air cadets to night flying."

"I'm not interested in your leisure flying activities, Carl," Joe responded sternly. "Now if the sortie had an immediate operational purpose, which I could justify it might be different."

"Well actually it does, sir," Carl responded. "We have heard that a new Russian Army vehicle overhaul facility is to open over at Weissensee. I would just like to inspect it from the air whilst we still have the capability to do so."

"Why then don't you let me come along, too, to take some photographs?" Joe inquired.

"That won't be necessary at this stage and anyway I want to bash the circuit on return to Gatow, which would be dead boring for you. I tell you what, Joe. I'll give you a bottle of German champagne, Sekt, to celebrate what may well be the Flight's last sortie ever, if you authorise me for a quick night flying trip."

"I don't think such behaviour is in the Queen's Regulations, but you win. I can't really stand between an A2QFI with a DFC and his duty or his generous nature, can I Carl?"

When Carl went to the Met Office the printed weather sheet for 1800–2400 hours forecast eight eighths stratus at five hundred feet in moderate to heavy rain with a wind from 230 degrees at twenty knots gusting to twenty-five. There was a possibility of stratus down to three hundred feet over heavily wooded areas with seriously reduced visibility. He called briefly at Air Traffic Control to notify them and Berlin centre that he was heading off North then Eastwards on a sector reconnaissance in the Weissensee area of Berlin returning directly to base across the centre of the city for some final night circuits at base.

By the time he reached the aeroplane Carl was already soaked. The crucial target map which he had drawn up was in the knee pocket of his overalls safely wrapped in polythene. The flight line despatchers well covered up in their all weather parkas must have thought he was mad.

As soon as he was in the cockpit everything became familiar but he used the Flight Reference Card for the pre flight checks to be sure. The faithful Gypsy Major engine coughed into life. Carl swung out of the dispersal fish tailing furiously and wiping away at the condensation inside the canopy to clear his view. The perimeter and runway lights were already on. Carl halted at the runway threshold, did his engine run-up and final checks, then called "Lima 50 ready for take-off".

In the strong wind the Chipmunk was airborne in a few score yards, surging upward, wallowing and weaving in the ground turbulence. By three hundred feet Carl was already in cloud. He had the perfect excuse for his ultra low level transit to Weissensee and with the wind behind him made good speed. He lowered a notch of flap to improve his forward view and manoeuvrability checking off the pinpoints from the map across his knees.

It might be an urban jungle below but it was certainly easier to navigate at a mere two nautical miles per minute than over the mountainous wastes of the Radfan in the Aden Protectorate at seven nautical miles per minute. No urgent radio call or unusual activity on the ground indicated that anyone thought there was anything untoward in his historic flight.

Soon the towering TV mast loomed to starboard and there were the track and parallel hedges, which delineated his landing strip. He was a bit close in but rather than edge out and be blown further downwind Carl chopped the throttle and did a tight curving approach Spitfire style. Lined up a few yards into the field he eased the control column back to its full travel just before all three wheels touched to a perfect three pointer. Keep straight, gentle braking on this uncertain surface, Carl said to himself. Then he saw it to his right. A Trabant East German car was just visible through the hedge. Would it be Hans or the STASI perhaps?

Carl skidded to a halt on the slippery surface and then slithered round retracing his landing run as far as he safely could. Out of the corner of his left eye he saw two hooded figures emerge from a gap in the hedge and dash half crouched towards him. He prayed they had the sense not to run in front of his aircraft. He would have to continue taxiing to the extreme end. He would need the field's full length to get airborne from the soft ground even in the strong wind.

To his horror he glimpsed flashing blue lights proceeding towards the halted Trabant on the other side of the hedgeline. Would the Trabant's driver have the sense to create a diversion to detain the police long enough to allow him to get airborne or would they fire at him first and deal with the car driver later he wondered.

With full rudder and judicious braking Carl slewed the aircraft into wind and slid the canopy back. The rain began trickling down his cheeks. He cut the throttle to idle as the two men approached. They ran up behind the trailing edge and above the tick over of the engine Carl heard the wail of police sirens, one seemingly almost alongside.

Amazingly Johann himself was at his elbow with Hans alongside. "Jump in. Straps tight," Carl shouted to Hans through the wash of the propeller and slammed the throttle forward leaving Johann to jump clear of the tail and fend for himself. There was no time for Hans to strap in properly or put on his electric hat. Indeed he was sitting on it.

Carl wondered if they would ever get airborne. The far end of the field was boggier than where he landed and they only just staggered over the trees. As they did so Carl felt a sharp jolt and an icy breeze on his cheeks. Glass from a hole in the windscreen and smashed instrument panel fell into his lap. The engine sounded rougher but they were airborne. He only hoped that his VIP passenger had not been hit and that the clearly labouring engine would keep running.

He did not need the broken directional giro. He knew the route and pinpoints by heart. After a gentle turn to port he saw he was on track, but would more trigger happy Vopos give the peppered Chipmunk its coup de grace. Endangering one of

His Majesty's aircraft would certainly be a charge impossible to disprove and a safe landing in the dark on the other side of the wall would not be easy. Carl noted the engine's oil pressure was falling ominously.

The Fernsehturm's dominance of the skyline made navigation easy even in the deepening dark. Beyond it he could see the illuminated death strip along the wall. Carl descended further to below the roof tops where he could. Engine failure would mean a crash not a survivable landing.

To his alarm Carl saw gun flashes from the top of the Brandenburg Gate. The overheating Gypsy Major in front of him began emitting a grinding, graunching groan. He took the aircraft still lower. Perhaps the riflemen would either desist from firing or wound their comrades on patrol below.

Then he was through the gap with the Reichstag and there was the flarepath of headlights lighting up the grass dead ahead.

He cut the throttle, banged down full flap and kicked the aircraft into a wild and extravagantly cross controlled sideslip perilously close to the stall to kill the last excess knots of speed and feet of height, lurched straight, yanked the stick fully back and waited seemingly forever. Seconds later there was a bone crunching bang and the dear old Chippie was down tail first but safely, if not intact, yet only with bullet damage to the nose, windscreen and cowling.

As soon as Carl stopped, the waiting illuminator cars surged forward and converged upon the Chipmunk. A pungent oily smell from the overheated engine was permeating the cockpit. He flung the canopy back and jumped out. A Mercedes diesel taxi style saloon drew up alongside. A hooded woman emerged and ran to the aeroplane's back seat. "Hans, you come with me now," she cried. It was unmistakably the voice of Sabine.

Carl looked carefully through the gloom to her car. Another cape headed anorak clad woman was at the wheel. "My God, it's Heidi," the realisation hit him hard. He was up to his neck in an unofficial enterprise whose clear operational success must surely terminate his job at BRIXMIS and their married officers' accommodation in Berlin within twenty-four hours at the most.

Carl could not escape the consequences but at least he must conceal Heidi's involvement if they were to have any chance of securing another Air Force posting which offered officers' married quarters or hirings. He was sure it was likely he would be Court Martialled and dismissed from the Service. If not he would have to do time on the most dreary ground tour the Ministry could devise.

Before Carl could even wish Hans Godspeed he was whisked away into the rainlashed West Berlin night. He himself hardly had time to take off his electric hat before a Royal Air Force Police Land Rover with a Squadron Leader and two burly white capped Corporals and a 'snowdrop' Sergeant on board arrived. "Flight Lieutenant Higgins, you are coming with us," the Squadron Leader announced in a threatening tone, which brooked no argument.

"What about the aircraft, sir?" Carl replied. "I can't just abandon it here in such a public place."

"You ought to have thought of that before you landed," the Squadron Leader retorted.

"But it was an emergency, sir. I had no option. The engine was about to seize."

"You tell that to the Inquiry. Now come along, Higgins. At once.

"Sergeant Perkins here will look after the aeroplane until the Queen Mary aircraft transporter arrives to take it away. You are accompanying me and Corporal

Henderson and Corporal Prentice to Gatow where you will spend the night in the Guard Room," the Squadron Leader went on. "In the morning we three will take you to BRIXMIS for you to give an account of these events to Group Captain Hannam. On arrival at Gatow you will be allowed to telephone your wife to inform her that you will not be coming home tonight although I am sure she will have guessed as much from the TV and radio news bulletins already. Your escapade has been dominating the airwaves this evening."

The Squadron Leader was as good as his word. He instructed the Sergeant of the Guard to let Carl ring home. "Heidi my love," he began. "I'm sorry to tell you something unexpected has cropped up at work. I won't be home tonight. Exigencies of the Service as they say and I expect they will have to take priority this weekend. I'll be in touch, sweetheart, just as soon as I know when you can expect me."

"I understand, dear," she answered calmly. Indeed she did and was prepared for the worst.

The 'cooler' behind the Guard Room was Spartan but tolerable. Carl felt as if his career had just gone full circle to his earliest Flight Cadet days when his supper arrived on a tray – the standard RAF meal he knew so well of bacon and eggs, baked beans and tinned tomatoes accompanied by two slices of white bread smeared with margarine washed down with a mug of milky brown oversweet tea.

Then he was full of hope for the future in spite of his heaving stomach when airborne. Now he just felt sick with disillusion. Why had he allowed himself to be exploited by Heidi's fanatical émigré friends? Why could not the Service be more flexible and realise that the worthy end of liberating Hans justified his part in the unorthodox yet brilliantly imaginative means of achieving it? After all the Other Side had no compunction about bending the rules of the game to secure their political and military objectives. Indeed such realpolitik or state cynicism was at the heart of their Marxist-Leninist doctrine. Why must the West always fight the Cold War with its hands tied behind its back? Surely he should be a NATO hero not an official arch villain, to be sacrificed to the pusillanimity of the Foreign Office.

After a breakfast identical to the supper he had consumed the night before Carl was virtually frogmarched to the RAF Police Land Rover by the two corporals with the Provo Branch Squadron Leader bringing up the rear. They accompanied him all the way to Brigadier Pearson's office. The Squadron Leader entered and quickly re-emerged.

"The Brigadier will see you now, Higgins. March in," he announced. Carl did so and saluted. Pearson and Hannam were sitting side by side behind a huge table. The Brigadier was perusing a brown file, which looked ominously like a compendium of Carl's personal assessments. Group Captain Hannam was desultorily flicking through Carl's report on his recent Mecklenburg tour and did not look up when Pearson began.

"Stand easy, Higgins. This is one of the most extraordinary episodes in the history of the Mission. I don't know of any officer who has more openly and fragrantly flouted Service regulations and the operational procedures which govern our work.

"Your Commanding Officer, Group Captain Hannam here is appalled by such blatant ill discipline and quite frankly feels betrayed and quite rightly so. Only recently I heard you argue on his behalf at the Commander in Chief's conference at Rheindahlen for the imperative necessity of maintaining the Chipmunk Flight for our intelligence gathering capability. After your actions yesterday the Soviets would be within their rights to prohibit any overflight of their sector of Berlin." The Group Captain nodded his assent.

"Indeed they have issued a formal protest," the Brigadier continued. "You, Higgins, have caused Her Majesty's Government the gravest embarrassment and even prejudiced the delicate political process of détente by airlifting a private West German citizen out of detention in the German Democratic Republic. The chances of your beloved Chipmunk Flight's being reconstituted now seem to me minimal."

"Obviously I take full responsibility, sir," Carl responded.

"That is not the point," the Brigadier went on. "You somehow have the luck of the devil, Higgins. Fortunately for you there appear to have been important mitigating circumstances. Your unauthorised operation has achieved some remarkably beneficial results for Western security. This mission has received congratulatory messages from the Heads of the German and Italian Air Forces.

"Even the C in C RAF Germany Air Chief Marshal Broderick telephoned Group Captain Hannam to express his appreciation. It would also seem that your exploit has been extensively reported in the British Press." The Brigadier reached over to the table behind him and produced a sheaf of newspaper cuttings. "'Aden Hero Rescues Prisoner behind Berlin Wall' is the headline in the Daily Mail. 'Undercover RAF pilot lifts Boffin to Freedom' writes the Daily Express. 'Aden Veteran in Heroic Berlin Airlift' shouts the front page of the Sun. Hannam you carry on now. Higgins is your man after all."

The Group Captain looked up wearily from the thick pages of the Mecklenburg Report. "Frankly, Carl, you've let me down and yourself as well as your Air Force colleagues in the Mission especially Joe Flanders who authorised your renegade sortie," he began. "You were not straight with me. The Mecklenburg Report is still inadequate and was clearly rushed. Instead of seeking to have it approved by me yesterday afternoon you deliberately left it with Sergeant Smithers to have it locked away in my office safe unscrutinised till Monday in order to go flying. As it happened I was in the office all afternoon and expected to be able to sign it off before going home."

"I can only apologise for all the trouble I have caused, sir," Carl replied simply.

"That does not help but very luckily for you, Carl, support for your madcap operation has been pouring in from the highest levels. Brigadier Pearson mentioned the AOC in C RAF Germany. However, no less than the Head of Defence Procurement at MOD in London rang me as well to express his warm commendation of your achievement saying that in case there were adverse disciplinary consequences for you he had intervened personally with the Air Secretary on your behalf.

"As a consequence," Hannam continued, "my friend Group Moxon on his staff who I gather is not unknown to you has sent me a signal saying that after consultation with Air Marshal Broderick you are not to be Court Martialled as I would have wished. Instead you are to report to RAF Uxbridge to serve as a barrack warden from next Monday. As the title suggests it is very much a ground tour. You are not to expect to assume a flying appointment for the foreseeable future. You and your wife will relinquish your Service hiring here forthwith. As the Brigadier said you have the luck of the devil, Higgins. If I'd had my way you would have been drummed out of the Service. Now dismiss."

Carl's life had already changed. No Service transport was laid on for him. He had to take a taxi back to the flat. He and Heidi had few possessions. Those were soon packed up and left with the duty officer at RAF Gatow to be sent on later. Heidi was surprisingly philosophical about her enforced move. She recognised it as the inevitable price for setting Uncle Manfred free.

"You've been short toured at BRIXMIS, my love," she observed, "but I certainly don't think your time has been wasted."

"I'm glad you feel like that, Heidi," Carl replied. "We now face a choice. Either we stay with my parents in Victoria till we can find permanent accommodation within range of RAF Uxbridge or you go back and live with yours in Bonn for a while. Alternatively if you can't bear to leave Berlin yet you could I suppose move in with Sabine."

"My decision is straightforward, Carl," Heidi responded. "My place whenever possible is beside you, my love. We go to England together. I'll ring British Airways at Templehof and book us on the next flight to Heathrow. Meanwhile you give your parents a call so we have somewhere to sleep tonight."

"I already have, my love, my mother is laying on supper for us on arrival and says we can stay with them for as long as it takes to get a home of our own again."

As the BAC One Eleven climbed out westward towards the air corridor across East Germany Berlin's romance, excitement, tension, surrounding lakes, forests and lighted death strip along the wall were soon left behind. Yet events in the divided city for Carl and Heidi as for so many of their Cold War generation shaped their destiny and directed it in a totally unexpected direction. Carl had gone to BRIXMIS to serve at the perilous interface between two ideologies and confronting military alliances preserved in permanently unstable equilibrium by the havoc each could wreak upon the other if deterrence failed. He now left Berlin a disgraced hero of that confrontation for a post as far removed from the dramas and dangers of his Mission's role behind the front line of the East West confrontation in Europe as it was possible to imagine. He came as an officer with a future. He left as an officer with a controversial past, which virtually ensured that he had none.

Carl's parents were at the airport to meet him and Heidi. "It's wonderful to have you both back," his mother declared. "We've been reading all about you in the papers."

"I'm not surprised they moved you," his father observed. "There's nothing the top brass hates so much as unauthorised success. Don't worry about it."

"Exactly dear," said his mother. "You always found when you were in Government Service that apparent setbacks turned out to be career opportunities. Reculer pour mieux sauter as the French say. I expect you'll find the same at Uxbridge, Carl."

"We certainly regard Uxbridge as an opportunity. We'll see if we can buy a little house West of London within commuting range of the HQs at High Wycombe and Northwood as well as the Ministry of course, which we can let out if we get posted away. This whole ungrateful business could be the making of us. I'm going to start house hunting round Uxbridge tomorrow," Heidi announced confidently.

She was as good as her word touring the Estate Agents of Uxbridge while Carl endured his first day at what in Lawrence of Arabia's day was known as the Depot. Now it boasted a declining RAF hospital, the Queen's Colour Squadron of the Royal Air Force and a square 1950s block, which held the Administrative Centre for the Service's hired accommodation in Greater London. The parade ground below where the Regiment did their drilling provided the sole visual relief to the anonymous ashen faced personnel who moved the paperwork on and periodically sallied forth into London's traffic to inspect some remote hiring, march in or out its transient Service occupants and ensure by dint of meticulous inventory checks that nobody marched out with the knives, forks and spoons in their pocket.

Heidi was tireless in her hunt for a proper home. They were determined not to live in a flat again. Carl needed the antidote of a garden to endure the stifling boredom of his daily barrack warden duties. Whilst Carl's friends and contemporaries were commanding Flights, being promoted, or preparing for the Staff College examination his days were spent chugging round the North Circular Road and remotest suburbs in his Volkswagen Beetle from one hired house to another or battling through the traffic jams to the hired flats of inner London.

He worked a six day week because he managed to resume on Saturdays his flying of air cadets on the Chipmunks of the Air Experience Flight at Cambridge. His fellow pilots there were sympathetic to his virtual ostracism within the Service and the Commanding Officer even let him borrow an aeroplane to fly himself up to the Old Cranwellian reunion.

It was a mistake. Others arrived in style in a more glamorous or operational aircraft including Douglas Bader in his Beech Travelair. Although Air Chief Marshal Broderick, the guest of honour, greeted Carl warmly in the bar after dinner few of his friends were there. His visit served merely to deepen his regrets and did nothing to put him in line for a decent posting back to full time flying on operational aeroplanes.

On his return from his nostalgic midsummer weekend at the College Heidi announced that she had doubly good news for Carl. "Dearest love," she began. "I'm to have a baby. Isn't it wonderful?"

Carl was thrilled beyond measure exclaiming in delight, "Heidi meine liebling. You have made me so incredibly happy. This is the best thing that has ever happened to me. My job may be dull but it keeps me at home which is exactly where I want to be my love, beside you and the baby, too."

"The other thing," Heidi reported, "is that I have found the ideal home for our family. Would you believe it? It is in London but in real country, too. It's a little cottage by a canal in a village called Harefield only a quarter of an hour's drive from RAF Uxbridge. It has a beautiful church called St Mary's, a hospital and a lot of rustic pubs you'll be glad to learn. It's a genuine English village. Because there's no tube or railway station the sprawl of London seems to have passed it by.

"What's more I think we can afford the place. It is a lock keeper's cottage and has two rooms downstairs, two bedrooms and a bathroom upstairs, a kitchen and lavatory at the back with a little garden in front leading down to the lock. There's a vegetable patch behind where we could grow our own. It'll be heaven for us and a wonderful home for the little one as well."

Carl pondered how as so often his present joy was born in destiny's apparent darkest moments. His work was certainly humdrum. He was passed over for promotion and he was far from sure that he would ever step again into the cockpit of a frontline aeroplane. Already he was having to call some of his Cranwell contemporaries sir. Yet he would not now exchange his lot for theirs although he was genetically programmed to drive himself on to overcome all obstacles. In his short married life with Heidi she had demonstrated incomparable courage and tenacity. Now God willing she would be vouchsafed the child she deserved and their life would be full.

Baby Max's arrival in the maternity unit of nearby Hillingdon Hospital took away much of Carl's disenchantment with his work. Heidi suffered no complications with their son's delivery and their home life in Harefield was by now well ordered. Carl realised that being a barrack warden was just a totally ordinary job like most others, but it had genuine compensations.

It involved no heroics, evoked no ideals but at least it paid the mortgage on their canal side home and for the new German au pair Louise whom Heidi had found on the recommendation of the German Air Attaché's wife. Above all Carl had not been forced to join any Ground Branch of the Service but remained nominally General Duties/Pilot, still potentially available for flying duties and as such continued to receive his flying pay, which he put into a fund for Max's education.

Carl might no longer harbour illusions that he would change history or achieve an illustrious career to high rank but he was conscientious and preferred to earn his flying pay through his weekly Chipmunk flying. Even with Max to look after Heidi was realistic enough not to demand, as many wives would have done, that he now give up his flying to help care for Max. In her German tradition the wife ran the home but acknowledged that her husband headed the family and his judgements had to be respected. Max grew vigorously and learned to walk early. His nanny Louise became so familiar an adjunct to the family circle as almost to constitute his young honorary German aunt.

Carl's routine was well organised. His colleagues accepted him as an odd ball. Who in their right mind would voluntarily work on Saturdays as he did they wondered. They knew his role was transitory. Soon his love of flying would see him called back to the flightline where he belonged.

At Uxbridge he had certainly amassed all the knowledge of a London taxi driver and had learned the rat runs and circuitous routes to avoid the traffic jams of Greater London. Yet he still yearned to be back in the air full time. It was his spiritual home as for so many of his flying friends; the only place where he felt truly fulfilled.

The call came sooner than he had imagined. One grey autumn morning as he was looking wistfully from his desk across the empty drill square watching a Pembroke climb out of Northolt the telephone rang in the Squadron Leader's office. "It's a certain Group Captain Moxon for you, Carl," he announced. "From Air Secretary's Department of MOD. Says it's personal. What's going on? Put up another black? Will you be staying longer with us here?"

"Can I take it in your office, sir?" Carl requested.

"Go ahead. I'll leave you alone. It's probably confidential. I've got to check today's marching out schedule with the chaps anyway."

Carl picked up the receiver. "Flight Lieutenant Higgins speaking."

"Moxon here. I must break some bad news to you. We've lost Flight Lieutenant Parker our QFI on exchange with the staff of the Air Academy at Risalpur. He had his tail knocked off by a student in a mid air collision and went straight in yesterday."

"What a terrible thing, sir."

"Did you know him?"

"Of course, sir. Freddie and I were at Cranwell together; in my Entry but different squadrons as I recall."

"The Pakistanis have been very understanding," the Group Captain continued, "by not expecting us to fill the vacancy immediately. It gives you time to do a quick refresher course and conversion to Jet Provosts at Manby, get yourself re-qualified as a basic QFI on the aeroplane at CFS and go out to Pakistan just before Christmas."

"In time for the Quaid i Azam's birthday, sir. How appropriate," Carl replied. "Is it an accompanied post?"

"I'm afraid not. It is a most unhappy experience for the Pakistanis to have to look after Parker's widow and children so they have stipulated that it must be a short unaccompanied tour, which is where you come in, Carl. You will be released early from your period of penance at Uxbridge and do a year on your own at Risalpur."

"Do you have a permanent home in the UK for your family yet?" Moxon went on. "Is it a place where they can live happily without you? Is it easily accessible for you to visit for your mid year leave?" he enquired.

"Yes on both counts, sir," Carl answered. "Obviously I must clear your proposal with my wife first, but I'm almost positive she'll be delighted for me."

"It'll be good to have you back in the old routine, Carl," the Group Captain responded. "With your boyhood experience of Pakistan and operational and QFI background you're ideal for this posting. Take advantage of it. No one else in the Air Force is nearly so well suited for the appointment. It could be the making of your career."

"Thank you, sir. I'm looking forward to it. Assume I'm on. I'll only contact you if it's vetoed by my wife."

CHAPTER 31

Carl returned home in some trepidation. Perhaps he had spoken too confidently to Moxon. Had he been justified to take a positive reaction from Heidi for granted? "It's my turn to break important news to you, my love," he began cautiously as he crossed the threshold. "They want to me return to flying. I've been asked to refresh, get re-qualified as a QFI and go out to instruct for a year at the Pakistan Air Force Academy at Risalpur. What do you think, sweetheart? It's flattering but do you think it's right for us and the family?"

"It's right for you, Carl dear. That much I do know," Heidi responded. "It would be wrong for you to be stuck any longer in that dead end job at Uxbridge and this new posting may be the only way out for a long while to come."

"I'm so glad you feel that way, sweetheart," Carl interjected.

"As for the family I'm not so sure: only time can tell," Heidi went on. "We will miss you terribly, but you must take it. If you don't you could regret letting the opportunity pass you by and I would not wish you to hold it against me."

"I thought you'd say that, Heidi darling and I thank you so much. I'll miss you and Max and our lovely home, too. It'll be painful to be separated so long especially with Max growing up fast," Carl replied. "However, I am promised a special foreign service supplement to my pay and a whole month's home leave in the middle of the year with the return air fare fully paid. It should help us to save more for Max's prep school fees."

"All right, my love, we're agreed. You go. When do you begin?" Heidi asked.

"On Monday at the School of Refresher Flying at Manby."

"Where's that?"

"In Lincolnshire. On top of the Wolds near Louth."

Manby was a sweet interlude. Carl could get home to Harefield every weekend. He relished the drives across the familiar Lincolnshire countryside. He either cut across the flatlands of the Fens. Or from Lincoln he drove through the increasingly undulating landscape towards the lofty church spire of red roofed Louth, which dominated the surrounding Wolds in whose gentle embrace lay the School of Refresher Flying.

Manby was an intimate traditional permanent station with a pleasant neo-Georgian Officers' Mes. The regime was straightforward; the atmosphere relaxed yet practical. The instructors had rather to supervise than to teach their experienced pupils.

Carl's QFI a crusty old Flight Sergeant Bryn Williams treated Carl with respect verging on deference. "Getting that bloke out of East Berlin in a Chippie must have taken some guts," he asserted before their first familiarisation sortie.

"I won't say that it was all in a day's work, but it was not so hairy as it sounds," Carl answered. "At least there were no hostile Tribesmen waiting to carve me up if I crashed as in Aden. The enemy forces were among the top brass of our own side."

It took only a couple of trips for Williams to send Carl solo in the sprightly Jet Provost Mark 4. Its performance was not much inferior to that of the old familiar Vampire and a lot better than that of its elder brother the venerable Jet Provost Mark

3 – a notoriously sluggish underpowered aeroplane universally dubbed as the 'variable noise constant thrust machine'. Flying with Bryn Williams was fun. He was only too happy to let Carl do everything interjecting occasional curt criticisms when required, but mostly he offered a running commentary of appreciation and benign encouragement interspersed with acerbic shafts of Welsh humour.

The refresher training was like a much compressed rerun of Carl's third year at Cranwell on the Vampire with a stronger emphasis on solo practice interspersed with occasional dual checks. The flying was undemanding and the course's remarkable mix of age and experience and of all ranks from Air Vice-Marshal to Flight Sergeant including retreads back in the Service from civil life meant that the leisure moments in the crew room were never short of entertaining anecdotes.

Carl had seldom been happier. At work all he had to do was fly, not perform the officer's usual station duties or exercise any responsibility save that in the air. At home Max was a delight. Louise the au pair remained cheerful and settled. Heidi had acquired a wide circle of socially aspiring young mums into which she fitted effortlessly. Their lockside home was rarely free of visitors at weekends and Max seldom wanted for company on expeditions to go feed the ducks and Canada geese along the canal.

During the working week which in effect only lasted from Monday morning till Friday afternoon or even lunchtime if he got his day's flying done in the morning, Carl was contented enough with joining his friends at the bar most of whom like him commuted at weekends back to their wives and families. Occasionally he ventured out to local pubs and one mid course evening invited himself to visit Jamie and Janey at their married Quarter at nearby Binbrook where Jamie was a Flight Commander on one of the resident Lightning squadrons.

There was a changelessness about the Jamiesons at which Carl could only marvel. They were clearly as deeply involved in Lincolnshire social life as ever. During Carl's visit their telephone rang incessantly and they evidently remained in close touch with their mutual Air Force contemporaries which Carl much admired. It was as if the life of their Cranwell Entry still revolved around them. They were full of news, not all of it good, however.

Peter Carrick was already at Staff College. He and Natasha had another child. Mark Driscoll was Deputy Leader of the Red Arrows down at Kemble. Although he still had not married again he shared a cottage near Peterborough most weekends with a dazzling blonde called Hazel. "Moxon who got you off the hook, Carl, and rescued you from barrack wardening at Uxbridge," Jamie went on, "is expected to become Assistant Commandant at Cranwell on promotion to Air Commodore. Grunt Gillespie whom you'll also remember from Chivenor is my own Station Commander here at Binbrook."

"All these are routine happy developments, only to be expected in each case," Carl replied, "but what is the bad news?"

"Brace yourself for it, Carl," Jamie responded. "Peter Lascelles is dead."

"I can't believe it. What on earth happened?" Carl interjected shocked and saddened.

"You know he quit the Service," Jamie explained. "Lizzie was financially very ambitious and wanted much more than Peter could possibly provide in the Air Force."

"That much I know, Jamie," Carl answered. "I think she was fearful that they would end up as her father had – of modest means and modest achievements, although I think she underrated Peter's capabilities."

"Anyway, he promised her that he could earn a lot more as an Airline Pilot," Jamie continued, "so he took himself to Cass College by the Tower of London to study for his Air Transport Pilot's Licence. They rented a fine flat in Kensington at vast expense, but no money was coming in. He could not stand the course – all useless theory about abstruse navigation, the technicalities of radio and radar, performance data and a host of subjects you would never use. All his Air Force flying experience counted as nothing.

"Lizzie became more and more critical running him down incessantly, moaning on about his failure and useless inability to provide the standard of living her friends' husbands did. When was he actually going to get that proper job he promised, she nagged. He was just a perpetual student and so on. Peter was devastated to find his wife was no longer even his friend. One day she just walked out with the child; must have had a lover no doubt. Peter sought the only solace he knew. He immediately returned to flying."

"Not back in the Air Force surely or did he go into the Fleet Air Arm?" Carl inquired.

"No he joined the Tiger Club at Redhill founded by some ex-Auxiliaries when their squadrons were disbanded. He had found that if you displayed their aircraft at shows you got free flying not only on the day but for the practices, too. He flew all sorts of types – Stampes, Betas, Zlins, Tiger Moths of course and the fabulous Pitts Special the most glorious aerobatic biplane ever produced. He became well known around the display circuit.

"When some ex Naval pilots asked if he would join their Pitts Special formation team sponsored by a cigarette company he could not resist."

"Not surprising. I wish I'd thought of that at Uxbridge," Carl observed.

"The aircraft is a delight," Jamie went on. "Peter even got a good salary.

"The last time Peter phoned us he said that although he enjoyed the team and loved flying the Pitts he still hankered after the Air Force and had approached to be accepted back even if it meant going down to Flying Officer again. He hoped to be sent to Manby to refresh and to be able to visit us."

"What happened then did he have a collision on his final civilian display or what?" Carl asked.

"The next thing, we saw was the black headline in the Daily Mail 'Aerobatic Ace Killed in Flight Test'. I still remember the wording of the article beneath. 'Experienced former RAF Jet Pilot Peter Lascelles was killed yesterday testing a new French display aeroplane. Mr Lascelles who was separated from his wife Elizabeth was killed instantly when his high performance monoplane lost a wing pulling out of a stunt manoeuvre in practice at Thame Airfield for next week's Battle of Britain displays. His next of kin have been informed.'"

Although it seemed ages since Carl had seen Peter and Lizzie, he felt extraordinarily bereft. They had been a glamorous couple and theirs was the earliest romance of his Cranwell days. Lizzie's association with Germany had gone back a long way as had his own. Peter was in his element at Laarbruch and when Carl was at Rheindahlen it was always reassuring to have real friends nearby. He could not lightly discuss Peter's death as he so often had the almost routine expurgation of so many familiar names from the Air Force List over the years.

Carl returned to the Mess at Manby in a more sombre mood than any he had experienced since the drowning of dear Angela in the forest swimming pool near Brilon. The questions came flooding in. Why had Peter allowed Lizzie to bully him out of the Air Force? Why had he not stuck with his studies for an Airline Pilot's Licence and got a secure co-pilot's job with an airline like so many who had left the Air Force for more money? What demon lured him into the Tiger Club – the only flying club, which specialised in air displays and then into the Pitts Special formation aerobatic team, the most spectacular and dangerous activity in civil aviation apart from competition aerobatics?

Obviously Peter realised that the thrill of pleasing airshow crowds could not last for ever otherwise he would not have applied to rejoin the Service. Why did he test the aerobatic qualities of an untried French aeroplane when he could have been safely back in his second home the Air Force and happily established at Manby refreshing among friends? Did Peter wish to prove to himself and to his estranged Lizzie that although he did not bring home much money his nerve to face down danger was undiminished?

If Manby was fun Carl's return to the Central Flying School at Little Rissington was even more delightful. The CFS was no more than an hour and a half's drive from Harefield. If he got fed up with the Mess he could spend the night at home midweek. As a special case en route to an individual posting to Risalpur, already an A2 QFI with over a thousand instructional hours in his logbook and the purple and white diagonally striped ribbon of the DFC on his chest, Carl was treated with a respect seldom accorded even to senior officers by the instructional staff on the waterfront of the CFS. Although he had not given basic instruction hitherto Carl found that his time on Chipmunks providing air experience to cadets had endued him with the sympathetic frame of mind to do his job well.

What made Rissington even better than Manby was not solely its proximity to Harefield and Heidi. It was the presence of Mark Driscoll at CFS. As an ex-member of the pioneering Yellowjacks Gnat formation team at Valley Mark had been one of the founders of the Red Arrows when he was sent to instruct would be Gnat QFIs at Kemble. He welcomed Carl's arrival at Rissington warmly.

Mark's irrepressible charm was wasted at the Mess bar of Little Rissington or in the crew room at Kemble. His ebullient personality was at its most delightful on his indefatigable girl seeking expeditions with Carl round the pubs of Bourton on the Water, Moreton in Marsh, Tetbury, Cirencester and Cheltenham. If Mark was the perfect leader, Carl was the ideal wingman for him on such seduction sorties.

Mark and Carl would return from flying and plan the evening's entertainment over tea in the Mess anteroom. Mark's loyalty to Hazel was unquestionable. He was with her unfailingly every weekend that the Arrows were not displaying but he simply loved the company of attractive, sensitive, intelligent women and they reciprocated warming spontaneously to his solicitous attentions.

Each expedition was different; each encounter exciting. For Carl the thrill of the chase in Mark's irrepressible company was intoxicating. Had Heidi known of these evening encounters in local pubs she need not have worried, not just because Mark logged up all the conquests but because their joint excursions were in transient search of the twinkling eye, the ready smile, the dimpled cheek, the silky hair and soothing voice of God's female creation which in more mundane company than Mark's went all too unappreciated.

The Cotswold idyll lasted several weeks but Carl always knew it could not go on for long. The exercises of his flying syllabus were steadily chinagraphed from the programme board. There were few unscheduled trips to interrupt his progress towards re-qualification, although he managed to wangle a cross country to St Mawgan to Maritime Farquie and a couple of air tests. His special treat was a ride with the CFS' own Jet Provost formation aerobatic team the Red Pelicans. This flight made Carl comprehend even more clearly the daily demands of Mark's role on the Red Arrows, the total trust in the reliability of team mates required and the lethal consequences of any error.

Towards the end of October Carl's Final Handling Test loomed. He did one more 'mutual' sortie instructing another experienced retread a Fleet Air Arm Lieutenant Commander Dusty Willcox, who had done his first instructional tour on Piston Provosts before becoming Senior Pilot of the embarked 801 Squadron on Scimitars. He had the merit of making deliberate mistakes, which Carl had to diagnose and rectify.

"For someone who's been away from serious flying let alone instructing for so long Carl that was pretty impressive," Willcox remarked as they walked across the pan to claim a well earned post flight coffee. "I even think you're good enough to operate from a pitching deck on a wet and windy night."

"Thanks for the compliment Willco," Carl responded, "I was almost thinking you'd be good enough yourself to be my wingman on an operation over the Radfan."

"I don't think extravagant compliments will get us through the Chief Instructor's FHT," Willcox commented.

"I agree," said Carl. "He's a stickler for a meticulous pre-flight briefing and obsessed with teaching recoveries from stalling in a manoeuvre."

"Not surprising," Willcox answered, "he trained on Balliols and found the technique essential from an early age to keep him alive."

When Carl and Willcox entered the crew room it was clear that something was wrong. The mood was grim. Their jocular banter seemed out of place and they fell silent. "Don't you two know what's happened?" a CFS trapper inquired over the top of the Air Pictorial magazine he pretended to peruse.

"How could we we've been airborne," Carl replied.

"The Red Arrows have had a collision at Kemble. Two killed. Mark Driscoll and a new boy called Doyle."

"I just can't believe it," Carl responded, "Mark was the total professional, the steadiest and most accurate pilot I've ever flown with."

"He may have been, but it didn't do him much good," the trapper observed coldly.

"How on earth did it happen?" Carl asked.

"Their opposition barrel roll went wrong apparently. Doyle got off line and clipped Mark's starboard wing inverted and that was it."

The Squadron Commander came through from his office and joined the crew room inquest. "You knew Mark better than any of us, Carl," he declared. "The Commandant and I would be grateful if you could drive down to Stilton near Peterborough where I gather he lived with his girlfriend Hazel. Could you break the news to her please?"

"Of course, sir, but only if I can have moral support," Carl demanded.

"I'll come with you," Willcox announced. "I've had a lot of practice in this in the Fleet Air Arm."

Dusty Willcox whose real name was George and Carl set off at once for Peterborough determined to get to Stilton before dark if possible. The autumn evenings were drawing in and they did not want Hazel to see or hear any news report of the Arrows' awful accident before they arrived. Carl flogged his faithful Volkswagen Beetle mercilessly with his foot on the floor virtually the whole way.

Inevitably the conversation turned to Mark. "What were the happiest moments of your time together, Carl?" Willcox inquired.

"There were so many, George," Carl replied. "It is hard to do him justice. At Valley when he took me in a Gnat through the aerobatic routine of the Yellowjacks including the opposition barrel roll, which seems to have done for him at Kemble. It was an unforgettable trip."

"Nothing since?" Willcox asked.

"Our time together on the Squadron at Khormaksar was very special. He and Moxon maintained a superlative double act leading tirelessly by example which inspired all of us. Then most recently here at Rissington, of course. We just had such super fun pub crawling and girl chasing. It was all totally light hearted and enchanting."

"Have you met Hazel?" George Willcox persisted.

"No, but from Mark's description and from what others say she seems to be quite a lady. She's been married before, but without children and is living well off her financier ex-husband's maintenance. The cottage was their weekend retreat, which she got out of the settlement when they split up. The other one who is going to be devastated is Mark's daughter. He doted on her and she adored him. She lives with her mother somewhere in East Anglia."

When George Willcox and Carl arrived at Stilton they faced the challenge of finding Hazel's home. Laburnum Cottage could have been anywhere so they called at the village Post Office for a description and directions. "It is a small two storey stone house with magnificent pink roses climbing up the trellis on the front wall. It's three away from the pub in this direction. You can't miss it," the postmistress explained. "Are you friends of Mark Driscoll by any chance?" She asked.

"You could certainly say that," Carl replied cautiously. "Thank you for your help. We must be on our way."

The little house was unmistakable and when they arrived Hazel was in the garden doing some desultory weeding. "We're friends of Mark," George began.

"I thought as much. You don't look like the tradesmen who call round here," Hazel replied. She was smaller than Carl expected, slim, neat, undoubtedly pretty and probably in her early thirties. Her voice was soft and geographically unplaceable. "Have you come far? Would you like to come in? Can I offer you a cup of tea?" she inquired.

"That's very kind," George Willcox answered. "We'd love one. The traffic was very bad especially around Oxford," he commented postponing for a few more seconds the dread announcement.

"So you're from Little Rissington are you?" Hazel went on. "Do have a seat. I'll go through, make the tea and bring you some of my latest cake. It's a raspberry sponge with the raspberries from our own garden. Mark's a master fruit grower."

"I can well imagine it. Remember we were on the squadron at Khormaksar together. I've always admired his many talents," Carl replied.

Hazel emerged from the kitchen with a silver tray complete with teapot, cups and saucers, plates and a large sponge cake with a thick cream and raspberry mixture separating its two halves. "It's surprising to see Mark's friends and colleagues mid week," Hazel observed. "Is anything wrong?"

"I'm afraid it is. You'll have to be very strong, Hazel," Carl replied. "We have all suffered a terrible loss. Mark was killed in a collision at Kemble this morning. You have lost the most wonderful man. We have lost the best of friends whom we admired more than I can express. It could not be worse."

There was no wail of grief from Hazel, no anguished cries or uncontrollable tears. Carl and George were almost shocked by the apparent calm of her outwardly unemotional reaction. "I knew it had to happen. I always expected this moment. Mark was too good to last. It was only a matter of time," Hazel mumbled hardly pausing for breath. "We were too happy. It was an unreal interlude. Life is never so wonderful. I tried to persuade him to stick to ordinary instructing, but he always replied that The Arrows were the pinnacle of his flying career and that for every member of the team there were a hundred other pilots who would like to take his place. He could not and would not let his Yellowjacks experience to go waste. He felt he had so much to offer."

"He most certainly did and it is the cruellest fate which took him away from us. It wasn't his fault. That much is clear." Carl explained. "Mark was bringing on a recently joined member of the team and training him up for the Arrows' famous opposition pair act. The new boy made a mistake, got out of line and hit Mark's wing at very low level. It was all over in a millisecond. Mark would not have suffered. We are so sorry Hazel. All of us at Rissington and Kemble offer our deepest condolences from the Commandant of CFS and all on the waterfront down to the men on the flightline."

"We will stay here for a while. We don't want to leave you on your own. Is there anything we can do for you, Hazel?" George asked.

"Don't worry I'll ring my parents," she answered. "They're living at Cambridge, not so far away. They're elderly but they can drive over to come and get me. I don't think I could face living here for a while. The memories would hurt too much."

"We understand. We are in no hurry to get on our way," George replied.

CHAPTER 32

Once requalified as an A2 flying instructor this time on the Jet Provost Carl's posting to Pakistan was almost instantaneous. He only had a long weekend at home before departure. Max was too young to realise what was happening but Heidi was particularly sad that Carl would be away for Christmas and was determined to celebrate it in Germany with her family.

She had acquired a part time job at the Goethe Institute in London giving German conversation classes. Heidi assured Carl she would be too busy to be lonely. "When you get back home for summer leave next year, my love, you'll find I've saved a lot of money to give us a really good holiday for once, something all my friends enjoy but we somehow have had too little time for," she asserted.

Neither Heidi nor Carl were good at fond lingering farewells at airports. "They only postpone and intensify the pain of separation," he insisted as she dropped him off at the departure gate at Heathrow.

Carl entered his new world almost before he left England. He joined a scrum of British Pakistanis and Azad Kashmiris mostly from Bradford, Birmingham and the Pennine textile towns by their accents jostling to be checked in first. Their baggage was voluminous, unconventionally shaped and haphazardly strewn about them. Children milled around and the incessant urgent chatter of Urdu conversation told of their excitement to be returning to Punjabi family roots in Rawalpindi, Jhelum and Campbellpur or to Kashmiri Mirpur by the Mangla Dam.

Carl with his first class ticket by courtesy of the Pakistan Air Force was privileged indeed. As soon as he revealed himself to the check-in staff of Pakistan International Airways he was treated as someone special and segregated far from the throng of returning immigrants.

A smart and deferential PIA ground attendant ushered him into the airline's VIP departure lounge. An exquisitely groomed and uniformed young Pakistani lady relieved him with deliberate courtesy of his passport and ticket. "I will see you to your seat, sir, when the flight is called. Just make yourself comfortable. There's a tray of special Pakistani sweets on the table, sir; a real delicacy if I may say so, just flown in from Karachi. Can I offer you a Jasmine tea or a mango juice perhaps? If you'd like to catch up on the news there's a copy of the Pakistani Times here and an English edition of the Daily Jang."

Flying first class in the PIA Boeing 707 was luxurious. The heavily laden aircraft took off into the autumnal gloom and bored up through the cumulus packed wall of an approaching front with its swept wings flexing vigorously in the turbulence like those of a giant heron. Once on top Carl admired the fiery sunset above the unbroken cloudscape below. He contentedly put his seat back and opened the classic book on the Pathans by Sir Olaf Caroe the last British Governor of the North West Frontier Province he had brought to keep him company on his journey and to speed up his intellectual acclimatisation to his future life at Risalpur.

Somewhere over the Alps Carl had his dinner – daintily cut cubes of chicken tikka with pilau rice and a herb laden yogurt, followed by Kulfi all washed down with several glasses of cold Murree beer. On arrival at Ankara to refuel in the depth of a hot Anatolian night a special vehicle whisked him away to a cool VIP lounge. Over the Hindu Kush breakfast was served. As dawn broke the big bird touched down at Rawalpindi/Islamabad airport.

At the open forward door Carl gazed out across the plain to the pink snow capped mountains behind. Innumerable crows seemed to be squawking. The scent of the sub continent wafted into his nostrils – an indefinable but emotive smell, which is unique to South Asia but whose replicas in other lands would in future years carry him back to this early morning in Rawalpindi when his great Pakistani adventure began.

As at Ankara a special vehicle appeared at the foot of the front door of the aeroplane. Its blue uniformed driver sat rigidly to attention behind the wheel. A bewinged Flight Lieutenant with eagled cap badge came to a quivering salute despite their equal ranks as Carl descended the last steps of the ladder.

"Flight Lieutenant Higgins, sir. Flight Lieutenant Shahid Malik at your service. Welcome to Pakistan, sir. Welcome to the Pakistan Air Force your new home. Come with me, sir. I'll get you through the formalities in next to no time. Meanwhile please relax here in the VIP lounge. What can I get you, sir?"

"Orange juice please Flight Lieutenant."

The furniture of exotic tropical wood was of the type universal in oriental VIP lounges. Wicker backed and bottomed chairs surrounded a gleaming mahogany table on which lay a collection of glossy magazines in Urdu together with the daily newspapers Dawn and Pakistan Times. The lamps were of the Arabian Nights variety, the carpets from the north-west Frontier and Afghanistan. A brass punkah fan rotated lazily overhead. A large portrait of the gaunt faced Father of the Nation Mohammed Ali Jinnah covered one wall matched by a photograph of the uniformed be-medalled President, General Yahya Khan opposite.

Carl hardly had time to finish his orange juice before Shahid Malik was back proudly handing him his passport. "Inbound formalities complete, sir. Your baggage is already in the vehicle outside. Our first call is at the Intercontinental Hotel where I suggest you can have a shower, a second breakfast and some rest. After lunch you have an appointment with the Air Adviser at the British High Commission. Then you can relax a bit more as your duties proper will begin tomorrow. I'll collect you at the Intercon at 0630 hours. You are due to report to the Commandant of the Air Academy Air Commodore Ahmed in Risalpur at 1730 hours."

"Did you say Air Commodore Ahmed, the late Yousuf Ahmed's father?" Carl inquired in surprise.

"You know the famous Shahid I Milat – martyr of the nation, may God's mercy rest upon his soul? One of the bravest fighter pilots Pakistan ever produced," Malik replied.

"Most certainly I did Flight Lieutenant. He and I trained together at Cranwell. I had the privilege, too, in those days to be introduced to his distinguished father," Carl explained.

"It seems that our Air Force has chosen well in inviting a true friend of Pakistan to instruct our young cadets," Malik went on. "I know that from one of Yousuf's former comrades they will receive the best training, sir. I have noticed the medals on your chest. I imagine you have flown many times in action."

"Indeed so, on Hunters against dissident Tribesmen in South Arabia," Carl responded. "They came under evil influences from abroad and chose the way of violence."

"I see you will soon understand Pakistan well," Malik answered. "Our Air Force has sometimes to use force to control miscreant elements in the tribal areas along the Frontier. We learned such methods from you before the Second World War. Air Control you called it and very effective it was, too; much better than the old-fashioned way of sending a punitive Army column, which was ignored by the miscreants as soon as it left their territory. With retribution from the Air Force they never know when their punishment is coming and cause the authorities much less trouble. The Governors of Baluchistan and North West Frontier Province are regularly sending messages of congratulations to our squadrons following such missions."

After a refreshing shower and substantial second breakfast Carl changed into uniform and went down to the entrance hall where the Pakistan Air Force driver was waiting for him. They soon left the bustling traffic of Rawalpindi replete with its jostling rickshaws, flowerily painted buses with ample racks on top for ramshackle possessions or precariously perched passengers, wobbly bicyclists and suicidally absent-minded pedestrians darting in and out.

Heading towards the distant mountains the broad newly built boulevards of Islamabad began to open up before them. Very soon they arrived at the iron gates of the British High Commission flanked on either side by two khaki clad, black beretted, hobnail booted, lathi wielding policemen with heavy side arms at their leather belted waists. A civilian security man scurried up to Carl's vehicle. The driver presented his identity card as did Carl. They were swiftly admitted and the guard ushered Carl to the reception desk.

The girl in attendance put away her woman's magazine, set aside her coffee and tried to appear bright and welcoming. "Flight Lieutenant Higgins I presume," she began. "The Air Adviser Group Captain Greenway is expecting you. I'll take you to his office." The well intentioned receptionist the bloom of whose youth was fading from too much boring duty in unpleasant climates, maintained a welcoming chatter.

"I hope you had a good flight, sir," she went on. "Were you met at the airport? Did they look after your baggage properly? It's so easily lost here. Are you comfortably installed in your hotel?"

"Everything's fine," Carl replied. As they mounted the stairs they passed stereotyped pictures of Britain. Carl spotted photographs of the Palace of Westminster, Chatsworth House, Lindisfarne, the Forth Bridge and Caernarvon Castle. One floor up was the door to the British Council offices with a Royal Shakespeare Company poster on it advertising a performance of MacBeth.

Soon they arrived at The Defence Section with its heavy steel double locked door at which they rang for admission. Another British girl not dissimilar to the receptionist in age and attitude let them in and took Carl straight to the ample office of the Defence Adviser. There he was greeted by a tall, greying, slightly stooped but rather distinguished looking Group Captain whose face was vaguely familiar from some posting in Carl's early days in the Service.

"Welcome to Pakistan, Higgins and welcome to the British High Commission," he declared. "I head the team of Service Advisers here. I have Squadron Leader Robert McNeil to help me specifically on the air side. You will report directly to him although nominally you are of course on the staff of the Pakistan Air Force Academy like all the other QFIs there. Your predecessor Flight Lieutenant Parker had many virtues. He was a brilliant instructor and the Pakistanis worshipped him but he didn't always keep us fully in touch with what was going on in the Pakistan

Air Force. I am told that you already know the Commandant at Risalpur Air Commodore Ahmed which can only help."

"It's very good of you to take so much personal trouble with me, sir," Carl replied. "I imagined that I would go straight to the Academy probably on the next PIA domestic flight up to Peshawar. Instead the Pakistanis install me overnight in the best hotel in town and you give me of your time to brief and welcome me."

"More than that," the Group Captain interjected. "You are going to make a courtesy call on the Ambassador and another colleague will fill you in on the strategic environment in which you'll be operating here."

Group Captain Greenway picked up the telephone and made a brief call. "My Deputy Air Advisor Squadron Leader McNeil is to join us in five minutes and I've also asked Colin Richards who is our resident expert on all things subcontinental to sit in as well. He'll put you in the broader picture," he explained.

While they waited for the other two to arrive Carl inquired about the A37. "What's it like as a trainer?" he asked. "Have you had a trip in the aircraft yet, sir?"

"No I haven't, more's the pity. I've had a ride in a Sabre and sat in a MIG 19 simulator but a flight on the A37 has eluded me so far. I'm told that it's not dissimilar to the Jet Provost – side by side seating, modest performance and forgiving for the student. Like the Strikemaster version of the Jet Provost it can also pack quite a punch if armed. As with the Strikemaster in Oman the Pakistanis load the Cessna A37 with bombs and rockets and then it becomes a useful counterinsurgency aircraft – ideal for use on the Frontier. You are advised to avoid those activities yourself, Carl. However, if such goings on do occur in the tribal areas we are of course always keen to learn about them."

Carl was impressed by Bob McNeil, an exceedingly young, tanned and fit looking Navigator with an Air Force Cross, which he had won with his pilot for nursing their burning Javelin back to base at Leeming after an explosive engine failure over the North Sea on a particularly wet and windy night. He clearly from his appearance was not spending too much time in the office now.

Colin Richards supposedly the Trade Counsellor was of medium height, nondescript of features, softly spoken and seemingly unemotional. "You should know Flight Lieutenant Higgins," he began, "that you have been posted to one of the most unstable parts of the world. In less than a quarter of a century since its independence Pakistan has been involved in two bloody wars against its larger neighbour India. It is my assessment that before that quarter of a century is reached it will be involved in another. Your role will therefore be sensitive as the effectiveness of the Pakistan Air Force is Pakistan's counterweight to India's military superiority in numbers and strategic depth."

Carl was impressed by Richards' calm delivery and cool judgement. He listened intently to his clear analysis. "Pakistan is more divided than ever," Richards went on, "not just geographically but now politically also. The recent elections saw Zulfikhar Ali Bhutto's Pakistan People's Party sweep the board in West Pakistan whilst Sheikh Mujibur Rahman's Awami League did the same in East Pakistan. The only cement which keeps the disparate halves of the country together is the Army but it is largely recruited in West Pakistan whose martial traditionalists have always despised the Bengalis as soft and untrustworthy. The President General Yahya Khan is riding two mustangs, which are beginning to canter in different directions."

"What's there about the situation on the ground or more pertinently in the air to affect me?" Carl interjected.

"In East Pakistan a low level guerrilla campaign has begun with a local armed secessionist movement called the Mukti Bahini attacking national targets with bombs and sniping. We suspect it is receiving clandestine support from India across the border," Richards responded. "Meanwhile the Indian Prime Minister is stepping up the bellicose rhetoric against Pakistan. For their part the Pakistanis are increasing the pressure on Indian occupied Kashmir with a heightened wave of violence by Mujahedeen terrorists whom we believe are trained and supplied by Pakistan."

"Where do I come into all of this?" Carl inquired again.

"In three ways," Richards replied. "First we want you to note any sign whatever you may detect visually, by word of mouth or documentation of practical Pakistani backing for Mujahedeen violence in Indian Kashmir. Secondly, please keep us informed of the tempo and orientation of the flying training programme at Risalpur. If the Pakistanis expect war to break out shortly they will step up their flying schedule substantially. Thirdly although the Air Academy's A37s could not be transferred to East Pakistan where the country's air defences would be overwhelmed early on in the event of war, these aeroplanes if armed could be a useful adjunct to a Pakistan sponsored uprising across the ceasefire line in Kashmir. If you observe any preparation of your aircraft or fellow instructors for such operations we will want to hear about it at once."

"It would seem that I am to be a bit more than a simple flying instructor," Carl responded. "I think I deserve special duties pay."

"You must be joking, Higgins," Greenway interrupted.

"Indeed I am, sir. I presume these responsibilities come with being a General Duties Officer on flying pay with an overseas supplement."

"Precisely so," the Group Captain replied. "However, if you submit good reports to Bob McNeil you will work your passage back to official favour and who knows a Flight Commander's job on a frontline squadron or a place at Staff College. Normally Bob will receive you here at the High Commission but occasionally you may have to meet him in the field. If you can wangle yourself visits to operational squadrons through Air Commodore Ahmed and the friends you'll make on the instructing staff we'd be much obliged especially if you can organise it for Bob to come along, too."

Because the timing was tight for Carl's meeting with the Commandant Shahid Malik decided that they should fly up to Peshawar rather than battle towards the Frontier up the Great Trunk Road through the mass of meandering oxcarts and the gaudy busses. When they arrived back at Islamabad airport the twin turboprops of the PIA Fokker Friendship were already running and the driver delivered them directly to the still open rear door. Two reserved places were awaiting them up in front in First Class.

Carl had already noticed that the old adage whereby the British were said to have bequeathed on partition democracy to India and a military tradition of efficiency and privilege to Pakistan seemed to be broadly correct. He had not enjoyed such respectful attention since his days as Swallowfield's ADC. The stewardess fussed around and favoured him shamelessly all the way to Peshawar.

"Peshawar must surely be one of the most magnificent airports in the world," Carl declared enthusiastically on arrival. The air was crisp, cool and clear not unlike Berlin's in autumn. In the distance were snow capped mountains, the notorious tribal areas and the Afghan border. A Pakistan Air Force jeep was at the rear steps. The aquiline featured weather beaten Pathan driver met them with a fearsome salute as they descended. Arrival at Risalpur's main gate was an impressive experience. A Hawker Tempest fighter from the Pakistan Air Force's earliest days bestrode a plinth opposite the gatehouse where the guards stamped powerfully to attention and delivered more quivering salutes as the jeep passed.

The layout of the base transported Carl back to the Royal Air Force of the 1930s. The kerbstones were individually painted an alternate black and white. Small groups of Flight Cadets with blancoed white Cranwell style capbands marched proudly and purposefully around. The fine Officers' Mess boasted a meticulously weeded garden, a croquet lawn and several tennis courts.

Clubs and comfortable verandahed bungalows for the families, spacious well laid out cantonments and impressive Officers' Messes ensured that successive generations of Pakistani officers also enjoyed a privileged life apart which their British predecessors had taken for granted. The bearer at reception refused to allow Carl to carry so much as his briefcase and took him to one of the finer senior officer's suites in the Mess with its own sitting room and balcony overlooking the airfield.

At the appointed hour Shahid Malik ushered Carl into the Commandant's offices. His Personal Staff Officer a moustachioed lean looking and correct Squadron Leader Akram Khan opened the conversation. "Are you keen on sport, Flight Lieutenant Higgins?" he inquired. "The Mess has a popular squash ladder and your predecessor Flight Lieutenant Parker was one from the top when he was so tragically killed. We also have instructors' teams for hockey and cricket."

"I've rather let my cricketing and squash skills lapse, sir," Carl replied, "and I haven't played hockey."

"Never too late to learn," the Squadron Leader observed.

A bell rang on the PSO's desk. "The ADC Flight Lieutenant Wasim Ali will take you through now to meet the Commandant," the PSO declared.

On Carl's entry the familiar friendly Air Commodore Ahmed advanced to greet him arm extended. "My dear Carl," he began. "How happy I am to be able to welcome you. When we so sadly lost Parker I remembered that Yousuf had said you were one of his most special friends at Cranwell.

"I got straight onto the High Commission and insisted that Parker's successor had to be you. I was informed that you were not even flying any more, so I said 'just get him up to speed and send him out here pronto. The Air Academy can wait for the right British Officer as long as it takes. Carl Higgins is my man.'"

"I am most honoured, sir," Carl replied genuinely affected by Ahmed's warmth. "It is such a privilege to serve here and under your command. It is the culmination of all I have done before. Your brave son Yousuf, God have mercy on his soul, was a fine example to us all, a true inspiration. I shall try to be worthy of his memory. Six long years after his loss I can only express my admiration for all Yousuf achieved and condolences to you, sir, and the family."

"It was the will of Allah. God the most holy, most merciful required his soul," the Air Commodore answered. "The martyrdom of Yousuf and so many of his friends saved our country. I am moved that you should remember him so vividly and with such affection. You must join the Begum and our family for dinner at the residence as soon as you have settled in."

Settling in for Carl was easy. His flying pupils were respectful and ultra keen. Converting to the Cessna A37 was a formality. His Squadron Commander Squadron Leader Mohammed Shah let Carl fly the aeroplane from start up to shut down and insisted on Carl's demonstrating low level aerobatics, which he duly performed in a smooth five minute sequence up a wadi North of base never descending below four hundred feet. "Very good Carl, safe and stylish," the Squadron Commander commented. "Here we set a minimum threshold of two hundred feet. I have control." Carl was impressed by his boss's panache and mastery of rare manoeuvres like a rolling circle and eye popping outside loop.

"We need to be able to operate confidently at ultra low level," Mohammed Shah explained. "Contour hugging is the best way to stay alive when we perform anti miscreant missions in the tribal areas."

"Is that often?" Carl inquired disingenuously.

"If I told you I would be revealing state secrets, but if you see some of our aircraft camouflaged you'll know there's a flap on," the Squadron Leader replied.

"When I do I'll ask if I can come, too," Carl replied. "Remember, sir, it's a familiar scene to me from Aden days."

After a fortnight of nonstop flying Squadron Leader Mohammed Shah summoned Carl to his office. "The reports on your instructing Carl have evidently impressed the Commandant. The Air Commodore invites you to dine at the Residence tomorrow night. Black tie and Mess kit required." Carl's heart leapt. What would he learn of Yasmin? Would she even miraculously be present? "Your friend Shahid Malik will drive you there," the Squadron Leader continued. "I am informed that the American Air Attaché and the South Asian Representative for Cessna Aircraft with their wives and the Governor of North West Frontier Province are also invited together with my wife and myself. It should be a very special occasion."

The avenue to the fine Commandant's residence was lined with fiery pine torches. Lofty turbaned retainers flanked the entrance. Through the open double doorway Carl spotted a welcoming group of four. An attendant parked Shahid Malik's car. As he and Carl mounted the steps Carl noticed the unmistakable, thrilling, slender and willowy figure of Yasmin beside a hugely imposing bearded man clearly of considerable authority on the left of Begum Ahmed.

The Commandant unwittingly eased Carl's potential embarrassment. "Carl my friend," he began, "I want to introduce you to my son-in-law Sardar Mohammed Asif Wasim Akbar Khan. He is Chief Secretary to the Governor of Baluchistan. Yasmin you will remember from our family visits to Cranwell and receptions at the High Commission."

"A pleasure to meet you both," Carl replied with studied calm politely shaking Sardar Mohammed Khan's hand and trying not to catch Yasmin's eye. However, he could not fail to observe her ruby and diamond necklace and gold emerald studded bracelets. Her fearsome looking bearded husband was evidently a man of some substance and no doubt a powerful figure in Baluchistan.

Carl had a place of honour at the magnificent dinner. On his left was the wife of the Governor of North West Frontier Province and on his right Sardar Mohammed Akbar Khan. Directly opposite him sat Yasmin with his Squadron Commander Mohammed Shah beside her. Shahid Malik was at the end of the table.

"Do you know why your instructor friend is here?" asked the formidable bearded Akbar Khan turning from the American Air Attaché's wife to Carl.

"I presume because the Commandant felt that I'd be more at ease if I had one of my fellow QFIs with me," Carl answered.

"Nothing to do with that," Sardar explained. "His father is Chief Martial Law Administrator in East Pakistan and is one of President Yahya Khan's closest allies. They both served in the same battalion in Burma at the end of the war and go back a long way together. Have you been to East Pakistan by any chance?"

"Actually yes, but a very long time ago. I spent some years in Pakistan as a boy. My father worked in the High Commission when it was still in Karachi," Carl replied. "We stayed in Sylhet with friends of Papa's for one of his leaves. They were among the last British tea planters left. I still remember the airfield there from which they used to fly supplies to China over the hump in World War Two. The planter's bungalow was light and airy with huge verandas overlooking beautiful tea gardens in rolling hills."

"Well that's what the Indians want to take from us, but we're not going to let them. They've got their eyes on the East Pakistan jute mills and the hard woods of the hill tracts behind Chittagong as well. Partition is still less than a generation ago and although Mountbatten or rather his wife Edwina fixed it for Nehru in India's favour they're still not reconciled to it," the Sardar argued forcefully.

At that point Yasmin leaned across the table gently reproaching her husband. "Remember our guest's not a politician my dear. These are our preoccupations, not his. I'm sure that just as Yousuf was he, too, must be mad about flying and good at it as well. Otherwise why would they send him here? Maybe the Governor will give us some political insights in his after dinner speech."

"Perhaps I do concentrate rather excessively on my flying, almost to the exclusion of everything else," Carl admitted. "In Aden I never tried to understand the political loyalties or nationalist affiliations of the various tribes. In Germany it was just so easy. One side of the wall were the good guys; the other side the bad. Here I expect it's much more complicated but my Squadron Commander on your wife's right has already shown me how well your Air Force can fly. I've seldom sat in on such an impressive display of low level aerobatics as his – low enough to knock a Pashtun miscreant's head off. That's a tactic I've seen used for real in Aden and it worked."

"I overheard that," Yasmin interjected. "I remember what Yousuf used to call it – shooting a line. You tell him, Akbar, about Baluchistan. I bet he's never been there and unless you have you can never believe how wild and exciting it is."

"I'm sure it's a dangerous place. I remember reading that there was a big earthquake in Quetta in the mid 1930s with thousands killed, but apart from that I know nothing," Carl admitted.

"You must come and stay with us. There's a lot to show you," the Sardar suggested. Carl felt a silky shalwar clad leg interpose itself boldly between his own. The surgings of desire were welling up inside him and he struggled to reply calmly.

"That would be very nice, sir, although I don't quite see how I would have the time. My boss quite rightly works me hard and if international tension is rising as you inferred, the pressure to push the Flight Cadets through more quickly will surely grow."

"I'm flattered but don't call me sir. I'm not the Governor of Baluchistan. I only work for him. However, I can tell you he does have his own official aeroplane, a Golden Eagle at his disposal. I'll get the Cessna man to describe it to you after dinner. My wife's father could authorise you to do a study visit to the Staff College at Quetta. Perhaps it would fire your desire to go to Staff College when you leave

Pakistan." Carl's desire was fired up enough already and leaving Pakistan was not on his mind. Even the prospect of mid tour leave at home had lost its appeal.

Yasmin's shalwar strokes to his calves and ankles intensified. Carl feared that her exciting ministrations would make his voice noticeably tremulous so he listened intently to Squadron Leader Mohammed Shah who was holding forth indiscreetly to Begum Ahmed. "We won't make the mistakes of '65 this time," he declared. "More tank battles in the Rann of Kutch will never get us anywhere. We have to tie them down in East Pakistan, suck the Indians in. Remember the Biharis are loyal. As Urdu speaking refugees the majority Bengalis always treated them as second class citizens. The Biharis are the people we should mobilise to counter the Mukti Bahini."

Begum Ahmed looked distant but still the Squadron Leader went on. "It's in the West where we can win decisively and rectify the injustices of partition once and for all. The Radcliffe plebiscite was always a fixed job. Our Kashmiri brothers across the ceasefire line are longing to be freed from Hindu rule. What do you think, Yasmin? You're supposed to be the expert, the brains of the Foreign Ministry's South Asia department."

"You know Squadron Leader we seek only peaceful coexistence," she replied.

"I've heard that so many times before," Mohammed Shah insisted. "I expect they said the same to you, Carl, about the Warsaw Pact when you were in Germany," he asked provocatively. "Did you believe it then?"

"Europe is very different, sir," Carl responded cautiously fighting off the rising blushes from Yasmin's probing legwork. "In Europe the Russians knew that if they tried to reunite Germany by force they would have to contend with armed intervention to protect West Germany not just by the Americans but by the whole of NATO as well. Here as I see it you have the USA and China as friendly powers but can you imagine the US Navy intervening in the Bay of Bengal to defend East Pakistan or China sending an expeditionary force across the Karakorams to help you in Kashmir?"

"What about the Russians then?" Mohammed Shah went on. "I bet they're trying to stir up trouble in Afghanistan even as we speak. They've developed a special relationship with India and keep supplying the Indians with modern weapons at knock down prices. They've always wanted direct access to the warm waters of the Indian Ocean and to keep China at arm's length in Central Asia. Under Admiral Gorschkov the Soviet Navy is getting global reach remember."

"I would not know about that Squadron Leader," Yasmin interjected again. "Our friend Flight Lieutenant Higgins will believe we're getting a war psychosis. We just hope that the President will be able to resolve the regional tensions in Pakistan without any foreign interference. I'm sure our traditional friends like the UK understand our situation."

"As ever the perfect diplomat my dear," the Sardar observed. "You're right of course, we wouldn't want Carl Higgins to get the impression that our Air Force can't wait to get back into action against the Indians. Let's try and agree dates for his visit to Baluchistan before the evening ends. By the way do you shoot, Carl?" Akbar Khan inquired.

"Yes, but I haven't since Cranwell days."

"Don't worry my friend. We have thousands of sand grouse and partridges just waiting for your arrival. They'll help you get back into the swing of it."

The Governor of North West Frontier Province a small wiry Lieutenant General originally an infantryman in the Frontier Force did not deliver the political after dinner speech Yasmin had anticipated. He gave crisp military compliments about the Pakistan Air Force and Air Academy in particular before going on to describe development projects in various tribal areas along the frontier – the Khyber Agency, Swat, Dir and Waziristan.

When it was over the ladies withdrew leaving the men to converse on their own facilitated by the contents of a very un-Islamic bottle of whisky. Carl wondered if he could have the chance to see Yasmin again before her departure. However, his hopes were raised by Akbar Khan's taking him aside on their way through to the drawing room to offer him some dates for his promised long shooting weekend in Baluchistan. When they rejoined the ladies they went straight to Yasmin. "Carl's definitely going to come and shoot with us very soon," the Sardar declared.

"I am happy to hear it," Yasmin replied. "We've always loved entertaining at home and we haven't had anyone from England to stay before, Akbar. You'll be able to reminisce about your time at Sandhurst and to tell him about your posting to Oman with the Baluch Regiment. After all he's an old Arabia hand like you."

"How do you know that?"

"Papa told me that Higgins had served with distinction in Aden and that his operational record there was one of the reasons he was selected to succeed Flight Lieutenant Parker."

"I see."

"There's a big difference though between you," Yasmin continued. "When your father died, God have mercy on his soul, you left the Army to take over the estates. Higgins, however, is as Yousuf was. I can't see that anything would induce him to leave the Air Force voluntarily. It's his life."

"You're a remarkably swift judge of character, Yasmin my love," Akbar Khan observed.

"I have to be in my job. International relations are the product of the interaction of personalities just as much of economic or material forces."

"Clearly our Foreign Ministry is lucky to have such perceptive feminine intuition at its disposal," the Sardar concluded.

After dinner Carl sought out the representative of Cessna aircraft a square jawed rugged individual from Wichita Kansas George Lange by name who was deep in conversation with the uniformed American Air Attaché. "Can I introduce myself?" Carl began diffidently. "I'm Carl Higgins one of the flying instructors here. You might like to know how much I'm enjoying the A37; one of the best jet trainers I've ever flown."

"Glad to hear it Lieutenant. Call me George," Lange replied.

"Tell me about the Cessna 421 Golden Eagle, George," Carl went on. "I'm hoping to have a ride in one soon."

"You're lucky. With two powerful low revving Continental engines and sturdy construction it's a very comfortable six seater with tables for the passengers to work at. It can actually carry seven people in all including one on the lavatory. The handling is completely straightforward. You'll love it."

Carl noticed the Sardar and Yasmin at his elbow. "I could not help overhearing your remarks, Carl, to my friend George and his backing up of my judgement. I advised the Governor to invest in a Golden Eagle" he confided. "When we come and get you I'll make sure his personal pilot allows you to fly the aeroplane. You'll come, too, Yasmin, when we fly over to pick up Carl for the weekend. Do you think our life is safe in his hands?"

"From what Yousuf told me Cranwell training is the best there is," Yasmin replied. "Anyway judging by the DFC ribbon I see on his chest Carl Higgins has obviously flown with distinction and courage in the face of the enemy so I doubt if a transit flight in a Cessna 421 twin piston from Risalpur to Quetta should daunt him too much even with VIPs like us on board."

"I agree my dear," Akbar Khan concurred.

"I've mentioned the plan to Papa," Yasmin continued. "He thinks Carl's proposed visit to the Staff College and the suggestion he convert to the Golden Eagle en route are very good ideas. He believes Carl ought to get a telephone briefing from the Governor's Chief Pilot beforehand so I took the liberty of getting his phone numbers. Here they are."

To Carl's amazement she put a folded piece of paper into his hand and the Sardar wandered off in search of another whisky.

"The first number belongs to the pilot Mr Mumtaz Ali, the second is mine," Yasmin whispered. "It goes straight through to the kitchen, not the hall and study which have the line my husband uses. I've told him that the kitchen phone is only for my Ministry messages so no one else can use it for security reasons. He respects that argument and the cook has learned to co-operate fully. You can ring me at weekends but call me Haseena in case our conversation is tapped."

Carl's mouth went dry and his heart was thumping. "I can't wait to call you," he answered.

"Do please, but be careful. I don't want to be stoned to death just yet – not at least until we've done enough to make it worthwhile. I must get back to the other guests. I see Mama is looking this way."

Next day Carl rang Bob McNeil in the lunch hour from the Mess phone booth. "Squadron Leader McNeil, sir. Carl Higgins here," he began. "I think it's time we met. I've got fully into the Academy's flying routine and you could advise me about what's been going on in the Royal Air Force. I'm out of touch with developments in the Service back home and in the wider world."

"Good idea, Carl. It just so happens that I was planning a trip to the Frontier this coming weekend," McNeil replied. "I particularly want to go up the Khyber Pass and call at the old British border base at Landikotal. Before I do so why don't we meet in the UK consulate building in Peshawar at 10.00 hours on Saturday? That's the day after tomorrow. Can you make it?"

"More than delighted, sir. I'll be there."

Next day Carl sought out his boss Mohammed Shah. "Glad to see you, Carl. Your pupils are doing exceptionally well. What can I do for you?" he asked.

"Just a small favour, sir. I have a routine liaison meeting with the Deputy Air Advisor tomorrow morning in Peshawar. Can I borrow a jeep and driver from the motor transport section for the purpose?"

"No trouble. Delighted old boy. Only too happy to oblige so long as your students keep passing their check rides with flying colours."

The driver by some homing instinct found the British consulate building in a maze of side streets and waited patiently outside. Carl showed his pass and was admitted to the small compound by a grizzly Pathan retainer and mounted the rickety stairs. Bob McNeil was already at the deputy consul's desk with a buff coloured folder in front of him. "Welcome Carl. Have a seat. Fill me in on what's up."

"I think I've struck gold," Carl began. "I've met the Governor of NWFP and the Chief Secretary to the Governor of Baluchistan who has invited me up to Quetta. At the Commandant's dinner last night there was much wild talk by senior figures who should have known better of Pakistan's intended subversion and probable armed intervention in Indian occupied Kashmir. It's a plan I must find out much more about. Luckily I've been invited to Quetta to visit the Staff College. I'll stay with Sardar Akbar Khan and his wife for the long weekend. I hope to meet the Governor of Baluchistan. I trust my hosts may prove indiscreet."

"I'm not interested in the details of your social programme," Bob responded. "However, you have a big advantage over me. I'm sure your Pakistani colleagues, friends and acquaintances will often have unguarded conversations among themselves in Urdu, which you can overhear and understand. They'll not all know that you're fluent in the language. I wish I was. I'm working away at it hoping to reach colloquial standard in the civil service language exam. I don't think I've a hope of qualifying as an interpreter. What else was being talked about at the Commandant's dinner?"

"They seem to want to avoid the mistakes of '65 if war breaks out again, Bob," Carl replied. "They know they can't defeat the Indian Army in set piece battles in the West and recognise they'll be swept from the skies in the East. The Schwerpunkt – forgive my German jargon – of the Pakistanis is to be Kashmir involving the insertion of freedom fighters in support of a Muslim uprising in the state.

"In East Pakistan," Carl went on, "they are counting on backing from the Urdu speaking Bihari minority although I have my doubts that they can effectively offset the Mukti Bahini's activities. In my view East Pakistan is not reinforceable and indefensible in face of Indian control of the sea and air."

"I'm sure you're right Carl," McNeil interjected.

"I'm trying to be asked to East Pakistan," Carl continued, "before the whole grumbling volcano of the subcontinent blows. Shahid Malik one of my best friends and colleagues who was also at the dinner is the son of the Chief Martial Law administrator in Dacca. I'm working on him for an invitation."

"Try and enable me to come, too," Bob requested. "I'm due to call on our Deputy High Commission in the city but securing permission to get out and about to visit Pakistani units is very difficult, which reminds me, Carl, of something. Don't you know Sardar Akbar Khan's wife?"

Carl tried to show no surprise. "Of course I do. Yasmin came to her late brother Yousuf's passing out parade at Cranwell."

"I gather she's a rising star in the South Asia department of the Foreign Ministry. Did she express any views on this at all?" McNeil enquired.

"Indeed she did. She insisted that peaceful coexistence was the official policy of the Government and was concerned that the bellicose talk of the military men around the table might give me the wrong impression."

"Thanks, Carl. How thoughtful of her," McNeil replied. "I must be on my way to explore the Khyber now. I hope we can meet again soon after your visit to Baluchistan. When is it?"

"Next weekend, God willing."

"It will be time well spent," Bob McNeil continued. "The Provincial Governor General Hamid Alam is another member of President Yahya's inner circle. He was his Intelligence Chief until they predictably fell out over East Pakistan."

"Why so?" asked Carl.

"Alam believes Pakistan should be a loose federation and not a unitary state," McNeil explained. "He's a Punjabi and did an attachment with the Bengal Rifles in Chittagong in the late 1950s. Since then he's never had a high opinion of the reliability of the Bengalis. He feels that East Pakistan should have virtually total autonomy leaving the Central Government only responsible for the Eastern wing's defence and foreign affairs."

"Sounds wiser than most Punjabis to me," Carl replied.

"He is. Listen to him carefully. He may be rusticated to Baluchistan now but he still has important friends in Islamabad. He is said to be coming back into Presidential favour."

After their conversation Carl returned to the Mess at Risalpur. The current weekend offered him no entertainment. Drinking as a pastime did not exist. Apart from Shahid Malik Carl had no real friends among his instructor colleagues. Only one recourse offered solace and brief respite from the gnawing solitude. He would summon up his courage and ring Yasmin.

Carl made his way to the pokey little phone booth under the Mess stairs. He felt his blood pressure rise as he dialled the fateful numbers – first for conscience's sake that of the Governor's Pilot. No reply. Then Yasmin's. A warm familiar cultured lady's voice answered. "Hello. Who's speaking?"

"Haseena it's you. Is this a convenient time to phone?" Carl began timidly. "Is the cook there?"

"No she's in the vegetable garden at the moment and my husband is out shooting so this is a very convenient time."

"What a relief. I imagined you might have a houseparty or be away for the weekend or on some local errand with Akbar. I can't believe how lucky I am."

"The good fortune is mine," Yasmin replied. "You say you'll be spending a whole year at Risalpur. We owe it to Yousuf's memory to keep in touch. They were such happy days."

"Unforgettable. They marked me for life," Carl answered.

"I know how much my husband Akbar is looking forward to welcoming you here," Yasmin continued, "I'm trying to persuade him to organise an overnight shooting expedition with camping under the stars. We'll bring horses and camels for you to ride between drives. I expect you rode camels in Arabia."

As Yasmin spoke seductively down the line Carl's burgeoning desire intensified and his impatient expectation for the next weekend grew.

"We can't wait to come and get you," she continued. "I'll be a traditional Pakistani lady transformed into the picture of modernity in my elegant new tight fitting green flying suit. I've started flying lessons in the 421 and Akbar permits me such vain exhibitionism. I say a pupil pilot must at least look professional and he cannot disagree."

Carl would not have known what to reply. The excitement made him breathless. It was as if Yasmin anticipated his difficulty.

"Must close," she announced. "Here comes the Mali, our gardener carrying an armful of vegetables and the shooting party are due back at any moment. See you at the airfield very soon. Bring tough boots. Akbar will probably want you to walk up the partridges and the terrain is rugged. He'll organise beaters to drive the sand grouse.

"By the way he's inviting Shahid Malik as well," Yasmin continued. "Shahid said his father had given him a pair of Purdey 12 bores for his twenty-first so you need not worry about a gun. I'm sure he'll lend you one of his. I look forward to taking a back seat when you're at the controls of the 421 on Thursday afternoon. It'll be the first time I've been flown by you."

"Goodbye Yasmin. You've made my day." Carl replied simply.

CHAPTER 33

Thursday's four sorties for Carl were all spinning and aerobatics. By the late afternoon he was weary from pulling so much 'g' and he looked forward to a gentle flight across the country's Western wilderness to Quetta. His weekend bag was packed and he put on his little used and unsweaty BRIXMIS flying overalls with the union flag badge to look his professional best. He and Shahid waited by the signals square for their hosts to arrive.

The 421 taxied to the control tower and Carl dashed across to greet it. The propellers had hardly stopped before a breathtakingly elegant Yasmin stepped out to make way for Carl in the co-pilot's seat. In her sleek green jumpsuit she looked like the model for a glossy magazine and far from the modest Pakistani female stereotype.

"All yours, Carl. We're so glad you could make it," she declared. Behind in the passenger cabin lurked her tribally robed and turbaned husband who was viewing his wife's fussy handover to the new co-pilot with some disdain.

Carl eased himself into the right hand seat up front beside Captain Mumtaz Ali with the four gold epaulette stripes that befitted a Provincial Governor's personal pilot. They put on their headphones and adjusted the bar mouth microphones expectantly.

"Remember my telephonic operating instructions, Carl?" Mumtaz inquired.

"Yes indeed. I'll fly the Shaheen, the Eagle like a twin engined Piston Provost making sure I don't over boost those well geared Continentals and remember to land tricycle style. Give me the flight procedures card please, Mumtaz."

Carl read out and actioned the proffered checklist, ran up the engines at the holding point and soon they were lined up ready to go. After a smooth double application of power they were away, cleaned up and climbing to their cruising altitude. "Nothing to it is there, Carl?" observed Mumtaz Ali. "You're as good as Yousuf Ahmed who was the best pilot on my squadron till I was lured from the Service after the '65 war by the Governor's irresistible rupees."

Soon they were approaching the grey agglomeration of disordered housing of Quetta.

"Let's show them the Governor's aircraft is back. Can I do a run and break and curved approach fighter style, Mumtaz?" asked Carl.

"Go ahead old boy, but don't exceed the undercarriage and flap lowering speeds. I want her down on her main wheels precisely on the runway numbers."

Carl dived gently building up speed to a point a third of the way down the runway, curled upward to port, eased back the throttles, down came the wheels, RPM lever fully forward, a touch of flap around the corner, full flap lined up and then the mainwheels caressed the runway threshold stripes in a perfect landing.

"You and Yousuf are truly one of a kind," said Mumtaz.

"Tell his sister. She'll be pleased," Carl replied.

On arrival at Quetta the party transferred to large jeeps and pickup trucks for the two hour journey to their host's estate. Carl had the privilege of travelling with Akbar Khan and Yasmin. She had decorously covered herself with a large Astrakhan coat for her return to the family home. They chatted happily en route. Akbar Khan was particularly forceful in his views.

"It's hardly surprising what's happening in East Pakistan. The Punjabis have taken the Bengalis for granted for years," he began. "They've been happy to siphon off the Bengali jute, tea and hardwood revenues but have put precious little investment back. It's even the same here. Baluchistan is woefully neglected. The Army appreciates the Baluch regiments and their bagpipe bands, but that's about it."

"Aren't you being a bit harsh, my love?" Yasmin suggested. "After all you're not without influence in Islamabad."

"Of course, Yasmin, but you're actually making my point. A handful of families like mine effectively run the Province and of course people like me are elected to the National Assembly year after year if they choose to run. Apart from the big landlords about no one is educated. I've benefited from my family and Army connections but Baluch society needs to change if significant economic development is to come here."

"Does that mean that if East Pakistan went its own way Baluchistan might seek to follow suit?" Carl asked.

"No, because our population is tiny and the Army would never let it happen, but there's a risk of extremist parties taking hold – like Jamaat Islami in NWFP. We Western Provinces look to Iran and Afghanistan and not just to Punjab and Sindh in the rest of Pakistan," Akbar Khan replied.

The Sardar was waxing eloquent. "If war does break out over East Pakistan I foresee much instability in South Asia for decades to come," he declared. "Once the Indians have got a compliant regime installed in Dacca they can turn their attention to us in the West cracking down on Muslim aspirations in Kashmir and perhaps connive with Afghanistan to nullify the Durand line international border settlement to foment a Pashtunistan straddling both sides of our Western frontier."

The conversation was becoming very interesting and Carl wanted to inquire further about what countermeasures Pakistan would take when they arrived at Akbar Khan's vast single storey ranch house. Bearers emerged from the shadows. Guests' luggage was spirited away to their bedrooms and dinner was announced for 8.00 pm.

"The Governor of Baluchistan, the Commandant of the Staff College, the Commander of the Quetta Pakistan Air Force base and my old battalion commander are all coming to dinner," Akbar Khan declared proudly. "My wife likes to entertain and in the Foreign Ministry socialising is luckily for her part of the job."

"You like it, too," commented Yasmin. "You are no recluse, Akbar. After all you were in the National Assembly and before that the Provincial Assembly. You're hardly an office clerk in your present work for the Governor. It's just that you like the country life and you rightly want to ensure that your family estate is properly managed. And there's the shooting of course."

"Yes indeed my love. We leave at 0630 tomorrow morning. Breakfast will be in the field at 0900 after the first drive," Akbar Khan declared.

Carl's room was some way from anyone else's at the end of the well verandahed guest wing. The hot water did not reach so far but he had always enjoyed cold showers. The Victorian plumbing provided a liberal jet of icy water. He was not going to let Yasmin down and donned his Saville Row tuxedo, magenta cumber bund, best silk double ended bow tie and shiny black patent leather shoes.

"Well dressed, well received" was one of his mother's mottoes he had never forgotten.

The dinner was even more lavish than Air Commodore Ahmed's and the conversation more uninhibited. Carl liked the Governor Hamid Alam. He was highly intelligent and kept asking him probing questions.

"What does the British Goverment think of the Bangladesh movement? Would they speak out against the secession of East Pakistan? Why do they always support India even though Pakistan was a British creation? Don't they realise that if Pakistan is allowed to break up, India itself might do the same in time? Don't they care that India is aiding and abetting Soviet Russia's objectives in South Asia?"

All the while Yasmin was maintaining her surreptitious footwork on Carl under the table making it hard for him to think clearly. He responded repeatedly to the Governor's cross examination that he was merely a flying instructor and not interested in politics. Why had he then met the Deputy British Air Advisor clandestinely on a Saturday morning at the UK consulate office in Peshawar, the Governor insisted. Service matters could and should have been discussed on the base at Risalpur. Hamid Alam's inquisition was becoming hot and Yasmin's probing leg strokes made it difficult for Carl to keep his composure. The Pakistani authorities clearly had him under surveillance.

Just before the toast was drunk a tall turbaned waiter handed a folded piece of paper to the Governor on a silver tray. He opened it and his face darkened.

"Ladies and gentlemen," he pronounced, "India has declared an air blockade. All Pakistan registered aircraft are prohibited from midnight from entering Indian airspace. The C in C of the Pakistan Air Force has stated that air communications with East Pakistan will henceforth be maintained via Sri Lanka."

"This is tantamount to a declaration of war," the Staff College Brigadier exclaimed.

"This will put a big strain on PIA who will have to pick up the slack. Most of the Air Force's aircraft haven't got the necessary range," commented the Group Captain from the Quetta air base.

After dinner when the men had rejoined the ladies Yasmin confided audibly to the Governor, "We had anticipated this in the Ministry. We have already got back to the West most of the aeroplanes from East Pakistan we can over the past week, except those vital combat aircraft essential in theatre. By the way I've been asked to call on the Chief Martial Law Administrator out there in the next few days to give him urgent political advice against any provocative act. We still hope diplomacy will prevail and that hostilities can be avoided."

"It affects me," Shahid Malik commented. "I don't want to be separated from my family in an emergency like this. I'll get my father to persuade Air Commodore Ahmed to have me posted to the resident fighter squadron in East Pakistan. Additional personnel are bound to be needed to augment the ratio of pilots to aircraft and they'll particularly want old hands like me with operational experience in '65."

The Scotch whiskey and Murree beer flowed freely and the Baluch pipe band played far into the night on the veranda outside before Akbar Khan finally brought proceedings to a halt.

"Remember its wheels rolling for the shooting part at 0630 sharp tomorrow morning. I've asked the principal piper to give us a reveille blast at 0600," he declared.

"Don't forget it's an earthquake zone everybody," warned Yasmin. "Doors and windows can jam just when you need to get out in a hurry so keep them unlocked and unlatched for safety's sake. We haven't had a tremor for several months but the last one was 5.7 on the Richter scale. The next could be worse."

It was not the baleful tones of a Baluch piper which woke Carl but the gentle caress of Yasmin's hand upon his cheek and her sensuous whisper in his ear.

"It's me, my love."

"Yasmin darling you're an angel of exquisite delight, but this is pure madness. You'll get us stoned."

"Don't worry, Carl. You can hear Akbar's whisky induced snores across the courtyard. He won't stir for at least another three hours. The watchman is in the gatehouse over half a mile away. The guard dogs who patrol the house know me well and make no fuss. The other guest bedrooms all look the other way and are in a different part of the wing."

Yasmin put a match to the nightlight and slipped swiftly beside Carl beneath the cotton sheets. What had he done to deserve such ecstasy Carl asked himself. Why was it that as a caring responsible husband and devoted father Yasmin still aroused such uncontrollable passion in him. His feelings for her outweighed all risks, potential disgrace, humiliation, punishment, retribution and the utmost personal danger. He knew that these intense perils for him were more than fully reciprocated for Yasmin. What was it that Mark Driscoll had said? "An impassioned heart will always overrule the wisest head and in the inner struggle between hormones and reason hormones will win every time."

The barriers of time, space and long separation were down. Both were married; both ostensibly happily so. Both realised they could never have married each other, but their unity of flesh and spirit seemed immutable. Much outwardly had changed in their lives since their first thrilling encounters in Lincolnshire, London, America and Yorkshire.

Their career aspirations were largely realised but the mutual longing to fill the void in their souls still remained. At 0500 she was gone. Akbar's snores had moderated and the first rosy tints of dawn were showing up the stark grey outline of the distant hills. Carl's nocturnal glimpse of paradise was dissolving fast in the light of a Baluchi day.

At 0600 hours the piper's call to action seemed a veritable lament. Carl dutifully donned his shooting gear, received his beautifully engraved Purdey from Shahid Malik and stepped with him into the final jeep of the convoy, which trundled punctually out across the pebble strewn wilderness of shrub and low thorn trees. At a cairn of stones all disembarked including from the leading pickup a distant Yasmin in her Astrakhan coat and knee length fur boots. The party duly formed into line and began the steady walk up for partridges with beaters filling in the gaps between the expectant guns with the dogs meandering excitedly behind.

The first two partridge walk ups were thrilling for Carl. The proceedings were on a totally different scale to the modest Saturday afternoon shoots at Barkston Heath aerodrome as a cadet from which he would be lucky to return with a brace of partridges, a wood pigeon, a pheasant, a rabbit or a hare. Akbar Khan's birds flew low and fast from the advancing line with coveys of partridges whirring away into the distant desert to a fusillade of shots from his eager guests.

As the guns moved forward the dead birds were picked up and the winged despatched by the grinning Baluchi beaters who exclaimed excitedly to Carl as each of his partridges plummeted to earth the Urdu refrain "Bohat acha, sahib, bohat acha" – "very good, sir, very good". Luckily Carl's interceptor pilot's aim was true and unlike others in the party he suffered no loss of face amongst the beaters.

Indeed at breakfast Akbar commented loudly to Yasmin, "Yousuf's old friend Carl Higgins seems a crack marksman my dear. I don't expect many of those miscreants in the jebels of South Asia escaped his Hunter's cannon. I well remember that in Oman my Baluch battalion had reason to be grateful to the Strikemasters of the Sultan's Air Force and their Cranwell trained pilots. Their precise strafing often to within a few yards of our positions got us out of many a sticky predicament."

The smell of the wood smoke from the cook's bonfire in the crisp morning air was exhilarating. Scrambled eggs served with naan bread and pilau rice had never tasted better washed down with strong sweet East Pakistani tea from the plantations of Sylhet. Around the blazing logs the conversation reverted to the Bangladeshi secession movement.

Governor Hamid Khan was adamant that it must not be allowed to succeed. "If we lose East Pakistan to the Bengalis it'll encourage the Pathans and Baluchis to go their own way, too," the General insisted. The Frontier Corps Brigadier agreed.

"The Indians have never given up their dream of splitting up Pakistan. Pashtunistan along and across the border with Afghanistan has been their aim for years" he asserted.

"I can't speak for the Ministry of course, Excellency, but I know there's a lot in what you and the Brigadier describe – the domino effect I'd call it," Yasmin observed. "I can't wait to get out to Dacca to see things for myself," she continued. "There must be a diplomatic solution short of full independence for Bangladesh if only Zulfikar Ali Bhutto in West Pakistan and Sheikh Mujib in East were not so intransigent."

"That's a very political observation to make if I may say so, Yasmin," Akbar Khan interrupted. "As far as I'm concerned I'd just like to get back to the colours if the balloon goes up. I know we can teach the Bengalis a lesson they'll never forget. They're only good for scheming, intrigue and politics: never have been a martial race like us. I'm still on the Reserve list you know."

"Don't you think it's time to move on, my dear," Yasmin replied. "The beaters are getting restive. Let's take our frustrations out on the sand grouse. This East Pakistan crisis has been a whole generation in the making. A further day or two of simmering tension won't make any difference. Anyway although the Indians may well be behind it all, they'll take a little while yet to get their act together."

A network of nullahs and a plethora of desert thorn bushes provided good cover for the guests at every drive. The lean swarthy beaters set off in the back of the big tyred pickups in wide encircling movements, lathis at the ready before disembarking and advancing towards the guns. Great flocks of sand grouse flew off ahead of them like darts, swiftly and straight.

By nightfall bulging sackfulls of birds had been collected and the plumpest selected for fireside consumption at the camp dinner. After the last drive at which Carl had achieved no less than three left and rights Akbar Khan led the hungry convoy off to a clump of lone pines for dinner and the night time bivouac.

Bearers and beaters cooperated to roast goat and lamb cutlets, partridges and sand grouse on spits above the flickering flames. Beyond the firelight the stars shone through the moonless night strongly enough to illuminate the desert floor. After the meal sleeping bags were laid over Baluch rugs upon the stony ground and the guests dispersed in order of seniority to the three camp fires.

Carl noticed Akbar Khan's Baluchi bearer unroll two sleeping bags beyond the farthest fire. The Governor's bag and those of his entourage and the senior officers were grouped around the biggest fire. Carl's and that of Shahid Malik were placed by their Air Force batman beside the smallest blaze in front of the assorted jeeps, pickups and cross country vehicles beyond which swathed in goatskins and ponchos the Baluchi attendants were sleeping amongst the bushes.

Akbar Khan's whisky induced snores were soon wafting sonorously across the campsite on the gentle desert breeze. By two in the morning the embers of the fires were dead. All movement around them had ceased. Carl's uneasy wakefulness was heightened by an irrepressible longing for Yasmin.

As so often in her married life Akbar's unislamic propensity for the whisky bottle had pre-empted any physical intimacy. Feigning a call of nature she slipped away from her noisily somnolent husband and tip-toed to Carl's sleeping bag tapping gently on the hood. Soundlessly but tremulously he admitted her to his side slipping her smooth silken shalwar down over her well rounded buttocks. If they were discovered together he felt sure that he would surely die but long before dawn she was surreptitiously off to her rightful resting place and Baluchi honour remained publicly untainted.

Next morning with calm formality tempered by a hostess' solicitude she accompanied Akbar Khan in his drive to the airport to see Carl and Shahid Malik off in the Golden Eagle back to Risalpur. "What do you do if war breaks out, Carl?" she ventured indiscreetly.

"I don't expect it will," he replied disingenuously. "I am sure that your diplomatic corps, President Yahya and even the most demagogic of Pakistan's politicians realise the risks to the country's integrity if things get out of control.

"Anyway I'll be better able to answer that question once I've returned from the trip out East, which Shahid's organising for me."

"By then I expect to be back in uniform," Akbar Khan interjected. "That is if I'm still slim enough to fit into my Baluch Regiment cherrypicker trousers."

CHAPTER 34

There followed for Carl a hectic week of flying instruction at twice the normal tempo during which rumours of war and wild scare stories spread thick and fast. Some said that the Mujahedeen had blown up a tourist houseboat on the lake at Sringagar in Indian held Kashmir. Others claimed that the Mukti Bahini had detonated a bomb at the reception desk of the Intercontinental Hotel in Dacca. Everyone agreed that Indian military aircraft were intruding into Pakistani airspace to a depth of five to ten miles on an almost daily basis. And so it went on.

Before the week's end Shahid Malik approached Carl as they strolled back to the instructors' crewroom after a formation detail.

"I've spoken to Papa, Carl," he declared. "We're on. There's a PIA 707 departing Karachi for Dacca at 2330 hours on Sunday night. I've secured a seat for you incognito in the back. Clear it with the Commandant here and your High Commission this afternoon please. As for me I'm going back onto ops. My posting to East Pakistan has been approved with immediate effect."

After the last sortie of the day Carl made his way to the Academy's Headquarters. Air Commodore Ahmed always worked late. He knew that success as Commandant offered him his final chance to reach Air Marshal. With war in the offing the quality of Risalpur's output could much affect its outcome. He also realised that a beleaguered Pakistan badly needed the help of bigger powers.

Carl's plea for a week's leave to go out East as the guest of the Chief Martial Law Administrator was therefore timely and most welcome.

"Delighted to give you a week's leave, Carl," Ahmed declared warmly. "My daughter's already out in Dacca trying to defuse things diplomatically. You're the sole non Pakistani we're allowing in and then only because you're combat experienced and an Urdu speaker. Your friend Squadron Leader McNeil is definitely persona non grata. A visit by him could be seriously misinterpreted. Things are definitely very sensitive and hotting up fast, I'm afraid. Even my son-in-law Akbar Khan has been recalled to military service at the age of forty-one. God speed, Carl. May Allah the all holy and merciful attend your important mission with success."

Carl snapped to attention, saluted and marched briskly out to join Shahid Malik' in the outer office.

"The old man says okay, Shahid," he began. "See you at Drigh Road, Karachi at the Guardroom at the main gate at 2100 hours Sunday. I've now got to clear this escapade of yours with the Brits."

After dinner Carl rang Bob McNeil from the cubby hole under the Mess stairs. After the usual mutual salutations he addressed the key issue.

"Bob," he continued, "I've been reading Fitzroy MacLean's Eastern Approaches, the book you recommended. I'm much enjoying it." The classic title was their code for Carl to undertake an East Pakistan reconnaissance.

"I do approve of your taste Carl. As tales of derring do in romantic places go, it's a literary masterpiece."

The Great Game in the Ganges Delta was on for Carl.

At the main entrance to the Air Force section of Karachi Airport Shahid Malik had organised passes for himself and Carl as well as a driver to take them to the VIP lounge. The PIA 707 was already waiting on the floodlit apron amongst a patchwork of glistening puddles from the afternoon's monsoon rain. Around it there was much activity on the part of the refuellers and turn-round personnel. A long line of shirt sleeved fit looking young men were patiently waiting their turn to mount the rear steps to the aeroplane. When they were all embarked Carl and Shahid were ushered in at the forward door.

The aircraft was full and no sooner had the passengers boarded than the sheeting rain resumed. Then they were off into the seemingly solid and impenetrable darkness at the start of the ten hour transit to East Pakistan overflying Sri Lanka on the way to avoid the risk of interception by Indian fighters.

Hardly had the wheels left the runway than a fearsome continuous bucking, thumping and heaving in the monsoon turbulence began. Glimpsing behind him into the large cabin aft Carl could see that the plain clothed Punjabi soldiery were unperturbed. No doubt they imagined flying always to consist of an interminable series of sickening thuds and jolts. They betrayed no anxiety. Allah the all merciful would decide their fate so there was no point in fretting about it even though any respite from the turbulence was impossible in the tropical latitudes where the rough weather extended far higher than the airliner's ceiling.

For Carl it was psychologically the longest flight of his life. Why had he so unnecessarily volunteered for this thoroughly unpleasant fact finding mission to an imminent war zone, he asked himself. His job instructing at the Air Force Academy was reasonably safe as befitted the role of a married foreign officer with family responsibilities and Risalpur was some distance from the front line if war broke out.

No doubt Bob McNeil and all at the British High Commission would be grateful for his report if he came back, but that was by no means a certainty. After all that the Bangladeshi secessionist militants had been through at the hands of the Pakistani authorities the Mukti Bahini would be no respecters of captured overseas military personnel on the Pakistani side regardless of their duties or country of origin.

A long spell behind Bangladeshi bars was by no means improbable for Carl waiting to be bartered perhaps for leading Bengali personalities trapped in West Pakistan at the outbreak of hostilities. Or he could even be traded with the Indian Armed Forces for personnel of theirs held by the Pakistanis, but that could take time.

Carl admired Shahid Malik's fearless and loyal personal commitment to Pakistan. Its unity was at imminent risk. His father held high responsibilities in the most endangered part of the country. As a Pakistani officer he had sworn to protect the Islamic traditions and way of life inherent in the creation and enshrined in the constitution of Pakistan. These could be lost at least in the Eastern wing if the ambitions of Hindu majority India were not checked. It was clear where his duty lay.

As the PIA 707 plunged down through the embedded cumulonimbus towards its final goal Carl reckoned it had no alternate to Dacca airport. He wondered what its weather minima were. Bangkok and Rangoon were surely now out of range. A diversion to India with a full load of soldiers was unthinkable. Dacca it had to be.

One thing alone made this perilous destination desirable to Carl. Somewhere amongst the inundated plains, flooded homesteads and rain sodden streets of Dacca was Yasmin; Yasmin away from Akbar Khan, away from the constraints of daily routine at the Ministry and now embarked on the nearest that the foreign service came to operations in the field with all the opportunity it offered for individual initiatives and unsupervised amorous extra curricular activities.

To Carl's relief the cloud base had lifted significantly and there was some respite from the torrential monsoon deluge when the 707 came in to land. The terminal building was filled with a chaotic throng of jostling humanity, but the shirt sleeved soldiers marched off briskly from the rear steps of the aeroplane to waiting lorries whilst Shahid and Carl were whisked away by staff car to the Chief Martial Law Administrator's residence.

The large building set in vast gardens seemed more like a fortress than a home. Rolls of barbed wire were strung around the perimeter. Tin hatted soldiers ponchoed against the almost incessant downpours patrolled the ample grounds. The gatehouse had been converted into a defensive strongpoint by sandbag emplacements and a couple of machine gun posts.

From these emerged the sergeant of the guard. He stamped out to greet them incongruously keeping his pacestick under the left arm as if on parade and saluting vigorously with his right. He scrutinised their identity cards whilst a rifle toting jawan kept a watchful eye on the proceedings and on the roadway beyond where the meandering rickshaws, countless beggars and decrepit vehicles, and listlessly wandering pedestrians all posed a potential terrorist threat.

Carl and Shahid soon satisfied the security conscious sergeant and were waved through to another impeccable salute. At the door of the house a lean imperious Bihari doorman with the most extravagant headgear opened the door of their staff car. He took their bags and announced deferentially.

"His Excellency is hoping you will join him and his officer guests for lunch, gentlemen. A member of the house staff will show you to your rooms so that you can have a shower and change after the long flight." Turning to Shahid he added; "Your father is waiting for you in the study, Mr Shahid. He is preparing the speech he must give after the luncheon."

The hall was dark, damp and hot. The water from the shower upstairs was tepid and did little to cool Carl down. He feared sweat patches would soon reveal themselves on his pale sand coloured uniform jacket. He hardly had time to dry himself and dress before a gong rang out. Carl heavy with jet lag descended the stairway towards the babble of voices beyond the open door of the drawing room.

The much medalled moustachioed Chief Martial Law Administrator advanced from his assembled guests to meet Carl.

"Welcome to East Pakistan, Flight Lieutenant Higgins," he declared. "It's a privilege for me to entertain an officer from the oldest and most famous Air Force in the world in our country's time of crisis. I know that my son Shahid was very happy you could accompany him here. While he'll be joining his squadron immediately we've organised a separate personal information programme for you – far away from the Air Force for once. They were very sensitive about the political and security considerations of having such an experienced British combat pilot with them at a time of maximum operational readiness and possibly actual hostilities. Instead the General Officer Commanding wants you to visit Army units on the ground to appreciate the threats they face, I also want you to see something of the country and the measures we have taken to maintain law and order in spite of the activities of subversive elements and miscreants."

As Carl pushed through the chattering group of VIPs they seemed not to have noticed him at all but he spotted the unmistakeable outline of Yasmin silhouetted against the grey window panes and the cascading rain beyond. His throat tightened, his stomach grew tense and his pulse raced.

Forgetting all caution he advanced towards her. She was in earnest conversation with a sallow black robed paunchy middle-aged Bengali, an Awami League politician, no doubt, he thought.

"My God, I never expected to meet you here," Carl blurted out, oblivious to her conversation. Yasmin jumped and reddened visibly.

"So you two know each other then do you," the Awami Leaguer observed. Before she could answer Carl tried to allay his suspicions.

"Her late brother Yousuf was a great friend of mine in the Air Force as is General Malik's son Shahid who has been posted here from Risalpur, at least for the duration of the crisis," he explained.

"He'll be in Dacca a long time then," the politician replied.

"So you're not worried about Indian intervention or the Mukti Bahini leading a popular armed uprising?" Carl inquired. "You'd better check with the Army. They run and know everything here. Or ask your friend from the Foreign Ministry," the Bengali answered.

"My job is to make sure that no one does or says anything provocative," interjected Yasmin diplomatically. "The British Flight Lieutenant has just got off the aircraft from West Pakistan. He must be very tired. Let him at least acclimatise before throwing him into the maelstrom of the East Pakistan crisis. He's a pilot not a politician after all."

The Awami Leaguer wandered off to join his colleagues leaving Carl and Yasmin visibly and embarrassingly alone. "Our destiny is extraordinary," she ventured. "Who would have guessed in those carefree days at Cranwell that dear Yousuf would die so young and that we should meet well over a decade later halfway round the world in Pakistan on the outbreak of war."

"I hope no one heard that," Carl replied beckoning furiously to Shahid Malik to come and join them. "Shahid, my old friend, I hope you know what you're letting yourself in for," Carl began as he approached. "Yasmin expects war to break out. You know that unlike in the West Wing there's no proper air defence system here, no effective network of fighter control radars, no adequate anti aircraft gun or missile defences, no diversions, no hope of reinforcement. Do you want to be a Shaheen, a martyr like her brother Yousuf?"

"How could you speak like that, Carl?" Yasmin objected. "I've never heard you sound defeatist before."

"My dear Carl. How unlike you of all people! You dishonour your DFC and belittle Yousuf's sacrifice," Shahid declared contemptuously. "My place is in the thick of the action where Pakistan needs me most and that is alongside my father fighting to prevent the dismemberment of my country," he added.

"Shahid is right," said Yasmin. "When you get out of Dacca, Carl, and see for yourself how disciplined and committed our Army is and how much our brothers of the Eastern Wing love Pakistan, you'll agree with him."

The lunch was a surreal affair with Senior Army Officers, politicians, civil servants and diplomats behaving as if complete normality prevailed in the country. Carl and Shahid listened to the conversation with growing incredulity. Yasmin could be heard entering into the spirit of the occasion with the best of them. Carl caught some of her remarks to the Australian Deputy High Commissioner and felt she surely could not believe what she was saying.

"My country is taking an increasing interest in Asia and can't be indifferent to the balance of power in the continent," the Australian began. "Our role in the Vietnam War showed that, but I doubt if we'd want to be involved in your crisis."

"It's not our crisis," Yasmin responded firmly. "We know the intercommunal difficulties in East Pakistan are being stirred up by the Indians even though since the Tashkent agreement ended the 1965 war we've been working consistently to improve relations with them," she went on.

"Even in Kashmir?" the Australian inquired.

"Any trouble there is caused by hotheads and fanatics not by us," Yasmin insisted indignantly. "The Soviets don't help either by always supporting India. Self-determination in Kashmir is long overdue. The United Nations called for it following the 1948 war after all."

"Don't worry. We understand your position and simply want to maintain positive relations with both sides. Pakistan and India are and always have been equally our friends," the Deputy High Commissioner replied.

More snatches of cross table dialogue heightened Carl's disbelief. An Awami League politician was holding forth to a senior Army staff officer. "The Punjabi elite has always underestimated us East Pakistanis," he claimed.

"I disagree," the soldier replied. "It is you East Pakistanis who have underestimated us. If India did attack the Pakistan Army would give the aggressors a bloody nose. They'd be seeking peace within a week."

"I'm glad to hear it," the politician responded. "After all we've suffered, first from the terrible cyclone this past winter and then from growing terrorist violence we really need peace to rebuild our lives."

After lunch all adjourned for tea and coffee. Carl managed to sidle unobtrusively up beside Yasmin.

"Don't you understand?" he enquired softly but urgently. "The writing is on the wall for East Pakistan. I wish I could get you out and back home tonight. You're effectively cut off from the Western Wing. The Indians didn't sever the direct air links with the West as an act of friendship. Their Navy and Air Force control the seas and the skies. In this festering pullulating pool of mud the constant bombings and shootings are hardly a goodwill gesture on the part of the local population. Hardly a single representative of a West Wing party was elected here to the National Assembly. The Awami League for all its professions of commitment to Pakistan I regard as representing the Bangladesh Secession Front."

"What a speech! Leave all that to us. Enjoy your tour of the country while you can," Yasmin replied calmly. "This afternoon I'm flying up to Sylhet and will stay in the Government Guest House. Shahid tells me you're going with the General's ADC to Jessore to visit a Baluch battalion on the front line near Benapole. I'll be back in the Intercon tomorrow night, Room 514. If you come at ten minutes past midnight my door will be unlocked. Beware. The place is teeming with guards, spies and secret police."

"I've said goodbye to Shahid," Carl replied. "His jeep is coming to take him to the squadron in five minutes. Our own transport will take us on our respective ways thereafter. Be careful war is nearly upon us."

Yasmin surreptitiously looked to see if the guests had begun to move to the door and turned back to Carl to whisper, "God bless you my love. I feel the hour of our final destiny is very close."

Carl warmly thanked his host the Chief Martial Law Administrator and boarded the waiting staff car with the ADC Captain Siddiqui of the Punjab Regiment. Open jeeps with Pakistani soldiers riding shotgun proceeded and followed them through the teeming streets back to the airport. At the entrance to departures throngs of distraught Biharis were held back by lathi brandishing police to let Carl and Siddiqui through to the check in area. "The richer Biharis are trying to get out to the West before the air shuttle closes down," the ADC observed.

"Hardly looks like a mark of confidence to me," Carl commented. "Rather different from the picture of normality that was painted at lunch."

"Lucky you weren't here two days ago," Siddiqui replied. "The Mukti Bahini set off a bicycle bomb amongst the would-be escapees killing six and wounding ten. Far from deterring them even more Biharis want to go West now. Anyway we're lucky. We have seats on the Skyvan to Jessore where the Baluchis will meet us and transport us to Benapole. There'll you be taken to the First Battalion The Baluch Regiment, which is commanded by Colonel Akbar Khan. He took over four days ago after his predecessor the regular CO was blown up by a roadside bomb."

"The Sardar, formerly Chief Secretary to the Governor of Baluchistan?" Carl exclaimed.

"One and the same."

"How incredible."

"Do you know him?"

"I most certainly do. Went shooting at his place only a few days ago. He said then he longed to be back with the Colours. I wonder if he reckoned he'd be on the front line quite so soon and commanding a battalion, too."

At the aeroplane Carl and the ADC were greeted by its Captain in nondescript green overalls whilst his co-pilot busied himself with the pre-flight inspection. In addition to some twenty passengers their possessions filled the cargo compartment lashed down with netting regardless of weight or balance. As the squat dumpy Skyvan held at the marshalling point a camouflaged Shenyang Mig 19 fighter trailing spray tore off into heavy rain charged clouds ahead of them. Did it already have Shahid Malik at the controls re-familiarising himself with the aeroplane on a sector reconnaissance in preparation for the impending air battles against vastly superior numbers? Could he possibly survive the Indian onslaught to come, Carl wondered.

The Skyvan lumbered forward and lined up on the runway. The twin turboprops' howl rose to a crescendo of sound. The fuselage buzzed in sympathetic resonance and they were away over the flooded landscape skimming beneath the lowering layers of nimbostratus. A few houses, trees, huts and homesteads remained above the water but not much more.

Just when it seemed impossible to imagine any town in this apparently limitless inundation a group of ramshackle houses and a runway appeared. The pilot carefully positioned the aircraft for a straight in approach to minimise the risk of hostile ground fire. Soon they were down and taxiing in.

A Baluch major in battle fatigues met them as they descended and introduced himself crisply. "Major Mohsin Khan, first Baluch Regiment, second in command to Colonel Akram Khan. It is my pleasant duty to welcome you to the battalion and to take you to our sector of the front line, which lies beyond the small settlement of Benapole. Luckily the road remains passable to motor vehicles unless the Mukti Bahini have destroyed any of the bridges or culverts. Anyway we have dinghies on board the jeeps if we need them and we can always radio for assistance if our route is cut and ask to be met on the other side."

Carl and Major Mohsin Khan travelled in one jeep accompanied by a jawan with a submachine gun. Captain Siddiqui came in the following shotgun vehicle bristling with riflemen. The one ahead had a mounted light machine gun and two more riflemen. In spite of the heat, mud, rain and watery terrain the Baluch soldiers were impressively alert and well turned out in starched shirts and carefully creased trousers. Only the major's denim battle fatigues looked more relaxed and in keeping with the tropical theatre.

On arrival at battalion headquarters, which were protected by numerous sangars and sand bagged defensive positions meticulously camouflaged with well draped netting, Carl was ushered into the command tent by the major. Colonel Akbar Khan was poring over the sector maps with the adjutant. The second in command announced the visitors. Carl saluted. Akbar Khan instructed the adjutant to continue planning the night's patrols and advanced to shake Carl's hand.

"How good to have you with us, Carl," he began. "How long can you stay?"

"Twenty-four hours, sir," he replied.

"In that case you'd better get kitted out to go on patrol right away. We've got half a platoon going out to see if we can take some Indian prisoners. The battalion on the left of the Ghurkhas opposite us has just been replaced. We need to know who by and preferably what their orders are. You won't be going with the contact section, but the follow up one. Its role is to cover the lead's flanks and rear and help it extract itself, its prisoners and casualties if any. When you return you can repair to the Mess Tent for dinner with me and to reminisce together about our weekend at my place."

Carl saluted again and withdrew. His minder an immensely tall, greying sergeant ushered him into the store tent where Carl donned jungle green denims, wet weather boots, a khaki beret and received a stick of charcoal to blacken up his face and hands for patrol.

"Take this, sir. It might come in handy," declared the sergeant handing Carl a Sterling submachine gun and two spare magazines, which Carl inserted in his webbing belt. "It's the British successor to the Sten and more accurate as you know. I expect you learned to fire it as a cadet, sir. It's also less prone to unintended discharges, which are the last thing we want on a snatch and recce patrol. I suggest you only engage the enemy in self-defence if you absolutely have to. Don't worry the jawans will have you well covered at all times, sir."

Precisely at sunset the sections moved out in single file, each divided as the paras would have said into two sticks of four. A subaltern led the first section from the front; the sergeant with Carl the second bringing up the rear. The plan was to assault an isolated advance observation post well in front of the main enemy position as night fell using the last light for the approach with the second section swinging in from a wide encircling move to the right to seize its defenders. The jawans advanced as noiselessly as cats. At the first pause the hawk-eyed sergeant pointed out to Carl the enemy OP and the main defences well hidden in the luxuriant undergrowth behind.

The second section began its outflanking move to the right with Carl feeling very exposed and vulnerable. He was sure the Indians must have seen the patrol's movement forward. Progress was slow through the waist high grass and the boggy ground underfoot was heavy going. However, the fading light helped to render their approach undetected though it made it harder for the sections to keep the man in front in view.

Carl wondered if the Indians could have laid mines or booby traps or set ambushes ahead of their lines but dismissed the ideas as figments of his hyperactive imagination. Just as he was beginning to gain confidence there were a succession of bursts of automatic fire and some single shots ahead in quick succession followed by much shouting.

"Get down and stay here, sir," hissed the sergeant who moved rapidly forward to investigate. At the same time a couple of flares went lazily up above the main Indian position. The defenders were already fully alerted by the firefight and commotion.

The sergeant soon returned grinning with excitement. "Our patrol has just caught half a dozen Mukti Bahini terrorists infiltrating Pakistan," he exclaimed gleefully. "We've killed one, wounded a second and captured three. Only one has escaped. We have no casualties though one of our jawans was hit on the hand. Luckily it's his left and only a superficial wound. He's still fit to fight. You don't knock out a Baluch so easily, sir."

"I never imagined you did, sergeant," Carl replied. "What's the drill now? Do I stay put?"

"The prisoners will be passing down the section shortly. The raid against the OP is obviously off but we'll take the Mukti Bahini back to battalion HQ for initial interrogation before being transferred to Dacca for our intelligence professionals to get to work on them," the sergeant answered.

"So you rate our patrol a success even though we seized no Indian soldiers, do you, sergeant?" Carl inquired.

"Not for me to judge, sir," the sergeant responded crisply. "The miscreants clearly must have come through the Indian lines so we have definite evidence of the Indian Army's planned collusion with these Bengali subversives."

"I never actually imagined otherwise," Carl retorted. "Such an extensive guerrilla campaign has to be organised with outside help or at least sanctuary. I know this from my time on operations in South Arabia."

"What's more the dead man was wearing Bengali Rifles uniform," the sergeant went on. "The wounded one, too, had on a standard Indian Army issue poncho and boots, but his beret was Bengali Rifles as well. These traitorous deserters are hand in glove with the Indians, but we'll make them talk and tell us when and where the Indian Army's attack will come in."

"You certainly need to find out," Carl commented. "This Indian build up can't be just for fun. If they went back to barracks now they'd lose too much face. Indira Ghandi would never stand for it."

The patrol returned to the battalion on full alert for nocturnal ambushes prodding their reluctant prisoners along with the point of a bayonet and careful to come in on precisely the right bearing to the spot in the defence perimeter where the sentries had been alerted to receive them. The roped up Mukti Bahini captives caused much jubilation amongst the expectant Baluchs. The wounded jawan went to get his hand dressed and after a quick shower under an upturned bucket Carl sought out the Colonel for dinner in the Mess Tent.

"Good show, Carl, my man. You've served well on your first combat sortie with us in best RAF tradition," Akbar Khan exclaimed. "Whether you're on the shooting field or out on foot patrol you seem to produce a good bag."

"I didn't actually fire a shot, Colonel," Carl explained.

"Don't worry old boy. You were there when the bullets flew. You saw how well my Baluch perform in contact with the enemy and the high quality of my NCOs, that's the main thing," Akbar Khan replied.

"Now of course," he went on, "we could have done with some pukka Indians to interrogate, officers preferably, but MB miscreants are the next best thing and they evidently operate together. You'll have to convey that message to your superiors in the UK High Commission. Not that I expect them to listen to you. They're too beholden to India economically and politically to acknowledge unwelcome facts let alone act on them."

Dinner was a simple affair under a hurricane lamp around a trestle table. The Colonel and Carl had the privilege of folding canvas chairs, Major Mohsin Khan, Captain Siddiqui and the Adjutant sat on piles of ammunition boxes. The menu was hardly deluxe being curried campo ration lamb stew and chapattis followed by tinned rice pudding.

"It's a difficult theatre for us to operate in," the Colonel admitted. "We can't use mobility to fill the gaps in our defences we're unable to cover unlike the West where much of the terrain is ideal for armour as in the Rann of Kutch. Nor can we rely on air power. We have no ground attack aircraft here, only a handful of fighters to try and keep the Indian Air Force off our backs. Anyway the weather in the monsoon is too dreadful to be able to count on air support. The countryside is full of informers against us and the Mukti Bahini harass our lines of supply. They attack any target of opportunity we allow them. What we do have in our favour is the decisive element – the quality of our troops whose courage, discipline and commitment are second to none."

"I agree, Colonel," Carl replied reassuringly. "In the short time I've been with you I've been deeply impressed by the demeanour and morale of your men. I understand now why you wanted so much to be back with the colours."

"You tell them, Carl, how confident we are when you return to the West," said Captain Siddiqui. "I fear many friendly nations have written us off but they're profoundly mistaken. Man for man the Pakistani soldier is worth two or three Indians, except perhaps for the Ghurkhas. They're in a different category."

"No doubt we'll have the opportunity soon enough to put all these speculations to the test," interjected Akbar Khan. "Before that there's all too little time to establish our defensive positions, set up the camouflage netting, test our communications with the artillery and Brigade, prepare our weapons and position our stocks of ammunition. I'll just share a moment or two with our British guest Flight Lieutenant Higgins."

The Pakistani officers withdrew and from beneath the table Akbar Khan produced a bottle of whisky. "What do you chaps say? How about a wee dram before we turn in? That's what the jocks used to ask when I was attached to the Argylls for an exercise at Sandhurst."

"A small shot to unwind at the end of the day is always welcome, Colonel, especially when we know the morrow will bring tough challenges," Carl replied.

"It most certainly will," Akbar Khan responded. "You probably think we're doomed. To be honest I don't care, Carl. What worries me is what might happen to Yasmin if she's still out here when the Indians come in. I can't see her getting diplomatic immunity from retribution at the hands of these Bengali barbarians. Have you any idea how many people they slaughtered when Bengal was partitioned in

August 1947? It doesn't even bear thinking about. That's why I'm lucky to be a soldier. At least I can die honourably. It's the code we know in Baluchistan and on the Frontier – defending our own by force of arms and our honour is our way of life."

"I saw Yasmin briefly in Dacca before coming here, Colonel," Carl answered. "Shahid Malik and I had a word with her at his father's official lunch the day I flew in. She seemed calm and full of confidence and was looking forward to going up to Sylhet. She and the other guests appeared remarkably optimistic. Perhaps these VIPs and those who see the high level intelligence know something we don't."

"I most certainly hope so," Akbar Khan replied. "From what our spies and the insurgents we bring in here tell us – by the way the little batch of Mukti Bahini you delivered are already singing to us like proverbial canaries to try and save their skins – we can expect a massive Indian Army onslaught within a week. They plan to capture Dacca in forty-eight hours, perhaps even earlier if they can win air superiority quickly and seize the airport. I'm telling you all this because you're a friend from a powerful country, which gave me a good training when I was young. It's pukka gen as you'd call it. I'm sure you'll use this privileged information wisely, Carl."

"I most certainly will Colonel Akbar. My affection for Pakistan has grown by the day and I want to help you if I can," Carl replied.

"I think you know enough to have made your visit here worthwhile," Akbar Khan declared. "Get your head down, Carl, and rest awhile. We'll transfer you to Jessore airfield at first light to catch the early morning Skyvan. If you hang around here any longer the aircraft may be requisitioned for use elsewhere as General Headquarters dictate."

"Thank you for your hospitality, Colonel. It has been a privilege to be with you, albeit briefly, but I've seen enough to know your battalion will acquit itself with distinction. You must be very proud of your men," Carl answered.

"I am. Oh, by the way, Carl, if you see Yasmin again do give her my love," Akbar Khan responded. "Tell her I'm fine although I would hope that by now she'll be winging her way home round Sri Lanka, that is if her Ministry has any practical sense, which I sometimes doubt."

"I shall do so, Colonel, if our paths cross before you return."

"As you say, Carl, my friend, God speed. In other words may Allah the all Holy, the merciful deliver you safely home. I'm sure they'll need your capable instruction more than ever at the Air Force Academy. What's more your friends at the UK High Commission will certainly want to hear all your news. I doubt if they currently have much clue as to what is actually going on out here on the front line."

"I'm sure you're right, Colonel," Carl responded.

"I'm going out on a night patrol myself in a few hours' time to be in position on the border when dawn breaks," Akbar Khan went on. "I need to monitor the situation there with my own eyes and to remind the jawans that I am no stranger to the combat zone. So I'll be away when you and Captain Siddiqui leave tomorrow morning. Two IC will accompany you to guarantee you're given priority onto the aeroplane and you'll be properly escorted en route to make sure the MB don't try any funny business along the road.

"Goodbye Carl."

"Goodbye, Colonel Akbar sir."

Carl was woken by the Colonel's bearer with a mug of hot sweet tea at 0330 hours. Heavy monsoon rain had set the battalion HQ awash.

"Breakfast in the Mess tent at 0400, sir," the jawan announced. "Two IC says that you and Captain Siddiqui are to be on your way at 0430 hours."

Despite his poncho Carl was half soaked on his fifty yard dash to the Mess tent. Nevertheless the scrambled eggs and chapattis were worth the wetting.

The task of his escorting shotgun riders would not be pleasant but at least the deluge should deter all but the most fanatical MB ambush layers Carl reckoned. Or would it lend them cover and additional safety from discovery he wondered. His military training induced a sanguine judgement but as so often it wrestled with his inwardly instinctive pessimism or fatalism in the face of danger.

On Carl's arrival at Jessore aerodrome a mêlée of lunghi clad locals jostled and fought for priority aircraft boarding even as far as the edge of the hardstanding. Here a cordon of heavily armed steel helmeted Punjabi troops maintained security with bayonets fixed. Major Mohsin Khan led the Baluch Regiment convoy straight through all the encompassing crowd of jabbering humanity desperate to escape the Mukti Bahini's vengeance and the much feared depredations of the invading Indian Army.

Major Mohsin Khan firmly addressed the Punjabis' subaltern of the guard.

"GOC's ADC and British VIP must pass now, lieutenant. Here are their IDs and the official authorisation of General Malik, Chief Marshal Law Administrator. Instruct your men to let the officers through." The lieutenant muttered some commands to the havildar. The guard sergeant bellowed orders out across the apron. Jawans' boots stamped. The ranks parted and their rifles' woodwork was loudly struck in salute.

On mounting the steps of the Skyvan Carl found to his surprise that the aircraft was almost full. Only two passenger seats towards the tail remained free. The rest were mostly filled with rotund self-satisfied evidently prosperous Bengalis who could afford the fare or the bribe to board. A lean looking Brigadier was sitting right up front with a red tabbed Lieutenant Colonel of the General Staff alongside.

Carl could see as they taxied away from the apron the desperate and increasingly despairing throng milling around and still pressing against the guard who remained commendably firm. It was a depressing vision of terrified humanity and did not bode well.

Soon they were airborne climbing hard to cruise below the cloud layer and happy to have left the border tensions behind. Suddenly the aircraft lurched. Carl could feel the impact as explosive bullets struck home. The interconnecting door to the cockpit flew open. To his horror Carl could see the captain in the left hand seat slumped over the control column. The co-pilot had blood pouring down his cheek from a massive head wound. His left arm hung limply at his side evidently unable to operate the engine controls even if he were still conscious.

Carl snatched a look outside. The starboard wing had a line of bullet holes from the leading to the trailing edge. Oil was pouring from the engine whose cowling was flapping in the slipstream. Ominously the port wing was coming up and the nose starting to drop to the right. A wail of terror rose form the previously somnolent Bengalis. The steward exclaimed, "Oh my God, oh my God." Only the staff officer acted.

The Colonel leapt into the cockpit, unstrapped the captain, seized him by his armpits and dragged him from the controls depositing him beside the astounded Brigadier.

"Anyone here fly an aeroplane?" he called down the cabin. By then Carl was already halfway down the gangway, slid to the Colonel's side and jumped into the vacant captain's seat. He took one look at the co-pilot who was by now unconscious.

"Lift him out of here, Colonel, and you sit beside me now!" he shouted.

Carl corrected the yaw and roll easing out of the dive just above the flood waters below. At least the flying controls still functioned. He throttled the starboard engine fully back and feathered the airscrew. The propeller blades turned and stopped in the angle of least resistance to the airflow. There was now hope of a safe landing unless fuel lines or tanks were ruptured or a consequent fire ensued.

Carl applied full power on the good engine and found that at almost full throttle he could maintain height. His left leg, however, was shaking with the effort of holding on enough rudder to avert another perilous yaw and subsequent plunge to earth.

"Put on the headset, Colonel!" Carl bellowed above the howl of the port engine and the thumping of the loosened cowling in the slipstream. To his relief the intercom still worked as did the radio. Carl flipped the selection switch to the final stud for the emergency channel and put out a MAYDAY call.

He was given a heading to steer for Dacca and a range. Carl judged their radar must be effective even to a low level. He ordered the Colonel to apply left rudder to keep straight with all his strength and began to assess calmly what to do having surmounted the immediate emergency. He began a methodical scan of the blind flying panel and checked the various system displays.

One glaring deficiency became instantly apparent. There was no airspeed indication yet all the cockpit instruments were undamaged. The pilots' bodies seemed to have absorbed the bullets which entered the cabin. He looked up and saw the exit holes in the roof. Of course they had been fired on the by the Mukti Bahini from below. He then studied the underside of the high wing. The starboard pitot head was drooping hence the lack of an airspeed reading and the flaps were riddled with damage and oscillated in the air flow. Carl could not risk an asymmetric flap deployment. Although he could find the approach speed in the flight reference card, without an airspeed indication he would have to call up for a formation approach to achieve a safe landing.

"Ask the Brigadier to go down the gangway, Colonel, to reassure the passengers," Carl instructed. "Tell him to inform them that the situation is under control and that we are going to land at Dacca as planned. Give your left leg a rest. I'll hold the rudder on for a while. It's a pity the rudder trim's not powerful enough to do the job for us. Anyway things are less tense now."

"I'm glad to hear it," the Colonel replied and spoke briefly to his Brigadier behind him.

"I'm getting homing headings from Dacca control and there's clearly no fuel leak as the contents are holding up well," Carl went on. "My main worry is getting the aircraft safely down, though the runway is long and the landing speed of a Skyvan modest. However, without a functioning airspeed indicator I daren't leave the approach to guesswork. I must keep a few knots in hand especially as with one engine out I'll need the rudder to remain effective all the way to touchdown."

The Brigadier did what he was told without demur and returned to report to Carl that the passengers were now calm and resigned to their fate. "Sorry to say, captain," the Brigadier also informed him, "the co-pilot has died in spite of the efforts of the steward and myself to staunch his head wound with the dressings from the aircraft's first aid box. Anything else I can do?"

"Not yet at any rate," Carl replied.

He advised Dacca control of their predicament and requested assistance from a shepherd aircraft onto which he could formate to bring the stricken airliner safely down. "Do you have any suitable lead aircraft?" Carl inquired.

"Only operational Mig 19s," control replied. "Much too fast. Totally impractical. There must be something else," Carl answered.

"Station Flight has an A37 Cessna – ostensibly a trainer but it's used as a hack, a communications aircraft. Would that do?"

"Still a bit on the fast side but with its gear and flaps down its approach speed won't be too dissimilar to ours on one engine and flapless."

"Roger message copied. We'll inform Flight Ops of your request and report."

About five minutes later Dacca control called up again. "The A37 is serviceable and being prepared. Flight Lieutenant Malik will be in command. He claims considerable formation experience with yourself in the aeroplane. Once airborne he will be vectored to your vicinity."

"Thank you, Dacca," Carl replied.

The weather began to deteriorate. Moderate rain was impairing the visibility. He put on the navigation and anti-collision strobe lights to facilitate a rendezvous with Shahid. How many scores of times had he done pairs recoveries to base through thick cloud thought Carl. This would be no different except it must be in line astern not the usual wingtip to wingtip since the Skyvan's high wing would obscure the A37 in a turn. He would position himself immediate behind but a little below Shahid's tail to avoid the A37's jet efflux and slipstream. Looking forward and upwards from the Skyvan's cockpit should pose no problems.

"Skyvan one from Shaheen Two." Carl recognised Shahid's confident tones immediately. "Have you straight ahead at two miles. Will pass down your starboard side and decelerate ahead. Call when settled in line astern."

Carl was pleased that Shahid had not even to be told that it must be an unusual line astern pairs approach. It was a pity they could not fight together. They trusted each other so well but those immutable 'exigencies of the Service' required that Shahid must to go to war without him, probably before the week was out.

Shahid duly drew up alongside and waved cheerily to Carl as he passed to starboard. Carl then eased into formation behind him close enough not to lose the A37 in the intensifying rain. Luckily the cloud base remained adequate.

"Skyvan one, I'll lead you overhead base as high as I can," Shahid transmitted. "Ops orders dictate a spiral descent onto the approach to reduce the risk from ground fire. Just hang in there. I'll call out the heights on finals and obviously overshoot just before you land."

"Roger, Shaheen Two," Carl replied. This was not going to be as easy as he had hoped especially as with one engine he had so little throttle to play with.

"Shaheen Two overhead. Descending," Shahid called. Carl could see the A37's airbrake deployment and a notch of flap applied. Shahid was clearly fearful he might get too far ahead on the way down.

"Keep the spiral tight, Skyvan formation," the Dacca tower warned. "One of our fighters has just reported ground fire on the final approach." The Mukti Bahini must be closing in on the capital Carl reckoned. Surely the end game had now begun.

Shahid started to tighten things up. The descending turns were now at some forty-five degrees. Carl eased the power back further on his good engine so as not to overtake the A37. Then he felt them as when climbing out of Jessore – the thwack thwack thwack of bullet impacts, this time on his port wing. He dared not look left, only ahead to maintain station.

"We've been hit again. Check port wing for damage, Colonel," Carl ordered.

"I see six bullet holes outboard of the engine and a trail of escaping fuel," the Colonel reported. Shahid must be told.

"Shaheen Two," Carl called. "Skyvan one hit by ground fire. Good engine okay but aircraft losing fuel."

"Roger Skyvan. Tightening up and steepening descent now," Shahid replied. The airliner's nose went down as Carl eased off more power increasing the bank to fifty degrees. He could hear the Bengalis wailing again in the back above his headphones.

"There's the cabin announcement button, Colonel. Get the passengers to cut the caterwauling," Carl demanded. "I can't even hear the R/T properly let alone think with such a hubbub and moaning going on."

"Straightening, straightening, go," called Shahid as he eased out of the steep spiral descent. Carl felt another series of jolts this time from the starboard wing. "What was that, Colonel?" he inquired anxiously.

"Cowling's detached completely and fallen off taking the loose flap with it, captain," the Colonel explained. Carl tried the ailerons gingerly still closely following Shahid who had his wheels and flaps down. The Skyvan responded normally. Anyway he could see the runway lights ahead.

"Order the passengers to tighten their belts and to brace, Colonel, as a wheel or tyre might be damaged and the touchdown could be rough," instructed Carl.

"I can only guess the landing speed."

"Shaheen one overshooting," called Shahid as he cleaned up and climbed away. Carl let the aircraft float just above the runway as he gradually reduced the power to idle. The Skyvan sank gently onto its wheels halfway down the runway. Carl turned off at the end and came to a halt. The port engine stopped. The fuel gauges told the story. The tanks were dry.

"Skyvan one clear, request tow to dispersal," he transmitted. He heard the passengers cheering and clapping behind him. Standing over Carl and the Colonel was the Brigadier.

"Congratulations my man," he bellowed above the passenger hubbub. "I'll see you get a medal for this."

A tractor delivered them to the apron where an Air Force ambulance took the bodies of the dead flight crew away. A smart camouflaged jeep with a single silverstar on a blue bumper plate drew up announcing the arrival of the Air Commodore.

"I wanted to congratulate you personally Flight Lieutenant Higgins," he began. "You have acted in the best traditions of the Royal Air Force and saved many lives. Come with me to the Base Commander's office."

There in addition to the Group Captain commanding Pakistan Air Force base Dacca, the Wing Commander Operations and Shahid Malik were waiting for him.

"Flight Lieutenant Higgins," the Group Captain announced, "by your professionalism and exemplary airmanship under fire today you not only recovered a valuable aircraft and saved its civilian passengers from certain destruction but also the Head of Military Operations of the Pakistan General Staff and his assistant. Pakistan owes you a debt of gratitude."

"Thank you, sir, but any officer would have done the same," Carl replied.

"We don't think so," the Base Commander responded.

"You are to fly back to West Pakistan tomorrow. The Commander in Chief of the Pakistan Air Force is to invest you with an award for gallantry – the equivalent of the UK's Air Force Cross. We cannot grant you Pakistan's counterpart to your Distinguished Flying Cross because although you earned the medal under hostile fire no war has been declared and anyway your role as a QFI at the Air Academy is strictly non combatant. Nevertheless your actions are worthy of the highest commendation. Incidentally the Commandant Air Commodore Ahmed has communicated his congratulations to you and your colleague Flight Lieutenant Malik."

CHAPTER 35

The Air Commodore lent his jeep and driver to transport Carl and Captain Siddiqui to the Intercontinental Hotel. Carl had hoped for at least another two or three days in East Pakistan and more chances to be with Yasmin before he returned. The culmination of all his anticipation would have to be compressed into one sole night. His longing intensified by the minute.

However, events were moving swiftly to a climax. The hotel was full of senior military officers. Yasmin would really stand out if she appeared. Waiting was hard but at least Carl's lonely dinner with Captain Siddiqui helped fill the time. It was interrupted by big bangs and the rattle of small arms fire in the distance.

"The Mukti Bahini's usual night time lullaby," Siddiqui commented dryly before excusing himself. "I've expended a lot of nervous energy today, Carl. You're used to in flight dramas. I'm not. I'm an infantryman remember. I'll get an early night if you don't mind. I'll let you know just as soon as I have a departure time for your flight back West. Goodnight."

Carl decided not to hang around. His presence in any of the public rooms of the hotel would only draw attention to himself. He did not want to be drawn into unnecessary conversation and perhaps be late for Yasmin.

He returned to his room, drew the blinds, hung up his uniform, had a shower and put on a clean cotton shirt and khaki trousers. Carl desultorily turned on the television. There were only two channels. One was showing President Yahya Khan giving a speech in Urdu to Naval Cadets in Karachi. The other featured a group of Bengali folk musicians. Carl opted for them, set the sound low, took out his current paperback – All Quiet on the Western Front – and timed his alarm clock for a midnight call in case he dozed off.

Carl duly did so but the clock performed its function well. He leapt to his feet, put on his shoes, passed a wet towel over his face and brushed his teeth in the bottled water provided. Gingerly he opened the door and checked for surveillance. No guards, minders or watchers were to be seen. He resisted the temptation of the lift. Unwelcome fellow occupants of the hotel might get in at any floor. Anyway the Mukti Bahini could cut the power. The city had suffered frequent blackouts of late at their hands.

Instead Carl took the emergency stairs to the fifth floor. He gingerly opened the communicating door and scanned the corridor. The coast seemed clear. He walked nonchalantly to room 514, took his key from his pocket and inserted it naturally into the keyhole pushing the door forward as he did so. Swiftly he shut it and chained it behind him.

Yasmin was beside the doorway in her silken night clothes. They flung themselves upon each other and embraced in quivering emotion. The excitement was too great for words for many minutes.

"You made it, Yasmin. Thank God you're safely back my love," Carl began. "How was Sylhet?"

"Beautiful. The tea gardens were glorious. The experience was a throwback in time," Yasmin replied. "One of the few remaining British tea planters Sandy Forbes and his wife Peggy from Dundee gave me tea in their bungalow. They must be well into their sixties now. The purple, magenta and orange bougainvilleas up the walls, the blue headed jacaranda trees in the garden and the view of the dark green tea clad hills partly swathed in monsoon mist were a delight. 'How can we go back to Scotland now' they explained. 'This is our home. We know no other.' What can you answer, Carl, and what will happen to them when the Indians arrive?" Yasmin inquired. "Presumably the new puppet Bangladesh Government they install will nationalise all foreign assets. I could not bear to speculate about the future for the Forbes. I wanted them to maintain their illusions as long as they can – at least for a few more days if they're lucky. I don't think they'll be harmed in any way, but I can't see them being allowed to stay on."

"When the Indian Army invade you said, darling," Carl observed. "Not if, but when. Your husband Akbar spoke to me in equally definitive terms, but he's not afraid I assure you. He says that the quality of his men will see him through."

"How is he really, Carl? Doesn't he know what he's up against?" Yasmin asked.

"Like all faithful Muslims I think Akbar's resigned to God's will," Carl responded. "But at the same time he's determined to bend it in his favour by acquitting himself in a manner worthy of Allah's approval."

"Yes, but he's been away from regular soldiering for a long time, Carl, and to be thrown in at the deep end by taking over the command of a battalion on the outbreak of war could hardly be a tougher assignment."

"I know, my love," Carl replied, "but as you must realise better than anyone he's more than capable. All that combat experience in Oman and his Sandhurst training will stand him in good stead. Anyway he's a natural leader born and brought up to it in Baluchistan and he's commanding his own people.

"What beautiful orchids, sweetheart," said Carl, "who bought you those?" changing the conversation and moving towards the bed. "Do I face competition Yasmin?"

"Don't be so silly my love. How would you think or say such a thing? One of your more inappropriate jokes. They actually came from the GOC's wife. I had tea with her today and she insisted I accept them. Her mali, the gardener, brought them round to the hotel earlier this evening."

"Was it wise to accept a gift via a strange man? A small bomb could have been planted in them. Did you check them?"

"You're getting even sillier now, Carl. Perhaps all the stress you've been under is finally getting to you."

"What stress, Yasmin?"

"Well you were nearly shot down today, weren't you, Carl, or have you forgotten all about it? I'm told you saved the aircraft and some very important passengers as well. It was wonderful that Shahid could guide you in."

"Who told you? Do you monitor everything that's going on?"

"It's my job isn't it? How can our government negotiate a successful peace deal on the basis of ignorance? Captain Siddiqui told me if you must know. The GOC's ADC doesn't go with you everywhere just to keep you company."

"I suspected as much," Carl replied.

"However, I'm glad my love that they're going to give you another well earned medal," she went on, "but it actually breaks my heart as well because I reckon tomorrow's PIA707 will be the last one out. I have received no departure instructions so I must stay out East and see it through. I had hoped we'd have a few more days, or rather nights, here together but the Indo-Bangladeshi High Command and our own Air Force's keenness to decorate you seem to have put paid to my fond dreamer's fantasies."

"Come to bed, Yasmin," Carl pleaded. "We were so happy in each other's arms when I arrived but then we allowed preoccupation with our duties to break the magic spell. If any lover thought when he stole the first kiss how a relationship could end love would be universally stillborn. As the Romans say carpe diem, seize the day, noctemque and the night added Carl lifting Yasmin bodily onto the sheets and rolling eagerly alongside her.

Their cares and fears fell away and mutual passion returned with a new intensity. Surely such madly illicit joy must bring its nemesis. Carl wondered why Heidi and their well ordered family life at home in Harefield and the prospect of more children to come meant so little to him. For Yasmin her role as Chief Secretary's lady, the Provincial chatelaine so much admired and respected in Baluch society counted for nothing now. They both longed only for a few more hours of complete self-giving bliss. Beyond that immediate necessity they had no more ambitions left.

At 0500 hours the alarm clock's urgent call rang out. As ever parting was too painful to prolong.

"I love you with all my heart. God bless you my darling is all I have to say," Yasmin whispered as Carl slipped away.

"I can't say more either my dearest Yasmin," said Carl after a last sorrowful kiss. "Wherever life takes you remember always that my heart is yours darling." The door clicked shut behind him. The corridor seemed deserted and the stairway clear as Carl returned disconsolate to his room.

What was the point of going to bed alone he wondered. A joyless dreary dawn was already breaking grey and wet over the drab dilapidated rooftops of Dacca. Yet the sodden streets were coming to teeming bustling life below. Carl would have a shower and be first down to breakfast.

The phone rang. It was Siddiqui. "Where have you been, Carl?" he expostulated. "We have been looking for you for the last two and a half hours. We searched the whole hotel. We wondered if you'd been kidnapped or bumped off by the Mukti Bahini. Police patrols were despatched for you all over Dacca. We rang the British Deputy High Commission in case you'd decided to spend the night there following a security tip off. The duty officer had no news."

"How could he? I've had no contact with them since I arrived," Carl interjected.

"Then we rang our intelligence staff," the ADC continued. "They knew at once. Appropriate action will be taken in the light of their information. You'll still catch your aircraft. It doesn't leave till 0830 hours, but you'll be leaving under arrest. I'm warning you as a friend, Carl. They'll be coming for you at any moment. You face charges of espionage for consorting in an unauthorised manner with an official of the Pakistan Government. By the way I never thanked you for saving my life in the Skyvan. Thank you, Carl. You're an exceptional pilot and a brave one, a really good friend, but a very unwise lover."

So it had all come to this. Carl felt totally winded, but at least he could perhaps still get out before the storm broke. He packed quickly and put on his tropical uniform. The door opened. A Provost Branch Squadron Leader and two towering Pakistan Air Force policemen entered. "Flight Lieutenant Higgins you are under arrest on suspicion of espionage. Put your officer's cap away and remove the badges of rank from your epaulettes. Come with us," the Squadron Leader ordered. Carl was frog marched out of the hotel and down to the car park and bundled into an unmarked staff car.

Memories of BRIXMIS came flooding back. Interrogation would not be pleasant. He might easily just disappear with a bullet in the back of the neck if he was lucky or be tortured to death if less so. Perhaps he would share the fate of so many Mukti Bahini suspects who vanished without a trace. This would be his posthumous reward for sharing the agonies of the death of Pakistan.

The Pathan airman drove at speed through the side streets scattering the bicycles and rickshaws and forcing dozy pedestrians to leap the stagnant puddles to the safety of the sidewalks. Carl's mind raced. How would they deal with poor Yasmin? Who had betrayed them?

Siddiqui knew nothing – at least until he made his unanswered phone calls, but as he admitted he would not have guessed. Of course they would not have looked for Carl in Room 514. It was unthinkable for an unaccompanied lady's room to be searched. It was unusual enough for her to travel alone. Surely to God they would not stone to death a Baluch Colonel's wife, the Chief Secretary's lady.

Then he realised. It was the orchids, the gift ostensibly of the GOC's wife delivered by the so called gardener, wired to record no doubt. The bugs would have picked up not just the ecstatic sounds of their love making, but their speculations about invasion timing. The taped conversation would indeed have been the stuff of espionage.

The staff car moved faster and faster through the Bengali crowds as the streets grew wider until the airport appeared. They stopped on the apron beside the 707 and got out. As they did so an air raid warning siren howled. "Warning, warning, warning," a tannoy boomed. "Air raid expected from North in fifteen minutes. Take cover. I say again, take cover. PIA personnel expedite 0830 hours Karachi service for immediate departure please. Doors closing in two minutes. Out." Carl was almost bodily lifted by the burly policemen towards the waiting airliner whose turbo jets had already whined into life.

Out of the corner of his eye he saw two Mig 19s move from their blast pens and taxi fast towards the runway with two more nosing out from the netted and sandbagged emplacement behind. Farewell my friend. God speed Shahid, thought Carl as the first pair of fighters roared off on their interception. The doors then closed and the mighty 707 followed them heading sturdily on stork like wings into a squall sweeping across the airfield.

They stayed low at about five hundred feet over the swamped Sandabans of the Ganges Delta till they reached the Bay of Bengal and began to climb steadily out of Pakistani airspace. Carl knew that his Royal Air Force career was finished, but at least he himself was safe.

On arrival at Karachi Airport the two Pakistan Air Force policemen never left Carl's side. They were met by a Provost Pilot Officer who had them ferried across to the military part of the airfield where he was held in the arrivals' lounge for two hours. "Arrangements have been made for your accommodation Flight Lieutenant," the Pilot Officer explained.

"As you will be aware Pakistan is now at war following Indian aggression," he went on. "Air Force Headquarters have decided that your case is an unnecessary distraction from the war effort. You are therefore to be repatriated at the earliest opportunity. Meanwhile you will spend the night in the Officers' Mess and remain in your room until you can be handed over to an officer of the British High Commission's Defence staff who will supervise your transfer home. It may take some time for the officer to arrive as he has to travel by road owing to the suspension of domestic civil air services for the duration of hostilities."

Following a simple curry for supper Carl was ready for sleep. The drama of his arrest and long flight from Bangladesh had exhausted him. He felt far from the war but wondered nevertheless whether the airport would be bombed, but dismissed the idea. The Indians were always careful to cultivate favourable public opinion worldwide and any civilian casualties at the airport would be counterproductive.

After about twenty-four hours' wait the young Pilot Officer who had taken over from the more daunting Provost Branch Squadron Leader entered Carl's room and announced. "The Air Adviser from the British High Commission has arrived Flight Lieutenant. I will escort you downstairs to meet him. An anteroom has been cleared for the purpose." Carl duly descended fearing the worst. If he were to be drummed out of the Service it were better done now he thought. He had no stomach for prolonged disciplinary proceedings back in England. Heidi at least deserved a happier home coming from him than that.

When Carl was led in the Air Adviser was already at a small table with a single straight backed wooden chair in front of him. "Group Captain Greenway, sir, good afternoon," said Carl coming to attention before him.

"Flight Lieutenant Higgins," the Group Captain began ignoring Carl's salutation, "in all my career yours is the worst case of totally irresponsible ill discipline I have ever encountered from any officer. Do you have anything to say for yourself, Higgins?"

"No, sir, and certainly not now," Carl replied simply.

"My misfortune is that I should have had to come all the way down from Islamabad," lamented Greenway warming to his theme, "and by road to deal with you when there's a war on and urgent work to be done by the High Commission's Defence staff and Service Advisers."

"I regret that, sir," Carl answered.

"Regret what Higgins? Your behaviour, which has been incompatible with your status as a commissioned officer or the serious inconvenience to which you have put me?"

"Both, sir," said Carl.

"Let me get straight to the point," the Group Captain continued. "To let your wild philandering lead you into an adulterous relationship with a senior Pakistani foreign service officer who is married to a highly respected officer of the Pakistani Army and civil service who has personally hosted you both at his home and at his battalion at the front is totally unacceptable. After your self-indulgent adventures our Pakistani friends will have second thoughts about ever accepting an exchange officer from the Royal Air Force onto the instructing staff of their Air Academy again."

"That indeed would be a loss to both Air Forces especially after Flight Lieutenant Parker's distinguished service," Carl observed.

"That's for both parties to decide," snapped Greenway. "You are to return to UK in the British Overseas Airways flight which leaves tonight. The Pakistani authorities as you may have guessed have decided owing to your exceptional airmanship in saving a Skyvan and the pressures of the outbreak of war to drop the fully justifiable charge of espionage against you. They have left it to your British superiors to take whatever disciplinary action is appropriate. To me falls that responsibility."

"Will I have the opportunity, sir, at least to try to explain what happened?" Carl inquired.

"It will not be necessary, Higgins." Greenway replied. "The facts speak for themselves. I have therefore concluded that you are to relinquish your commission with immediate effect. On arrival in England you will return to civilian life without any gratuity or terminal leave. Your conduct has been as I said before incompatible with your status as a Royal Air Force officer. You are lucky to escape a Court Martial. It would only have caused your family pain and have an inevitable outcome."

"Do you want my report on developments in East Pakistan before I depart, sir," Carl asked.

"Not much," the Group Captain replied tersely. "However, before I leave for Islamabad I will bring you up to date with the progress of the war," Greenway continued. "The paper you were preparing for Squadron Leader McNeil has been overtaken by events and is now superfluous. Colonel Akbar Khan's battalion the First Baluchs was virtually annihilated in the first twenty-four hours in the big Indian offensive through Benapole to Jessore and beyond. About half the battalion are casualties and half were taken prisoner. Colonel Akbar Khan was very seriously wounded. He refused to leave battalion HQ until it was overwhelmed. He lost an eye and a leg in a mortar burst and was captured by the Indians."

"At least the Mukti Bahini didn't get their hands on him, Thank God," interjected Carl.

"His wife Yasmin, however, is dead," the Group Captain went on without emotion. "A bomb detonated beneath her official car as she left the Intercontinental Hotel car park for work on the morning of your departure. She was critically injured in the blast and suffered eighty per cent burns. She died in hospital six hours later. Her vehicle was in a secure area and could not have been tampered with by the Mukti Bahini. The explosion had all the hallmarks of an inside job. We believe it to have been the work of Pakistani intelligence. She had become an embarrassment and paid the price."

Carl felt the blood drain from his face. His hands began to shake and he found it hard to breathe.

"As for your friend Shahid Malik," the Group Captain continued piling on the agony. "He shot down the first Indian aircraft of the war. He intercepted a raid coming in from the North as you left, destroying a Hunter and damaging a Gnat. Unfortunately for him the second wave of Hunters caught him and his wingman as they were recovering to base out of ammunition and very low on fuel. Shahid was on finals with his undercarriage and flaps down when the Hunters pounced. He cleaned up and tried to pull away in a hard turn to port but a well directed burst cut off his tail and he span in. His number two seeing his leader's fate ejected downwind and parachuted into the drop off point for passenger departures."

Carl was so shell shocked he could hardly reply and certainly did not want to comment on the destruction of the dream he had been living. "What about my kit, sir?" was all he could say.

"Your possessions will be returned to you in the UK in due course," Greenway replied. "That's it as far as I'm concerned, Higgins. After this unpleasant interlude I must return post haste to my duties. Pilot Officer Hukam Dad is resuming charge of you and will see you through departures. Good day."

"Goodbye, sir."

The Pilot Officer ushered Carl upstairs again to his room. He sat on the hard chair and began to shake. He could not weep. He could not cry out. By his impetuosity he had destroyed the most courageous and whole hearted of lovers any man could wish for in a manner so horrible that he wondered how he could endure the guilt ridden years ahead. Carl could not conceive of a world without Yasmin. True he had only rarely been able to see her but he had always known in the recesses of his innermost spirit that somewhere she was there for him and if ever they could be together it would be as it had always been.

Yet he had destroyed not just one love but two. Except in the case of total war he knew he would never again be recalled to the cockpit by the Royal Air Force. Flying had sustained him ever since he had conquered his airsickness at Cranwell, a triumph which anyone less dedicated could never have achieved. Flying had been at times the inspiration at others the solace and consolation, which underpinned his personality and place in the world. Now he would have to set it permanently aside unless he took up the challenge of display flying, which Peter Lascelles had briefly and tragically espoused, or accept the mind numbing servitude of flying for an airline.

Finally how could he face Heidi? What could he say? Even more difficult would be to respond to the questions of her gallant and dedicated father. Would the Air Force reveal to them why his services were no longer required? He must have a better alternative to Royal Air Force flying before he was reunited with his family. His parents would be surprised, too, but perhaps less so. They at least understood what Pakistan was like and the perils of the murky world into which his passion for Yasmin had so imprudently impelled him.

After what seemed the longest and unhappiest hour of Carl's life Pilot Officer Hukam Dad knocked at his door and entered with his two formidably built companions.

"It is time to go Mr Higgins. Come with us. The British Overseas Airways VC10 leaves for London in fifty minutes," the Pilot Officer instructed. The tall finned floodlit Speedbird awaited on an empty apron. The terminal, too, was virtually deserted. Only the departure lounge was filled with expatriate Britons hurrying home. Pilot Officer Hukam Dad was waved through passport control with Carl. "I must just see you onto the aeroplane," he explained.

No sooner had they reached departures than a familiar yet unplaceable individual approached Pilot Officer Dad. "Would you mind," he asked, "if I have a brief word with your friend?"

"By all means, but please make sure that he doesn't miss the aeroplane," Dad replied.

"Mr Carl Higgins," the familiar figure began. My God he's recognised me flashed through Carl's mind, then, I remember who he is, Colin Richards the political and strategic briefer at the induction session at the High Commission on arrival. "I think you may soon be looking for gainful employment. Just ring this number when you get back to the UK and ask for a certain Mr Medway. He'll probably invite you round to Carlton House Terrace for a chat and if that goes well could have need of your services."

"Thank you very much. You are a friend indeed, Mr Richards."

"And I suspect you are a former aviator now much in need," he replied. With that he disappeared into the crowd as unobtrusively as he had arrived.

"Now it is time for me to take my leave, Mr Higgins," Pilot Officer Dad explained. "Just show your boarding card to the PIA girl please. I'll see you up the gangway. Before you go I have a souvenir from the Pakistan Air Force for you." He slipped a long silver container into Carl's hand.

"Thank you Pilot Officer," Carl replied. "You've looked after me well in unhappy circumstances. Goodbye."

"Goodbye, Mr Higgins. It has been a privilege to have you in my charge."

Form the top of the steps Carl cast a last lingering look over the Sindhi desert. He inhaled a final lungful of the odorous Pakistani air and listened for a farewell squawk from the ever present crows before entering the aeroplane to find his seat by the tail alongside the cluster of four mighty Rolls Royce Conway engines, which were to speed him home.

Carl opened the box. In it were a medal and ribbon, a miniature of it and a scroll. He unrolled it. It was a citation. It read: "To Flight Lieutenant Higgins, DFC, RAF in grateful recognition of his gallantry and exceptional airmanship under hostile fire leading to the safe recovery of a valuable aircraft and its passengers."

Carl began to shake uncontrollably as the jets opened up to fully cry. Their take off roar filled his soul and tears ran down his face wetting the parchment citation on his knees. The Speedbird rapidly gained speed and soared powerfully skyward towards Risalpur, the Frontier with its jagged snow capped mountains and wild Afghanistan beyond.

THE END